PRECURSOR

A NOVEL ABOUT UKRAINIAN PHILOSOPHER HRYHORIY SKOVORODA

This book has been published with the support of the Translate Ukraine Translation Program

UKRAINIAN BOOK INSTITUTE

PRECURSOR

A NOVEL ABOUT UKRAINIAN PHILOSOPHER HRYHORIY SKOVORODA

by Vasyl Shevchuk

Translated from the Ukrainian by Yuri Tkacz

First published in the Ukrainian as "Предтеча (Григорій Сковорода)" in 1969

Proofreading by Gareth Pugh

This book has been published with the support
of the Translate Ukraine Translation Program

**UKRAINIAN
//IIIBOOK
INSTITUTE**

Book cover and interior book design by Max Mendor

Cover image: (Detail) Painting of Hryhoriy Skovoroda
by an unknown artist, c. 18th century

Publishers Maxim Hodak & Max Mendor

www.glagoslav.com

ISBN: 978-1-914337-52-9

First published in English by Glagoslav Publications in November 2021

A catalogue record for this book is available from the British Library.

PRECURSOR

A NOVEL ABOUT UKRAINIAN PHILOSOPHER HRYHORIY SKOVORODA

Translated
from the Ukrainian
by Yuri Tkacz

GLAGOSLAV PUBLICATIONS

CONTENTS

VASYL SHEVCHUK

THE FIRST NET

For ten days now Hryhoriy had been imbibing the thick air and could not slake his thirst. Back there, beyond the Carpathian Mountains, it had been more delicate, more benign, but it had not borne the smell of the steppe, it had not refreshed his soul. For ten days he had lain on the cart and not taken his eyes off the poplars, the birches, and the cherry orchards which swathed the bright palaces and peasant houses with tiny windows in a greenish-white froth. For three long years while in the parks of Tokay and Vienna he had dreamed of his native cherry blossom, warm southeasterly winds, a sky filled with the spring songs of larks and the evening warble of young girls. There were times the boys would sit down, sigh, grieve a little and sing softly: "Oh, heigh-ho, mother, oh heigh-ho, mother..." while he stood and wept. Surrounded by paradise, he nevertheless flew on the wings of the song to his native Chornukhy, to Kyiv.

The wheels creaked, the horses ran tardily, and a pink wisp of dust meandered behind the carts. Not yet like the dust of summer, when one could not see the world, but more like the smoke emerging from a pipe.

"It's humid, there'll probably be a shower," Nychypir piped up, pulling his hat onto his forehead, and spurred on the horses to catch up to the train of carts: "Gee-up, gee-up, my little falcons!"

Bending over, propping up his head with his hand, he began to croon a song. Without any words, barely audible. He was like a sack of songs.

And what a voice he had! How well the lads had sung in the seminary or the bishop's choir, and yet next to this peasant from Chornukhy those famous choristers were simply billy goats, laughing stocks.

> *Oh, a fire burns upon the hill,*
> *In the vale a Cossack lies still...*

Hryhoriy could not work out whether it was Nychypir singing or whether the song had surfaced from his own heart.

> *Cover'd his eyes with nankeen cloth,*
> *'Tis a young Cossack's just desert...*

Horsemen appeared out of the blue. They checked their fiery steeds and pranced alongside the cart. Zaporozhian Cossacks[1] – formidable men with moustaches, tanned by the elements.

"Where might you be travelling?" the oldest grey-haired fellow asked, rising in his saddle.

"To St. Petersburg, from Hungary!" Nychypir replied cheerfully. He pushed his shabby hat to one side.

"A-ah, little foster children! Little gentlemen *hetmans*[2] who wash the feet of chickens!" the horsemen guffawed.

"And you don't wash them?" Nychypir half-closed one eye.

"After we've washed them, the chickens can't find all their feet!"

"Eagles, eagles!" Nychypir continued to gush.

"And how is His Illustrious Majesty Rozum?[3] Still at the skirt, or is he already separated?"

"Don't get too carried away, boys, we've got Vyshnevsky in the coach up ahead there – his majesty's colonel."

....

[1] Zaporozhians – Zaporozhian Cossacks, literally meaning Cossacks 'from beyond the rapids' [on the Dnipro River].

[2] A supreme Cossack leader.

[3] Reference to Count Kyrylo Rozumovsky (1728–1803), a Ukrainian Cossack who served as the last *hetman* of Little Russia, as Ukraine was then known.

"You don't say!" The grey-haired Cossack raised his hands. "And is he thick with thalers?" he asked, exchanging glances with his lads.

"We haven't counted them... Weren't graced with the honour."

"P'raps we should shake this little colonel, my dear children?" The old Cossack turned up his moustache dipped in milk.

"Let's shake him, father!" the 'children' called out amiably and made their horses rear, prepared to attack the coach.

The Cossack leader raised his hand, checking the hotheaded young men.

"*Auri sacra fumes!*"[4] he said in Latin. Then, adjusting his sabre, he looked at the aristocrat's sleeping coach and sighed sorrowfully: "These grapes are too green for us, brothers."

Hryhoriy wanted to ask the old *otaman*[5] where and when he had studied, but was not quick enough.

The Zaporozhians set off into the fields and soon disappeared into a deep ravine overgrown with oaks.

Hardly had the dust kicked up by the Cossack horses settled, when a detachment of hussars appeared unexpectedly from a wood, which loomed a mile up the road. Stopping the train of carts, the Poles asked Vyshnevsky something, and half-leaning out of his coach, the fellow pointed a finger in the direction the Cossacks had just disappeared.

"What a bastard!" Nychypir muttered. "Small wonder they say a crow will never peck out another crow's eyes."

"Don't worry, they won't catch them," Hryhoriy said, feeling an anxious concern in his heart for the falcons who were flying over the steppe somewhere toward their dear Cossack fortress – the Sich. "They won't catch up... *Nec deus intersit!*"

"What did you say?" Nychypir wrinkled his forehead.

"May God not intervene!"

"Heigh-ho, His eyes have long been covered in cataracts. The things that are happening in the world today, and He won't even lift a finger..."

"The Lord preserve you, uncle! What are you saying?!"

....

4   A damned craving for gold! (Latin)

5   A Cossack chieftain.

"Let Him listen," Nychypir looked into the deep azure sky. "My grandfather and father were free men. And yet I've become a serf, a human draught horse to be traded! I've been bought and sold three times already..."

He grew silent, dropped his head onto his chest and did not spur on the horses, even though their cart was lagging behind the rest.

Skovoroda became pensive. He unbuttoned his blue camlet coat and bared his chest to the ever so slight breeze. They were entering the forest. The high pines strained their branches into the sky, fighting for every ray of sunshine. The weaker ones perished, and even those which victoriously straightened their shoulders lost those branches which remained in the dark shadows. The law of nature! People were like these trees too...

"Gee-up! Gee-up!" Nychypir called out, waving at the horses with an oak whip handle (he had purposely lost his whip, taking pity on his ashen steeds) and launched into a merry song. But soon he launched into one which made Hryhoriy's heart ache.

> *The brethren they are a-grieving,*
> *That heavy chains have bound their feet,*
> *Oh now, dear brethren, surely we*
> *Are lost until eternity...*

"Eh, Hryshka, Hryshka!" Vyshnevsky's footman hollered, as if summoning people to a fire. He turned his horse around behind the cart and, carelessly playing with his whip, ordered: "Off you run to the landlord!"

"Go and tell his nobleness that I'm no dog and make no habit of running after coaches," Hryhoriy snapped back.

The footman blushed crimson, raised his whip... but did not lash out. Tugging at his reins, he squeezed the horse with his spurs and galloped off as if the devil was chasing him.

Nychypir let out an ululation and waved the whip handle over his head. The horses set off at a gallop.

Pines and pyramidal wild pears smothered in white blossom sailed past.

The forest rumbled, laughed, and filled with the clatter of wheels.

They stopped at noon. The horses were unharnessed, set free to graze in the forest clearing, along which crept a narrow little stream overgrown with dense leafy herbage, willow, and alder. Birds were singing everywhere.

Motley hoopoes struck their kettledrums, an oriole screamed out and a nightingale's warble filled the grove. Large black crows flew over the clearing like evil spirits and cawed hoarsely.

Having drunk from a spring bubbling out from the base of an ancient alder, Hryhoriy slowly made his way to the colonel.

"At last, you've come," the fellow growled angrily. And scratching a Russian wolfhound behind the ears, said: "Doesn't it seem to you, Hryhoriy, that dogs and servants are made of the same dough?"

"Just like lords and pigs. Everything is made of matter!"

Vyshnevsky stared goggle-eyed at him. Then he bawled angrily at the footman:

"Why are you prancing before my eyes?! Go and help with the meal!"

Having vented his anger, the colonel cheered up a little, half-closed his eyes, and said: "Inordinate pride does not become one.."

"Neither does the lack of it."

"To a serf, let's say, there's not an ounce of good as a result of it, only harm."

"A proud person cannot be a serf."

"So that's it! What will you order him to be then?"

"Either free or a nothing."

"What about God? He created the slave and the lord..."

"God created man."

"And divided him."

"That was the work of the Pharisees, to please the nobility."

Vyshnevsky groaned, fingered his moustache à la Peter[6] and adjusted his staff sword. Fetching a handkerchief, he thunderously blew his nose.

"Such thoughts are worthy of shackles or cudgels," he said icily and smiled: "However, I'm a good fellow and respect learned people..."

"These grapes are still green," Hryhoriy interrupted him.

"What have grapes to do with it?" Vyshnevsky failed to understand.

"Those were the words of a fox unable to reach a bunch of grapes."

The colonel shrugged his shoulders. He trampled the fiery-yellow flowers and young sorrel with his riding boots. Hryhoriy walked alongside him, eyeing his interlocutor sullenly, and listened to the forest. A titmouse twit-

....

6   Moustache similar to that worn by the Russian tsar Peter the First.

tered somewhere nearby, a woodpecker hammered at a tree, the water in the stream gurgled away…

"Actually, I didn't call you to argue," Vyshnevsky said. "Sometime tonight or in the morning we'll reach Kyiv. What will you do, what business do you have to attend to?"

"I have no idea," Skovoroda confessed frankly.

"Do you have land or cattle?"

"There is a little patrimony. In Chornukhy, in the Lubny Regiment. I've an older brother there."

"Well, farming is a worthy, honest occupation…"

"But one not at all suited to my nature," Hryhoriy added.

"And what is?"

"I'm still not sure…"

"Come with me to St. Petersburg. They badly need learned people there who know the language and have studied the sciences. You won't regret it. You'll earn a title, estates, money!"

"*Omnia mea mecum porto.*"[7]

"What did you say?"

"That such riches are of no use to me."

"Saints above! Who's ever been harmed by wealth and titles?!"

"Those who intrinsically live in poverty, but are rich in spiritual peace."

"They have the Academy there, famous scholars, great people!" Vyshnevsky said feverishly. "And what is there here? Thick-skulled peasants, priests and Cossack elders who pride themselves on the size of their backsides, but eat borsch[8] from the same bowl as the peasant!"

"Each of us must get to know his people, Lord Vyshnevsky, and thus discover himself," Skovoroda replied calmly.

"So, you won't come along?!" he asked in disbelief.

Skovoroda smiled and spread out his hands.

"This is the first time I've seen a dolt who's prepared to exchange a commander's warder[9] for a shepherd's staff!" the colonel's voice thundered through the clearing.

....

[7] I carry all my things with me. (Latin)

[8] A beetroot-based soup with many other vegetables; variable, according to region.

[9] A truncheon used by a commander-in-chief to signal orders.

"As for me, it's better to be a shepherd at home than a commander in foreign parts..."

Vyshnevsky groaned. He shattered a pyramidal ant's nest with the toe of his riding boot.

"Your illustrious excellency, lunch is served," the footman ran up and stood to attention.

"Coming!" the lord retorted angrily and turned to face Hryhoriy once more.

"Think about it. Don't let good fortune slip through your fingers!"

"I've already heard that from the lips of the empress herself," Skovoroda said firmly. "And yet, here I am... Alive and not regretting it."

Vyshnevsky waved his hand and stepped toward the carpet on which the meal was laid out.

Hryhoriy threw off his coat, spread it out in the shade and laid down on his back. The sunlight was blinding through the sparse, still yellowy-green leaves. His ear caught the ring of a mosquito, or perhaps some other unknown God's creature which was lurking somewhere in the undergrowth nearby – small, unseen, but alive, in a tiny droplet of the world, who knows why... True, everything in the world had a sense and a logic to it, but it was often hard to perceive its reason for existence, as it was with people... However, it was possible! Everything was subordinate to the human mind...

He smiled, recalling his dispute with the German, who had attempted to prove that the world was unfathomable. The essence of metaphysics...

"Hryhoriy, come and eat!" he heard from afar, as if from another dimension.

It was Nychypir calling. Presently his figure blotted out the sun and his face spread into a grin.

"You're no angel, Hrytsko, you can't survive on the breath of the Holy Spirit alone..."

*　*　*

After they had lunched and the train of carts set off again, doubts and vacillation began to beset Hryhoriy's soul. Who in Kyiv was waiting for him? His old student friends were by now scattered throughout Ukraine or even the entire Russian Empire, from Zaporizhia to the White Sea... The instructors had disliked him for his harsh judgements and irreverence toward the letter and dogma before which they bowed their heads... St. Petersburg... Lomonosov was there. And in a few years, he would be joined by his former friends from Leipzig – Hrytsko Kozytsky[10] and Mykolay Motonis[11] – for where else would they go?

"Gee-up, gee-up, my falcons!" Old Nychypir spurred on his ashen steeds. He wasn't old in years, but in appearance he seemed to be almost a grandfather. Sweat ran down his brown neck. His soiled shirt was stirred by the wind, which spurred on the train of carts and carried the dust somewhere toward Kyiv, where a black cloud hung on the distant horizon. What a strange wind – it was blowing toward the cloud, rather than from it...

Slowly his thoughts returned to St. Petersburg and Kyiv. Temptation was always seductive... Palaces were more easily spotted than poor hovels... However, happiness was not contained in palaces, but in freedom! The Cossack was like the wind, he could fly across the steppe in whichever direction he pleased... Besides, whom would he teach in the capital? The sons of courtiers? To whom would he impart his painstakingly acquired knowledge, which he had gathered like a bee in the boundless field of human wisdom? The empress? The nobility? And let the buckwheat sowers, that is, the peasants, obediently place their tufted heads in yokes like oxen, not even guessing that apart from the furrow, this world also had steppes, and liberty, sharp sabres, and philosophy?!

> *Oh, steed, my fair steed,*
> *With mane of gold indeed...*

Nychypir launched into song once more, for it was just as necessary to him as the air he breathed.

Skovoroda closed his eyes and his childhood came flooding back...

...The air was fragrant with pears, birds, and clouds. Ripe *dulia* pears[12] hung from branches like golden droplets. Fluffy baby birds screamed joyously

....

[10] Hryhoriy Kozytsky (1724–1775) – Ukrainian writer and statesman in the Russian Empire.

[11] Mykola Motonis (?–1787) – Ukrainian writer, translator, philologist, a leading light in education in Ukraine.

[12] A very tasty pear variety, popular because of its high yields and winter hardiness.

for the whole world to hear and flitted from bush to bush. And way above there in the sky sailed those shaggy white ricks of hay...

Small Hryhoriy placed a flute to his lips and it sang, laughed and wept. It sang about his father who had returned from an expedition to the mountains. It laughed at his brother Stepan, who had the day before climbed onto father's horse and had fallen off after making the Cossack yelp "*Poohoo, poohoo!*" And it wept after his grandfather, who had told him interesting and scary tales about the Swedish attack, how Chornukhy had been defended from the enemy, and how its last brave defenders had perished in flames...

Young Hryhoriy turned in the direction of the village and seemed to see the church crackling in flames, inside which the barely living, wounded, but not yet defeated Cossacks had locked themselves. He could see his grandfather's grave, the cross on it, and the periwinkle flowers...

"Look, look!" Stepan yelled and dashed past on his jet black horse. He had learned to ride it, after all! His shirt was billowing in the wind, happiness sparkled in his eyes.

Watching his brother ride off, the small boy lay face down and began to daydream…

The grass was tall and thick. When you looked through it at the steppe, toward the Mnoha River glistening here and there among the reeds, it was not at all hard to imagine that you were grown up and on horseback, wielding a sabre or riding with a *bandura*...[13] Riding slowly through the fields, playing and playing, with the Zaporozhian Cossacks listening to you and the feather grass lapping like a river in flood... The horse under you was not jet black, or grey, but golden, the same horse which had once drowned in the river when it had been deep, clear, and navigated by Cossack boats...

"Hrytsko-oh! Hrytsko-oh!" Mother called from the yard. "Come and have some lunch!"

Hryts turned his head, but did not see his mother, spying only the roof and the stork in the nest atop the house. The bird spread out its wings and chattered something with its red bill, as if also summoning Hryts. It was very, very wise, this stork... But Hryts had no desire to head home. He had

....

13   A Ukrainian plucked string instrument. In the 1700s it had 5 to 12 strings and was similar to the lute.

already eaten so many sweet pears that he could do without food for a whole week.

Beetles and ants crawled sedately over the grass; here and there green grasshoppers leapt nimbly. The speckled ladybirds made their way to the tips of stalks, and suddenly took off, flying into obscurity. Or perhaps it only seemed that they disappeared into boundless space...

Geese screeched on the river. Hryts strained his ears and suddenly heard the drawn-out, resounding neighing of the golden-maned horse. It was over there near the river, in the marshes!

Hiding the flute down his shirt front, the small boy jumped up and ran in a beeline through the gardens down to where the gentle Mnoha River lurked in the reeds and willows.

His heart beat madly. The thorny stubble cut into his feet, but he kept running, feeling nothing. His ears heard only the neighing, which died away, then rang out again over the river, like a taut string.

The reeds rose in a wall, a forest. In a minute the sky, the sun and everything in the world had disappeared, except for their knobbly stalks, narrow leaves and fluffy panicles. All around there was serenity and silence. Not even a mosquito let out a squeak...

A breeze sprung up out of nowhere and suddenly the reeds became like flutes, enough music for the whole world to hear!

Someone struck a tambourine. Then silence again. In the depths something was snorting hollowly, sighing, groaning...

It was the horse!

Hryts ran out of the marshes, found the path to the reach where their boat was moored, and raced for all he was worth along the narrow cutting in the reeds. His soles were pleasantly pampered by the cold, damp, springy earth. Gallinules and mallards rose fearfully and, like the ladybirds, immediately disappeared into the vast spaces of the world. His grandfather had said that there was no end to the world, in the same way as stars could not be counted.

The boats were tied up like tethered horses.

"Gee-up, gee-up, my falcons!" Nychypir called out merrily, waving the whip handle about, and turned to Hryhoriy: "Why are you so deep in thought?"

"I was recalling the past..."

"Good for him who has something to recall!" Nychypir sighed sadly, pulled his hat down over his forehead and launched into a new song:

> *A plane tree by the water's edge,*
> *Leans out over the shady sedge;*
> *Pained by injustice in his land,*
> *The Cossack stands head bowed...*

Hryhoriy made himself more comfortable on the cart and again slipped into reminiscences of the distant past...

Lord Almighty, how long the winter nights had been in St. Petersburg! As soon as dusk fell, the choirmaster's attendant appeared and passed on the order to hurry to rehearsals or to the gallery of one of the palaces, where a court ball was to take place. Toward dawn the boys returned to their choir dormitory, tipsy and merry, collapsing fully clothed onto their rough-and-ready beds and fell asleep. They awoke sometime toward evening, dined hastily and again ran off to please the nobles with a Franco-German musical mish-mash, so loved by the empress, the *frauleins*, and the choirmaster – a Holstein German.

Hryhoriy had had a real battle with this diehard German. He had fallen ill one day and did not turn up for rehearsals. The choirmaster sent the music to him and ordered him to learn the *wunderbare kleine Pastorale*[14] for that evening. Hryhoriy ran his eyes over the pages and hurled them onto the table. What liars – no shame or conscience! Where had they seen such shepherdesses and shepherds, loveable cherubs who frolicked like baby doves in the colourful meadows? What about the rain, the cold, the knee-deep mud! There were times when you suffered, clothed in an old sack, like a chained pup. Or when the biting wind of autumn dashed about the steppe, carrying dust, straw and leaves...

Taking the *bandura* down off the wall, he ran his fingers over the strings and grieved after the fields, the forest, and his native Mnoha River.

....

14 Wonderful little pastorale. (German)

There followed a second and a third song... He sang and wept, and soared over his native steppe as a strong-winged falcon, unable to delight enough in its beauty, unable to drink his fill of its healing fragrances...

"Now that's our song!"

Hryhoriy covered the strings with his hand and turned around at the voice. Heads bowed, lackeys, cooks and coachmen stood silently in the doorway. His neighbour from Chornukhy, Nychypir Dolia, was heading toward him, arms spread out.

"What winds bring you here, uncle?!" Hryhoriy rejoiced at the sight of his visitor.

"An ill wind, Hrytsko," Nychypir said. They kissed three times. "Whatever blows for us now, it's always from the wrong direction!"

"Oh, how true, how true." He was supported by the wretches who did not dare enter the room of the court choristers. The spark of freedom still glowed in their souls, weak, faint, like a death scream, and equally eternal, like the evening star...

"Come in, good people!" Hryhoriy invited them. "Why are you standing there in the doorway?"

Exchanging glances, they moved inside and again became silent near the door.

"Well, how are our people back there? Alive and well?" Hryhoriy asked.

"I haven't been home for three years," Dolia said sullenly. "I'll probably be a vagabond until the day I die..."

"You should marry."

"What for, Hrytsko? To breed more serfs?!"

Nychypir sat downcast, the lackeys, cooks, and coachmen sighed in silence, knowing they would never see their children free...

"Play for us, Hrytsko!" Dolia handed him the *bandura*. "But a merry one!"

"Which one do you want to hear?" Hryhoriy asked softly, for his entire soul was one big wound. Without waiting for an answer, he began the one his grandfather had loved to sing:

> *The lass stood in the doorway,*
> *Winking at the Cossack lad...*

Nychypir straightened up and joined in:

> *Come here, my dear Cossack,*
> *Come here and love me truly.*
> *Joy of my life,*
> *Joy of my life!*

Suddenly the choirmaster appeared in the doorway. The court staff scattered, as if blown away by a wind. Only Nychypir remained standing there.

"*Bist du denn krank?*"[15] the German raised his lorgnette. "Instead of high French you rehearse *deine barbarischen Lieden!*"[16]

Tearing the *bandura* from his hands, he took a swing and smashed it against the bed end. Nychypir rushed toward the choirmaster, but Hryhoriy immediately barred his way.

"A *bandura* can be smashed," he said with restraint, "but a song – never!"

"Ha-ha!" The choirmaster pulled a sour face. "What song is he, him primitive!"

"Part the seas – a frog is coming!" Nychypir snorted.

"*Was sagst du?*[17] I frog, I?" The haughty German bristled. "Hey, who there?" he called out, rushing up to the door.

This began to smell of trouble. Running up to the choirmaster, Hryhoriy lightly slipped his hand through the fellow's arm.

"My brother is with the Third Section of his Excellency Rozumovsky," he whispered, nodding in Nychypir's direction.

The diehard German took a deep breath, mumbled something in fright, and bowing before Dolia, dashed out the door...

....

15 Are you sick? (German)
16 your barbarous songs! (German)
17 What did you say? (German)

"Why are you guffawing?" Nychypir asked, holding onto his lambskin hat, which the raging wind tried to snatch away.

"I remembered the time we duped that German."

"In St. Petersburg?"

"Aha."

"Did that powdered mongrel ever run!" Nychypir called out. Meanwhile the wind tore off his shabby hat and rolled it off into the fields. "Whoa, whoa!"

He dropped the reins, jumped off the cart, and gave chase to his hat.

"Go on, bark, bark!"

"Strewth!"

They were laughing on all the carts. Vyshnevsky's long-legged wolfhound had shot out of the coach and, joining in the chase, pounced on the ill-fated hat, tearing it to shreds.

"Don't worry, his lordship the colonel will have a new one made for you," Skovoroda tried to comfort Nychypir after he had settled back on the cart and grabbed the reins.

"God willing, he won't have time," Dolia grumbled sullenly and yelled: "Gee-up, gee-up, my falcons!"

Hryhoriy did not ask what such words were meant to imply. He could see for himself, could sense with his soul that a decisiveness was maturing in his compatriot, a new kind of unknown essence, a sullen force. On the eve of great changes and great upheavals, people always seemed to be reborn, blossoming wantonly with all that was best and loftiest in their hearts. Nychypir Dolia had neither beauty nor money, nor liberty. He only had his enchanting voice, which he had inherited from his parents, from the Chornukhy nightingales, whose singing and twittering had imbued them with a craving for love. And he sang. He had sung yesterday, and the day before, but today a flood of melodies, sorrow, grief, and joy flowed from his bosom. Even now he was sitting, eyes closed, quivering all over like a skylark:

> *Oh, a slender stalk upon the field*
> *Trembles in the breeze...*

Vyshnevsky had mentioned that the Holsteiner German was now himself lauding Little Russian songs and ballads, and fussing over *bandura* players, as if they were made of porcelain. Small wonder! The empress had awarded one of them for his virtuoso playing with nothing short of a noble title.

She was somewhat strange, this omnipotent woman... She would make one man a noble, and then turn hundreds into serfs, livestock. She said that she fervently loved Little Russia, its songs, culture, and soul, and yet the famous Lavra printing shop in Kyiv had been forbidden to print anything for so many years now, save for those books which had already appeared in print in St. Petersburg or Moscow... Words and deeds. How far apart they stood! And the more power, the more might a person had, the less truth, the less sincerity there was in their words. Everyone played a role, but quite often it wasn't the one for which they were born. Temptation, the greed for wealth and fame, a privileged existence, led people astray, into the territory of others, where they themselves suffered and tormented those close to them.

Lord, what happiness it was to return to one's path after straying!

It had been a golden autumn back then. Rain was already falling on St. Petersburg, while the sun still shone in Ukraine, the sumptuous shoots of winter wheat were like green velvet and on the meadows and flooded fields the birdlife gathered for its sad autumnal games. Here and there the maples were already burning with cold flames and Indian summer hung out its silvery cobwebs on the dry broom grass by the roadside...

The carts of the court servants stretched behind her majesty's coach like the train of a gown. For so many days now, she had sat by the window admiring the landscape of woods and meadows, the tidy houses and streets of Cossack villages smothered in cherry orchards. Each evening, when they stopped for the night, she bid the court choristers and bandura players be summoned, and for a long time she listened to the songs born on this land by this proud though genial, sonorous people. And once, right near Kyiv, a local Cossack officer, after arguing with a tsarist minister, assembled lasses and lads from the nearest houses in place of the court choristers, and gave such a concert that the sovereign willed that they all be taken into her choir. And only after the officer had pleaded with her did she let them go, giving each a gold coin.

They had entered Kyiv on a sunny Sunday morning. Bells announced their arrival. Priests, townsfolk and subjects stood in crowds near the bridge and along the ramp. A detachment of cavalrymen dressed in bright green tunics embroidered in gold met the distinguished guest near the Dnipro River and pompously accompanied her to the Lavra church, where Elizabeth[18] was staying.

Back at the ramp Hryhoriy had jumped off the choristers' wagon, turned right and made his way toward the suburb of Podil through the golden forest along the Dnipro. Above him the old oaks and maples spread out their mighty arms and carpeted the path with fiery yellow leaves. They rumbled, rustled, tried to tell him something, but the bells gave them no opportunity, tolling throughout the city. He embraced the trees, patted them, told them about the longing which had gnawed away at his heart; he spoke to them without words, with his soul, and the thick-barked giants understood everything. They too had their aches and pains, but they had grown deep into the ground and feared neither storms nor landslides.

Under a wildling tree he gathered some ripe pears, stuffed them into his pockets and relished them, enjoying them all the way to the Academy.

And in the Academy, he had been immediately mobbed by students and instructors alike, who hadn't forgotten him yet, and inspected his sumptuous clothing from the capital, asking how things were there. Hryhoriy became so emotional that he could barely answer their questions, telling them about his life in the royal court, complaining about his fate, which had spurned him and had taken him along a foreign path. Slipping their arms through Skovoroda's, the zealous brethren immediately set off to find the rector.

"Gee-up, gee-up, my falcons!" Nychypir sang to the horses and flicked their wet backs with the reins.

"For some reason you're very cheerful today, uncle," Hryhoriy called out.

"Because I'm celebrating today! Gee-up, gee-up, there are no wolves to spur you on!"

....

[18] Elizabeth Petrovna, also known as Yelisaveta or Elizaveta, was the Empress of Russia from 1741 until her death in 1762.

"Is it maybe your name-day?"

"God no... Oh well, maybe yes! I'm newly born!" Nychypir guffawed. And he sang about the steppe, about liberty, which was like that firebird, attracting people, but not allowing itself to be caught...

The sacred truth! How much had been said of this firebird at the Academy... When the boys got going in the dormitory, the dispute would last until morning. Some shouted that everyone should go off to the Sich, the Cossack fortress, as they had done under Khmelnytsky, join the army and achieve freedom in battles fought with sabres, while others maintained that one could achieve destiny for the commoner and the Cossack peacefully, quietly, through knowledge and the education of the nobility in a spirit of brotherhood. Hrytsko Kozytsky had been the loudest among them. Pale, terribly thin, with a high forehead, he stood atop his bed and yelled resolutely into the excited crowd of students:

"All evil in the world stems from ignorance! Where knowledge and wisdom reign supreme, the whole of society benefits, from the elite to the commoner!"

"Nonsense!"

"Lies!"

"Such a miracle cannot be!"

"What about Yaroslav?[19] And Julius Caesar?!" Motonis shouted, flushed. There hadn't been an instance yet when his buddy hadn't supported him, refusing to contradict even a single word. Castor and Pollux! Though not brothers, these two were Dioscuri, of which there was a dearth in this long-suffering land of the Polianians.

"Knowledge and scholarship are the best weapons!" Kozytsky proclaimed passionately. "And our duty is to serve scholarship, humanity, and thus fight for a better lot for our land."

"Our brethren have opened schools from Chernihiv to Tobolsk, but it hasn't made the nobility any better!"

"They've even harnessed the Cossacks into yokes!"

"Made nearly all of them bonded people!"

"Offer the nobles a finger and they'll bite your arm off!"

....

[19]   Yaroslav the Wise (983–1054) – Rus' prince.

There were shouts, a tumult, until someone called out that it was dawning. The Dioscuri were the first to go to bed and fell asleep quickly, as if on cue. Every student could sleep through lessons in class with a light heart, but not these possessed two, who took in knowledge the way sand absorbed ink.

They had been sent off to study in Leipzig, as if it was in the far-flung reaches of the world. Having earned some money through *vertep*[20] puppet shows, the philosophy students organised such a merry send-off for them that the whole of Podil marvelled.

The Hudovych brothers, in whose retinue the boys intended to travel, were to leave early on the Saturday morning. On the Friday, sometime around noon, the full Academy choir assembled in the dormitory and thundered with a hymn. And then kegs of mead and spirits did the rounds. Soon the already tipsy brethren rolled out of the monastery in a crowd and, arms around Hrytsko and Mykola, burst into the nearest tavern, tossed out the drunks, downed some mead and launched into a doleful song. Having obtained a fiddle, a dulcimer and a flute from the tavern-keeper's wife, they launched into a *metelytsia*[21] dance with such gusto that bottles fell off the bar. And then they proceeded to a second, a third, and a fourth tavern.

Sometime toward morning, having kissed everyone goodbye, Hrytsko and Mykola bowed before the Brotherhood Monastery and the Academy, and went up Borychiv Rise to the Upper City, where the counts Hudovych were staying. And they seemed to melt into thin air after that. For six years people said they were supposed to be studying at the university in Leipzig...

"Whoa, whoa!" Nychypir yelled and pulled on the reins. Carried away with his singing, he had nearly run his horses into the cart ahead.

The waggon train stopped. The cloud still loomed black up ahead, but the wind had died down. In the distance the deep-red sun was diving into a blue expanse of forest. Chafers buzzed. In the pinkish sky mallards flew in impetuous pairs.

The footman galloped up and gave the order to stop for the night.

....

[20]   An ancient Ukrainian mobile puppet theatre, performing religious and humorous plays.

[21]   *Metelytsia* – (literally 'snowstorm') a Ukrainian folk dance which abounds in choreographed figures of a spinning nature, symbolizing a snowstorm.

They camped near a tavern some ten miles from Kyiv. Putting the horses to pasture, they had dinner and went to sleep: some slept on the carts, some on the grass under the lindens. Nychypir hobbled the horses, took a horse blanket and his grey German coat bought for him in winter by the lord, and went off into the night. But before Hryhoriy had made himself comfortable on the cart, he returned – now without the horse blanket and the coat – strained his ears and asked softly:

"Going to St. Petersburg or staying in Ukraine?"

"I still haven't decided," Skovoroda said, jumping down off the cart.

"Well, think, think hard then," Nychypir said. "If you happen to be in Chornukhy," he added after a short silence, "then visit my sister in Kyzlivka. She's the only family I have left..."

"I'll drop by to see her."

"Tell her I've gone off to find grandfather..."

"What's the matter, have you decided to die?" Hryhoriy took a step forward.

"Many a loaf of bread will perish before then!" Dolia laughed somehow fiercely. "Well, good health to you," he whispered and slipped off. But he returned straight away, hugged Hryhoriy, pressed him close, kissed him on the cheek and disappeared again into the darkness.

With sinking heart Hryhoriy watched him go: his compatriot would pull some fine stunt on this night. He felt alarmed and a little saddened that Nychypir hadn't opened his heart to him, hadn't asked for advice or help. He didn't trust him, considered Hryhoriy to be only partly on his side, or perhaps even a nobleman... He wanted so badly, so painfully to call out to Nychypir, to talk openly, sincerely with him, brother to brother, Cossack to Cossack. But was it worth meddling in the current of life, forcing one's friendship upon others? Perhaps everything should be allowed to continue along its natural path and the gods should not interfere, as the Romans had said?

He lay on his back atop the cart, cupping his hands under his head, and listened to the night. The horses smacked their lips in the damp meadow. In the willows which swirled near the pond way past the tavern, a nightingale was cheering its small lover, and in the village on the far side of the lake musicians kept playing the *holubets*, the *horlytsia* and the *metelytsia*.[22]

....

[22]   Ukrainian folk dances.

Once again, he recalled the boisterous send-off for Hrytsko and Mykola. To tell the truth, it had pained him then that he himself was not venturing off to foreign lands, where there were probably so many interesting, new, fresh things to do. Perhaps it was because of this that he found himself in Lord Vyshnevsky's mission, which had gone off to study the Tokay vineyards and winemaking. He had seen Vienna and Offen, spoken with people renowned for their scholarship. But throughout these three years he had never forgotten his own land: blood-soaked, drenched in sweat and torn apart, its steppes, ravines, cities and villages, and commoners, who strove to attain liberty and, like a chained Prometheus, were unable to do so. He had thought much about them, impatient to see them again, to breathe his native air and sleep under a Ukrainian sky, just like now – with a nightingale's song, the whisper of a breeze redolent of blossom, ploughed fields, and grasses... One needed to have a stone for a heart to live unfettered among foreigners in a foreign land!

The musicians grew silent. Countless sheep ran out onto a boundless velvet field and only the shepherd was late: he had caroused somewhere or had fallen asleep in the clouds, which had spread out on the horizon like a black spectre...

Finally, the fields became fields, and the sheep became sheep... He recalled Okip Outcrop near Chornukhy, the meadow beside it, and their forest, which was called Sava's. And Sava, his father, sharpened his scythe and, spitting on his rough muscular hands, began mowing his strip. The scythe swished, sighed, rang, and the juicy, lush grasses fell merrily at the edge of the strip, still not suspecting that this was their end, their demise...

A lark hovered above in the loftiness of the sky. It could not be seen, only its song was audible...

"Hey you, philosopher! Come on, wake up there!" someone shook him angrily.

Hryhoriy sat up, opened his eyes. The furious red mug of the footman seemed to float out of a mist.

"Where's your countryman Nychypir?!" the footman grabbed him by the clothes on his chest and drew him up.

Hryhoriy grasped the impudent hand and yanked at it so hard that the nobleman's henchman fell to the ground.

"A-ah, so that's your game!" the footman strained through his teeth and, getting up, drew his pistol.

Hryhoriy jumped down to the far side of the cart.

Who knows how this would have ended, had the boys not come running and defended him?

"You're all rogues!" the footman shouted. "It isn't enough to hang you all!"

"What's with him?" Hryhoriy asked when the footman headed back toward his master, still cursing. The colonel was already awake and, covering himself with a coat against the cold wind, watched the uproar from his coach.

"Nychypir's run off. Took a horse, a saddle, and a sabre, and took to his heels without leaving a trace!" the freckled coachman carting the wine explained. "Made off for the lower reaches of the Dnipro River, probably to join the Zaporozhian Cossacks."

"Went off wherever he pleased," another muttered sullenly.

Slipping his feet into his shoes and throwing a coat over his shoulders, Skovoroda went off into the fields; he wanted to be alone for a while. It had long since grown light, but it was still grey, for the black cloud seemed to have broken its tethers and was flying, spreading its wings across half the sky. The wind was growing stronger, bending trees, tousling their branches, carpeting the pond with pinkish-white blossom.

"A fine wind," he recalled Nychypir's words. "If he's off to the Sich, he'd be quite some distance away by now."

He envied Dolia. He too wanted to fly across the steppe on a jet-black steed, to breathe in the freshness of the wind and sense freedom with his whole body.

> *Oh steed, my fair steed,*
> *With long mane of gold...*

The first drops fell. Lightning flashed. A ploughman standing in a field nearby crossed himself hastily, glanced at the cloud, and again pressed down on the plough grips. The oxen moved along leisurely behind a small boy who walked on ahead, his white shirt billowing in the wind, his pants pasted against his legs. He took no notice of the wind or the rain, which was beginning to come down. He looked gloomily, heavily somewhere into the distance and measured the earth step by step, sagene by sagene.

"Socrates," Hryhoriy said quietly and stood under a linden tree, for the downpour had begun in earnest. The ramous lightning ripped through the sky more and more often, the thunderclaps became ever louder.

"Hryhoriy, hurry into the tavern!" voices called out from the road. "Hryhoriy!"

He did not answer. The meeting with his native land, the nice memories and Dolia's escape, the ploughman, and the clatter of thunder – everything had combined, merging into a single whole, which expanded his chest and filled him with strength. As if alive, the spreading linden trembled from the lightning and the wind. Its thin spring crown was no protection against the rain. And the rain came down in a wall, obscuring the horizon, the tavern, and the villager and the little boy with their oxen. It seemed there was nothing in the world except for the linden tree, the thunder, and the lightning. The burgeoning solitude was frightening, but his soul was cheered by that philosophical unseen unity between him and the world, which he had just fathomed.

Forsooth, perceive yourself and you will perceive everything! He did not remember whose bit of wisdom this was, but he was certain of its verity. The trembling of the linden was his trepidation, the claps of thunder echoed in his soul as if in a heavenly dome, the rain imparted a ticklish foreboding of rebirth, as if he, Hryhoriy, was that tiny seed which contained the future of humanity, forests, birds, and everything else which would perish, only to be reborn in the same image...

The rain stopped suddenly. The sun flashed and the earth glistened with spangles, seething with fragrances, everything strained upward. The ploughman stood in the field waiting for the land to drain, the oxen ruminated, and the boy watched the swallows which were already scraping the sky like black lightning. Steam hung over the fields drenched in sunshine. Coming to their senses after the rain and thunder, birds began to resume their chatter. The hoopoe piped away and the oriole played its flute...

"Hryhoriy! Come along, we're leaving!"

He heard them, and yet he didn't. He looked, listened to nature blossoming after the rain, and his heart moved ever further away from the bustle, the haughty notions and the weal with which Vyshnevsky tried to lure him to St. Petersburg. What was all this compared to freedom, to the life he strove for, and the right to reason?!

He threw back a wet lock of hair off his forehead, hung his coat over his arm and headed toward the train of carts.

THE SECOND NET

Hryhoriy had been absent from home only three years, but how much water had passed under the bridge, and how many good and bad changes had taken place! Without having bidden their younger son farewell, his father and mother had passed away. His sister-in-law had given birth to a girl, and her boys had already grown up and now tended cattle and rode horseback no worse than grown Cossacks. And his brother had changed too. He no longer jabbered like a mill, and now spoke staidly, demurely, stroking his moustache as he brought a glass to his mouth. True, after Hryhoriy told him that he entertained no intentions of farming and let him retain all the land and property acquired by their father, Stepan beamed joyously and yelled out: "Dash into the larder, wife, there's another hunk of bacon there somewhere!"

Hryhoriy felt both sad and happy when he recalled this meeting with his brother Stepan. Sad, because it was the first time he had seen him in the firm grip of land and prosperity, but also happy, for once more, at the crossroads of life, he had not followed his older brother along the most travelled path, which destiny had prepared for him, but had chosen his own path. Even though it was difficult and thorny, it suited his temperament.

For two long months he wandered about the Hetmanate[23] lands, with books in his bag and grief in his heart. He was like that stalk in the field. No one cared about him; he had no one to confide in. Each person had his own life, his own troubles, sorrows and joys. Only his friends from the Academy rejoiced at his arrival, as if youth itself was visiting them from years past, from Kyiv. Oh, how many embraces there had been in the summer, how many memories shared and tears shed! Though a student's life was not easy, it was still preferable to the vanity dominating the world, the eternal turmoil, disease, and fear for one's own welfare, the fate of one's children...

....

[23]   Hetmanate – the Cossack state.

He sighed, adjusted his bag so it wouldn't dig into his shoulder, and stepped off the road to make way for a cart rattling up behind him. He was delighted to be like a bird in the sky, free as free can be, a vagrant Cossack for whom the steppe was his home, the grasses his bed, and the sabre his wife. True, he had no sabre... However, he had books, knowledge and wisdom, which humanity had nurtured within the hearts of its better sons, from the wise Hellenes to Prokopovych.[24] And what in this world was superior to wisdom?!

"Whoa! Whoa!" someone shouted frantically beside him. "Who do I see there?! Is this a mirage, Hrytsko?!"

Hryhoriy shielded his eyes against the sun and on the cart which had drawn up alongside him he spied a giant in Cossack dress, with a lambskin hat pushed to one side.

Jumping down from the cart, the Cossack embraced Hryhoriy and kissed him awkwardly on the nose and cheek.

"I thought you'd already vanished somewhere in foreign parts!"

Only now did Skovoroda recognise the giant as the Mykyta who had been nicknamed Stork in the dormitory because of his long legs. He was also overjoyed at this unexpected, though welcome meeting.

"Whither and whence?" Mykyta asked briefly, without releasing Skovoroda from his embrace.

"To Pereyaslav..."

"Really?!" Stork threw up his arms.

"To teach in your Collegium..."

"But that's wonderful! My nephew's studying there and we have a future student running about without pants back home! And our instructors aren't exactly among the wisest... Why have we stopped? Let's go!"

He grabbed Skovoroda about the waist and dragged him over to the cart. Once they had made themselves comfortable and the horses set off, he fell back, grabbed his pistol and, with a shout of *"vivat professores!"*,[25] fired into the deep blue sky.

....

24   Feofan Prokopovych (1681–1736) – Ukrainian theologian, writer, poet, mathematician, philosopher, translator, rector of the Kyiv-Mohyla Academy (1710–1716).

25   Long live the professors! (Latin)

Frightened, the horses surged forward at a gallop. Trees and stooked sheaves of wheat flashed past.

"How about you, serving in the army?" Hryhoriy asked after his spirited fellow classmate had quietened down a little and put away his pistol.

"A lieutenant!" Stork struck his breast.

"Oho!"

"Why, am I some country bumpkin?! What stops me from being a Cossack?"

"I can't get used to the idea," Hryhoriy said softly. "So thin, long-legged..."

"Like a stork!" Mykyta guffawed, lifted a finger, wrinkled his forehead, and announced in Latin: "*Tempora mutantur, et nos mutamut in illis!*[26] Isn't that so, teacher? You were the first among us!"

"You're not the man you used to be..."

"Small wonder! I've tasted freedom! Thanks to the Empress and God, Cossackdom is revelling again!"

"A bitter beggar's piece..."

"Have you seen the *hetman*?" Stork asked fervently. "He's an eagle! A philosopher! One like that will defend our freedom! And we'll help him."

"Tell me, Mykyta, does the *hetman* have many serfs?"

"A few thousand."

"Wow, that's a regiment of Cossacks, perhaps two..."

"You always were a strange one, Hrytsko," the lieutenant replied after a silence.

"Can freedom be defended by someone who himself enslaves others?" Hryhoriy asked.

Mykyta pulled his neck in. Turning away, he examined the reigns intently, coughed, and whipped the horses. It was obvious, he had his finger in the pie too. Throughout the Hetmanate lords and lordlings were raking land, estates and commoners under themselves, including their own relatives. And Rozumovsky, that Cossack son who was now a count and a *hetman*, the brother of the empress' lover, blessed all this, this 'freedom' of the Cossack officers, while playing the father defending Mother Ukraine and her poor orphans from the St. Petersburg court dragons.

---

[26] Times are changing and we are changing with them! (Latin)

"Here it is, our miracle of a city!" Mykyta pointed into the sun-bathed distance.

Girded by a blue-green belt, a walled city was perched atop a hill. In the misty sky above it floated crosses and church domes aflame with gold, as if competing with the sun. Fishing boats rocked lazily on the Trubizh River, horses grazed in the meadow, and near the walls, under the willows, there were graceful white figures of women and strips of linen spread out on the grass in the sun.

"Have you been in Pereyaslav before?"

"Never had the opportunity."

Mykyta stretched out on the cart, supported his head with his arm, and began recounting everything he knew about his home town. However, only every second word reached Hryhoriy, for he sat as if bewitched, taking in the beauty not only with his eyes, but with his whole being, which had suddenly become buoyant and insensible, like mist over a dawn meadow. His soul was filled with a foreboding of something new and joyous. Like all vagrants, he too had a niche in his heart where there lurked a desire for certainty, to have his own corner in this uneasy, cruel world, his own piece of bread, albeit stale, and even enjoy the smile of a girl's lips...

"Have you fallen asleep there? Wake up, Hryhoriy!" Mykyta shook him.

Still smiling because of his daydreams, Skovoroda glanced at him and asked with his eyes what it was that he had wanted to ask him.

"Who invited you to the Collegium?"

"The bishop, through Father Hervasiy."

"What will you be teaching the offspring?"

"Poetry."

"Oho!"

"Why not? I'm no country bumpkin, you know!"

At the crossroads the horses turned toward the city of their own accord and, thumping over the new bridge, made off at a faster gait along the well-travelled road on the dam wall.

Mykyta stopped the perspiring horses outside his grace's residence, adjusted his hat, and said: "Well, here we are. Go through the gate, there's a door on the left there and you'll spy the bishop."

In the city Mykyta became staid and reserved. He seemed like any other respected lieutenant, not Stork.

"Once you've settled in," he added, "come and visit. It's not far, near Mykhailivsky Cathedral. We can down a chalice or two, recall our Kyiv days and the Academy!"

"I'll drop by, Mykyta," Hryhoriy said hurriedly, slipped his bag over his shoulder and said farewell: "Good luck!"

"In good time!" Mykyta called out and waved.

Moving his heavy, stiff legs Hryhoriy made his way under the pale-blue arch of the gate and entered the courtyard. On his right he saw the dark shape of a wrought-iron oak door in the pale-blue wall, and further on were windows and more windows; up above was a high iron roof and white cherubic clouds. To the right was an orchard, a well, stables, and a gilded light coach.

He suddenly felt scared for some reason, imagining the face of the bishop whom he had seen back in the Academy, and stopped dead in his tracks. Lord Almighty, what would he say to him? How would he prove his ability to teach squires the great wisdom of composing poetry? Mentor of youth, Hryhoriy Skovoroda, the son of farmer Sava! Is this not blasphemy, Hryhoriy? Do you wish to play someone else's role in the theatre of life? Don't tempt fickle fate! Before it is too late, leave this yard, this city and, having blessed your vagabond path, go forth among the people, play the flute, teach people to do good and grow wise. Wisdom is boundless! And yet, having grabbed its miserable crumb, you are insolently prepared to mount the pulpit and deliver its maxims...

Near the gate he met Father Hervasiy. The father superior embraced Hryhoriy, kissed him as a close friend, and asked: "Been to see Iosaf?"

"Not yet…"

"Then off you go! This is his little temple!"

The rounded, lively Father Hervasiy pattered along like a woman; he recounted, inquired, rejoiced at the pleasant meeting and cheered up Hryhoriy without letting him utter a word. He led him indoors, bade a novice inform his grace that he had a visitor, and said in parting: "I will go and tell them to prepare a decent cell for you."

The chamber Hryhoriy was standing in was high and spacious. Benches hugged the walls, in the corner under the icons stood a large table covered with a luxurious tablecloth, and there were several deep, comfortable armchairs. And also, an icon lamp. Its meandering crimson light illuminated

Sabaoth's face, then, with a flicker, crossed to the Holy Mother or The Precursor standing at the edge of the desert, setting a crowd of heathens onto the true path...

"Is it you, Hryhoriy?" the bishop appeared in the doorway. He blessed him and motioned him into an armchair. Sitting opposite, he spoke softly but clearly, as if fearing that his interlocutor might not comprehend something and leave without quenching his thirst, like a traveller who had not drunk at a well because there was no shadoof. He was thin, delicate, his long hair fell onto his shoulders. Almost unchanged from several years earlier. Except that he had turned a little greyer.

"I've heard that you recently visited foreign parts."

Skovoroda nodded.

"So, what did you see? Whom did you meet? How did you enrich your mind and soul?"

"I was in Tokay, Vienna, Pressburg, Offen... I travelled quite a few roads and spoke with all kinds of people..."

"With the Orthodox? Or with Lutherans and Catholics?"

"I did not inquire. Similarly, no one asked me my faith." Skovoroda smiled. He understood what his grace was intimating: afraid that he had absorbed too many foreign ideas. "They don't revere the church there very much at all," he added on purpose. "Even though they have faith in their hearts and pray to the Lord..."

"It is merely half a step from Protestantism to heresy," the bishop intoned and moved closer to the point: "Father Hervasiy told you that we need a teacher who knows poetics and can teach our students how to compose and comprehend poetry. I've heard that you have knowledge and experience in this difficult area, so I've agreed to your coming and saved a place for you. Watch out that you are worthy! Try hard. Don't begrudge your powers or knowledge. And so that you have someone to emulate..." He opened a drawer. "...take this book – very wise, though still unpublished. It was given to me by the author himself. Guard it like the apple of your eye and draw wisdom from it!"

Iosaf rose and came up to the newly appointed poetics instructor, who also jumped to his feet and stood, clutching the book to his chest.

"Don't be frightened," he took him by the arm and smiled. "All of us were once green and young when we began our good deed..."

"I'm very grateful," Hryhoriy began, but the bishop interrupted him: "Wait, what about your ailment? You stammer, don't you? I recall the bishop in Kyiv wanted to ordain you a priest!"

Dropping his gaze meekly, Hryhoriy replied: "I was healed, father…"

"As soon as you left the Academy?"

"The ways of the Lord are unfathomable…"

"Well, may the Lord go with you!" The bishop smiled without any malice. "Go to the Collegium, read Konysky, pray, think. The first lesson is tomorrow!"

When Hryhoriy emerged into the courtyard, illuminated by the evening sun, a monk, who had been dozing on a rock by the gate, came toward him. Sullen, grim, with a large mane of hair and a bushy beard, he would have frightened the living daylights out of Hryhoriy, had he come across him in the twilight.

"Follow me," he told Hryhoriy and trudged off toward the gate.

Skovoroda felt a pleasant lightness throughout his entire body and soul, a sense of joy and self-assurance. He already loved his future pupils, curious and thoughtful. He burnt with a desire to impart not only what he knew, but also those things which he would come to know, for he understood how much there still was that was inscrutable, and strongly believed in the immense power of the human mind. He did not miss the fields, the endless roads, the hot days and the sad nights, cool as spring water. It was wonderful here too! Such a high sky, such parks, such a sluggish river way beyond the city walls, the osier, the meadows… How nicely the sun went to bed, spreading out a sheet of forests and covering itself with a cloud…

He caught up to his sullen guide, touched his shoulder: "Look, father, what beauty!"

The fellow didn't let out a single mutter. He walked along, indifferent and unmoved. Turning into the monastery grounds and passing the church, he stopped by an old stone building with narrow windows, opened a weather-beaten door. In the small hallway stood a bucket of water and a wooden mug. Stepping over the holes in the floor, the monk entered one of the cells, letting Hryhoriy inside, and left in silence, dissolving like a wisp of smoke…

A small bare table stood under the icons, and on it stood a candle in a candlestick turned out of wood. By the wall was a trestle bed covered with coarse fabric. There was also a stool and that was all.

Hryhoriy placed the *Poetics* manuscript on the table, slipped his bag onto the windowsill, and removed his coat. He lay down on the trestle bed and sighed with relief. All day he had been on the road! Even the sun had tired of warming the earth; its crimson reflections were dying away on the sill. The heavy twilight grew thicker still…

Even though he hadn't had a crumb to eat all day, he had no desire to seek out the refectory. He grabbed his coat, slipped his hand into a pocket, and pulled out a stale hunk of bread he had been saving since the day before yesterday, just in case. He breathed in the smell of bread, fields, ripe rye… Biting off a large mouthful, he began to chew on it without hurrying, without succumbing to the body's desire to assuage his hunger as quickly as possible. Mice were rustling about somewhere, squeaking: they had smelt food. He broke off a small piece of bread and tossed it into a dark corner. He would not be satiated by that crumb, yet for them it would be supper.

Finishing the bread, he lay down and listened to the silence. It had become completely dark. Only the window was grey and in places the paint on the ascetic, stern, divine faces of the icons still glinted.

Suddenly he sat up, reached for a flint and some tinder. He struck some fire and lit the thick wax candle. Sitting down on the stool, he opened the book. Latin, Latin! Everything was familiar, already heard before… This was the very same book Konysky had taught them from at the Academy!

With a sad heart he turned the pages and imagined the classes, the boys, and the professor's face: a high forehead, wise, with two warts to the right of his moustache… God, it was all the same! The years had moved along, passed under the bridge. Life flowed like a river: everything changed, lived and was renewed – the world, its people, and even wisdom. That which had once seemed inviolable truth, set in stone and immovable, was today merely ashes and dust.

He closed the book. This was no way to teach poetry! Back in the Academy they had sought new directions, studied German and Polish poems, Trediakovsky[27] and Lomonosov, discussed why the simple songs of the common folk touched everyone's soul, why they lived on through the ages while the panegyrics of philosophising rhymesters were written in vain –

....

[27]   Vasily Kirillovich Trediakovsky (1703–1769) – Russian poet, essayist and playwright who helped lay the foundations of classical Russian literature.

and died in vain. He still wasn't sure where the truth lay, where it was to be found, but he was certain that he would not be teaching using that petrified method. As Heraclitus[28] had once said, one can never step twice into the same water in a river!

Blowing out the candle, he felt his way over to his spartan bed, removed his shoes, lay down and immediately fell asleep, as he had trained himself to do in the dormitory.

He woke as dawn was beginning to break, dressed, washed by the window outside, and went off to roam about the city. Thoughts came to him when he felt unfettered, surrounded by nature, under the heavens. Then you felt you were the crowning glory of nature, its best creation. Thoughts soared like falcons, the lungs breathed in the fresh morning breeze, and the soul glowed with that primordial bliss, which was the least treacherous.

Pereyaslav was still catching up on its sleep. There was a dead silence in the city. He could only hear ripe apples occasionally falling onto the resilient earth of people's yards and sleepy birds squawking, sensing that morning had arrived, but still unable to rouse themselves. Under the fences there was already the occasional pile of withered leaves, straw, and dry vines of trailing plants: summer was passing. Another month or two and it would be swept away, snuffed out. Then the homeless could do little else but sit down and cry, for frosts were no joke… Well, thank God he now had a roof over his head, shelter, work, pupils, and friends. Everything that one needed!

He descended the ramp to the city gates, which were already open, and came out onto the banks of the Alta River, stopping in amazement. The old spreading willows standing in the mist looked as if they were in water. They hung down in heavy clouds over the narrow meadow, ready to dump a deluge of leaves onto the earth. And beyond the ravine and the mist, on the yellow-grey slope, horses dozed, as if they were suspended in the heavens...

The water in the river was clear, sluggish. It flowed, barely stirring the weeds overgrown with green moss, without any eddies or turns – like a sorrowful song.

From the mists, from the distance, came the sounds of neighing and lip smacking. The heavenly horses immediately became alert, raising their heads...

....

[28]   Heraclitus of Ephesus (535 – circa 475 BC) – pre-Socratic Greek philosopher.

Skovoroda shuddered: once more his soul began to throb with that testamental, distant half-legend and half-truth, which he had taken with him from home as his only and most precious treasure. What if that magical golden horse had become bogged in the mire here, drowned by our ancestors who had found themselves in an implacable storm?

Again and again, he heard neighing and snorting. Descending the ramparts, he ran deliriously along the narrow, shallow river and stopped where the Alta joined the fast-flowing Trubizh River. Hemmed in by the water and the cliff, he checked his heart and listened. Nothing anywhere. Only mist and silence. And a solitary guelder rose bending over the misty mirror of the river, admiring its beauty. Further on more bushes of guelder rose burnt red... What beauty! Red clusters of berries against the grey willows, and the first rays of sunshine which broke through from behind a church dome, piercing the mist, the water, and even the berries laden with juice, or perhaps the blood of warriors who had fallen in bloody battles on the banks of the dreamy Alta...

The horse could not be heard.

Glowing from the exercise, Hryhoriy took off his coat and hat, went down on his knees and bent over to wash with water from the river. Still straining his ears, he rested his gaze on the reflection of his face. He had grown haggard during the summer – his cheek-bones were protruding, his eyes had become sunken. His nose had grown longer, his forehead higher. His hair was bleached from going about a long time without a hat. Luckily, he had had a haircut in Lubny. Even though it had been a 'bowl' haircut, at least he wouldn't be entering the auditorium looking like a long-haired hermit! In the auditorium... For a poetics class... Was this really true, or just some fanciful dream? Yesterday he had been a vagrant Cossack, homeless and unneeded in this world, and today he was a teacher, a mentor of youth!

He washed hastily and wiped himself with a handkerchief. Picking up his coat and hat, he made his way back to the city gates. The mist cleared slightly. He could now clearly see the cows and sheep crossing the bridge on the far side of the Alta together with the herdsmen, still sleepy and sluggish. A horseman galloped into the city flashing a sword hilt or a pistol in the sunshine. Geese cackled, rejoicing at the water and the new day. Hammers, flails and pestles pounded away. Tardy wisps of smoke rose into the sky from chimneys...

The world settled down to its daily routine, its daily bustle.

At an intersection of two streets, he came across Mykyta and a pupil.

"Well, how did it go?" the lieutenant rushed up to him. "Did the bishop bless you?"

"That he did."

"Well, thank God for that. Ivas, come here!" he called to his nephew, who was standing nearby. "This is your new teacher – Hryhoriy Savych Skovoroda."[29]

Ivas bowed to him.

"And this is my nephew," Mykyta poked the small lad in the chest. "A smart lad! And so quick with Latin – leaves me for dead!"

"In which class?" Hryhoriy asked the pupil.

But Mykyta wouldn't even let him open his mouth: "In poetics, of course!" He grabbed Hryhoriy about the waist, screwed up his eyes and twirled his red moustache: "Come to my place and we'll have a glass of mead or spirits! It's not far. See that house with a shingle roof and the two poplars? That's my place. And what a wife I've got, Hrytsko!" he smacked his lips avidly.

"God bless you, brother," Hryhoriy thanked him. "I'll come by and we'll have that drink, only not now. I've got lessons! And I'm trembling like an aspen and anxious…"

"All the more reason to have a drink!" The lieutenant threw up his hands. When I go to Hlukhiv, I down a mug for courage to face the clear eyes of the *hetman*. Ivas! Ivas!"

"He's run off to the Collegium," Hryhoriy said genially. "And it's time for me to go too."

"Pity, pity," Mykyta drawled. "Then I'll go and have one myself in the name of the Father, the Son and the Holy Ghost…"

"Amen," Skovoroda finished the sentence and said goodbye to the merry lieutenant.

Poetry! Wherein lay its kernel, its great mystery revealed to the select few? There are thirty ways to write poetry, and the thirty-first way is the

....

[29]   As a mark of respect and in formal situations a person was addressed by their given name, patronymic and surname. Acquaintances might use merely the name and patronymic. Family and close friends would use the diminutive form Hrytsko.

way you will write it. During the ten years that he studied in Kyiv, piles of poems were scribbled down. Everyone wrote, but where were the poets? Still unborn, or tottering under tables, or were they already studying, befriended by muses?

Perhaps they were here in the Collegium, awaiting his advice, his exhortations... New Homers and Virgils! There were thirty ways...

Near the Collegium he was joined by Father Hervasiy, who blessed him for the work ahead and accompanied him to the classroom.

Finally, Hryhoriy was left face to face with his pupils. They sat silently, well-behaved and attentive, eyeing their new teacher. He smiled and the class sighed with relief.

"Gentlemen, friends!" Hryhoriy began his lecture. The students exchanged glances and became agitated. "Latin is a fine language," he answered their silent question. "The great Romans speak to us in this language, together with today's eminent men of scholarship. Praise and glory to the wise! But why should we borrow other people's water, when we have our own well – deep, pure and inexhaustible? You are all the future shepherds of your people, poets and warriors who will stand guard over freedom and wisdom. The people are mighty with you, and you are mighty with the people. You are not homeless Ivans without a family tree, but Cossacks whose grandfathers routed the Polish gentry and shook The Porte.[30] You are the descendants of brave, cheerful, generous, clear-voiced Ruthenians, who won glory from the Pechenegs, the Cumans, and Byzantium.

"Poetry is no cunning toy, it's a spiritual sword; stunning and sharp in the hands of the skilled, and only a hunk of ordinary steel in the hands of those incapable of wielding weapons.

"We must master this craft. And master it we will!

"There are thirty ways to compose poetry, but the thirty-first way is yours. That is, of course, if the muses have not deserted you."

He spoke enthusiastically, noticing neither the passage of time nor the fact that soon both doorways were packed with teachers and students from neighbouring classrooms. He spoke about the essence of poetry, about the eminent poets of all peoples and all times, from Ancient Greece to Prokopovych and Lomonosov. He shared his doubts about the old canons

....

[30]   The Ottoman Empire.

of poetics and called on his pupils not to expect ready truths from him, but to think for themselves, to seek, compare, and forge new paths. He finished his lecture with the words of the blind bards who bore songs and ballads throughout Ukraine, just as the wind carried seeds, stopping people's hearts from becoming overgrown with the thistles of unruffled serenity.

The students were enchanted, and he himself did not have his feet on the ground: he was not standing under the heavy arches of the auditorium, but was in the kingdom of the spirit, in the macrocosm of the goddess of wisdom.

He recovered only on the trestle bed in his cell. Lying there, he was relieved that the frightening first lecture was behind him. He was dissatisfied that he had been too reserved, and ardently aspired to impart to his students in two hours everything which he himself had taken years to collect in his homeland and in three foreign countries.

A merry sunbeam played hide and seek in the cell. It would disappear, and then reappear again on the filthy old floor, luring people out into the sun, into the open fields of lush grass, where there was a fresh breeze, but the sky was already faded.

He sat up on his hard bed and felt an irrepressible hunger. Find the refectory, for you've earned your daily bread, Hryhoriy!

In the twilight of the hallway, he bumped into the lieutenant's nephew.

"Mister teacher, the bishop is asking for you."

"Well, there you go! And I was about to go and have breakfast."

"He ordered that you come at once."

"Let it be so," Hryhoriy sighed. "When the body is hungry, it's not half bad, but when the soul thirsts – that's real trouble… Where is he, Ivas?"

"In his palace. Father Hervasiy said he was fuming…"

"Then I'll have to run!" Hryhoriy joked.

"And take along the *Poetics* his grace gave you."

"What on earth for?"

Ivas shrugged.

With a sense of foreboding, Skovoroda returned to his cell, grabbed Konysky's book under his arm and hurried out.

Iosaf sat in a chair under the icons. He nodded in answer to the greeting and asked: "So, have you forgotten your Latin?"

"I trust not."

"Then why transform the Collegium into a playground?"

"I didn't invite the students from other classes," Skovoroda heaved his shoulders.

"I invited you here to teach poetics, not to amuse us with interludes!"

"But you weren't there, you didn't hear…"

"Like the Lord, the bishop knows all and hears all," Iosaf said viciously.

"I didn't notice anyone laughing," Skovoroda frowned.

"Our students are well behaved," the bishop said. "Besides, I must remind you that this is no country fair, it's a Slavic Greek Latin school, a temple of scholarship and wisdom…"

"And therefore?"

"Therefore, the sweet sounds of Latin must resound here."

"Everything is fine to a certain degree and at a given point in time…"

"Wisdom can have no degrees."

"But Latin is no equivalent to wisdom," Hryhoriy remarked in reply. "There is just as much nonsense written in this language."

The bishop's face became covered in splotches.

"Do you realise what you are saying? The great Romans…"

"But we are not Romans. And we are not great," Hryhoriy added slyly. He was beginning to enjoy this argument, this unexpected amazing dispute.

The bishop leafed through his papers for a long time.

"Give me back Konysky," he raised his thorny grey eyes. "I was told… What's this?!" he asked angrily on opening the book.

"Must be mice." Hryhoriy became embarrassed.

"How did you dare?!" the bishop thundered.

"I didn't take a single bite."

"Blaspheming? Without this book we are as if without arms and legs! What are we going to use now to teach the great wisdom of poetic composition? The damned animals even took no pity on the title," the bishop grieved, leafing through the unfortunate book. "Now we might as well head for Kyiv. Perhaps they'll write one for us there. Or give us a replacement text."

"I can write one," Hryhoriy said softly. "Please allow me the honour!"

"You?" the bishop said forcefully, and smiled. "Well then," he added, eyeing the impertinent fellow sullenly. "As they say, may the Lord help our calf. Give it a go! Show me what you have in a week. Meanwhile Father

Hervasiy will take your students peacefully through the gardens of the Bible."

The bishop rose decisively. There was none of the affability and courtesy with which he had spoken the day before, as he saw Hryhoriy to the door.

The sovereigns of this world love everyone to succumb to them without reservation, in silence. Convinced of their boundless authority and infallibility, they radiate majesty and acknowledge no verity other than their own. To them the sensible are meek, a friend is servile and unworthy, and an enemy is one who doubts, seeks and thinks.

Feeling shattered, Hryhoriy left the bishop's chambers and wandered off through the autumnal city. He avoided the fallen yellow leaves which burnt here and there in the narrow streets like splinters of sun. He breathed in the tantalizing scents of hot meals and overripe pears, and philosophised. He turned over the pages of his life like a book unfinished, but long since begun. Nonsense! The world did not need him as he was, the way nature or God, or simply his parents had created him. Everyone tried to remould him in their likeness, to alter him like an ill-fitting coat or a hat that is the wrong size. Those who were as pliant as wax were rolling in clover. The sons and grandsons of freedom fighters were becoming lords, trading in conscience and commoners, no worse than the Polish aristocracy or the Muscovite courtiers. They raked and snatched, tearing the long-suffering, blood-soaked land into pieces. The grandsons of knights bartered freedom like those whores lounging about the taverns, selling their luckless bodies.

From the steppe, from the north, a wind burst into the city, raising dust and withered weeds.

A cold wind! One that stripped leaves for fun, breathed of snows, and drove vagabonds and animals into burrows…

He pulled down his hat and buttoned his coat. Not so much against the wind dashing about the streets as against the future which stalked him with Iosaf's savage frosty eye.

Still so tender, so merry early that same morning, the city now appeared foreign and gloomy. The half-blind old buildings, the squalid stalls and the neglected, peeling churches oppressed the soul. And the beggars and cripples, dirty and ragged, were like spectres out of hell… They grew in number each year, these disinherited wretches. But maybe they were happy? Satisfied with the necessities and neglecting the superfluous. Was not happiness contained therein? One could eat one's fill of goose and dream of swan, or one could chew on a stale crust of bread and be satiated. .

This impetuous cold wind was permeated with stubble, winter crops, leaves, mushrooms and bread. In the steppe outside the city, it was even more biting, chilling people to the bone. It was good to have a sheepskin coat and boots for the winter. But this required money, and no small sum at that! A teacher's pay, of course...

Suddenly he felt so alone and alien, wanting to sit down and cry. He looked about to see where he had wandered so absentmindedly, and turned to the right toward two poplars which towered way beyond the square. Mykyta was a good-hearted lad, he would not spurn him. He would even be delighted to see him. For he too was probably suffering for lack of close friends. The Lord gave us friendship. Or maybe not the Lord, but people! The best way to make a free man into a slave, an apostate, was to force him to fear his close friends. The solitary were wild animals or gods. And gods were few and far between, while heinous animal-people were blind. Bastards without mind or honour had multiplied throughout Ukraine like weeds in an unsown, neglected field. Stem by stem they had destroyed the brooms which swept rubbish out of houses. And people stood and blinked like rams in an abattoir. The Lord turned away the proud, showering His grace upon the meek... To hell with the blockhead's meekness and Judas' grace!

Mykyta was rubbing down his stallion. He ran a horse comb over its raven-black coat and kept repeating: "Stand still, horsie. We'll rub you down nicely, and then you'll gleam like a newly minted coin. To a Cossack, his horse is like a dear brother."

The stallion kept glancing at him with its big black eye and, as if in agreement with the lieutenant's thoughts, neighed softly and shifted its feet.

"A fine horse you've got there!" Hryhoriy said, after perching on the stile.

Mykyta swung around abruptly, beamed with joy and, resting the horse comb on the stallion's back, shouted for the entire household to hear: "Onysia, dear, come and greet a dear guest!"

He embraced Hryhoriy as if he hadn't seen him a whole lifetime, kissed him, and placing his enormous hand on his waist, led him off into the house.

On the porch they were met by a beautiful lively young woman, who bowed and came up to Hryhoriy with a high white bread on a wooden tray.

"We welcome you warmly," she said, blushing all over and dropping her eyes.

In the hallway, when Onysia had run off to fetch some food and drink, Mykyta pulled off Hryhoriy's coat and, blissfully rubbing his hands, whispered: "Well, did you see my lovely wife?! I barely managed to tame her and snatch her out of Lokhvytsia! The swains buzzed around her there like bees around honey!" He turned up his ruddy moustache and screwed up his eyes. "The Pereyaslavians and I scattered them all and I seized her from under their very noses! It's been two years and they're still angry with us... Hark, here's my dear wife again with her mead and spirits!" He called out, noticing that his wife had returned. "Set it down, Onysia, for our guest is probably hungry as a dog..."

"Mykyta, you should be ashamed, using such language in front of strangers..."

"Who, him, a stranger?" The lieutenant hugged his wife. "We sang together for two years for alms.[31] Whenever we launched into "May the Peace of Christ Dwell in Your Homes" the kindhearted aunties would give us their last coins, and treat us to mead or spirits. Those were the days," he sighed and grew sullen. But then a short while later he came to life, kissed his wife on her pink ear and grabbed a faceted bottle. "Sit down Hryhoriy, and we'll down a glass or two, so that destiny doesn't pass us by!"

Hryhoriy sat down, unable to fend off the invitation. He at once felt relaxed and cheerful here. All the bitterness seemed to have magically evaporated.

The hostess brought out some borsch, hot and fragrant like a meadow in June.

"Well, here's to us!"

"To us!"

"Ooh, a good potion! Down it in one breath, Onysia!"

She waved her supple swanlike white arms about, smiled through a twinkle of tears, and invited them to partake: "Have a bite of something. There's aspic here and lardo."

....

[31]   All year round throughout their studies, students would visit houses after sunset and sing hymns to receive alms in the form of money, food and other necessities.

Skovoroda tucked in. The vodka passed through his body in a wave, splashed into his head and feet, and filled him with languor. Of course, they would never have served such delicious borsch or lardo in the monastery refectory...

Mykyta poured a second glass, sliced up more bread and, waiting until Hryhoriy finished a slice, raised his glass: "Let's drink a second one, brethren, so the first one isn't lonesome!"

"Farewell, dear mind, we shall meet again tomorrow!" Hryhoriy added.

"Forsooth!" Mykyta called out, downed his vodka and kissed his wife. "They say you raised all hell, Hryhoriy! Ivas came by and said the Collegium is still buzzing..."

"Why, aren't the students pleased either?" Skovoroda grew wary.

"They're in raptures! But the instructors are angry, because they are being pressured into conducting all lessons in our native tongue! You played quite a trick there!" Mykyta roared with laughter.

"The bishop has already upbraided me."

"Ah, spit on him!"

"Mykyta," Onysia piped up reproachfully. "He's a cleric..."

"I'll refrain, my dear, by God I will," the lieutenant placated his wife.

Onysia again invited Hryhoriy: "Go on, eat up, or your borsch will go cold. The host of this house will talk anyone into the ground. Last year he brought in some beggar, sat him down to lunch, and quizzed him for so long about where he'd been and what he'd seen, that the poor fellow went and fainted. And then in spring..."

"Onysia, love," the lieutenant interrupted her craftily. "His borsch is getting cold..."

Hryhoriy ate the hot dish and it made him more intoxicated than the alcohol. It was a pleasure to listen to this chirping couple, to admire their happiness, and even to be a little jealous. They already had their snug haven, their rock, their firmament. While he was being blown about by the winds of life like a ship which yearned for distant shores yet to be reached by anyone.

After a third glass, over roast meat, Hryhoriy began to complain about the world, his fate and the bishop, whose mind was set like a cart wedged against a stump.

"Don't worry, Hrytsko!" the lieutenant moved closer to him. "A priest's tongue is like a Petrivka day.[32] All right, all right, love, I won't any more, by God I won't," he apologized, and then turned to Hryhoriy: "It'll all pass, you'll see. And if not, you can come here. You won't die with Mykyta," he beat his breast. "I heard that Tomara is looking for a teacher for his lad. Well, and our little Bohdan's growing up too." The lieutenant hugged his wife.

"And how old is he?"

"One year old next week!" Mykyta exclaimed. "Leading the life of a Cossack at his grandma's."

"Oh! A student already."

"Preparing for the Academy! Listen, you haven't forgotten how to play, have you?"

"I don't think so."

"Then let's pound out one of our songs!"

"'May the Peace of Christ Dwell'?"

"May it suffer a fit!" The lieutenant waved his hand about hopelessly, took down a violin off the carpet on the wall and handed it to Hryhoriy. He took a *kobza*[33] for himself, ran his fingers over the strings, knitted his brows, and began:

> *Oh there, Bohdan, oh Bohdan, Zaporozhian hetman,*
> *Why are you going about in black, oh in black velvet...?*

Skovoroda ran his bow across the strings and the violin grieved and lamented like a Cossack mother on the battlefield...

"I can't, Hrytsko!" the lieutenant tugged at his shirt. "It makes my heart bleed..."

He dropped his head onto his chest, remained silent awhile, and then suddenly, with a flick of his locks, launched into a merry song:

> *Reeds crackle and crash,*
> *Marsh waters do splash,*

---

[32]   St. Peter's fast, or Petrivka, is a brief fast which begins a week after Holy Trinity. It is summer then in Ukraine and the days are short.

[33]   A favoured string instrument of the Ukrainian Cossacks, having three to eight strings.

'Tis uncle lugging,
A perch off to auntie…!

Skovoroda returned to the Voznesensk Monastery in the moonlight. The streets were quiet and deserted, although boys could be heard singing beyond the ramparts on the Trubizh River. Here and there lights burnt in windows covered with branches. A hasty horseman clickity-clacked past and dissolved into the evening gloom. He heard the voices of the guards at the gates. Somewhere a girl let out a scream and roared with laughter…

Lord, what majestic tranquillity! Flooded in moonlight, the city rested. Having put their children to bed, women finished their labours. The men read books, drank mead or spirits, or simply chatted, after having stuffed their pipes full of tobacco and lighting them with the night lamp. Lads sought their match, girls who had flowered during the summer like sumptuous roses, awaited their intended. The monks were already asleep, or praying, while some of the younger ones had gone off in search of fun. The boarding students slept, agitated by Hryhoriy's words, his disobedience…

God, he had come to like this city and these people! He so wanted to remain here at least until it grew warmer, until the summer, to open his agitated soul to the still innocent youngsters thirsting for truth, he wanted to fathom their thoughts and their aspirations!

Well, stay then. No one is driving you out. Only renounce your truth, your faith and your own self. Do not reason, do not think. Perform the will of others and munch on your bread…

It was so painfully hard. His thoughts dashed about like horses frightened by a thunderstorm.

He entered his cell, struck some fire and lit a candle end. Taking off his coat, he sat down at the table. Staring into a half-dark corner, he remained stock still.

He was tired of thinking, of weighing things up, of finding a way to have his cake and eat it too.

Soon he got up, took his inkwell, pen and paper from his bag. Moving the candle closer, he dipped the pen in the ink and, with a heavy sigh, wrote diligently on the first sheet: "*Praecepta de arte poetica.*" Just like in Konysky's book. He read the title and winced. Though he respected the professor, he could not remain in the shadow of his thoughts, tastes and views. Standing water grew fetid. Only good-for-nothing pupils tagged along after their teachers all their lives without ever attempting to outdo them. He was a good-for-nothing too, a donkey who had exchanged his intellect for a warm stall and an armful of hay! He threw down the pen and grabbed his head between his hands.

Exactly a week later he placed his *Poetics* on the table before the bishop. It was written in the Ukrainian language. A book like no other.

Iosaf pointed to the armchair and began to leaf through the book, reading only certain pages here and there. He knitted his brows more and more, and pressed his thin bloodless lips closer together. At last, he stood up, closed his eyes, and grew rigid.

"So then, you don't wish to toil with us here?" he asked after a while, without moving.

"If I had no desire, I wouldn't have come," Skovoroda said calmly.

"Then why do you write such nonsense?"

"This isn't nonsense."

"What then?"

"Thoughts about poetry and guidelines as to how it should be written. I've explained it simply, so that everyone can understand."

"Simply is not necessarily wisely," Iosaf smiled.

"I am relying on the judgement of experts that everything written in my poetics manual is essentially correct, exact, and based not on empty chimeras, but on the nature of this art." Skovoroda rose from his armchair.

"That's lofty philosophising!" The bishop stung him with his gaze. "You've forgotten that the Lord detests the proud, the judgement of experts," he muttered. "Well, I'm judging." He screwed up his eyes. "Everything must be rewritten and taught as tradition dictates."

"*Alia res sceptrum, alia plectrum!*"[34] Skovoroda laughed.

Throwing his head back against the armchair, the bishop closed his eyes and sat this way for a minute or two. Then he rose, threw the manuscript back at Hryhoriy and added angrily: "Be arrogant, if you please, but not in my house!"

He got up and left without saying goodbye.

---

[34] The shepherd's rod is one thing, while a shepherd's flute is something quite different! (Latin)

Skovoroda slipped his ill-fated book into his shirt front, surveyed the room with a misty sorrowful look, and quietly headed toward the door.

Well, that was that! An end to anxiety, doubts and hopes. The trap had snapped shut, although it had not managed to catch the bird. Once more you are free as free can be, Hrytsko! A vagabond Cossack for whom the steppe is your home, the grass your bed, and the book your wife... He felt sorry for the students, but did not yearn for captivity. Without the right to think, to seek verity and to speak the truth, life was not worth living!

He passed the Collegium where lessons were in progress and Father Hervasiy was explaining the Bible to his students instead of poetics, and then turned right toward the building where he had left his flute and bag.

Outside the door, which was already locked, the same frightening monk stood waiting for him. Indifferently he handed him his bag and made no move to leave, as if fearing the ex-teacher might try to break the door down and occupy his squalid cell.

Skovoroda threw his bag over his shoulder and removing his hat, bowed to the guard: "Good health to you, uncle!"

The monk did not bat an eyelid. He stood like a stone idol, without feelings, silent. The Lord's mute servant. Maybe still alive, possibly already dead...

Hryhoriy turned around and proceeded to the gate, still feeling the fellow's penetrating, weighty stare on his back.

Outside the gate, in the street, he looked one last time at the stone Collegium, adjusted the bag more comfortably on his back, and set off into the autumn weather, which was already consuming the city, heading off into an unknown whose name was the future.

THE THIRD NET

The end became the beginning. Seed rotted away after fresh, vigorous greenery emerged from it. Death and birth, being and eternity... There was this flow in human life, this endless replacement of one thing with another: merriment with sorrow, health with infirmity, hopes with despair. And vice versa. Just like milestones: where one ended, another began.

In Pereyaslav, after the bishop had driven him out of the Collegium, Skovoroda had gone to the lieutenant and spent the winter with him as if in paradise. True, he had bought neither a sheepskin coat nor boots. Well, that was nothing! His coat was still in one piece, and as for shoes... It was approaching summer now, not winter. And there would be money! Lord Tomara would not want his son's teacher to go about barefoot like a stork. He would pay him an advance. And if he didn't, there was no need to go and bow before him. Hadn't he gone about barefoot in the past! In the old days people removed their boots as soon as the snows melted and put them on again with the first frost... It was already spring! Maybe it was early and unreliable, but it was spring all the same. The sun was blinding, the last snow had retreated to the deep ravines and hollows, the rivers seethed like Cossacks at a black council, and the birds had arrived...

Mykyta was a fine friend! He had broken Tomara after all. The fellow had been piqued by the teacher's disobedience and his dispute with the bishop. You see, he was sick and tired of all these vagrants and rebels...

Skovoroda smiled. He felt easy and cheerful at heart. Back near Helmiaziv the beginnings of a song had been born in his soul, and it would not go away still. Whistling like a lark. Then dying away, then again chirping and warbling.

Lovely spring, ah, 'tis here!
Fierce winter, ah, 'tis past...

He found it funny himself: it was as if someone was sitting on his chest, unable to rejoice enough at the bright sun, the larks, the overflowing rivers and the winter wheat which flourished with verdant shoots across the steppe expanses!

The road was like black dough kneaded with melted water and sun, firmed by the warm spring wind. The path, which wound in a ribbon along the dry side of the road, was a saviour.

Solitary ploughmen could be seen here and there on the grey hillsides. Rooks circled over a black wedge of ploughed land. And above the road, above the drooping stubble, the indefatigable skylarks fluttered, head into the wind, weaving the thread of a song, infinitely long and gentle. About what and for whom were these heavenly minstrels singing? About the blue sky, the earth, or about the joy of spring which gurgled in their small breasts like water in a whirlpool? Who would fathom them, who would answer their sincere ballads?

Or perhaps they were simply happy with song, flight, wind, clouds, and required no words of rapture, or understanding, no audience! Suspended in rays of sunshine, they continued to toll a hosanna for the sun, the sky, the fresh green shoots, the ploughmen, the gravemounds, and the solitary traveller. They did not hear that he was singing too, that there was an April tumult in his breast too, a plethora of emotions, but they must have known that only perhaps a dead man would not break into song in the fields in springtime!

In a shallow gully alongside the road, the still orphaned transparent forest was howling in the wind. Howling like the sea or the Dnipro River, when a violent storm made mountains of its waves.

He stopped and strained his ears. There was something melancholy and menacing in that howling murmur, in those restless, leafless boughs. It seemed as if the trees were raising their arms, groaning, begging the heavens to send them blessed peace, green buds, and leaves, and the multitudinous clamour of birds, and insects, and animals – everything that was the bounty of summer.

His step was heavy as he emerged from the gully. He kept moving his swollen, weary feet and dreamed deliriously of a settlement, rest, and a mug of water or beer.

A horseman appeared on a hilltop in the steppe. He stood there a while, as if contemplating where to go, brought down his whip and his horse raced down, as if borne on the wind. Drawing closer, he removed his grey hat and greeted the traveller.

"Cossack, is it far to Kovray?" Hryhoriy asked.

The young fellow stopped his horse and smiled: "No, not too far. A mile or two – depends how you walk!"

He cocked his hat and dug his spurs into the horse. He shouted something, let out a whistle, and was off like a gust of wind.

Skovoroda quickened his step. When one knew the distance, it seemed easier to walk and the miles didn't seem so long.

Soon after, he spied a church from the hilltop, a large nobleman's residence, and on both sides of a winding creek stood houses and sheds. On the slopes beyond the creek was a forest, and above it, windmills in the sky, not far from the burial mounds. They were flapping their wings, as if trying to fly off, but never quite managing to.

Hryhoriy squinted – and imagined it had become summer. The village was drowning in cherry groves and willows. The spreading old oaks stood up to their knees in verdant grasses. Bees buzzed in a mighty choir in the blossom-covered lindens. A cuckoo called out. And nightingales sang...

With a sigh he drove away the mirage, adjusted his hat, assiduously did up his buttons, and began the descent into Kovray.

Tomara's yard was fenced like a fortress. Dogs growled behind the palisade. When Hryhoriy entered the yard, they raised a furious baying and rushed at the stranger.

A graceful blonde girl ran out of the building, grabbed a switch and waved it at the dogs: "Kudlay! Mars! Be quiet this minute!"

She angrily stamped her small foot, shod in neat yellow shoes, and the dogs grew silent. With their tails between their legs and throwing guilty glances at her, they sidled away from the gate and lay down, resting their heads on their enormous paws. True sphinxes!

"Black-haired lass, is Lord Stefan at home?"

The blonde girl snorted and, splashing her azure gaze at him, fired away as if she was strewing dry peas: "I'm blonde. And the lord is at home. What shall I say? Who are you? Where are you from?"

"Mariana, who is that annoying the dogs?" a chesty, drawling voice called out, and a young, but already stout woman appeared in the doorway.

"Someone asking after the lord!" the girl answered and moved away, covering her eyes with a dense shroud of lashes.

"Go and prepare lunch," the woman bid her and rested her arms on her hips, as if about to launch into a dance. Letting Mariana pass inside, she took two authoritative steps forward and stopped. "Why do you want to see the lord?" she asked forcefully, in a tone bordering on derision and amazement.

"I'm from Pereyaslav. I've been summoned by Stefan Vasyliovych to teach his son," Skovoroda said softly. He became perplexed, and hunched his back.

"You're a teacher?" she asked and burst out laughing. "What will you teach him? How to beg? Or how to go about in shoes and still leave toe prints behind?"

Skovoroda looked the sumptuously dressed woman up and down, and replied: "All that glitters is not gold. Or as they say in our Chornukhy, the mushroom boasted that it had a nice hat, but what of it, when there was no head underneath."

The lady was flabbergasted. Without answering back, she swung around and resolutely returned to her chambers. If after this a footman brandishing a whip had come running out, Hryhoriy would not have been at all surprised.

However, a short while later Tomara himself appeared on the porch. He was slender, tall, with a handsome Hellenic nose and flaxen-blue eyes. With a cursory, patronising look he sized up the vagabond in worn-out shoes and a coat which long begged to be replaced, and asked sternly: "Who are you?"

"Skovoroda. Hryhoriy Savych."

"My, the times!" the lord grimaced. "So hard to tell an instructor from a beggar..."

"But then the elders can be seen from a long way off," Hryhoriy answered in kind. "They strive to get up high. May the ladder, perchance, not break..."

"You're a witty one," Stefan smiled. "What languages do you know?"

"Latin, Hellenic, Old Hebrew, German, Polish..."

"*Sehr gut, sehr gut,*" Tomara raised his hand and saluted. "*Meine Mutter ist eine kurländische Adlege aus dem Familie von Brinken.*"[35]

....

[35] Very good, very good. My mother is of Kurlandish nobility from the house of von Brinken. (German)

"Oh, so you're a real lord then!" Skovoroda could not help himself. "Not any old lord, but one with blue blood, thoroughbred."

Tomara drew his black, almost bluish eyebrows together and riveted his gaze on the insolent fellow's face.

Meanwhile a stooping, long-unshaven Cossack came out onto the porch. Crumpling his shabby hat, he asked timidly:

"So how about it, Lord Stefan? I've got children, a wife – if you don't help me, I'll have to go begging."

"Come next week, Brus," the semi-aristocratic Kurlander remarked angrily and, without a word to Skovoroda, disappeared inside the building.

"Oh woe, woe is me!" the pitiable Cossack sighed, pulled on his hat and trudged out of the yard.

"Can I perhaps help you, uncle?" Hryhoriy asked, but the fellow only waved his hand in despair.

Hryhoriy watched the stooped figure disappear and sat down on a bench, not knowing whether he should wait, or leave, having been left with egg on his face, as the saying went.

He felt painfully melancholic: no one had yet slighted him like this. The Cossacks had gone to rack and ruin! Were these knights, fighters for freedom, and defenders of the wronged?

"Mister Teacher!" Mariana called him, having noiselessly run out of the aristocratic mansion like a weasel. "Come and have lunch!"

* * *

Skovoroda met the small Tomara only about a month later, after the trees became covered in buds and the birds had reappeared.

"Greetings, Vasyl," Hryhoriy offered his hand, as if to a friend.

"This is your teacher, son," her ladyship interjected immediately. "Hryhoriy Savych."

The lordling threw him a sullen glance and immediately grew silent, curling up into a ball like a hedgehog.

"You're not sick are you, Vasia?" his mother asked with agitation, worried by such a sudden change.

The small boy shrugged his shoulders and then very sadly surveyed the yard, the orchard, the creek, the forest, and the hill. He had spent almost the entire winter with his grandmother and had probably missed Kovray, where he was born and where he grew up. The lordling was no longer that small, some nine or ten years old. Intelligence shone in his eyes and wrinkles gathered on his high forehead, as if he was a grown man. He had studied a little and probably had memories of those studies, which were akin to Turkish slavery.

"Vasyl, could you come with me into the forest beyond the creek?" Hryhoriy asked.

"But he's hungry and tired!" her ladyship said, pressing her son close. "Let him have lunch first and a nap, then he can go."

"I'm not hungry, mum," the small Tomara came to life. "And I slept on the cart."

Skovoroda resolutely took the boy by the hand.

Near the gate the young lord broke free, turned to the left, behind the icehouse, and ran off into the orchard. Hryhoriy left the yard and headed for the dam along the embankment. He was certain the boy would catch up to him. At this age children no longer suffered compulsion, they wanted to resolve things for themselves, without encouragement or nannies. And this was no whim; this was human nature, the law of preserving oneself as an individual, as something unique. To break a person's will, to make of them a mute implement incapable of reasoning – this was the greatest crime!

Even from afar he spied the lad. He had already reached the dam and was sitting in the shade of the yellow-green willows, awaiting his teacher.

"My, you're a nimble lad," Hryhoriy praised him.

Vasyl did not even look at him. He would dash off, and then stop again, then walk staidly like an adult. In a clearing on the far side of the creek, where Herculean oaks had sunk their feet into the ground and supported the sky with their crowns, he froze for a moment in rapture, and then dashed up into the sun-drenched thickets and disappeared, dissolving in the flood of greenery.

Hryhoriy sat down under an enormous sessile oak, pulled out his flute and began to play a melody about spring, about the first grasses which had broken through the litter in the sunlit patches and reached toward the sky, about the golden willows and the blue water, which so reminded him of Mariana's merry eyes. And over the pond, over the forest, over the still cold, indifferent oak tree sailed impressive blinding-white clouds, driven by a gentle breezy wind…

Sensing someone's intense gaze, Skovoroda turned and noticed the boy, who was hiding behind a nearby linden.

"Come on here, Vasyl!" he called out to him and played a dance tune. He could play naturally, as if he was reading music, only when he was face-to-face with nature.

Vasyl drew closer and stood under the oak tree near where the teacher was sitting. Hryhoriy heard the boy shuffling in the leaves, breathing hard. Without turning around, he played the *kozachok*,[36] and then the *horlytsia*. Suddenly he launched into such a sad melody, that he himself became emotional and almost shed tears.

After he finished playing a silence descended on the forest. The boy did not move. Even the birds stopped twittering, as if fearing to sing their song after such music.

"How did you learn to play?" the lad asked timidly.

"From my grandfather, when I was small."

Vasyl grew silent, thinking. Then he sighed: "We don't have a grandfather… He went to Crimea on an expedition and died there."

Hryhoriy felt sorry for the lad. He offered him the flute and suggested: "If you would like to learn, I can help you. Within a year you will play no worse than me."

"Really?" the small fellow exclaimed. "You're not joking?"

"*Docendo discitur!*"

"What did you say?"

"Through teaching we learn ourselves. That's Latin. Do you know how to say 'forest' in Latin? No? *Silva. Magna silva* – a large forest. Latin is the key to wisdom. The beautiful works of the great Romans are all written in Latin, including all the medical books and those dealing with philosophy."

As he was talking, Hryhoriy got up and slowly moved through the forest. Vasyl listened intently, still clutching the flute. Occasionally he ran ahead of Hryhoriy and looked into his eyes, as if not believing that there were such intelligent, such gentle people, as he now imagined his teacher to be.

....

[36]   A Ukrainian folk dance, originating with the Cossacks.

After they had emerged from the forest and had almost reached the top of Kravets Hill, they heard a resounding woman's voice from below calling them home.

"Mariana's looking for us," the lad said regretfully.

"Well then, let's go," Hryhoriy said. "It's probably time for lunch." Cupping his hands to his mouth, he yelled at the top of his voice: "Oh-ho-ho-ho!"

They met Mariana in the hazel thickets.

She was dressed fit for a festive day. Her blouse burnt with red-black poppies, on her head she had a light-blue ribbon and azure violets, and on her feet small neat boots. She was a marvel to behold!

Vasyl ran up to her, hugged her, pressed close and began to boast that he would be learning to play the flute and to speak Latin.

Mariana stroked his wiry hair and looked at the teacher with a faint smile. But Hryhoriy suddenly grew quiet and walked with his head bowed, as if he was searching for a coin on the ground.

"Hryhor Savych, why are you so sad?" she asked, not without a hint of wile in her voice.

"I'm not sad, my dear," Skovoroda smiled. "Why should I be sad?"

"Then maybe you're angry with me?"

"You guessed."

"Why?" the girl stopped dead in her tracks.

"Because you are... like the sun..."

"Well, there you go!" she burst out in happy laughter. "I'm not to blame!"

Gradually she grew silent, lowering her blue eyes. Meanwhile Vasyl had run off to visit some little nest, and they descended toward the dam together.

"Wait till her ladyship catches you walking about the forest with a young man, you'll get an earful," Hryhoriy joked to break the heavy silence.

"Oh-oh, I'm scared!" Mariana flinched like a bird and laughed once more. "She sent me off herself, and even tied the ribbon in my hair."

"You have a mistress then and the lord is quite a fellow," Hryhoriy said, moved by such tenderness in relations between the lady and her domestic servant.

For a long time, the girl said nothing, but then grimaced bitterly, like a child, and suddenly asked: "Are there really good lords?"

Hryhoriy blushed with shame.

"Hryhor Savych! Hryhor Savych!" the small Tomara shouted, catching up to them. "There's already a small speckled egg in the nest!"

*　*　*

Though the village of Kovray was not large, it somehow transpired that the wretched Cossack Skovoroda had met in Tomara's yard did not appear before his eyes again until Whitsuntide. Hryhoriy had already forgotten about him. And suddenly he came across Brus in the reeds in Staroselshchyna. The Cossack stood leaning back against a hollow old willow, waving his arms about and talking to himself.

"Good day, uncle! Come to get some greenery?"[37]

"A-a-ah, mister teacher!" Brus raised his eyes with difficulty. "What greenery... I'm carousing from sheer joy!" And he sang:

> *Hey, he that's drinking, pour him a glass,*
> *And he who's not drinking, let him be!*

He yanked up his pants, which failed to sit on his stomach, since it was pressed hard against his back, and wiping away the dirty traces of tears on his cheeks with an awkward black fist, he began to praise the landlord: "What a fellow, that lord! He solved my misfortune after all. Didn't leave a close friend in trouble!" Breaking out in guffaws, he continued his story: "See, it wasn't in vain that my granddad Ovsiy covered the lord's old grandpa with his own chest to shield him from the *hetman*'s sabre. Otherwise the dear colonel would have been lying buried somewhere near Bendery now, in a foreign land, an intruder forgotten by everyone." He sobbed softly. "As it was, he returned with glory, brought back prisoners and a cannon. And he was also permitted to kiss the fair hand of his majesty!"

> *Oh, the turtle-dove maiden,*
> *Nestles up to the Cossack...*

....

[37] During Whitsuntide (Green) week, based on an ancient Slavic fertility festival, people adorned their houses with greenery.

The merry great-grandson of Ovsiy Brus launched into a dance. Last year's dry reeds crackled under his feet, greasy sludge flew in all directions, while he planted his feet enthusiastically, fiercely, into the bosom of the mute earth, as if wanting to reach its heart, to unburden his pain and sorrow, his bottomless grief.

Hryhoriy could see that Brus had not gotten drunk out of joy. The fellow soon quietened down, toppled back into a lush bush of guelder rose, and began to weep bitterly.

"Behind my back, the lord said, you'll feel as safe as if you were behind a wall... Oh God, for thirty-two roubles! A horse is worth fifty..."

Skovoroda sat down beside him and said agitatedly: "What's the matter with you, uncle? What grief has befallen you? Come what may, it doesn't befit a Cossack to weep."

"And a serf?" Brus asked sullenly.

"Well..."

"But I'm a serf, a serf from now on!" The fellow drummed his chest. "Together with my wife, and children, and grandchildren, and great-grand-children!"

Skovoroda grabbed Brus by the shoulders, shook him vigorously and shouted into his ear: "What are you babbling?! Have you had too much to drink or are you out of your mind?"

"Oh, if only, if only, mister teacher." He grabbed his head in his hands. "But I'm completely sane. They could have taken the land, the house... Well, at least this way the children won't have to crawl away to sleep under strange windows."

"You sold yourself to Tomara for the debt?!"

He made no reply and sat there, rocking to and fro.

"Well, what choice did I have?" he said after a while. "I borrowed from him once for farm implements and to build the house. A lord's kindness is like a wolf's friendship. Well, and so he gobbled me up!"

"What about your Cossack friends, your neighbours?" Hryhoriy flew into a passion. Everything seethed in his bosom from indignation. "Are they looking on peacefully, like sheep, as a fellow man is being bludgeoned with the butt end of an axe?"

"Cossacks there were, but not anymore," Brus waved his hand. "Some are in the yoke, others are still being pressed into it, and still others are bursting out of their skins to clamber upon the wagon, to grab a whip and to spur their brothers on. Hey! Haw! Gee!"

He rose with difficulty to his feet, took a bottle from his pocket, uncorked it and, taking a look at the crimson setting sun, fell upon the bottle. Finishing it, he gasped, wiped his lips with his hand, and hurled the bottle into the river.

"Some fellow, that lord," he guffawed. "Helped me out of my misfortune, and even gave me money for a bottle of vodka!"

He swaggered, looked malevolently at Hryhoriy, and tore at the old dirty shirt on his chest: "I'll go now and gladden my wife and children with the news: the Almighty has sent us happiness! Ha-ha-ha!"

Roaring with laughter, the wretch moved across the meadow toward the enormous, blood-soaked setting sun, which he was seeing for the last time as a free man.

Hryhoriy raised his hands to the heavens: "Lord, where are you looking?! For what have You sent such a heavy punishment upon this suffering earth, these unfortunate people? Do You have a rock in Your bosom, or do You bathe in those tears which flow in rivers!? If You are wise and almighty, Lord, don't allow these Pharisees do away with freedom, for they utter honey-sweet words and then crucify people through their deeds! Slaves do not become the earth, and only those who are indifferent to its future stand there guarding slavery. Don't be a Pilate, who washes his hands at a difficult hour, when the Cossack tribe is bearing its cross onto the heights of Golgotha!"

But the heavens were silent. Large clear stars shone joyously, resembling girls who had come running out upon the azure valley of the sky. The sharp-prowed boat of a new moon surfaced upon the gilded mists and the nightingales began to warble and twitter.

Somewhere on Kovray Meadow girls and boys sang out to one another. There were Cossacks there, and freedom...

The next day after mass, Hryhoriy assembled nearly all the male residents of Kovray on the church atrium and told them about Brus. They stood in silence, heads bowed, like maidens at a betrothal.

"What's the matter gentlemen, lost your speech?" he raged, indignant at their indifference. "Your brother, your comrade is perishing!"

"He won't perish under Lord Stefan," the village elder finally piped up. Though a free Cossack himself, he was one of those who looked Tomara in the mouth like a loyal dog. "Bah, he'll live even better!"

"E-eeh!" whistled the young fellow Hryhoriy had encountered in the gully on his way to work in Kovray. "The lord's favour rides a swift horse!"

"Don't venture where angels fear to tread, Ivan," he was stopped by a staid Cossack from Kovray-Meadow. "Let your moustache grow out first."

"Intelligence is found in the head, not in a moustache," the lad snapped back.

"It's God's will, that Brus became a serf," the priest announced, stroking his luxurious beard. "And it doesn't befit mortals to interfere in God's designs."

"And what about 'thou shalt not covet', father?" Hryhoriy asked.

The priest was lost for words at first, but then looked Hryhoriy in the eye and answered: "The Bible, mister teacher, is a rock of wisdom which not all are given to digest..."

"From this day on, father, having heard your sermons, I will be of the same opinion." Hryhoriy did not remain in debt.

Tucking in his cassock like a wolf would its tail, the priest made off as fast as he could for the landlord's manor.

"Let's go, brothers, before Stefan sees us!" the village elder grew anxious.

"Right, right" He was supported by the wealthy men.

"The priest will snitch on us all the same!"

"And what about Brus?!" Hryhoriy blocked their path. "Fear the Lord, people!"

"Well, what can we do?"

"We can barely make ends meet ourselves."

"We're all deep in debt!"

"And we'll all end up like him..."

"Lots of people live in serfdom, the devil won't take Brus either!"

These faces, the church, and the clouds – everything at once melted and became all jumbled up.

"And you are the descendants of knights who defended their brotherhood and freedom in bloody battles?!" Hryhoriy asked angrily. "You're being drowned, destroyed like pups, and you don't even dare break free, let alone yelp! Take off your sabres, you're not worthy of wearing the weapons of your grandfathers and great-grandfathers! There are yokes upon your souls!"

"Now don't go on, or we'll count your ribs for you!"

"Clucking away there..."

"He speaks the truth!"

"Rubbish!"

"It's slander!"

"Just think, that lord is no bigwig!"

"If we want, he'll get a fico with poppy seed in place of Brus!"

They spoke out, argued, as if at a black council. When it began to smell of fisticuffs, Hryhoriy pulled out some money, raised it in the air and shouted: "I'm giving a rouble!"

There was silence. The men wheezed, coughed, and exchanged glances. However, they did not hurry to pull out their purses.

"Me too!" Ivanko ran up. "Those who've gone about in the skin of a bondsman will not wish it even on an enemy."

The ice was broken. With grunts the fellows gave money one after another, even borrowing money to throw into the reddened straw hat which Hryhoriy was holding.

"Tomara will have a fit."

"He'll bite himself on the calves!"

"And grab us by the hair..."

"His arms are too short for that."

"We need to send one of the boys to fetch Brus."

"True, true. Bring him to his senses!"

"We'll all go to Stefan. He won't dare go against the community..."

"Everyone, all of us!"

"Of course. As the saying goes, in company – even death..."

"One can break a mallet across your back!"

"Mister teacher, perhaps this will be enough?"

"Here, let me!" Ivanko ran up, took the straw hat and, sitting cross-legged on the knot-grass, began to count the thalers, half-copecks and three-copeck pieces, and the gold coins.

The throng listened to his count in silence. Their swarthy faces were strained, as if before a battle, some had drops of sweat on their foreheads.

With each rouble added to those already counted, the men sighed more easily and cheered up.

Skovoroda forgave them their fear of their own destiny, and their blunt indifference to other's grief, and their unearthly, somewhat reclusive, sad tolerance of servitude. He admired them, was overjoyed at their unity, which had flared like gunpowder in the dark night of bitter discord. God, such a people – gentle, wise and, heroic – if only they stuck together, they could overcome all calamities and rise to the same heights as the Ancient Greeks!

"Thirty-four!" the Kovray Archimedes announced.

"Will you look at that – enough to pay off his debt and buy vodka for everyone!" the elder said. "Give me the remainder, I'll run down to the tavern."

By the time they had regained their senses, he was rushing past the fourth house. There you go! One fellow took fright and took to his heels. The community pot had cracked.

"To Lord Stefan's!" Ivanko called out, raising the straw hat with the money. "For Brus' freedom!"

They filed in one after another through the narrow gate. Decisive, hushed, filled with a sense of brotherhood, dignity and self-respect.

Tomara came out sullen and menacing. He rested his hand on his sabre, surveyed the crowd and asked: "What has God sent you here with?" He grimaced in a smile: "Such respected visitors…"

"We've brought Brus' debt," Ivanko said and offered Tomara the money.

The fellow folded his arms on his chest.

"He settled his account yesterday."

"With what? His freedom?!"

"Let that not bother you."

"You'll soon have us all in your web!"

"You're growing rich on our poverty!"

"Clambering toward nobility over our backs!"

Tomara wrenched his sabre from its sheath. All the same he did not give in to temptation. He took a piece of paper from his pocket and showed it to the throng.

"It's written here in Brus' hand that from now on he's a bondsman, my property…"

"Judas! For thirty silver pieces you've put your brother into slavery!"

"Hang the fellow!"

"Burn him with his spawn!"

The crowd was boiling. Here and there sabres glinted. There was the smell of blood in the air.

And just then Hryhoriy moved resolutely up to Lord Stefan, grabbed the piece of paper almost by force, ran his eyes over it to check that it was Brus' document, and hurried off toward the gate. Leaving the straw hat with the money at Tomara's feet, the throng followed him out, still buzzing.

"To Brus' place!"

"To the tavern!"

"There's still powder in the old powder-horn, eh!"

They rejoiced like children. They sensed the might before which even their money-grubbing magnate was nothing, a mere illusion of power, a Kurlander hatchling draped in silks and woollen cloth.

*   *   *

Water Nymph Week[38] was warm and mild. Each morning the sun rose brightly, and after lunch heavy clouds gathered over Kovray and watered the earth with thunder, downpours, and lightning. The grain grew tall and lush, cherries grew plump with red juice, and the greenish, still small apples bent the branches of the trees ever closer to the ground and were astoundingly fragrant toward evening, so much so that, after the thunderstorms, they made one's head spin. And the nights... What nights these were! Tender, dreamy, adorned with the pink blossom of stars, permeated with the fragrance of herbs, filled to the brim with intoxicating fresh air and the twitter of nightingales!

There had never been such a miraculous summer in Hryhoriy's life, such amazing nights, and such bliss, which expanded his chest and made him hold his breath. Even Lord Stefan's offensive silence and the landlady's contempt after the Brus fiasco left him feeling indifferent; it was like those storm clouds, which shielded the sun for only a moment or two. His star, his Mariana, shone for him! The lord's blue-eyed housemaid had broken through the ice in his soul like a warm spring breeze, stirring, disturbing and breaking the banks of

---

[38] The week after Trinity Sunday, when water nymphs were said to walk upon the land.

an irrepressible blue tide. Wherever he went, whatever he did, he saw before him the mirage of her blouse covered in red-and-black poppies, her cheerful, tender gaze and the flaxen hair of her plait. With alarm, and yet with joy, he lent an ear to the miracle which was unfolding in his heart, and more and more often he dreamed of simple human bliss.

In the evening, on the ancient women's festival of Bryksy,[39] when the boys and girls gathered on the far side of the river opposite the dam to bid the water nymphs farewell for another year, Skovoroda found Mariana at one of the bonfires, took her by the hand and led her off into the night.

Ivanko saw them off with a very sorrowful look, and then called out merrily into the gloomy darkness: "Mariana, take care of the teacher, or the water nymphs may steal him away!"

"Watch out they don't steal you!" she called back.

"Who needs me?" the poor lad sighed.

> *Oh, a young maiden runs along, she runs,*
> *A water nymph chasing her quickly...*

The song rose into the heavens and sailed off over the sleepy forest, the steppe, and the mists on the river...

Cowering, Mariana snuggled up to Hryhoriy and whispered: "Do you think all the water nymphs have disappeared or are they still roaming about?"

Hryhoriy made no reply. Instead, he embraced the girl's shoulders and pressed her close to himself. Mariana grew still, like a fledgling bird, and stopped breathing.

Almost with every minute the darkness grew brighter and the sky became higher. The bonfires burnt away behind them and indistinct shadows kept growing, and then suddenly decreasing in size.

Occasionally bats or nocturnal birds swept overhead and the nightingales sent their songs and trills across the pond. It was as if the ones in the village orchards were competing with the ones who had grown accustomed to life in the forest.

"They say a lad was tickled to death in Pishchana..." the girl spoke again.

....

[39] An ancient festival celebrated on 12 July. On this day men had to satisfy a woman's every whim.

"By whom?"

"The water nymphs..."

"How can something which doesn't exist tickle someone to death?" Hryhoriy asked and let out a laugh.

"But water nymphs do exist. They walk about on land all week long..."

Around the bonfires they were singing a new song:

The water nymphs, we saw them off, we saw them off,
So they would not return, not return,
So they would not trample our green fields of rye,
Chasing after our fair young maidens...

The nightingales and the singing, and the beat of their hearts fused into a single fairy-tale melody, which elevated the soul and the body, as if on mighty wings.

In a fit of rapture, Hryhoriy stopped in a forest clearing, turned the girl around to face him and, without letting her out of his embrace, whispered emotionally: "Mariana, my darling – will you marry me?"

"Yes," the girl replied simply.

Hryhoriy almost burst into tears of joy. He took the girl's bright face between his palms and asked: "But do you know that I've nothing in the world, apart from my soul and my flute?"

She nodded.

"That like a bird in the heavens, I neither reap nor sow?"

"Those who reap and sow don't always have bread, Hryts."

He became speechless, amazed at her earthly wisdom. Peering into her deep eyes, which reflected the stars, he asked after a while: "And you're not afraid of marrying a Cossack who is as naked as the bough of a tree?"

"You're a powerful hero. You have a good mind... Well, and besides that, you are free."

Suddenly Hryhoriy seemed struck down by thunder. Mariana was a slave, a serf, the lord's possession!

In desperation he pressed the girl close and, choking on tears, said: "What about the lord and lady? You're a... You're a..."

"They'll let me go, they'll take pity on me," the girl said hollowly.

"I'll see the lord in the morning and ask him."

Something tore free in his bosom and fell like a cold rock. He didn't have a skerrick of hope. Such a lord had yet to be born!

"No, I'll do it myself," the girl said softly. She freed herself from his embrace. "I'll plead with the landlady. She's from my parts and even something of a relative. Surely she'll show us mercy."

Speechless, sad, as if taken down from the cross, they returned to the dam where bonfires were still burning, and the boys and girls were celebrating a farewell to the fairy-tale spirits of summer:

> *A little cuckoo came flying*
> *Out of a dark-dark wood;*
> *She perched and sat,*
> *Then cooed 'how's that,'*
> *In a small green garden...*

* * *

Driven by thoughts and doubts, Hryhoriy woke the next day before daybreak and crossed the river into the steppe, toward Platkovshchyna. He yearned for open spaces, distant horizons, an impetuous wind, and freedom. During hours of bitter indecision, anxious contemplation, and pressing decisions, he hated being in the close confines of houses and forests, and dashed out into the fields, where it was easy to breathe and thoughts soared like falcons.

The cold dew pleasantly caressed his feet still warm from bed; the morning crispness poured strength into his bosom and drove away his sleep. A majestic serenity reigned supreme everywhere. The grasses and flowers were slumbering. The greenish-grey thick rye stood straight and still, like Cossack regiments before a bloody battle...

Suddenly the first bird woke and let out a squawk. It was followed by a second, and a third. And a minute later everything had come to life, woken up, chattering, filling the air with song and sounds. The earth rejoiced at the new day, the bright sun had returned from its long nocturnal wanderings, like a father returning home from market.

His father had always brought back raisins and bagels, dividing them equally among the children, without leaving a crumb for himself. He watched the boys tuck into the titbits and smiled into his moustache. He would bring something for his wife too: either a colourful woollen kerchief, or boots, or a wrap-around skirt. He would hand the presents out to the children and then call out to their mother: "Palazhka, take a look what I found entangled in the sloe!"

Stuffing their treasures into their shirtfronts, the small boys picked up the kerchief and, admiring it against the light, kept asking one before the other, if there hadn't been anything else there, where he had found it. Merry devils danced in father's eyes, while mother grumbled good-naturedly:

"There's already snow on your temples, but just as you were never staid, so you remain to this day."

Snow on his temples... Hryhoriy's own winter was still on a distant golden pond, but his youth had long ago been scattered all over the place: in the Academy, beyond the Carpathian Mountains, along well-travelled roads. The wind drove destinies about like tumbleweed... Alone in the whole wide world! At times it was horrendous: not a sincere friend, no wife and children, no refuge... Die and there will be no one to remember you with an angry or kind word.

He ascended the steep embankment to the open steppe. A large pure sun splashed onto his face. The earth shone, glittering with sparks.

Squinting, Hryhoriy filled his lungs with air and let it out noisily. God, what beauty, what unfettered freedom! Unlike this simple miracle, the daily bustle of the city brought no peace, but corroded away the soul like rust working on iron.

He sensed himself filling with the tart feeling of oneness with the grass, the sun, the eagle which had risen into the sky from a nearby grave mound on the fresh morning wind... He even choked. The words appeared of their own accord and he burst into song:

> *Ah meadows, meadows verdant green,*
> *Meadows streaked with flowers' sheen...!*

But then grew silent, having realised an incoherence, a disparity between what he was thinking and seeing, and the words of the song being born in his soul. For a moment it even appeared that it was someone else singing. He looked about and smiled – all around him there was solitude and stillness. He felt his body splitting in two. What absurdity – to think in vernacular and to compose verse in highbrow academic language![40]

He took out his flute and played the same song, continuing to refine the melody, to perfect it. He played as he walked across the virgin steppe, through grey waves of feather grass. He was consumed by the music, every fibre of his body and soul was humming.

> *Ah, you pure torrents of water!*
> *Ah, you verdant grass-cover'd banks...*

He came to his senses only after seeing a girl standing before him. He barely recognised her as Mariana. However, for a long time he couldn't understand a single word of what she was saying, although he could see that she was talking, laughing, and crying.

He finally caught her quick cheerful words: "…the landlord will give us land and a house."

"To whom? For what?" He shrugged his shoulders.

"For us, of course, for us!" Mariana tousled him. "And horses, a cart, and a cow in calf! The landlady was so overjoyed, as if she was my own mother. Well, and Lord Stefan promised to throw the wedding! Aren't you happy, Hrytsko?"

"I'm happy, darling, of course I'm happy!" Hryhoriy embraced the girl, realising at last that the talk was about him and Mariana. What a fiancé! This was absurd. While singing, he had forgotten that he was meant to get married.

"I must run, there's lots of work to do!" The girl knitted her brows. She stood up on tip-toe, kissed her betrothed and, blushing, ran off.

"Mariana!" Hryhoriy dashed after her. "What about freedom?!"

"They said there'd be freedom too!" She waved her kerchief at him and ran down the slope.

Seeing his sweetheart off with a long tender gaze, Skovoroda wandered slowly on. Well, that was that. His vagabond days were over, trudging the thorny sloe of paths to truth and struggling for justice where it had long

....

[40]   At the time Ukrainian spoken by people differed from the language books were written in, which was more formal and akin to Church Slavonic.

been driven into the ground and covered with heavy stone slabs lest it be resurrected. Everywhere there was vanity, chaos, and corruption. Only in the natural world, in a blade of grass, in the sun, in the eternal replacement of old with new, was there the spirit of Minerva,[41] law, and harmony. The deuce take you all, you hypocrites and Pharisees, who lead your close ones astray through your raving, always ready to sell not only a friend or a teacher, but even your native land for silver coins! He would sow, harvest bread, nurture children, and draw serenity and wisdom from the springs of love, harmony, and natural beauty. As Virgil had put it, *O fortunatos nimium bona si sua norit agricolas.*[42]

Moving up the slope, avoiding bushes of sea kale, he reached the top of the grave mound, breathed in the fragrant air and looked into the distance. From now on his soul would enjoy its desired peace! Like most people, he would have a roof over his head, a fertile field to cultivate, a cherry orchard, a well, and two endearing suns – one in the sky, and the other in his home. He imagined Mariana in her own household and was deeply moved. In their free time he and his wife would read wise books and play – he on the flute, she on the *kobza*, or they would sing. And later they would open a school and teach children for free...

Meanwhile a newly-born tender song again quavered in his heart. It was about the golden morning, the forest and the fields, about nightingales and larks, which woke the earth in the morning.

Hryhoriy's soul swelled with buds. He turned to face the sun, and sang in bookish Ukrainian:

> *Oh, perish there, my heavy thoughts,*
> *In those crowded bustling cities!*
> *With my piece of bread, I'll die*
> *In a city just like this...*

* * *

---

[41]   Roman goddess of wisdom.

[42]   Oh, they would be overjoyed, if they knew their good luck, those farmers!

Never hasten to rejoice, for sometimes happiness escapes from one's hands like a bird from a snare.

The little blue-eyed sun, which was to have shined for Hryhoriy all his life, set before the bright cosmic sun had finished traversing the high summer skies for the third time.

The evening before, they had sat in the orchard on the river and dreamed of their future happiness. It was pleasant and serene. Stars big and small grazed lazily on the blue field of the sky; a crescent moon hung over Platkovshchyna like a shepherd. Nothing prophesied a storm. But the following day...

Having set Vasyl a part of Cicero's speech to learn by heart, Hryhoriy stepped outside to greet his beloved with the joyous new morning. He did not go looking for her in the landlord's chambers, but sat down on a bench under a young apple tree near the path leading to the icehouse. She would pass by on her way to fetch some beer or fish...

Chinese geese, introduced by Vasyl Stepanovych, wandered about the yard, nipping at the knotgrass. Near the stable, Persian ponies pawed at the ground – they too had been brought here at one time by the colonel from Sulak or Derbent. The young men were loading up a cart. Ivanko was among them. He had avoided the teacher since Bryksy, but now he glanced in Hryhoriy's direction for some reason and smiled quietly into his short black moustache. He had probably recovered his senses, become reconciled to his fate, realizing that she would not be his...

"Mariana!" he jumped to his feet, seeing the girl as she hurried along the path, head bowed.

She shuddered, for a moment beamed her familiar pleasing smile, but then grew sullen, looking like the world before a thunderstorm.

"Mariana, darling..."

"Good-day, mister teacher," she whispered, without looking up. She stepped onto the knotgrass and, passing around her betrothed, ran off to the cellar.

Feeling his heart and chest grow numb, Hryhoriy watched her hasty movements at the icehouse door, and then stared at the black hole which had swallowed up the girl and did not release her for an insufferably long time. He could not understand what had happened, could not believe that she had swept past him like a cloud...

Meanwhile Mariana emerged from the cellar. She replaced the heavy lock on the door, furtively wiped her eyes and, lifting up a pot, raced across the knotgrass where the geese were feeding.

"Wait, Mariana!" Hryhoriy tried to intercept her.

She did not reply, as if she had not heard him. Her plaits flashed like the white wings of a gull, and she disappeared into the maze of the house. She had been, and was no more. Like some demon she had disturbed his spiritual calm and left him in despair's embrace.

He could already sense – in fact he was almost certain – that this was a new twist of fate, and he suffered terribly because he could not understand the reason for all this. The events and actions which had surfaced as a result of this chaos weighed down heavily on him. The worst evil was unfathomable, incomprehensible, without any logic.

In agony the whole day, he reflected on the previous evening, analysing his words and actions, and lay in wait for Mariana to find out how he had angered her. She had run away from him, as if he were the plague. She had become an unfathomable stranger, not at all like the blonde weasel who had become his best friend during spring, his hope for a better future.

It was already growing dark, when he finally caught up with Mariana by the well on the riverbank. She tried to run away, but Hryhoriy grabbed hold of the buckets and refused to let go.

"This is no way to act, my darling," he said reproachfully. "I'm no leper, after all, for you to be so afraid of me."

She dared not look at him, wouldn't even raise her eyes. Her lean narrow shoulders became stooped like an old woman's and she shuddered ever so slightly. It seemed she would fall to the ground at any moment under the weight of some grief, never to rise again, never to bless the world with her azure smile.

"Forgive me, if I've done anything wrong," Hryhoriy whispered. "But don't torture me, don't make yourself suffer. Tell me the truth, to my face. I understand that I'm not a good match for you, I'm plain, stubborn, restless, poor..."

"Stop it, stop it!" the girl dropped the buckets and covered her face with her hands. "Go, leave me alone!" she begged tearfully. "Otherwise, I'll drown myself, do you hear?"

Dumbfounded by her delirious screams, Hryhoriy recoiled.

"Leave the village, go to the ends of the earth!" the girl sobbed.

"Such fervent love!" he said bitterly. "And here I am foolishly torment-ing myself. God, can the whole world be a delusion, and the people mere shadows, slipping through one's fingers like sand?! Everywhere there is hypocrisy and treachery..."

"No, stop!" Mariana straightened and took a step toward him. Her eyes were filled with tears, despair, and inexpressible grief. "Don't talk like that," she said. "Don't lose faith in people..."

"Tell me then what happened?"

"I... I haven't betrayed you." The girl wiped away her tears. "I'm just the bird which is tied by its leg inside a cage to lure others in. Escape, run away, Hryhoriy!"

He came up to her, hugged her, and kissed her forehead. She lifted her swollen, bitten lips and tear-filled eyes up to him and whispered: "Farewell, my Hryts, my grey-winged dove, my bright-eyed moon..."

"I'm not bidding you farewell! I'm not going anywhere!" Hryhoriy yelled. His soul wept tears, screamed its grief out loud.

"And you'll become a bondsman?"

"God won't allow that!"

"God scorns us. For serfs there is only the landlord's will..."

"Let's run away together! To Zaporizhia. Or the Polish side."

"The hetmanites[43] will catch us and torture us to death."

"Then let's wed. To spite the hetmanites and the Lord!"

"You're crazy." Mariana brushed him aside. "Captivity is death for eagles."

"But that's for eagles!"

"Farewell," the girl said softly, but sternly. She filled her buckets with wa-ter and bore them into the night, which approached like a horde of savages. "Farewell, Hryhoriy!"

Skovoroda leaned against the log wall of the well. He swallowed burn-ing tears. He was not weeping, no. He had turned to stone, swathed in inky darkness, sorrow and pain. Those vampires, those degenerates! They had sowed the earth with bones and were reaping the rewards of slavery now! The foul-smelling snakes, they had gobbled up freedom and were

....

[43]   Subjects of the Cossack Hetmanate or Zaporozhian Host which existed in Central Ukraine between 1649 and 1764.

excreting fetters! Those Judases, they had crucified their own mother at the crossroads!

*　*　*

From that day the world grew dim. Summer was in full bloom – the buckwheat was flowering, scythes rang in the grasses and grain ripened on the stalk, but for Hryhoriy a grey autumn might as well have appeared. Everything which had once impressed him, provoked fresh thoughts and new songs, had suddenly paled and faded. The forest, which had reminded him of flowing locks of hair, had simply become the landlord's forest, the pond became a stretch of water which turned the landlord's mill, and the steppe was land which increased Tomara's prosperity and power. Even Vasyl, his quiet, talented pupil, now no longer seemed a lad with a curious gaze and a kind, sincere heart, but was merely an immature landlord, the future owner of Mariana and hundreds of other souls. He would grow up, sense his might and power, and would also begin to rake everything in sight under himself. Sloe trees, obviously, never bore pears...

Hryhoriy would have left this loathsome settlement, had he not signed an agreement for a whole year and he didn't want to be the one to break his word.

It was broken by Lord Stefan.

In a few days a rumour spread through the village: Ivanko was marrying Mariana, who was meant to have wed the teacher. No one knew for certain, but they said that apparently Skovoroda had refused to marry her because of the small dowry. The gossips whispered that the teacher had no desire to cover for other people's sins...

The landlady was furious. She stopped Hryhoriy as he made his way to explain a new lesson to Vasyl, rested her hands on her hips and hissed: "Why are you disgracing my Mariana, you son of a bitch?!"

"I'm not disgracing her."

"I'm offering you land, a house, a cow, horses – and that's still not enough?"

"You'd do better to grant her freedom."

"Why, you scoundrel!" the landlady burst out. "You'd rather take your wife by the hand and set off with bags to tease the dogs on the byways?!"

"Please grant her freedom!"

"I'll give you two more heifers, and a porker!"

"Freedom for Mariana."

"There won't be any freedom!" the landlady hollered.

"But she's a relative of yours..."

"Even if she were my own mother I wouldn't let her go! And you, you blessed fool," she hissed fiercely again, "you'll die like a dog by the roadside."

"A good day to your house, lady!" The village elder appeared at an opportune moment. "Is Lord Stefan at home?"

"No, he's not," she growled. "He's gone off to Pidstavky."

"Then I'll drop by later."

"You can wait, he should be back shortly!" she barked angrily and hurried off into the bakery to give the bakers a roasting.

Vasyl was already at his books. He rose and greeted his teacher. He looked warily at Hryhoriy (he'd probably heard the altercation), fetched a quill from a drawer, and began to sharpen it with a curved gilded dagger.

Hryhoriy heaved a deep sigh, realising that he could be teaching a whole classroom, instead of pussyfooting around this one fledgling.

"Well then, Vasyl, have you finished reading about the gladiators?" he asked, controlling his hostility.

"Aha. I even translated it," the boy said jubilantly.

"And you understood everything?"

The young lord nodded.

"Tell me how to translate *gladius*?"

"Sword."

"And *pugnus*?"

"Fist."

"What a smart little lordling," someone whispered. "And so small."

The Kovray village elder was standing in the doorway.

"Can I help you, uncle?" Hryhoriy asked tersely.

"It's nothing… I was just curious. I only studied one winter, and even then, I was taught by a drunk deacon."

Skovoroda waved his hand and turned toward the young lord.

"The gladiators – who were they?"

"Combatants who fought in the arena. Before the start of their battle, they shouted: 'Greetings, emperor, those about to die salute you!'"

"And what did they actually think? Was it what they shouted?"

"Of course. They were slaves." The boy shrugged his shoulders.

"You reason like a hog's head!" Hryhoriy said. "So according to you, slaves die joyously with a leap?"

Vasyl frowned. He gouged the fine surface of the Polish-made table with his dagger and wheezed like a hedgehog.

"Leave the table alone!" Hryhoriy grabbed the dagger off him.

He noticed that the village elder had slipped away, and sighed with relief: he hated it when outsiders were in the classroom.

"Alright then," he said peaceably. "Let's continue. Today we will learn the passive state..."

The landlady burst in like a whirlwind and screamed: "You cad! Miserable ragamuffin! You're the only hog's head here! My son is a blue-blood aristocrat, and you're not even worth his little finger, you cad!"

She fell upon the young lord, kissing his head and cooing: "My good boy, my little baby... Don't worry, little bird, I won't let you be tormented! Come along, my baby, I'll get you some dumplings..."

Clucking away like this, she slipped her hands under the boy's armpits, and lifted him like a gladiator dying of his wounds, leading him into the chambers.

"I don't want to eat yet, I want to stay here!" Vasyl bellowed, but in vain.

Hryhoriy sat down on the bench, grabbed his head in his hands and groaned: "Oh, Lord! Why have You punished Your people so grievously, Your mortal creation, taking away their intellect?"

Only after lunch did the young men find Hryhoriy in the orchard and they took him to see the landlord.

Tomara was sitting there, looking like Julius Caesar. Tanned, trimmer as a result of the endless travels between settlements and his various other holdings, which were scattered across practically the entire Hetmanite lands. He was majestic, formidable. Knitting his black, brush-like brows he announced: "Forgive me, Hryhoriy, you're a good teacher, but I must refuse your services. Here, take a thaler for the road. It's a pity, of course..."

"The wolves took pity on the mare," Hryhoriy said.

Tomara rose abruptly, hurled the worn silver thaler onto the table and quickly marched out.

Vale![44] The end, and a fresh beginning once more... Something had died, and something new was born. No, it had not died, but became trans-

---

44   Farewell! (Latin)

formed into an unfading memory to be retained in the heart forever. The past is our greatest treasure, our spiritual shield, our sterling experience. A person with only the present in them was like a sapling without roots.

Without realising it, he found himself in his room. He placed his coat in his bag, covering it with his books and flute, and stepped outside. Near the columns he paused for a while – he could not leave without looking once more into the faded eyes of his love, his earthly sun, which had set without shining its fill. It would surely rise and shine once more, but not for him. It would shine for Ivanko, or perhaps someone else. The ways of the Lord were unfathomable... So was aristocratic whim.

"The landlady sent Mariana off somewhere," a voice said quietly beside him.

Turning around, he met the young man's gaze.

"Well, good health to you, Ivan." He offered the lad his hand.

"Don't be angry at me, mister teacher," the fellow said, hanging his head. "I love her too – I love her madly!"

Hryhoriy swallowed the lump in his throat.

"Respect her, don't insult her, and don't let her be mocked. She's one of a kind..."

"I'm ready to die for her!" The swain flinched.

"Farewell."

"Farewell. May the Lord protect you!"

Grey clouds flew over Kovray, heading west. On either side of the road, the landlord's boundless wheat was swept along in the wind like a sea, rustling quietly with ripe golden ears. A quail was crying somewhere. Bumblebees droned away. Swallows scraped the heavens with their wings...

"Hryhor Savych! Teacher!" he heard suddenly. Someone was running after him, waving his arms about and begging him to stop.

Skovoroda took off his hat to cool his head. At once he smiled: holding onto the drop-crotch of his trousers, Brus was catching up to him.

"So, he threw you out after all... The thrice-damned magnate," Brus said malevolently, catching his breath. "Ivanko told me... I couldn't believe it! Where are you off to?"

"The world is a big place."

"P'raps you could live with me? Like a blood brother, a true father..."

"No, I'll be off. God bless you, brother!"

"If things get tough, you're dearly welcome – my last piece of bread is yours."

Skovoroda was moved. He began to say his goodbyes hastily.

"May fate be good to you!"

Brus grabbed the teacher's bony hand and kissed it.

"Come on, what are you doing, uncle?!" Hryhoriy flinched. "Aren't you ashamed? I'm no priest."

"I will kiss your footprints," Brus said emotionally. "I have become a man again."

Hryhoriy embraced him, thrust his lips into Brus' smoke-permeated moustache, and made off into the steppe toward the sun like a drunk. He did not turn around, but he seemed to see the village, the forest, the river, and the windmills, and even Brus, who stood and wept. Farewell, my past! Good day to you, my future! Who knows what you will be like? What paths will take me there?

He stopped. Really, which way should he go? The earth spread before him in all four directions, above him was sky... He was all alone!

There was just him, the earth, and the sky.

But then there was freedom, liberty! He could do what he wished. If he wanted to walk, he could go right ahead and walk, if he wanted to lie down, he was free to do so. And to write poems he merely had to take out some paper and write! Beauty and harmony! Lucky man, he had that which many people yearned for, for which they struggled, going to their deaths, facing torture!

He adjusted the bag on his back, slipped his well-worn lambskin hat into his shirtfront, and walked off with a sweeping gait, as if he knew exactly where he was going, which path to take.

In the distance, beneath the sun hanging over the azure Supiy River, golden-maned Cossack horses were racing off somewhere, and their melancholy neighing carried across the bronze of the late afternoon steppe like the tolling of a great bell, like a melody:

O vita nova![45]

....

[45]   Oh, new life! (Latin)

THE FOURTH NET

His fate was probably to blame. As if through a whirlpool, he kept being drawn again and again into the wide world, into the irrepressible bustle of life and science. Half the Academy had already been lured across to St. Petersburg and Moscow, where Lomonosov had stirred up the putrid mud of illiteracy and stopped up the gullets of the Germans, who had croaked for so many years about the utter ignorance of the descendants of the wild Scythians. They had forsaken their alma mater and had set off to learn, to teach others, to grab titles and support the heavy vault of the throne with their heads. It was as if a storm had passed over old Kyiv. The miserable brotherhood, which had only the sonorous sounds of Latin to their credit, renounced their near and dear ones, the steppe and their already scanty freedoms for postings in Russia.

Hryhoriy made himself more comfortable, stretched out his stiff legs. One could see even a speck of dust in another person's eye...

Only a year had passed since he had discussed the sceptre and the whip with Vyshnevsky and, having wandered his fill, he had set off into the arms of destiny, to seek happiness. No, he wasn't looking for personal happiness, he only strove to be useful! He saw the world, its past, and peered into the future; there was a treasure in his heart which he felt duty bound to pass on to people, to make them see with their mind and soul, to teach them to think and to understand themselves, nature, the universe. What a disgrace, what a tragedy – we have lost the ability to reason! We sleep and curse when we are woken, when we are encouraged to open our eyes... Oh Lord, forsooth, no prophet is accepted in his own country!

Come what may, his coach was racing northward.

The coachman, engaged in Tula, was unsociable, reticent, and only in the evenings did he quietly sing sad songs, each one resembling the other.

The houses they passed were sullen and dark. There was not an orchard in sight.

Hryhoriy began to feel insufferable sadness. He looked back at Kalihraf, who had been dozing almost the whole way, and moved closer to the coachman.

"Whose village is this, uncle?"

"What? It's the Naryshkins!" he answered in Russian.

"And are there any free men here?"

"What?"

"Do all the people belong to the landlord?"

"Well, of course. Gee-up, gee-up, my swift ones!" He waved his whip over the horses.

"And are you yourself a serf or a free man?" Hryhoriy did not relent.

"We're all bondsmen of the Demidovs..."

"And what's your landlord like, is he good?"

"He's good, knows his business," he drawled in Russian, and looked askance at his interlocutor.

"Doesn't ask for food when he's asleep," Hryhoriy added.

"What?"

"Would you want to become a free man?"

The coachman shrugged his shoulders and whipped the horses with the reins.

"But to be on horseback, brandishing a sabre."

"Stop pestering him, Hrytsko!" Kalihraf suddenly spoke out. He had already woken up, this devil of a tempter in priest's garb, who had dragged Skovoroda away with him on his travels. "He has no idea what it means."

"Gee-up, gee-up, my swift ones!" the coachman called out in Russian. The horses set off at a gallop, dust rose in a cloud behind the coach.

Skovoroda sat next to Kalihraf, to discuss serfs and freedom, but his companion closed his eyes once more. Was he asleep or just pretending?

"Freedom is immortal. *Vita sine libertate, nihil!*"[46] Hryhoriy announced fervently. Kalihraf didn't even bat an eyelid. Not even a wrinkle trembled on his tanned face, framed by the thick locks of a beard. He now strangely resembled Jesus Christ! Volodymyr... But what had been his name before he was baptised? At the Academy he had been occasionally teased as Itsko or Shmulyk. He had abandoned his family and tribe, taken up the Orthodox

....

46   Life is nothing without freedom! (Latin)

faith, graduated, and was now going to Moscow to the Greek Latin Academy to teach philosophy to the brotherhood. Hryhoriy was curious to know how the fellow felt spiritually. Was there inner peace and harmony? Had he been able to thoroughly plough over his soul and sow it with new seed, without any cockle weed of the past?

In Pereyaslav he had been grabbed by Mykyta, who plied him with vodka for three days and on the fourth saw him off, and not alone, but with Hryhoriy. That damned Hayster! And he slipped them a small barrel of mead, so they would have something to drink along the way.

"Is it not time for us to receive Communion, squire?" Kalihraf suddenly remarked, as if hearing Hryhoriy's thoughts. "Something's scratching in my gullet and there's a glittering chalice of mead floating in the ether before my eyes."

Skovoroda fetched the small barrel from the hay and slowly pulled out the swollen bung.

"In the name of the Father, and the Son, and the Holy Ghost." The young priest crossed himself and, lifting up the barrel, fell upon it like a calf to an udder. "Sweet nectar, ambrosia!"

Hryhoriy took the already light vessel from him and went to have a drink too, but unfortunately the lieutenant's gift was not bottomless.

"He, who forgets about his close friend, will forget to wake for the Last Judgement." He hurled the barrel into the hay.

"What, there's no more ambrosia?!" Kalihraf opened his eyes, as if it wasn't him who had just drank the last drop.

"It's gone, disappeared…"

"Just as smoke disappears!" He sighed piously and nudged the coachman in the back with his foot. "Ahoy, respected fellow, is there a tavern nearby?"

"Two versts away, near Lipitsy," the coachman said without turning around.

"Well then push your swift ones hard, old chap!" Kalihraf woke up completely and began to wave his arms about: "Gee-up! Gee-up!"

The tavern stood in a birch wood at the base of a small hill. Lashed by rains, fiercely plucked by winds, it showed its ribs like a vagabond drunk who had caroused his fill.

"This is it?" Kalihraf expressed doubt, having already hung his feet over the side, ready to dash off to the source of merriment.

The coachman nodded, pulled the reins taught as a bowstring and, having stopped the horses, said in Russian: "The owner ran off in the spring, so the landlord recently rented the tavern out to a Jew."

Hesitating for only a moment, Kalihraf jumped down, adjusted his cassock, and, assuming an air of triumph, headed pompously for the door. Hryhoriy followed him. The coachman tarried, fetching the horses some hay.

Curious alert eyes appeared in the half-blind windows. Dressed in a gaberdine and wearing a skullcap, the old tavern-keeper came running out to meet his guests, bowed low and gabbled away: "We welcome with much kindness! How was the trip? Do the gentlemen desire vodka, mead, or perhaps Hungarian wine?"

"Some mead, you sow's ear!" Kalihraf interrupted him angrily. He pushed the door open with his foot and dived into the dark entrance. The tavern-keeper rushed in after him, swept the crumbs off a table and placed two brass chalices already filled with a fragrant potion.

"Call this mead? It's dishwater!" Kalihraf barked after tasting it. He hurled the chalice to the ground and began screaming: "What are you plying us with, Jew?! Roll out a new barrel!"

"*Weis mir*, this instant, this instant!" The old tavern-keeper began to fuss about. "Rebekka! Motel!"

"What's the matter, are you crazy?" Hryhoriy asked Kalihraf after taking a sip. "The mead's all right, no worse than Hayster's."

"For diehard drinkers it's a miracle," he said, squinting craftily. "But we're respectable people, gentlemen, philosophers!"

The mead turned bitter for Hryhoriy. In the devilish twinkle which appeared in his comrade's eyes for a moment, he sensed contempt, derision, an allusion to his wandering life...

Meanwhile, the tavern-keeper had filled the chalices from a new barrel and brought them to the angry guests on a silver tray.

"Well, this isn't too bad..." Kalihraf cooled down a little. "Where did you get it?"

"In Romny, from Lord Markovych himself."

"There's a cask in the coach outside," Kalihraf said in a burst of generosity. "Fill it full for the road. But from this barrel."

"But of course, of course." The tavern-keeper hid behind the tray. "Would I deceive such a lord?"

Having finished his mead, Skovoroda fetched the thaler from his pocket which he was saving for a rainy day, handed it to their host and quickly walked out of the tavern.

They passed through the village in silence.

The coachman, who had partaken as well, began to sing but struck the wrong note, began to cough, swore, and began to hum to himself.

"The Oka River!" he announced after a while, when down below among the cliffs they spied a river shimmering in the sun. "And over there is Serpukhov." He pointed with his whip beyond the river. "E-eh, my swift ones!"

Taking fright, the horses charged down the steep ramp, the coach began to shudder and sway from side to side.

"Hold them, slow down!" Kalihraf grabbed hold of the pleated reins. "Slow down, or we'll have an accident!"

"Eh!" the coachman only cocked his sheepskin hat.

Reaching the bottom the horses turned sharply to the left, the cart teetered, there was a sharp crack and, having ploughed a wide furrow, it stopped on the meadow near the water.

The coachman sobered up immediately. He jumped down nimbly and loped off after the wheel which had overtaken the horses and splashed into the water. Luckily the bank sloped gently here and the water was shallow and sluggish.

"Stupid fool, you heavenly tsar's oaf!" Kalihraf raged, running around the cart. "Where are you fitting it, you dumb bell-clapper? Can't you see, the axle's broken."

The coachman let go of the wheel, scratched about in his sparse hair and glanced at the sun which, having lowered its rays into the pinkish-grey river, was preparing for bed.

"Ye-e-eah... The axle will have to be..."

"And how long will this take?"

"We'll have it fixed by morning, that's for sure..."

"Faugh! The pox on you!" Kalihraf said despondently and turned to Hryhoriy: "Let's go to Serpukhov for the night, and he can fetch us tomorrow."

Fetching a bag with minimal provisions, they made their way to where two carts loaded with hay and a crowd of boys and girls were waiting for the ferry.

"Ahoy, respected sir!" Kalihraf called out to the coachman. "We'll be spending the night in the monastery across the river near the stagehouse!"

"In the men's or the women's monastery?"

The priest spat on the ground in reply.

"In the women's, of course!" Hryhoriy added and laughed. "My, we've got a witty coachman."

"Like a battledore from Kozelets," Kalihraf grumbled angrily.

Having blessed the girls and boys, he proudly stepped first onto the solid old ferry which had just arrived at the jetty, stopped by the railing, shook his hair and grew silent, like a prophet communing with the Lord.

Skovoroda was last to board. He felt anxious and sad, recalling Kovray and Mariana. Would they again meet in this life? Or maybe in the after-life...?

Interesting… Where was the real world? Here on earth, or somewhere up there, in the heavens? Copernicus had kept silent about this, as had Galileo and Bruno...

Slowly the ferry set off. The thick water pushed off in elastic waves, glittering with gold. The bank swam towards them, with its fortress walls and churches. A bell tolled somewhere, followed by a second, and then a third, and then a solemn, sorrowful ringing filled the encroaching twilight.

The soul was filled to the brim with reverence, a mute enchantment with the beauty of the world, the magic of the water, the sun and the sky...

The great bell grew silent and out of the silence, perhaps from the water or the sky, was born a miraculous song which soared over the azure reaches, over the banks and meadows:

> *Don't you blow hard there, like tempestuous breezes,*
> *Eh, don't you rustle at all, my green-green forests of home,*
> *Don't you rustle at all, my green-green forests of home,*
> *Eh, let a fair maiden enjoy herself in the orchard...*

"My-my," Kalihraf smiled wryly. "Just like Jews during the Feast of Tabernacles."

Skovoroda drew close and asked in a low voice, so the *muzhiks* who had settled down under a nearby cart could not hear them: "Why are you sulking?"

"Who, me?" Kalihraf feigned surprise.

"Well obviously not me."

"It's your imagination, Hrytsko. Archangel trumpets are singing in my soul. It is filled with peace and grace…"

"Then why are you roaring at everyone like a hungry lion?"

Kalihraf grew sullen. "Who did I roar at today?"

"The tavern-keeper…"

"Oh Lord! But he's just a Jew!"

"He's a human being."

"They're a damned tribe, extortionists!"

"And don't you yourself hail from this tribe?"

Turning crimson, Kalihraf yelled: "I'm Orthodox Christian, do you hear! And don't relegate me to those tormentors of Jesus!"

"I'm not. I'm simply curious," Hryhoriy stopped him.

"Curious about what?!"

"I don't believe that a person who has scorned his people, his faith and language, can enjoy spiritual peace…"

"Well, that's heresy now. Are you trying to persuade me to return to Judaism?"

"No, I'm simply saying that all things are beautiful in their own place, when they are natural, pure and genuine."

"Then why do you resemble a mangy cat in your faded garments and ragged hat?" Kalihraf guffawed wickedly.

"This is an unworthy way of conducting a conversation," Skovoroda said calmly. "We are talking about the soul, not the garments."

"Those with money and prosperity also have spiritual peace!" The priest stuck to his guns.

"Nonsense. There's a folk saying for this: a peasant house isn't beautiful for its corners, but rather its pies. Wealth is inside us, not in money, estates, or titles."

"You're like a small child, Hrytsko," Kalihraf said patronisingly. "A stupid little kitten who won't acknowledge the lion's superiority…"

"As for me," Hryhoriy refused to remain in debt, "it's better to be a real cat rather than a lion with an ass' soul."

The ferry ploughed into the riverbank. On a cliff nearby burnt the domes and crosses of countless churches. The sun was still shining up there. But grey twilight was already settling upon the valley below, on this very placid river.

✳ ✳ ✳

Moscow greeted them with a cold wind and a low sullen sky. The city area across the river, having separated itself from the south with a wide new rampart, strove amicably upward. Here and there among the orchards and pastures rose buildings of stone. In the distance Ivan the Great was scraping the clouds with a bright cross, and all around him majestic tsarist churches flaunted themselves, while the sharp spears of the Kremlin towers stood as if on guard.

"What beauty, what might, Lord Almighty!" said Kalihraf, raised up on his knees in the hay. "I never dreamt such a place existed."

Thirteen years earlier Hryhoriy too had been quite impressed by this sight, but now he calmly accepted both the impregnability of the walls, the majesty of the churches, and the sumptuousness of the villas of princes and other St. Petersburg dukes, who loved to upstage the old Moscow capital.

"Will I really be living and working here?" The future instructor rejoiced like a child. Gone in a flash were his respectability, haughtiness, and merciless formidability, with which he had frightened mere mortals from Pereyaslav to villages on the outskirts of Moscow. "Why, oh Lord, have You so generously graced me, your humble servant Itsko from the Podil, who, having torn the millennial fetters of the Talmud, has found this sacred, true verity?! I thank Thee, oh Lord..."

"Volodymyr, stop this act, people are watching," Hryhoriy whispered to him.

Kalihraf flashed an angry eye at him, but obeyed. As they passed along the stone bridge over the Moskva River, there was a throng of gossips, paupers, and aristocratic-looking gawkers. While skilfully husking nuts, they absentmindedly studied everyone who moved into or out of Moscow, exchanging words among themselves or with passers-by, sometimes cursing or muttering rather bawdy jokes.

They did not let Kalihraf pass without comment either.

"Hey, look brothers, a miracle!" some wit called out.

"Where, where, Petrukha?"

"The Lord has heard our tearful prayers and sent us a priest!"

"What's the matter, Petrukha, aren't there enough priests in Moscow?"

"Not a single one..."

"Slanderous people, blabbing such nonsense," Kalihraf grunted angrily, pulled his head into his shoulders and hid behind Hryhoriy's back.

The Collegium or Slavic Greek Latin Academy was located in Kitay-Gorod, in the Zaikonospassky Monastery.

Having passed Red Square, the coachman turned right, into the tumult of the marketplace. The multitude of things they sold here! Olives, books, sugar, lemons, beds, fish, wine, caviar, stockings, saddles, furs, Chinese trays, gingerbread, men's overcoats, boots... There was a clamour, a rumble, laughter, curses, shouts... People swore oaths, tugged at coat flaps, followed the coach and tried to give away 'for practically nothing' goods for which there was no equal in this world.

Kalihraf couldn't sit still. Pushing the hay apart with his feet he leaned over and grabbed one thing or another, asked the price, smacked his lips, offered half as much. His large, slightly bulging eyes burnt with enthusiasm and joy. It seemed as if the holy father was about to jump off the coach at any moment, tuck up the skirt of his cassock and disappear into the market, like a fish into the sea.

"What's the matter, Volodymyr, your nature bursting to get out of its cage?" Hryhoriy asked. He asked without any malice, in jest, however Kalihraf rolled into a ball, grew quiet, hiding behind the incarnation of the prophet. He sat pouting like an owl, did not utter a word and took no notice of the market crowds.

"Whoa, whoa, my swift ones!" the coachman called out when they reached a new gate. "Well, this is where your Saviour is, the one who stands behind the icon."[47]

Crossing himself three times, Kalihraf rose, shook the hay off his cassock and spoke to Hryhoriy, as if he was his servant: "Grab the travelling bags, the cask and bring them into the yard. I'll go and find the rector."

The Collegium looked wretched here. There were signs of fire on its dark-grey walls. The small dirty windows looked out onto the world with mute longing. From the depths of the cramped yard came the smell of old cabbage soup, tainted meat and overly sour bread. Only the churches stood proudly and sumptuously, like princesses in a throng of servants. The priests and monks were looked after as well. But as for the seminarians – oh

....

[47]   Literal meaning of the name of the monastery.

Lord! – they barely dragged their feet. Thin, uncombed, in overcoats off stranger's backs, they crawled about in the shadows like sinful souls in hell.

Hryhoriy looked back on the already-closed strong oak gate and hoisted the bag onto his shoulder. The earth burnt his heels, the walls pressed in on him, his heart shrank in anticipation of something grievous.

Kalihraf emerged cheerfully from the archimandrite's cells. He could barely contain his joy. However, the smaller the distance that separated him from his companion, the more his joy turned to gloom.

"Well, how'd it go?"

"Things are fine with me, but with you…" Kalihraf said sadly. "The holy father says…"

"And the Lord be praised for it!" Hryhoriy expressed his joy.

"Of course, it's all God's will," Kalihraf drawled meekly. "However, I spoke with the prefect…" He screwed up his left eye, as if taking aim. "…and he said, if there was a good gift forthcoming…"

"Oh, don't take any sin upon your soul!" Hryhoriy joked. "Have you forgotten that a camel will sooner climb through the eye of a needle, than sinners will enter the kingdom of heaven?"

"But we'll repent…"

"Well, I'm off then," Skovoroda said resolutely. "Take care! *Vale!*"

"Stay here, Hrytsko!" Kalihraf stretched out his hands imploringly.

"*Noli me tangere. Alea jacta est!*"[48] Hryhoriy stopped him. He adjusted his bag and hat and made his way to the gate. "Fare thee well, and good luck to you!"

Kalihraf raised his hand and froze. In sorrow, or perhaps contemplating whether this strange, free soul was worth luring into a cage, this soul which fearlessly flew off into obscurity once more.

Only on Red Square did Skovoroda slow his step. Phew, he was in a sweat! He had run as if a pack of wolves had been after him. Why, from whom? He was unable to say. But as soon as he emerged from the jostling of the narrow merchant streets into this wide, almost deserted space, he felt relief. Humming a merry song, a melody which was born in his soul with the sudden change in mood, he slowly made his way across the square. To his right the Kremlin walls and towers rose almost to the clouds, and

....

[48]   Do not touch me. The die is cast! (Latin)

straight ahead, near the descent to Moskvoretsky Bridge, like some band of giants in multicoloured turbans, stood the enchanting, handsome Cathedral of Vasily the Blessed. Against the backdrop of the cathedral, like a wart on the smooth body of the square, loomed the frightening Lobnoye Mesto, now forgotten by everyone. For ages the tsars and boyars had quartered freedom here.

Hryhoriy turned to the right to bypass this horror, and ask a gentleman coming toward him: "Tell me, good sir, where is the university here?"

The lord looked this brazen fellow in an old overcoat up and down with a formidable gaze and said mischievously: "It used to be here before," he said, nodding in the direction of the Lobnoye Mesto. "But more recently, since about the past twenty years, it's been on Bolotnaya Square. So off you run, they'll teach you a lesson or two there!"[49]

A witty fellow, this devil of a gentleman!

He asked three other people, who were more simply dressed, but failed to learn anything. They would have been glad to help him, but they didn't know themselves.

Finally, he spied two fashionably dressed dandies near the cathedral. Staring up at the colourful domes, they spoke among themselves. Drawing closer, Skovoroda heard German being spoken and asked: "*Sagen Sie bitte, wo ist hier die neue Universität?*"[50]

The fellows turned around and froze in astonishment.

"Skovoroda! Hryhoriy!" they exclaimed together and, spreading their arms apart, they advanced toward him.

Lord Almighty, these were the Dioscuri, Hrytsko Kozytsky and Mykolay Motonis!

Having kissed each lad, Skovoroda hugged them tightly, as if afraid that it was a mirage which would melt at any moment.

"Well, how are you, where are you ensconced?" Kozytsky asked. He hadn't changed at all – thin, tall, with a fervent glint in his blue eyes.

"I'm here right now," Hryhoriy replied.

"But where are you staying, where are you working?"

"Nowhere."

....

49   The square was frequently used for public executions.

50   Can you please direct me to the new university here? (German)

"You're not joking, are you?" Kozytsky asked and grew sad and reflective.

"God's honour."

"We were told you were in the Collegium in Pereyaslav," Motonis drawled sorrowfully.

"I sure was, but no more. The bishop drove me out for my lack of knowledge of poetics."

"Poetics?" Motonis asked, and laughed.

"But no one knows it better than you!"

"And what about you two?" Skovoroda embraced them again. "Here already or still in Leipzig?"

"Still there. The Academy is paying for our studies," Kozytsky said.

"The German Academy?"

"The St. Petersburg Academy. We've come back to get more money and buy clothing..."

"For which we swore to serve it eternally," Motonis added, stretching out his hand, as if placing it on a Bible. He was stocky, wiry, and for this reason probably seemed like a mighty oak beside his gangly comrade.

"My, you're lucky fellows!" Hryhoriy was truly envious. "Studying for so many years..."

"Listen," Kozytsky interrupted him. "Why don't you come along to St. Petersburg with us? There's a dire need there now for teachers, pupils, and any educated people in general. The palace has finally realised that it has to rely on wise heads, not on hackles and slavery."

"Oh, lads," Hryhoriy sighed. "There have yet to be rulers who would be on friendly terms with wisdom! Minerva is proud, and from time immemorial emperors have respected those who can crawl nicely and lick Caesar's feet."

Turning around to see if anyone was listening, Kozytsky began fervently: "No, no. Luckily these are different times and different rulers! One intelligent and virtuous advisor close to the emperor can do the people more good than a whole regiment of freedom fighters."

"Skovoroda, you can't put all tsars on the one pedestal with Herod," Motonis interjected.

"Ah, not only emperors like Herod, but even good ones aren't worth much."

Kozytsky cowered. Motonis wiped the sweat away from his face and suggested:

"Let's go to the tavern, brothers, and pay Bacchus his due respect for this unexpected meeting!"

They went off, embracing each other and, amazed at such a strange sight, the Muscovites stopped and watched them go. Really, where was it heard for gentlemen and commoners to walk about the town like that! They entered a decent tavern, called a *kabak* by the locals, or a 'drinking house'.

They were given vodka in a carafe and cabbage patties on a wooden plate. Motonis grunted, filled up the glasses and announced: "To our alma mater!"

They drank the toast. Kozytsky gasped for a long time, then picked up a patty so carefully, as if it was a butterfly, and tucked in.

"Well, how's Kyiv these days, how's the Academy?" he asked.

Hryhoriy only waved his hand.

"And the Lavra printing works? Are they printing books again?"

"No way. It's a lost cause..."

"But they promised to give them permission!"

"The lord promised to give me a fur coat, but I have only his words to keep me warm."

Kozytsky knitted his brows.

"Time for another one, boys," Motonis picked up the carafe. "Have you come across any of the old boys?"

"How could I not! Throw a stick at a dog and you'll hit one of our brethren," Skovoroda smiled.

"Where's Mykyta Haister? He was so thin and tall..."

"Mykyta's a lieutenant in Pereyaslav..."

"Really!"

"I spent the winter with him. And I've just come from his place."

They were brought fried fish, which filled the whole tavern with the smell of onion and garlic.

Motonis inhaled the air with his nose and melted into an avid grin.

"Now this is what I call a snack...!"

"Tell me, Hryhoriy," Kozytsky picked up his glass, "what's happening in Ukraine. How are the Cossacks doing and their freedoms?"

"Freedom is dying there, lads. The landlords are trading people, drawing estates and wealth together, ready to give away not only their country and freedom for a noble title, but even their own mother."

"Such are the times, Hryhoriy," Kozytsky said. "If our own don't do it, intruders will..."

"A fellow countryman's yoke is no easier."

"The vodka is begging to be drunk!" Motonis called out. "To our meeting, may it not be the last!"

"So, what do you intend to do?" Kozytsky asked after they had chased the drink down with some fish.

"Don't know. P'raps I'll find shelter in some collegium..." Skovoroda shrugged his shoulders.

"Hryhoriy, go to the capital, St. Petersburg!" Kozytsky said passionately. "Those that are in power or will be in a year or two must be taught lofty notions, virtues, humanity, and a taste for freedom, equal rights for all social strata. We must teach them! And not avoid service, ranks, positions. For if we don't, then others will take control and turn power and might against all goodness and truth, whom God and our consciences have bidden us to serve!"

"Of course people must be taught, but which ones?" Hryhoriy answered. "As for ranks, positions and virtuous intentions – that's all hypocrisy, a desire to rationalise one's greed for glory, wealth, creature comforts. Those who have given their right hand, will give their left as well. One can't serve two gods without defiling one of them."

"You're wrong, Hryhoriy. If we are being summoned, we must answer their calls."

"Man must reason..."

"Time for a third!" Motonis said firmly and nodded in the direction of the tavern-keeper who was eavesdropping on their impassioned conversation. "We came across Liashevetsky today," he said briefly.

"Kyrylo?"

"Yeah, Kyrylo. So grand and wise. No joke – he's now the vicar of the Trinity Lavra of St. Sergius!"

"We talked about you with him," Kozytsky added. "He remembers you. Perhaps you could go to teach in his school?"

"Eureka!" Motonis exclaimed. "Kyrylo will accept you with open arms."

"He's probably still in Moscow," Kozytsky said. "Let's hurry to the bishop's palace!"

No matter how the boys hurried, they missed Liashevetsky. He had departed shortly before. However, fortunately, the vicar's carts had tarried for some reason and Skovoroda, being Father Kyrylo's friend, was triumphantly placed on the most comfortable cart.

They said farewell, as if forever. There were no promises of letters, meetings or rendezvous. They were aware that having crossed so unexpectedly, their paths would once again diverge for years to come, perhaps even a lifetime. Though they didn't show it, they found it painful to have to wander about the world, to philosophise like hawkers from the Podil in Kyiv, while their ancestors had drawn their sabres and tried their luck in battle. They rambled about the world, seeking honour and sustenance, while their mother country was sweating away, with no one to hand her water and say a kind word.

They kissed and furtively wiped their tears.

Soon after the carts set off.

*　*　*

Father Kyrylo was not too overjoyed at the stranger's arrival. He got up from his desk, where he had been writing something, blessed the new arrival, sullenly offered his hand to be kissed. But when he saw that Hryhoriy made no haste to fall upon his miracle-working rings, he raised his brows angrily and asked in Russian: "What has God sent you with?"

He was tall, formidable, with thick red hair surrounding his sharp face like a nimbus.

"I'm from Ukraine, father, the name's Skovoroda," Hryhoriy said.

The vicar looked at him sharply and turning red, melted into a generous smile.

"Now this is a miracle! And I thought it was some pilgrim... Forgive me. I didn't recognise you, by God!"

He came up, embraced Hryhoriy and sitting him in an armchair, indicated toward his desk: "I'm composing a sermon. We've a great procession of the cross tomorrow. There'll be a mass of people. Many coming specially from Moscow to hear me preach! Always makes them sob terribly, both common and noble folk – everyone. Even the poet Sumarokov wept..."

A novice entered and invited them to the refectory.

"Come along, Hryhoriy, let's satisfy our growling stomachs!" the vicar said merrily after the novice had disappeared. "Remember our meals as students? Oh, it's quite different here! If our brothers were let in here..." He rubbed his hands avidly and guffawed: "They would have been pleased!"

The tables really did bend under the weight of the food. On enormous plates lay mountains of bread, patties, meat, and various fish. There were cabbages, pears, apples...

Having blessed the brethren, the vicar hastily mumbled a prayer, made the sign of the cross over the food and sedately sat down at the head of the table. He motioned Hryhoriy to the vacant chair beside him.

"What church festival is it today?" Hryhoriy asked in a whisper, once the meal had begun.

Liashevetsky shrugged his shoulders and glanced at the steward-monk on his right.

"An ordinary day. Why?"

"Nothing. You obviously like to fast..."

The vicar threw a proud eye over his flock and said: "We have a hundred thousand serfs."

Skovoroda's food stuck in his throat. Barely managing to swallow it, he asked in sheer amazement: "Are you joking? Or is this true?"

"Ha-ha-ha!" the vicar guffawed and explained to the monks who had stopped champing: "Our guest doesn't believe that we have a hundred thousand bondsmen!"

A soft murmur spread through the resounding refectory. Wheezes, smiles, greasy faces, jokes.

"And two hundred thousand odd *desiatynas*[51] of arable land," the steward-monk added calmly.

"So, you can remain with us, you won't die!" the vicar said and winked.

"Ho-ho-ho!" the brethren guffawed.

Hryhoriy strained every muscle in his body, almost exploding with words of reproach and anger. But he managed to stop himself at the last moment and said forcefully in a low voice: "I am not worthy of such honour... Thank you."

....

[51] *Desiatyna* – unit of land measure, equals approx. 2.7 acres or 1.1 hectares.

The monks got their backs up, but they gradually calmed down and once more set about the tasty dishes.

After lunch the vicar took Skovoroda to the upper level, 'into the cupola', as they said here, where the famous monastery library was located.

Greedily, Hryhoriy took in this unbelievable luxury. Wherever one looked there were books! On the darkened old shelves and the tables, in chests, and in piles on the floor. Small and large, old and new, printed and handwritten, in expensive bindings and tattered ones without bindings...

"Here is the source, the living well of wisdom," Liashevetsky gestured with his hand. "Come ye, thirsty of spirit, and drink, drink to your heart's desire!"

Skovoroda picked a book off the shelf and brushing away the dust, began to leaf through it. It was a collection of short Greek poetry. He stopped at the wise words of one of them and translated it aloud:

> *Time must be caught, for all things soon grow old,*
> *In one summer, a kid becomes a shaggy goat.*

"You know your Greek well," the vicar said, glancing over his shoulder. "And we sorely need a teacher..."

Hryhoriy remained silent. Like a miser in a chest of coins, he rummaged about in this literary gold, noticing neither the flow of time, nor the impatience which had overcome Liashevetsky, who was unable to remain standing still.

Finally, the vicar took Skovoroda by the arm and said decisively: "Come along. I'll show you our monastery. These folios won't disappear anywhere. After the school bell sounds you can come here every day, if you like, and read until evening. And if you still can't quench your thirst, grab some candles and stay the night! There's even somewhere to sleep here."

Even though the procession of the cross was scheduled for the following day, the monastery was already crowded, resembling market-day in Lubny.

Hushed, fearful, and inexpressibly impressed by the agglomeration of stone walls, and churches, the pilgrims wandered about the monastery, prayed to the Lord, bowed, bought candles, crosses, and various other knick-knacks to guard them from disease and enemies, for these were from a place agreeable to the Lord and closer to heaven than their sinful villages.

Taking no notice of the crowds, Liashevetsky told Hryhoriy about the founding of the Monastery, about its defence in the times of the False Dimitry.[52] After they had passed the pond overgrown with willows and came up to a church, he took his guest by the arm and said reverently: "The Cathedral of Assumption. See the chapel? Under it lie the remains of Tsar Boris Godunov, his wife, daughter, and son."

Soon after he stooped before another church.

"And this one was built by our dear old compatriot Oleksa Rozum, or Count Rozumovsky as he later became known. It was blessed the year before last. The empress herself was present – you should have seen Oleksa! A real aristocrat, a proper nobleman. All decked out in silk and gold. Led the empress about, sent the ministers running like hares..."

He was not speaking loudly, but with such envy, that he grew sweaty and short of breath.

"You've probably long been dreaming of becoming a bishop, no?" Hryhoriy joked.

However, the vicar did not laugh, he did not answer in the same vein. Instead, he pushed his chest out and said dreamily: "For everything there is God's will. If it is His wish, He will bestow this grace upon me too..."

"What about the synod?"

"They like me in the synod for my sermons... And my gifts..." He crossed himself and changed the topic: "The Smolensk Mother of God icon is in this church. People come to see it from all corners of Russia because it performs miracles. The previous year two fellows possessed by demons were healed, and three sterile women gave birth to babies whose faces resembled Hers..."

"I see you don't recognise me again, Kyrylo," Hryhoriy said mirthfully. "I'm not a pilgrim…!"

"Why, aren't you a believer?!"

"Yes, I am a believer," Skovoroda laughed. "Such monks can heal not only a woman, but a fig tree as well!"

Kyrylo knitted his brows, angrily shook his 'aureole' and smiled. "I see you still have the knack of ruffling feathers."

....

[52]   There were three pretenders to the Russian throne in the early 1600s who claimed to be Tsarevich Dmitry, the youngest son of Ivan the Terrible. The real Dmitry had died in 1591, most likely assassinated.

"You once had a sharp tongue yourself."

"In ten years, it got worn down, erased. It's like an old whetstone now," the vicar sighed sorrowfully. "Think it's easy to please both God and the people?"

"Then don't try to please them."

"And what about the order? And the habit of constantly being respected by those around me? And my approaching old age?"

"Most precious of all is spiritual peace and harmony."

"You can't be satiated on spiritual peace alone, Hrytsko."

"Bliss lies not in satiety, Kyrylo, but in kindred toil, in the certainty that you are living according to truth, without harming others and not allowing anyone to deaden your soul."

"Unfortunately, this world is no paradise," the vicar disagreed. "Each person looks out for himself. They yell about conscience, spirit, and love towards one's neighbour, yet they snatch what they can for themselves. And according to you, I must stand to one side, look on and bear all this in silence? No, thank you nicely! I'm no fool. When the rest become more pious, then I'll gladly follow suit."

"But you're a preacher, a pastor!"

"Well, I preach, denouncing greed, dishonesty, baseness, and all the sins of this world."

"And yourself?"

"And myself I live as best I can!"

"And people believe your words of deceit?"

"I don't know. They weep..."

"Out of grief?"

"Why don't you ask them?"

There was a commotion, hasty steps, raised voices. The pilgrims surged like sheep to the main gate, crowding in among the three churches. Gradually they calmed down and made way for someone.

"What's happening there?"

"The ascetics are off to pray," the vicar said hollowly.

Soon after, a group of monks emerged from the crowd, which had parted devoutly. They were dressed in flowing black woollen cloaks, which dragged behind them for five cubits. On their heads they wore high black hoods, while in their hands they had thick staffs instead of croziers. Around their necks each had a bell and, what's more, with a length of rope attached. All of them were draped with beggar's sacks, icons, and books.

A menacing echo spread through the crowd: "Make way, make way for the holy fathers!"

Hryhoriy spat on the ground, for among the 'holy fathers' he had recognised several of the monks who had recently been gorging themselves in the monastery refectory, guffawing joyously that they had an opportunity to fleece people.

"They're hypocrites, monkeys!" Hryhoriy announced angrily.

"It's time for me to go to church," the vicar said hastily. "Go and see the steward-monk about a cell."

"If you'll permit me, I'll stay the night in the library, up in the cupola."

"As you wish! There's a trestle-bed and blankets there."

Liashevetsky wanted to add something else, but he only waved his hand and hurried off to the church, which was filling with a stream of pilgrims and ascetics.

Bells tolled, calling people to pray and to repent. The cool, pre-autumnal twilight was already descending... Darkness crept into the soul.

He made his way into the refectory.

The thin young novice who was preparing dinner humbly listened to Hryhoriy's request, fetched two candles and, lighting one of them, handed both to Skovoroda.

"Shall I bring you dinner?" he asked in an indifferent, almost other-worldly voice.

"There's no need, thank you."

It was already completely dark in the library. Finding the old candleholder, Hryhoriy dripped a little wax into it, stood the candle in it and went off to find the trestle-bed. It was nestled in a niche, behind a small table piled high with rolls of paper and books. There was even an inkwell here, and quills. True, the inkwell had long been dry, like the desert sands.

Hryhoriy threw off his bag, coat, and boots, which Mykyta had given him in Pereyaslav, laid down on the trestle-bed and took the nearest book off the table. It was Erasmus, a great luminary of truth, liberty of spirit, and brotherhood. Hryhoriy began to leaf through his brilliant *In Praise of Folly*, which he had read back in the Academy. However, the monks, the vicar, and the crowds of pilgrims played on his mind, together with everything he had heard and seen during the past half a day spent in the Monastery. Oh Lord, Jesus, Son of God, what has become of your apostles, your prophets and servants! Day and night they pray in the temple and endlessly rattle away into the Psalter. They build churches, monasteries, chapels. They wander off to Jerusalem as pilgrims... So holy to look at, but in their hearts, they are completely lawless! Ambitious people, pimps, merciless and intolerant... Oh, such hypocrites!

He put down Erasmus. The trembling flame of the candle glimmered and flickered. He placed his coat under his head, stretched out more comfortably and picked up several books at once. Plutarch, Seneca, Cicero... Verily a live-giving spring of wisdom!

He fell asleep toward morning, after the second cock had crowed...

...And immediately stepped onto the poplar-lined street in his native village.

There was a great summer festival. People walked about with bottles and glasses, laughing, singing, weeping, and dancing. He was given a large chalice of mead and a red apple. Musicians were beating out the *horlytsia*, and the dancers kicked up a whirlwind...

Suddenly he found himself in a palace where powdered curly-haired gentlemen and ladies were making merry. Affected, cunning, and greedy, they smiled benignly at one another, removing their masks and admiring their impeccable looks before a large mirror. It seemed as if Hryhoriy was some invisible, fleshless ghost in their midst.

Finally, some unknown force led him inside an enormous church. And together with the deacon he began to conduct the liturgy. In the choirs the choristers sang in drawn-out voices: "Holy God, holy and mighty, holy and immortal, have mercy on us..." Meanwhile, the priest walked about the church with a plate and snatched money from the hands of the female pilgrims, while the cantor cleaned out the pockets and purses of the men.

Suddenly he smelt something burning. Hryhoriy entered the sanctuary and stopped dead in his tracks. Priests and monks were gorging themselves here on the flesh of animals and fowls. And those for whom this was not enough were roasting a person in black over a large fire. Hryhoriy screamed in fright...

He woke up. Lying there, covered in sticky cold sweat, he tried to recall where he was.

Dawn was already shuffling about the library. A pink glow filled one of the windows...

He remembered where he was – and felt awful. For the world, for himself, for his native land which he had left so recklessly at such a difficult, bad time. The summer of freedom had passed; the last leaves of human rights were dropping off the trees. They scattered like rats from a sinking ship! Diving straight into their holes. Sons of the people, wise men! Who would defend the poor commoner now, who would become the cochineal shield between them and the nobility, teaching people truth and verity, which the magnates had hidden behind seven locks?

He rose from his bed, regretfully surveyed this kingdom of books and began to get ready. Immediately he felt freed and easy inside. It was always like this. When he reached a decision, he would feel serene, sharp in thought and spoken word, ready to endure the endless miles, the destitution, the solitude, the thirst and the hunger.

He went down into the refectory. He had wanted to ask for a piece of bread, but changed his mind. The novice was asleep on the bench, and he felt awkward about taking some. So as not to wake the lad, he carefully removed the latch and, pushing open the heavy iron-clad door, stepped out onto the covered porch.

A mist hung grey among the willows above the sleepy pond. On the lawn around it the poorest of the pilgrims were asleep on spread-out coats. People were already roaming about here and there. Someone was washing by the well out of a trough. An old fellow with a beard like a billy goat's was kneeling and praying, looking at the golden crosses which were already burning in the slanted rays of the sun.

Putting on his hat, Hryhoriy ran down the moist steps of the porch and made his way toward the gate.

Dressed in a cassock, but armed with a sabre and two pistols, the sullen guard wordlessly slid open the bolt and pushed the door with his foot. Hryhoriy stepped outside. Squinting because of the sun, he filled his lungs with fresh air. Back onto the road, toward the warm south!

Blessed be the great path home! It was easier to die there, than to live in foreign parts.

THE FIFTH NET

Who would have thought that Iosaf had not forgotten about him? So many years had passed, and yet he still remembered him. Having put aside their earlier disagreements, he had sent Father Hervasiy to find the vagrant teacher and invite him to Kharkiv. And he also let it be known through the Father Superior that Hryhoriy could teach the students as he saw fit. A miracle, no less! Either the world had changed during these past six years or the bishop had become greater friends with wisdom after becoming bishop of Belgorod. Or perhaps it was one and the other. One lived a single day and seemed to change so much as a result of it. Man never stopped learning and a single life was not enough to discover everything, to perceive the world completely...

They were already expecting him in the Collegium.

"Hryhoriy Savych?" the prefect asked, rising as soon as Skovoroda crossed the threshold of a cell choked with books. "Kordet Lavrentiy." He offered his hand and smiled painfully. "A humble monk, a lover of muses and a teacher of philosophy."

He had a pleasant, resounding voice, gleaming brown eyes and jerky boyish movements.

"Hervasiy told us about you. Sit down, please."

He cleared a place on the bench, spread his arms apart as if apologising for the importunate intruders in leather bindings, and returned to his crude oak table.

"Have you heard? The Russians have routed Frederick II at Kunersdorf!"

"So what?"

"Well, it's a victory for us too, because there were four regiments of Cossacks fighting there!"

"And how many widows and orphans has this victory in Prussia left us?"

Kordet grew thoughtful. He looked to be thirty-five, although he was probably younger. The monk's cassock never made anyone appear more youthful.

"You've been assigned the poetics class," he said shortly after and smiled. "Porfyriy Kraisky, the archpriest, wanted to take the class for himself, so I had the honour of proving to him that versification and the crafting of secret petitions is not *wszystko jedno*."[53]

"Well, he'll have you for dinner now, colleague."

"He'll choke!" Kordet's eyes lit up. He resolutely closed the book he had been reading on Hryhoriy's entry and suggested, "Come along, I'll show you to your cell. True, it's not quite a cell, simply a quiet nook in the *museum*, that is to say our library..."

"Great, father!" Skovoroda said gladdened. "Four years ago, I almost wept, leaving just such a nest."

Lavrentiy grew sullen.

"I beg you earnestly, don't call me father, it really annoys me..."

"Forgive me, I had no idea..."

"This is the Collegium," Kordet remarked, nodding in the direction of a three-storey stone building. "And further on is the dormitory, or, as some call it here, the grey-nutritive building. And way over there is the monastery's refectory. By the way, have you had lunch?"

"I don't eat lunch."

"Neither do I, when there's nothing to sink one's teeth into!" said Kordet. "Let's go first and have a bite of whatever the Lord's sent, or more correctly the rector, and then we can retire to our cells."

"Thank you, but I haven't eaten lunch for four years now," Hryhoriy grew perplexed. He did not like to boast about his life, to tell people how modest he was, how tolerant and almost saintly.

"In the name of what? To deaden the flesh?" Kordet asked in amazement.

"No, on the contrary. Surfeit does people more harm than a small amount of scarcity."

Kordet grumbled something. He looked askance at the new teacher and turned toward the exit from the monastery. Just before the gate he turned right, led Hryhoriy into a squat stone building and, opening the door to a small cell, said not altogether courteously: "You can nurture your future relics here, I'm off to have lunch."

"May the Lord help you!" Hryhoriy called after him.

....

[53]   One and the same thing. (Polish)

"I think I'll manage to chew the food myself, my teeth are still strong!" Kordet replied from the doorway and hastened out of the library.

Skovoroda smiled. He was a fine lad, this prefect-philosopher. Sharp, frank, sincere... Oho! There was a real bed here. And even a bowl for washing, a towel, a bucket of water, and a mug. And on the table stood a large new candle in a nicely turned candlestick.

Hryhoriy placed his bag on the bed and, untying his collar, washed away the dust of the road. It was clear spring water. The towel was soft and fragrant, as if in a peasant house. A sweet wave of bliss and peace spread through his body. The soul craved open spaces, it was like a living spring, filled to the brim with music, with words of gratefulness to those who had seen to the creature comforts of the unknown teacher, and even accidentally, or perhaps purposefully, had given him a place to live about which he had dreamed so much. For him this was more comfortable than any nobleman's chamber.

He took the flute from his bag, lay back on the bed, closed his eyes and began to play and play...

> *Oh, snows lie up in the mountains.*
> *Waters lie still in the valleys,*
> *Poppies bloom along the roadside;*
> *Oh, they are not small red poppies,*
> *They are darling young* chumak[54] *men.*

When he opened his eyes Kordet was standing in the doorway. He was agitated, tears glistened in his eyes.

"Hryhoriy, you have a God-given gift!" he said eventually in a simple intimate way and, closing the door, ran up to the bed. He took the flute, turned it this way and that and asked: "Where did you buy such a magical instrument?"

"Nowhere. I made it."

"Really?"

"It's the truth..."

....

54   A trader, who carted principally salt and fish from the Black Sea coast to markets throughout Ukraine.

"And you know the notes?"

"Yes."

"Hryhoriy, you're a veritable treasure. We have no one here to teach the boys singing!" Kordet raised his arms. And he said in a burst of generosity: "Come along, I'll show you our deserving garden!"

Apart from the churches, there was nothing much to see in Kharkiv. And as it was, Hryhoriy had already seen the best one, the Pokrova Cathedral, for it stood in the monastery grounds near the Collegium. Therefore, so as not to offend the prefect's patriotic feelings, Skovoroda waited a while, before asking forgiveness and suggesting: "Let's go into the fields instead."

Kordet grew silent, not having finished the story of how the church of St. Nicholas had been built.

"Across the Lopan River we have a small cottage," he said demurely after a while. "There's a forest there, a hill, and a bubbling spring..."

"Is this far?"

"No."

"Then let's dash across the Lopan!"

They descended the narrow Bursatsky Rise, passed the solid old gate and the half-filled wide moat.

"The fortress is falling apart," Hryhoriy said. "Don't the Tatars reach Kharkiv anymore?"

"When they did, the Moscow tsars mollycoddled the Cossacks," Kordet sighed. "But now they take us for granted. Colonels are appointed like hussars!"

He ran down to the river, jumped into a boat, and picked up a paddle.

"The Tatars are quiet now," he said after they had reached the middle of the river. "But the *haydamaks*[55] still harass the magnates. Not in Kharkiv itself. This last Whitsuntide they swooped down on the settlement of the *hetman*'s aide-de-camp, leaving feathers flying!" He waved the paddle about like a sword and almost tipped the boat over.

"Take it easy, or we'll sink like pups in a pond," Hryhoriy joked.

"I can swim!"

"So can I."

---

[55] *Haydamaka* – a rebel who took part in the national liberation and socio-political movement against enslavement in Right-Bank Ukraine in the late 18th and early 19th centuries.

Kordet rose from his seat and began to paddle standing up. The paddle bent from the strain and the boat flew like an arrow.

"O-ho-ho-ho!" Kordet called out in a high-pitched savage voice.

Mallards rose in fright from the reeds. And on a meadow in the distance a lone mower raised his hat and waved in greeting.

Near the far bank Kordet turned to the left and manoeuvred the boat into a tributary or sooner an arm of the river, thickly overgrown with reeds and willows. They moved along slowly, barely able to push their way through the undergrowth. However, after a while Kordet could stand such torment no longer and, hurling the paddle into the bottom of the boat, he nimbly jumped out onto a patch of yellowish sandy shore.

"Jump here!" he called out to Hryhoriy and disappeared in a flash, as if falling through the earth. But hardly had Hryhoriy taken a few steps, when he heard his companion's voice up ahead: "This meadow is ours. We graze cows here and mow hay for the winter."

Shortly they emerged onto the wide meadow which had been visible from the river. Mature, freshly-mown grass covered the ground, bumblebees buzzed over nests disturbed by the scythe. But the mower was nowhere to be seen. He had been and gone.

Hryhoriy quickened his step and caught up to Kordet, who was kicking the hay apart so that it would dry faster.

"Where's the mower?"

"Probably mown his fill and trudged off home," Kordet said without turning around. "The grass is thick and has been left to stand too long – half a day's work here will tire you out completely. The house and the well are over there." He pointed toward the setting sun, where a wall of forest stood at the base of a hill (just like in Kovray!). "We spend the night here occasionally, when we tire of the city hustle and bustle."

Skovoroda squinted and saw the river, the dam, heard Mariana's voice...

"Hryhoriy!" he suddenly heard nearby. "Hryhoriy!"

He turned around – his compatriot Nychypir Dolia was running toward him with a limp!

Kissing three times, emotional, they stood in silence, then embraced again and, laughing through their tears, began to talk. Actually, this wasn't a conversation, but rather a hail of questions, an irrepressible whirlwind of joy.

"You're not brothers, are you?" Kordet eventually interjected and they grew silent.

"This is a compatriot of mine from Chornukhy!" Skovoroda said happily. "Well, and besides that we spent three years together in Hungary. And I thought you had run off to Zaporizhia," he turned back to Nychypir.

"You're a soothsayer," Dolia melted into a grin.

There was something comical about him... Aha, there was stubble on his head where a forelock should have been!

"And where's your forelock, uncle?"

Nychypir looked at Kordet.

"The barber shaved it off, Hryhoriy." And he smiled: "But I still have my head! And how are you, what wind has brought you here to these Slobodian parts?"

"He is going to be a teacher in our school," Kordet said hastily and suggested: "Let's go into the house, brothers. We have some aqua vitae there. Uncle Nychypir, you haven't finished it off yet, have you?"

"It's alive and well," Nychypir buzzed. "Did you drop by to see my sister?" he asked Hryhoriy. "How is she getting along there, jumping up and down with joy?"

Skovoroda tripped. He had wanted to nod affirmatively, but was unable to.

"She's dead... Hauled off to a debtor's prison, and it was rather frosty."

Nychypir gritted his teeth.

"Damned magnates," he said angrily after a while, crumpled the straw hat he was carrying in his hands, and groaned. "They're ready to skin their own father for money. Oh God, will there really be no retribution?! Will they not suffer for our tears and blood! What sort of people are we?"

"We're just osier switches, and no one can be found to tie us together," Hryhoriy said.

"Thoughtless sheep shorn by every passer-by," Kordet added.

"Where are you looking, wise scholarly heads?!" Nychypir clenched his fists.

Lowering their gaze, they roamed across the meadow, silently turning over heavy clods of reproach in their minds and were unable, dared not, utter a single word in their own defence. Of course, they could have expressed countless reasons and circumstances for the current state of affairs, but this wouldn't have made them or their people feel any better. The noose was being drawn ever tighter around the necks of the people, and no one had the strength to wrench it off. A few more years, and the raven's caw would signal an end to Cossackdom...

After they had entered the house and a glass had done the rounds, Skovoroda asked Nychypir: "How is Zaporizhia, uncle? Is freedom revelling there at least?"

The Cossack waved his hand in despair.

"Only at night, perhaps, among the poor foot soldiers. Usually we saddle the sumptuous nobleman's horses and dash off to pay the Tatars or the Polish aristocracy a visit...!"

"What about our own?"

"Sometimes." Dolia smoothed his moustache. "We pull down their baggy pants and whip that spot which becomes overgrown with fat. Then they immediately come to their senses and rediscover their brotherly generosity – ready to give away everything!"

He laughed.

"Though they can sometimes feed you a bullet or two," he said after a while, and wriggled his foot about. "If it wasn't for him," he nodded in Kordet's direction, "I would have long been sipping vodka in paradise and following it down with dumplings."

"C'mon, I didn't do anything." Lavrentiy lost his composure. "They wouldn't have found you anyway..."

"I would have croaked it in the forest there," Nychypir said and handed Kordet a full glass. "God bless you, brother, I'll never forget what you did! God Almighty, when I appear at the Sich, they'll all run away! They think I'm dead and buried..."

He broke off suddenly, hung his head, sighed sorrowfully and launched into song:

> *Hey, once upon a time there was freedom,*
> *But in these times, there's only misfortune,*
> *But in these times, there's only misfortune;*
> *My dear old heart and my head ache badly...*

They returned toward evening. Kordet was taciturn, hunched over. It seemed he was anxiously waiting to see what the new teacher would have to say about the *haydamaka* from the Sich. Even though the fellow was a compatriot, who knew what thoughts were in his head...

"My heartfelt thanks to you for saving Nychypir," Hryhoriy placated him. "If only everyone..."

Kordet would not let him finish.

"I would have burnt and butchered them myself! The damned extortioners, the traitors! They suck up to the tsarina for a piece of rotten cloth... Faugh!" He struck the calm pinkish water fiercely with the paddle and asked: "Tell me then, tell me for God's sake, where is our pride, our honour? We are Cossacks, fearless Ruthenians who did not yield to the Tatars, the Polish nobles, or the Turks. But as soon as some two-bit lord arrives from Muscovy, we begin to wag our tail and run, tripping over each other, to denounce our brother and fill our purse with those wretched silver coins. And how we shy away from the common folk, as if they weren't people, as if they didn't have a heart or a thought, as if they have long been destined to be the manure which makes our nobility flower!"

Hryhoriy listened and was amazed at the similarity of the fellow's thoughts to those of his own. He spoke as if he was aflame, sparks flying. Old oak trees burnt this way, when they were struck by lightning…

The archimandrite Kostiantyn Brodsky was waiting for them in the monastery. He was also the rector.

*　*　*

On the eve of lessons in the school Skovoroda was summoned by the rector. Kostiantyn was dressed in a *klobuk* and skufia. He was flabby, grey-haired.

"Sit down, Hryhoriy," he announced indifferently, without any intonation. He finished reading a large stiff sheet of paper, picked up a quill and affixed his long fancy signature to it. Then he took Skovoroda's manuscript of lessons from a drawer and offered it to him. "I've become acquainted with it," he said hesitantly. "Well, it's interesting... You have my blessing. May the Lord help you!"

Skovoroda rose.

"Wait a moment," Brodsky raised his dry old hand. "Tell me, Hryhoriy, who imposed a penance on you and for what reason?"

"You're mistaken, father," Skovoroda replied politely. "I don't think I've even sinned..."

"Then why do you fast, eating only once a day, avoiding company?"

"Is that a sin?" Hryhoriy asked tersely. "As long as some eat too much, some must fast."

"And human company?" Kostiantyn growled shortly thereafter.

"Father, those who wish to reason must strive for solitude. Well, and apart from that," he screwed up his eyes, "the company here is much too grand and noble for me. I'm from poor Cossack stock, a black sheep, as they say..."

"These are the words of the evil one," Kostiantyn said stiffly. "You are noble with erudition. And you have a high rank."

"Of course, a teacher..."

"I wasn't referring to that," the rector raised his voice. "Her Highness the Empress conferred upon you the worthy rank of court choir soloist."

"I'd forgotten about that," Hryhoriy drawled.

"Off you go," Kostiantyn waved his hand dismissively. "No, wait! Here, take this money, go down to the merchants' row and buy yourself a new decent set of clothes. A *kaptan*[56] coat, a camisole, woollen pants. Because you look like a beggar."

"I feel fine in these clothes..." Skovoroda began.

"Go, go, Hryhoriy! I want to see you looking like a newly minted coin tomorrow!"

Hryhoriy stepped outside. Amazed at such generosity and kindness, he pressed the money into his hand and wandered off to his *museum*. Nothing less than a miracle! He was welcomed in Kharkiv as if in his own home. Given work, shelter and new clothes.

Why, for what reason? By whose grace...?

"So, what did Brodsky want from you?" asked Korcet, who was on his way to see the rector.

Skovoroda opened his hand with the money.

....

[56]   *Kaptan* – from the Turkish 'kaftan', traditional outerwear in the shape of a robe or coat usually made from carmine-coloured woollen fabric.

Kordet let out a whistle.

"He told me to buy a *kaptan*, a camisole, and everything else which a teacher should have."

"Congratulations," the prefect sighed. "I could have given you mine, if you were a little shorter. Having had to pull on this damned garb." He poked his finger at the cassock and sighed again. "Enjoy yourself! But watch out, lest the traders cheat you!" he called from the doorway and disappeared into the dark antehall.

Leaving the *Poetics* manuscript in his room, Hryhoriy left the monastery. The cold heavy gold dug into his pocket. He had never had such a large sum of money, even though he had lived almost forty years in this world. He felt unaccustomed, confused. He felt as if he was wearing something inappropriate or was revealing naked flesh somewhere, and sensed that all the passers-by were eyeing him with condemnation. Several times, villagers, probably in Kharkiv for the first time, wanted to ask something, but changed their minds and hastened on their way. Even the old blind minstrel sitting outside the scribe's building and singing in a long-since hoarse voice, suddenly rested his thin, almost black hand on the strings.

Hryhoriy took out a rouble and placed it in the hat. The old man flinched, quickly fingered the money and hid it down his shirt front.

"Sing me a song, grandpa."

The minstrel adjusted his old instrument, tightened one of the strings and said subserviently:

"Just one moment, one moment, dear sir..."

Skovoroda grimaced. He wanted to say that he was no lord, but a destitute fellow too, with nothing apart from his flute and several books to his name. But he wasn't quick enough. Clearing his throat, the minstrel began a song about how Empress Elizabeth granted freedom to the Cossacks and *Hetman* Kyrylo.

Hryhoriy continued on his way. In his heart he felt a painful melancholy. He passed stores, kiosks and once more tried to reclaim his spiritual peace and harmony, which he had lost after seeing the rector.

The fair celebrating the Feast of Assumption was in full swing. There were about ten times more people prowling about the city than on ordinary days. They had come from all over the place: Cossacks, townspeople and commoners, traders, lords and lordlings from Slobodian Ukraine and cities in Russia, which began beyond Ostrogozhsk and nearby Belgorod.

Hryhoriy viewed the humanity in this Babylonian multitude as if in a theatre. Everyone seemed equal here: no one was beating anyone and forcing them to hand over the fruits of their labour. People haggled, poked about the market, sealed deals with drinks... In actual fact there were chasms everywhere. That little lord there who was examining a new carriage had grown wealthy and wanted to change his turn-out. And that one (my, how he had decked himself out!) had probably been to the capital, received a village in appreciation of his faithful canine service, and was now seeking a craftsman to build him a mansion. A trader bent down to the ground before a moustached hussar, even though he himself could probably buy a whole regiment of them. Some Cossack on his last legs was offering up his sabre – his last weapon. There was a commoner in bast shoes and without a hat, who had brought along an old mare that could barely stand up. Lordlings and officials in expensive camisoles were guffawing at him, poking the nag in the ribs and demanding that the owner mount her and ride her at a gallop. The wretch stood downcast and down his cheek – tanned and covered in dust – ran a bitter, burning tear.

Hryhoriy pushed through the pack of jeerers, bought the nag off the fellow, and leaving his purchase with him, disappeared into the crowd. They called out to him, but to no avail.

He felt relieved, but suddenly realised that he would be unable to buy himself an aristocratic outfit! Not because he no longer had enough money, but because of his nature, because of that great affinity he felt with the poor, which brought him boundless strength and faith in a better future. Forsooth, know yourself, and you will know happiness.

At ease, smiling, Hryhoriy entered a store, bought himself some pants – wide, blue ones on a drawstring, some good Cossack boots, a shirt, a belt, a hat, and an ordinary grey peasant coat.

The trader's eyes bulged when he saw the teacher take off his fine German overcoat and put on the simple peasant coat.

Leaving his old clothes in the store, Hryhoriy stepped out onto the crowded market street and headed off for the Collegium. He seemed to have grown younger some ten or twenty years! He took big, easy steps. His head was filled with morning clarity, and his soul was awash with joy.

My, Kordet would be amazed! And the rector? He would castigate him. Or perhaps even drive him out. It wouldn't be the first time... Happiness was not in the rank or position a person achieved, but in the person himself! The bishop would probably summon him and begin lecturing him about how one needed to live, so as not to anger the Lord and irritate his beloved slaves, who enjoyed Paradise on earth. All was the vanity of vanities! The worst torment was one's conscience. With a clear conscience, and peace and harmony in one's heart – Jupiter could rage!

However, he entered the Collegium grounds with trepidation: he hated terribly to cause people unpleasantness.

*　*　*

But misfortune always appears when it is least expected. Like a thunderstorm in June – sudden and unbidden.

In the spring, after the orchard was in blossom and the school holidays had begun, Hervasiy invited Hryhoriy to come to Belgorod. Skovoroda did not sit around waiting for a reason to leave and that very same day, placing his chattels in a bag, headed off north.

It was a warm, serene day. The road ran through the forest, dipping and rising, while in the misty shroud on the plains the quiet Kharkiv River glittered like a sabre. The larks sang. They were invisible, and so it seemed as if it was the clear blue sky quavering away. From the tall hills drenched in blossom and grasses, colourful brocades of fields, woods, ponds and meadows spread before the eyes in all four directions. At the foot of almost every hillock running water flowed into the river, a gully, or a ravine. Curative, fresh, sun-drenched water...

Having managed some twenty-five versts, Skovoroda stopped beside a small spring in the riverbank. He lay his bag on the ground and removed his straw hat, a gift from Nychypir Dolia before the fellow had left to join the Cossacks. From what springs was he drinking now? Had he reached the Sich? Although even there, as they said, there was no freedom now for the poor...

He filled his cupped hands with water, splashed it in his face. Ooh, sheer bliss! A stream of water trickled into his bosom. Hryhoriy took off his shirt and washed the dust of the road from his chest and neck. He then drank till he could drink no more, dressed and stretched out on the green grass in the shade. The sun blinded him through the young willow leaves, as if flirting with him. Without waiting for the evening, two nightingales began to compete in the thickets by the river. Here and there cuckoos counted someone's years, a hoopoe struck its tympani, and a turtle-dove babbled away.

He closed his eyes. God, what more of a paradise could people wish for! But no, they churned about, forging fetters for their neighbours. Freedom-gobbling brutes! Like hawks they soared through the sky seeking out their bloody prey.

> *Oh, you yellow-breasted bird,*
> *Do not build your nest up high...*

The words of a new song were being born. And the melody seemed to come from the nightingale's roulades or perhaps the calls of the oriole, resembling Aphrodite rising from the foam. Life was simple, unsophisticated and an indissolubly kindred part of the sky, these woods, this spring, these birds, and of this day, this blossom, this crystal-clear brook, and that dense sycamore tree way over there on the hill, whose branches were being twisted by the wind...

He failed to notice a corpulent, elderly priest drive up to the spring on a cart.

"Whoa, cursed beast!" The holy father fretted and, throwing his cross onto his back, grabbed the horse by the nose. "Stop, stop, you Lucifer!"

The horse stepped back, rearing its head, but then struggled toward the water again.

Finally, the priest's patience ran out and he called to Hryhoriy: "Hey there, you scoundrel, come here and hold the horse while I take a drink."

"Perhaps I had better hold you and let the horse have a drink first?" Hryhoriy asked, getting up.

"Do as you're told, imbecile," the priest grunted angrily and, handing the horse over to Hryhoriy, fell upon the spring.

"Father, where did you learn that I was a scoundrel and an imbecile?" Hryhoriy asked cheerfully.

The priest croaked deliciously, wiped his lips with his hand and waved his hand for Hryhoriy to let go of the horse.

"At your age, my chap, smart people don't go about on foot."

"A logical, though erroneous judgement."

The priest slapped his sides with his hands.

"Woe is me, and what would you know about logic? What's the matter, did you sleep off a drunken spree outside the Collegium Monastery?"

"Of course," Skovoroda retorted. "Even wise Pliny once said that *omne perire tempus, quod studiis non impertias*, to wit: lost is the time you have not used for study."

"Skovoroda?!"

"Aha."

"Please forgive me." The priest began to fuss, perplexed. "I took you for a vagrant peasant unwilling to walk behind the landlord's plough…"

"And I have no desire to do so," Hryhoriy said.

"You plough the untouched and fallow fields of the soul, mister teacher, and sow them with the grain of knowledge. Your fame is spreading already."

Now it was Skovoroda's turn to grow embarrassed.

"Are you from Kharkiv?" he asked, in order to change the topic.

"Been to market. And now I'm off home, to Starytsia. And where might you be headed?"

"Belgorod."

"My God, that's on the way! I'll give you a lift. And if we're late, you can spend the night in my home! The old woman will be glad. My nephew studies in your Collegium. Such a smart lad. You probably know him – Mykhailo Kovalynsky. He's finished second year."

"Unfortunately, I don't." Skovoroda spread his arms apart. "I taught poetics."

"I implore you." The priest folded his meaty arms across his chest. "Please make the acquaintance of my nephew and have a few words with him. He's a glorious lad, aye!"

"I surely will," Hryhoriy promised and picked up his bag.

"Shall we be off then?" the priest asked.

"Let's!" Hryhoriy jumped onto the cart.

No matter how they hurried, they were still late and Hryhoriy spent the night with Father Petro in Starytsia.

The following day, having thanked him for his hospitality and promising to drop by again shortly, Skovoroda set off for Belgorod, which was close by.

Father Hervasiy received Hryhoriy in the archimandrite's cells. He greeted him like a brother, squeezed Hryhoriy in a tight, strong embrace. He had grown even sleeker, more rotund. He was gleaming, like a steer in autumn.

"I've heard, I've heard, Hryhoriy," he said as he caressed his guest with his eyes, "how you've taken Kharkiv by storm. What a fine fellow! Didn't put me to shame."

"I only... It was nothing." Skovoroda recoiled.

But Hervasiy took him by the shoulders and sat him on the stool before him.

"How thin you are, Hrytsko! But don't worry, I'll fatten you up here..."

"I'm not worried," Skovoroda managed to interject. "As long as my soul is healthy."

"If the soul is the wine, then the body is the wine-skin." Hervasiy raised his finger and laughed. "So, how was it?"

"Good."

"They didn't wrong you, did they?"

"No."

"A bit tight with money?"

"Not really."

The archimandrite grimaced – something about the conversation wasn't to his liking, but exactly what Skovoroda failed to understand.

"You're an odd fellow, after all, Hrytsko." Hervasiy smiled meekly. "Do you really have no wish to achieve happiness and distinction?"

"But I'm happy already, father," Skovoroda said fervently. "There's work, pupils, books – enough for three unfortunates!"

The archimandrite said nothing, either hesitating or thinking something over. Suddenly he asked: "Tell me, Hryhoriy, why aren't you a monk yet?"

"Because I'm not worthy..."

"Well, but would you like to be one?" Father Hervasiy cheered up.

"I really don't know. To become a novice at my age.. "

"We'll accept you into the order straight away. I've spoken with the bishop."

The archimandrite rose. Hryhoriy followed suit.

"I'm not ready, I'm much too sinful," he said decisively.

"Hryhoriy," Father Hervasiy took him by the arm. "We're all sinful. And you've long been living like a real ascetic."

"This is so unexpected. I need to think it over..."

"Strange fellow! What's there to think over? Iosaf himself bade me to accept you into the monastic order. In a year or two you'll become a prefect, then a rector."

"God bless you. But really!"

"You are the wisest – you should be in command!"

Hryhoriy wiped away the sweat.

Regaining his senses after the praise, which depressed him, he said passionately: "No, I can't. Thank you for the honour, the friendship, but monastic life is not to my liking. At least not now. When I sense that I am ready, I will come and let you know, and drop to my knees. Then you can place the monk's hood upon me and dress me in a skull cap. But at present – no."

"You're a child, Hryhoriy. You don't understand simple things. The bishop is offering you honour, wealth, respect. Can you imagine being a rector?"

"Will the hood give me extra wisdom? For the essence is in the head..."

"It is easier to live without a head now, than without a monk's hood and a skullcap," the archimandrite said angrily.

"Maybe for someone striving to reach the top," Skovoroda noted. "But I have only one worry, father, to die with all of my wits intact."

The archimandrite grew sullen.

"Let's go see Iosaf!" he announced after a while and proceeded to leave the cell.

Skovoroda followed him. He already knew these efforts would bear no fruit. They would set upon him together and drive him into the monastery walls, like hunters driving an old wolf into a ravine. The mighty had grown unused to tolerating freedom alongside them. It irritated them, like a speck of dust in their eye. They feared it, for where there was freedom, there was reason, and a desire for truth and dignity. It was easier to control slaves. There was no need for intellect then, the sword and the whip were enough.

"Wait here," Hervasiy said after they entered a large room. Countless old portraits hung on the walls. They were all bishops, pious-looking old men in expensive, lavish vestments. All in the same style, like identical twins.

"You may enter!" Father Hervasiy called out, peering out of a side door.

The bishop blessed Hryhoriy affably. He had grown older, his grey hair had turned yellowish, his eyes and cheeks were sunken.

"Father Hervasiy tells me," he began softly, hoarsely, "that you refuse to enter the monastic order. Is this true?"

"It is."

"Why?"

"I'm afraid."

"Of what?"

"Of losing a treasure."

"What treasure?" He exchanged glances with the archimandrite.

"The last one I have remaining – my freedom."

"You'll be deprived of it sooner without a monk's hood. Some lordling will enter you into his register, and you can kiss your name goodbye."

"But I'm a Cossack."

The bishop chortled.

"And I have the rank of court chorister."

"Hryhoriy," the bishop began sincerely in a brotherly tone. "Take a closer look at me – I'm already old and frail, very soon the Lord will call me into his sumptuous chambers... Who will I leave the flock to, who will I hand the diocese over to? Who will stand on guard, wielding God's word like a fiery sword, stemming the flow of greed, injustice, and squabbles? Perhaps him over there?" He nodded in the direction of Hervasiy. "He's a good, loyal shepherd, but a far cry from Cicero, or even Konysky! Kordet or Brodsky? Or perhaps Kraisky?"

"As long as there's bread, teeth can be found," Hryhoriy remarked.

"Of course, they can." Iosaf smiled wryly. "But which ones, whose?"

"It's a great offer, Hryhoriy," Hervasiy interjected. "Such an opportunity comes once in a lifetime, and even then, only for one in a hundred thousand of us."

"Verily!" the bishop intoned. "You'll have wealth you never even dreamed of. And respect, authority, and power! Coaches, horses, gold!" The bishop seemed to grow younger, filled with vigour once more. "Whether you walk or ride, the people will view you as God, they'll run after you, kissing your garments, your hands. You bless the brethren and sense the angelic wings growing as you take up a position beside the Lord's throne."

Skovoroda got up and, barely able to contain his indignation, said in a voice hollow with anger: "You want me to join the already teeming numbers of Pharisees?! Eat your fill, drink sweetly, dress lavishly – and live your monastic life! I'm not your fellow-traveller. You preach love toward one's neighbour, whereas in fact you love only yourselves. You rant about free conscience, yet you are as intolerant as the Eastern despots, and in God's name encroach upon the honour and life of the heterodox. Each day, each moment, you assert that our faith is the only true one in this world, and yet you fear lest someone express even half a doubt. And this is supposed to be the essence of a righteous man?!"

"Hryhoriy, come to your senses!" Hervasiy called our fearfully. "Remain silent, you poor wretch!"

"Who then will tell you the truth, who will remove the cataracts from your unsatiated eyes? You've grown big bellies, dressed yourselves in silks, broadcloths, and gold, and you bless violence, torment and slavery!"

"Hryhoriy, fear God!" Hervasiy wailed again.

Raising his hand and looking askance at Hryhoriy, the bishop said stiffly: "Accept the monk's habit then, stand at the head of the diocese and show the shepherds how to live, cleanse the true word of this defilement..."

"Even Hercules would be unable to clean out your Augean stables!"

"Heaven preserve us!" Hervasiy whispered.

The bishop sat gritting his teeth, examining a Gospel bound in silver and gold.

"What are you trying to achieve then?" he asked at last.

"A life intimately bound to the soul, to Nature," Skovoroda responded animatedly. It seemed to him that Iosaf agreed with him. "The essence lies not in the monk's hood and the order, but in magnanimity, in the serving of truth and man, in knowing oneself, and struggling to overcome such passions as self-esteem, greed, excessive pride, conceit. Know yourself – this is the ultimate commandment, our alpha and omega. Otherwise, we become mere cattle!"

Grimacing like a martyr, the bishop focused his cold grey eyes on Hryhoriy.

"Very grandiloquent, my good fellow," he said with restraint. "Your thoughts verge on heresy." He stopped Skovoroda with his raised hand, for the fellow wanted to contradict him. "Of course, your words bear a scrap of verity, a small truth… However, the great truth in the name of which we live and struggle, tramples the smaller ones, sacrifices them. Together with those who cling to them," he added forcefully.

"This is hypocrisy!" Skovoroda burst out. "Once a mother kills her children, she is no longer a mother. Having committed maternal filicide, she becomes a putrid corpse!"

Iosaf closed his eyes, as if defending himself, and once Hryhoriy had grown silent, he pronounced: "In our Collegium there is a tradition that all teachers are monks or priests, and we cannot, we do not have the right to violate this ancient custom..."

"You mean, 'be arrogant, if you please, but not in my house'?" Hryhoriy asked, recalling how the bishop in Pereyaslav had driven him out.

"Don't rush. Think it over. There's a whole summer ahead of you," the bishop said in reply and closed his eyes again. "Go now, rest after your journey. Father Hervasiy has prepared a comfortable, sunny cell for you."

Hervasiy stood up and made his way to the door in silence.

Left alone, Hryhoriy was besieged by a swarm of thoughts. And neither the magnificent cell, in which it wouldn't have been a sin for the bishop himself to stop, nor the books so dear to his heart chosen by Hervasiy himself, were capable of dispelling the mournful ache in his chest. Back there in the bishop's chambers everything had been simple, clear-cut, but here, on his own, the clear, pure water of his unshakeable convictions and judgements was covered with the duckweed of doubt. Who are you, to speak with the bishop as an equal? They found you, warmed you, let you feel the joy of a full life, of the association with youth, and you repay them with unpleasantness, extreme disobedience. You are like that wolf, which remains insolent no matter how much it is fed! *Homo novus*, who has attained life, but seeks the truth in it. Instead of taking existing dogmas and covering your shame with them, living for the sake of pleasure, you keep digging, seeking, philosophising! Your temples are covered in silver, and yet you still torment the soul with a desire for truth and freedom...

He spent the night tormented by doubt. Awaking before sunrise, he left the cell barefoot. A light breeze pleasantly caressed his chest. In the park behind the church the birds welcomed the approaching sunny day. The oriole probably exerted itself most of all. It seemed to be luring someone, calling them, and was engrossed in song, in expectation of morning and sunshine.

Driving away thoughts about his own fate, which had irritated him badly all night long and stopped him from sleeping well, Skovoroda wandered off into the park. Actually, it was a small courtyard which had been barely squeezed in between the bishop's palace and the cathedral. The city was growing beyond these walls. However, here too, inside this fortress, new buildings and offices appeared, squeezing out the parks and gardens into the suburbs and fields.

Hryhoriy left the castle through the double south-eastern gate. And immediately came face to face with the sun. It was rising over the boundlessness of meadow and forest, hurling rays into the sky. On the hillside the dew changed colour, glistening; lower down, in the valleys, it lay lavishly, covering everything with a dull bluish grey tinge, still dozing, covered with a blanket of mist.

One could breathe freely and easily here. Weakened during the night, exhausted by endless churning thoughts, his body once more filled with miraculous strength, the sunshine, blossom, and bird songs revived him. It suddenly seemed as if it was someone else who had left the city that morning, while he had been standing here an eternity, like this earth, like the oak tree which had spread its ample crown upon cushions of mist. This feeling was so overwhelming, that he dared not take a single step or even wriggle a toe, so as not to tear his roots. Only after a herd of cows had been driven out to pasture did he leave the road and wander along the wall to the river.

Thoughts, thoughts... The year had passed like a song! How emotional he had been coming to class, and how he rejoiced, seeing the mute rapture in the boys' eyes at his words, his down-to-earth, friendly attitude toward everyone without exception. And the evenings spent poring over books! The candle burning straight, soft, tender twilight in the corners. Hellenes with high foreheads joined him at the table, majestic, proud Romans, Frenchmen, Germans – all of them sages and philosophers, engaging him in debate and discussion. The wisdom he had drawn from those evening discussions, how he had enriched his mind, his soul... Or the times spent on the river in May when the choir students, putting aside their hymns and psalms, launched into:

> *Hey, 'tis not thunder rumbling over the steppe,*
> *'Tis Sirko, the Cossack otaman,*
> *Calling out to his brotherhood from the Sich...*

He was moved to tears about the books and the pupils he would have to leave behind, the hours he and Kordet had sacrificed to reflection, the quest for truth and that firmament which would not allow his people and native land to perish.

Perhaps, had he become a monk, he could have shown people what a member of the clergy, a true believer, should have been like, and been able to take on the Collegium or the diocese. He could have set an example of integrity, humility and courage in the struggle for the hearts of his fellow man.

No, no! This was fear talking, this was abjuration, self-deceit, the aim of which was to rationalise his desire to submit to the will of the strong to retain a miserly scrap of comfort!

And what if instead of you the order were to be embraced by a base person, an animal with a beast's soul? Would their sins, their villainous deeds not fall upon you? You had the chance to stop them and you didn't.

But there was not just one of them, their numbers were legion! You would become lost among them, like a drop in the ocean. Soon enough you would become like one of them or die a martyr. These were hypocrites who lived by lies. They had transformed the great faith of the oppressed into a shield for their greed and vainglory, into the scourge of the people and liberty...

He stopped on the white cliffs. The mist had melted away and the world shone with a smile. Down below, the river bore along its azure-white waters into the steppe, meadows and hillocks flourished – everything was warmed by the sun, bathed in a warm downpour which had toiled hard all of the previous evening.

Hryhoriy suddenly imagined that next to him, or perhaps even inside him, he could hear the rustle of that mighty sycamore, which had towered over the river near the spring, where he had quenched his thirst the day before yesterday. A wind gusted from the east, tried to tear the shirt from his body...

A melody surfaced, having been born near the brook under the willows:

> *Tempestuous winds come gusting,*
> *Breaking the sycamore's arms...!*

Recalling how Father Hervasiy had suffered the day before, he laughed long and heartily.

He lay on the grass on the clifftop, peering into the clear spring sky, breathing in the intoxicating air and revelled in the warmth, the beauty, the serenity. Somewhere nearby a shepherd was playing on a horn. Geese were screeching. Horses neighed in the meadow below.

Exchange all this for a monk's cell? Sell the blue sky for the ceiling of a palace? Give away a clear conscience, and in its place take on the sins of all the clergy, their lies and deception? Never! Even if his grace went raving mad, to hell with him!

Let those torment themselves,
Who struggle to reach up high...

He sat up, embraced his knees and listened to the words of a new song being born inside him, about a yellow-breasted bird, which did not chase after vanity and glory, but strove to live quietly, wronging no one in the world and not letting itself be abused. Happiness had no place, country, order or home – it was in the soul, inside us, with us forever and everywhere!

Returning into the bishop's yard, Skovoroda collected his belongings and went to tell Father Hervasiy of his final decision.

The archimandrite was unable to see him. Or had no desire. Only at noon, when Hervasiy emerged to see the petitioners who were awaiting him in the foyer, did Hryhoriy humbly bow his head and say firmly: "Father, bless me for the road."

Looking somewhere off to the side, Hervasiy silently made the sign of the cross over the recalcitrant teacher and turned his back on him.

Hryhoriy left the archimandrite's chambers and put on his straw hat. Where to now? Pereyaslav once more? Or perhaps Kharkiv? Kordet could find him a tutor's job somewhere... No, no. He was more than satiated with the world – this prostitute without shame or conscience! To Starytsia perhaps? Father Petro had invited him. It was close by, and it was lovely there – forests, meadows, water. Peace and quiet... He could build himself a hut in a grove by the stream and, like Horace, serve the muses, reasoning and admiring the beauty of immortal Nature... It was a wonderful idea!

Throwing the bag over his shoulder, Hryhoriy set out of the city. He walked briskly, joyously, even though he felt anxious. A new life lay before him! Scholarship! Freedom!

And solitude...

The solitary man must be a king or a beast, as one of the wise Romans had said.

Which are you, Hryhoriy Skovoroda?

THE SIXTH NET

Solitude is the blessed time of philosophy. In the bustle of life, thoughts are like butterflies: they are born, tremor with colourful light wings and disappear, perish. Man must reason and perceive the world. For how will he then differ from animals, birds, even trees? *Cogito, ergo sum.*[57] Death arrives when one stops reasoning and becomes a wordless, mute creature, which anyone can skin to make a pair of boots.

Solitude... However, it too is not enough for happiness. People were attracted to people. The community was like a magnet, attracting, providing work for hands and minds, sharing social experience, absorbing it. Like bees we gathered the nectar of thoughts from everywhere and brought it to the common hive of human intellect.

For fifteen months Hryhoriy lived in the quiet, amiable Starytsia. And on the sixteenth, after the children had gone off to school and the birds had set off for the distant warm regions, he hoisted his bag onto his shoulders and set off for Kharkiv.

The seminary students greeted him joyously. They crowded around him, tanned, lively, friendly. Questions flew thick and fast, and most often they asked if he would be living with them and teaching them poetics. Hryhoriy answered them, laughed and felt the ice slowly melt inside his soul. Seeing quite a few new faces in the crowd, he asked, recalling Father Petro's request: "Is there a Kovalynsky among you, boys? Mykhailo Ivanovych?"

"Yeah! Yeah!" they called out in unison, parted ranks and pushed forward a slender dark lad of fifteen. He grew embarrassed; a light rouge played on his gaunt cheeks and his long, curved eyelashes trembled. A high forehead, wide bushy brows... Suddenly he noticed the lad's gaze – deep and penetrating! For a moment it seemed to Hryhoriy that he was looking into a mirror and seeing his own eyes there. Astonished and even somewhat

---

[57] I think, therefore I am. (Latin)

frightened, he cast an eye over the crowd of students who were laughing, telling him something, and asked in a strange, distant voice: "Are you Kovalynsky?"

"Yes..."

"Father Petro's nephew?"

"Aha."

Hryhoriy saw the lad as if in a mist and could barely hear his scanty, brief replies. Had the lad said that he was Hryhoriy Skovoroda, he would not have been surprised, would not have contradicted him. Lord Almighty, could it be that You have taken pity on a vagrant Cossack and instead of sending him a son, sent him a bosom friend, a wonderful young soul, to which one could give all one's love, and all one's wisdom acquired over forty years?! He had prayed for this in Starytsia, when black clouds hovered over him. And God had heard him! His thoughts flew like Cossacks on horses. He kept smiling, then knitting his brows, his eyes glued to the spot where Mykhailo had just been standing, but where there was no one now.

The seminary students had gone off somewhere. Had the bell summoned them to classes, had someone dispersed them? Or maybe they had scattered, noticing that their teacher, this ascetic and bibliophile, was communing with God, oblivious to his former students...

"Hryhoriy!" Kordet called him, stepping out of the Collegium doorway. "Good health to you, brother! What wind has brought you here?"

Humbly he let himself be embraced, meanwhile watching with emotion through the walls as Kovalynsky ran into the classroom and, sitting at the front desk, found his book, took out some paper, dipped his quill in ink.

"What's wrong, Hrytsko?" Kordet tugged at his coat. "Not ill, are you?"

"No..."

"Staying with us for good or only visiting?"

"Who knows?"

He was drawn into the Collegium, to where Mykhailo was. He was drawn there uncontrollably, to the point of pain in his chest. Passing around the father prefect, he headed for the doorway like a sleep-walker. However, a few steps later he turned to the right and quickly left the monastery.

He recovered only near the willows by the Lopan River. Leaning back against an ancient black-barked trunk, he looked for a long time at the water laced with willow leaves and listened to his own soul. Something strange was happening there. Painful waves of joy came rolling one after another, splashing into his chest, his head, filling his body with zeal, strength, and energy. Nothing like this had ever happened to him before. Except perhaps when he had fallen in love with Mariana... No, that was something quite different. That was youthful tumult, a vigour for bliss, advancement. But this was a craving for continuity, a desire to win the duel with time, with death itself, which ruined everything we took so long to build, with such effort. Everyone yearned for eternity. Some through deeds, exploits, others through children and grandchildren, and still others... No, he was not dreaming of eternity. It wasn't for mortal fame or heavenly bliss that he had avoided wealth, awards, struggling to understand his own essence, people, nature, and the world as a whole. There was no other way for him. To go about in lavish garments, when thousands of his brother compatriots were glad to have a coarse grey peasant coat? To bathe in glory, when your people are bound, quaking with fear, crippled?!

He got into the nearest boat, moored on the muddy bank. Closing his eyes, he again saw his new friend. He was already certain that this youth would become like a son to him from now on.

The water tenderly splashed and babbled among the boats. Fish jumped out of the water. On the far bank near the mill small boys were tending a herd of cows. A bonfire was burning...

He would be Mykhailo's guide and inspiration. He would cultivate his vernal soul like a ploughman tilling a fertile field, sowing it with the grain of wisdom. The number of decent-hearted, worthy, free-willed men grew progressively smaller. Some, by oppressing others, subjecting them to slavery, lost their human face and began to resemble vampires, who lived off other people's blood. And others, onto whom the yoke was placed, were stunned, exhausted and salted through with sweat, growing silent in a kind of frightening metamorphosis, dying or becoming draft horses – mute, meek, painfully defenceless and forlorn. Who would save them, who would teach them to perceive their unservile essence, their innate ability to turn mountains upside down, perform heroic deeds which even Hercules would have envied? Decent-hearted, honest sons of the people, radiant with the fire of scholarship, warriors of the human soul and truth!

He wanted to dash off to the monastery, but forced himself to stop. No need to be feverish, Hryhoriy – pacify your tempestuous heart and act as befits a man, not a small child. Who are you? A transient, homeless teacher. How will you approach your good friend, how will you win his love, his trust?

He tormented himself with thoughts, doubts and all the same continued uphill into the city. He knew not what would happen to him in an hour, or tomorrow. But he was certain that his life would assume a new sense and meaning. Nothing in the world was eternal, only aspirations and notions, and only then if they entered the flesh and blood of the people and became a banner passed on to sons, grandsons, and great-grandsons.

Short of breath and red-faced, Kordet stopped him near the *museum*.

"Where have you been roaming? I raced around the whole city. You seemed to have disappeared into thin air!"

"I did disappear, I went down to the Lopan." Skovoroda smiled. "Starting to miss me?"

"Like a cat misses the broom," Kordet mumbled and said cheerfully: "The rector is calling for you!"

"What for?"

"You need to come. He'll tell you himself. God, I was afraid you'd already dashed out of Kharkiv! Come on, let's go!" He gave Hryhoriy a nudge in the side and winked: "There will still be time to talk our fill..."

This time Father Kostiantyn met him more affably. Blessing him, he began to question him about what he had toiled over in quiet Starytsia, what had brought him to Kharkiv, and in the end he put the question point-blank: hadn't he tired of the life of a hermit?

"I don't know, father," Skovoroda admitted frankly. "I can't seem to decide myself."

The rector remained silent for a while and, raising his sorrowful grey eyes, suddenly said: "Hryhoriy, perhaps you could return to our Collegium?"

Skovoroda grew tense. Would there be talk of the monastic order again?

"And Iosaf?"

"He gives his consent."

"As a secular teacher?"

"Whatever you like."

"A teacher of poetics?"

"Choose for yourself." The rector smiled benignly. "Anything from infima to philosophy!"

"May I teach syntaxis?" Hryhoriy asked, rejoicing that he could teach his new friend.

"Please do." The rector rose and then caught himself: "Although, we have no one to teach Greek..."

"I agree, father, I'll teach both of them!" He was so overjoyed at the opportunity to see Mykhailo each day, that he was ready to take on all the subjects.

"Well then," Father Kostiantyn said with relief. "Let it be so. You can occupy your former cell. It is still free."

"I'm off. God bless you, father," Hryhoriy whispered, moved by such kindness, and quickly left the rector's office.

*　*　*

Who knows what they had told the boy about him, only Mykhailo began to avoid his new, incomprehensibly wise and fervent teacher. Hryhoriy noticed this, his soul ached and he patiently waited for the opportunity to have an open, frank talk, without leaving things unsaid, as befitted two blood brothers, two Cossacks.

In early spring when the sun was shining brightly over Kharkiv and playful gurgling streams ran down the narrow snow-covered streets, they bumped into one another at the monastery gate. Kovalynsky had wanted to slip past, but Hryhoriy grabbed him by the elbow and stopped him.

"It seems to me that you're angry at me. Is that true?"

"No."

"Then why do you keep avoiding me?"

"I'm not avoiding you..." the lad said softly and even attempted to look the teacher in the eye. But he was unable to, and quickly looked away, blushing.

Skovoroda felt sorry for the lad. He was ready not to demand the truth from him, but he could not leave the young soul in the hands of know-nothings. Pretending not to notice his confusion, he embraced the boy's shoulder and suggested: "Let's go down to the meadow, Mykhailo, and pick some pussy willows."

The youth silently agreed. The slushy wet snow shifted under their boots, the sun blinded them, reflecting from the flowing water, the windows, the sky. The air was intoxicating, gentle, permeated with thawed snow, bark, maple sap...

"Do you like spring?" Skovoroda asked after a while.

"When it is warm and green."

"I like it even as it is. Blessed is the time of rebirth, when life which has been lurking in buds, seeds and roots awakens, musters its energies and willpower, to rush upward with youthfulness and lush greenery out of the previous year's rotting litter. God, what could be more joyous!"

He stopped, pressed together a large snowball and hurled it at the monastery wall. Happily screwing up his eyes, he bent over to get more snow and yelled: "Watch out now, lad!"

Mykhailo ducked and the snowball landed like a cannonball into a puddle.

"People are watching us," Mykhailo said with reproach.

"So what?"

"It doesn't befit staid people like us to act this way..."

"Nonsense. It doesn't become us to do evil. But to be merry, to rejoice at friendship, the sun..."

"But we're not small children."

Jumping over a fast rivulet of melt running down Bursatsky Rise, Hryhoriy went down toward the gate. He felt painfully vexed that some fanciful clerical-aristocratic philosophy was firmly entrenched in Mykhailo's head and that there was no way to drive it out, to melt the ice which had kept them apart for six months, destroying the tender shoots of a budding friendship. However, the situation spurred him on to overcome the obstacles. He had fought all his life with misfortune, hunger, violence, stupidity, lies, and other terrible harpies which stopped people from living happily. Even with himself, his flesh, which gave him quite some trouble, not submitting to the will of his heart and mind. Without struggle there was no life, no progress. Everything immobile, steadfast, forever determined by someone, was dead.

"You are not right, Mykhailo," Skovoroda said, after they had passed the gate. "One should not be ashamed of one's joy, one's earthly happiness."

The youth turned around, spread his arms apart and smiled: "I don't seem to see anything happy around us."

"What about me? And you?"

Mykhailo burst out laughing.

"Happy is our colonel, Lord Kulykivsky!" he said after a while. "But we are forsaken by God, perhaps even damned."

"Kulykivsky admitted as much to you?"

"I know it anyway. If I had his baton, his estates, villages, and more than a thousand bonded people, I would be happy too!"

"That's foolishness, lad," Hryhoriy said sharply. "Is happiness really to be found there?"

Mykhailo did not relent: "In expensive clothes, replete food and drink and in various pleasures!"

"Tell me, who is happier," Hryhoriy asked, "a magnate who can't sleep nights because his neighbours' fertile land irritates him, or a poor devil who dines on his last piece of bread and snores for the whole house to hear?"

The youth grew thoughtful.

"The magnate, I suppose..."

"The tailor who loves sewing or the general who does battle during the day and relaxes in the evening playing a flute, because he has dreamed of becoming a musician since childhood?"

"Who knows…?"

"Or take Plato, Socrates, Titus, Marcus Aurelius? Did estates bring them happiness?"

"They were all wretched," the boy said decisively.

"Why is that?"

"Because none of them had Christ in their heart and did not pray to the Lord..."

"But they prayed to verity!" Hryhoriy exclaimed irascibly. "And God is verity!"

"According to you they are all holy men?"

"You guessed it. Men whose example we should follow!"

"If only Father Porfyriy heard this," Mykhailo said forcefully.

"Father Porfyriy is ignorant."

"Our archpriest, Porfyriy Kraisky?" the boy asked in fright.

"Like a block of wood. He's missed out on intelligence, and God forgot to place a soul inside him."

"But he's a priest, and priests have the blessing of the Lord!" Mykhailo turned red.

"The Lord's blessing is upon all social strata, or more correctly, everyone is equal before the Lord, everyone is worthy of happiness, and only those be damned who, not having understood themselves and not having trusted their nature, have taken on roles for which they are ill-suited. They have rushed off after the flash of glory, honours, after that deceitful shimmering mirage which brings tears instead of bliss."

"What you're saying is weird," the boy said, alarmed. "In your opinion both the tsar, the nobleman and the bondsman are all made of the same stuff. While perfection, with which the upper classes…"

"A person's perfection lies in how capable they are of bringing benefit to their fellow man."

Mykhailo walked along, hands slid under his beet-red belt, and stole glances at the refreshed, excited face of the teacher.

"Why don't you attend Greek classes?" Hryhoriy asked peaceably.

"The rector forbids me."

Skovoroda stopped.

"The rector forbids you?"

"And my uncle too…"

"Why? What's the reason?"

"So, I don't meet with you…"

"Oh, those people!" Skovoroda raised his arms. "Abominable vipers!"

He turned back toward the city with a decisive step, without hopping over puddles and brooks.

Mykhailo could barely keep up with him, even though he was running at a trot.

"But we haven't picked any pussy willows!" he called out to stop the teacher.

Skovoroda waved his hand dismissively. But soon after he regained his senses, waited for Mykhailo to catch up, and set off more slowly.

"What hypocrites. Stupid, empty heads," he said with regret in his voice. Everything seethed inside him. If one of those impotent shepherds had come this way now, he would have pummelled him, even though he hadn't laid a finger on anyone to date.

"Look, look over there." Mykhailo whispered fearfully and immediately hid behind a gate.

Splashing through the puddles in his boots, Porfyriy Kraisky was hurrying up Bursatsky Rise! He was in so much haste, that he kept tripping.

Skovoroda entered his *museum* like a black cloud. That philosophical calm, that stoicism with which he had earlier greeted misfortune and joy, all had gone out the window! He threw his coat onto the bed, hurled the boots under the stove and paced about the room like a caged animal. Thoughts swirled about, his soul was bleeding. Mothers must suffer this way when they learn that someone wants to take their child away.

Turning around he saw Kordet in the doorway. The fellow was reading, holding a large blue sheet of paper, and smiled.

"Listen, Hrytsko," he announced, without taking his eyes off the sheet. "Will it be more scathing like this:

> '*Resplendent is the colonel sitting in Kharkiv City,*
> *But more resplendent would he be lying under Kharkiv.*'"

"It's good, my word, mister prefect," Skovoroda praised him. "That's right, Kordet, tear off the mask from this most beautiful and most repugnant prostitute: the world!"

"What's the matter with you, Hrytsko?" the prefect grew alarmed. "Have you caught cold?!"

"No."

"Hurry, get into bed!"

"I would, my friend, if I could hide there from hissing vipers..."

"You've a fever, Hryhoriy," Kordet whispered, grabbing his friend by the shoulders and sitting him on the bed. "Lie down, lie down... I'll fetch a healer."

Hryhoriy lay down and smiled.

"Why don't you call Father Porfyriy?"

"Does he cure the evil eye as well through magic spells?!"

"I'll cast a spell in his ear, so he doesn't poke his nose into other people's business!"

"A-ah, you're angry," Kordet drawled in disappointment.

"I am fuming, red-hot, like a hunk of iron in the forge!" Skovoroda sat up on the bed. "You know, they forbid the lad to study Greek, to have discussions with me! And Father Kraisky snoops on us like a hound. Faugh! Fun and games!"

Kordet remained silent. He settled down on the stool near the table and read through his cutting poems.

"Perhaps you should leave the lad in peace," he announced quietly.

"He's my comrade, a close friend!" Hryhoriy flew into a passion.

"Are there none among us worthy of being your friend?"

"There are, there are. You, for example. But there is no one like him. He is like a son to me, like another me!"

"People are saying that you are leading him astray, in the vein of the Ancient Greeks," Kordet said and blushed.

It was as if someone had hit Hryhoriy over the head with a pole. The window, the bed, the table and his guest slowly began to spin around. He took a deep breath and laughed.

"Verily, if the Lord wishes to punish someone, He takes away their mind!"

He fell upon his bed and felt a fear for his friend press in on his heart. What would happen to the lad when the ignorant ones 'opened his eyes'?!

He needed to get up, to run off and warn him! No, no. That was not the way. It was better to say nothing, not to meet... What about the lad? What about me? Solitude, dark thoughts... Stupid, tiresome discussions... Banquets, gossip... God Almighty! To fall from the heights, inhabited only by eagles and deer, into the mire among the swine...

"Here, listen to the epitaph I came out with this morning, Hrytsko," Kordet piped up:

"Spit, traveller – for here lies Porfyriy,
Who sent accusations to the synod..."

Hryhoriy turned over onto his stomach and groaned.

"Please leave, Lavrentiy, I need to be on my own."

* * *

For two months Skovoroda did not talk to Mykhailo, never came face-to-face with him. The gossip and slander died away. But Father Porfyriy's forever watchful eye did not rest.

Disheartened, Hryhoriy grew close to a poor ten-year-old seminary student named Yasha Pravytsky, visiting him when the lad was ill, and paid to have some boots made for him.

However, he could not reconcile himself to relinquishing his good friend to dark forces, the ignorant crowd of priests. He wrote letters to Mykhailo, so that he could better master his Greek and Latin; from afar, through other people, he watched enviously which books the lad read, whom he associated with, who his friends were. And he suffered. Letters were letters, but irrepressible youth, the enticements of the world and customs would take their toll... In the end, he could bear it no longer. Recalling the experience of the first zealous Christians, who gathered secretly at night in the catacombs or in wild thickets, Hryhoriy decided to meet with Mykhailo somewhere outside the city in the evening.

Agitated, he took some paper and ink and sat down at his table. He dipped his quill in the ink and wrote in Latin:

Greetings to you, my treasure! My most precious Mykhailo!

I have probably seemed coarse and irritable to you all these days. But how can one not suffer, my friend, when I have had wrenched from me one of my greatest joys and pleasures. If you were located somewhere safer, I would have fretted less. But as it is... For what am I to do in life, what do I fill my soul with, what do I care about? To worry about nothing, not to suffer, means not to live, to be dead, for anxiety is the movement of the soul, and life is about motion... Only now have I perceived that you are not of the same breed as hawks, but of noble eagle blood, so soar toward lofty ideals and, despite the bats with their love of darkness, reach for the sun.

I have come to like you so much, that even were you to become my enemy, I could not detest you. You continually remain before the eyes of my soul, and whatever good things I think about, whatever I do, it seems to me that I can see you beside me. You appear before me when I am on my own, you are my companion and comrade when I am in public...

Oh, if only one could write as much as one thought!

As soon as we parted after the gathering, my soul was suddenly overcome with pity for you and a strong desire to see you, and I felt sorry about not having invited you into my museum. Believe me, my good soul,

Having read through the letter, he folded it in four, dripped some wax onto it and affixed the seal of a deer. He called over young Yasha, who was sitting in the library, and sent him off into the city with the letter, to Kovalynsky's home.

They met near the boats under the willows. As Hryhoriy was making his way toward the river, Mykhailo jumped out from behind a hollow old trunk and roared like a bear. Skovoroda purposefully let out a scream and covered his face with his hands.

"It's me, it's me!" the youth called out.

"Christ, protect me!" Skovoroda crossed himself. "I thought it was a wolf…"

"A wolf doesn't roar, it howls."

"I was so scared, I couldn't make a thing out."

"Were you frightened, really?" Mykhailo asked warily.

"Of course!"

"No, you're joking… But I'm scared… Of wolves. bears, vampires, witches, devils, and ghosts."

He looked about fearfully – it was already growing dark.

"Nonsense."

"Yeah, nonsense," the youth whispered. "There was a witch living in our settlement recently. She milked the cows and braided the horses' manes."

"It's all old wives' tales."

"Grandpa Stepan got in league with the devil and couldn't die. The poor fellow screamed, pleading with God to die, while the devil and an angel fought over his soul at the head of the bed…"

"If such battles were fought over each soul, there'd be as many angels in heaven as there are sparrows in Kharkiv!"

"He was laid out on the floor, and they cast spells over him," Mykhailo continued in the same vein. "The old man finally died, but he still wanders about in this world…"

"Who filled your head with such rubbish?" Skovoroda stopped. They were walking along between the city ramparts and the river. "Human life is like a garland: with a beginning and an end. From the earth you come and to the earth you return. Once a person has died, they are not given the power to rise and move about, similar to rocks, iron and clay..."

"What about the spirit, the soul?" Mykhailo asked in a whisper.

Hryhoriy did not reply for a long time. He walked along, deep in thought, alone with his doubts, vacillations, and reflections. The soul... What was it, really? Consciousness? The spirit? Or perhaps the ability to reason? Who invested man with it? God or matter itself...?

"I don't know, my friend," he said at last. "To me this is still a mystery, hidden behind a murky veil... I'll tell you one thing, though: the soul is at one with the body. And when the body dies..."

He took out his flute, with which he never parted, turned to the right into a narrow clearing outside the city and played a heavenly melody, recently learnt from an itinerant minstrel.

They soon reached the cemetery. Mykhailo had wanted to dash down to the river, but seeing that the teacher calmly continued walking, he followed in his footsteps.

A crescent moon had already risen and long shadows from the crosses bound with sashes covered the ground, as if the dead had crawled out of their graves and stretched out to warm their bones in the cold rays of their nocturnal sun.

Skovoroda stepped over the graves as if they were sheaves and, without even turning around, began to speak about music.

"The soul is probably music. What is this flute made of? A small piece of wood. But when you play it, you seem to swoon, to rise on the wings of the muses..."

Waiting while Mykhailo caught up to him, Hryhoriy sat down on an old grave, leaned back against a blackened oak cross and offered the boy his flute.

"Play something, while I listen."

Mykhailo took it, without breathing, and pressed it to his lips.

"I can't. I haven't any breath for some reason," he said in a suppressed voice. "I'm short of breath after coming up the hill..."

"You should walk more. You sit over your books too long. There must be moderation in everything, young man," Skovoroda announced without a hint of jest. "Sit down and listen. I recently gave birth to a song..."

He made himself more comfortable, cleared his throat and began singing in bookish Ukrainian:

> *Oh world! Ignorant world!*
> *Your hope lies in kings!*
> *You think this shore is impeccable?*
> *A wind will scatter this dust...*

"A wonderful song!" The boy rose and began to try out the melody on the flute.

"Not like that, not like that!" Skovoroda could not hold back and took the flute. He played it slowly, clearly.

"Just like in church!" Mykhailo did not relent. "Sends a shiver up one's spine..."

"If you want to really enjoy it, listen to it from afar." Hryhoriy stood up. "Stay here while I go into that wood."

Before the youth could utter anything, he moved away, weaving about among the graves. He listened... No. Mykhailo was not running after him. He was holding his ground! He would overcome his fears this one time and be rid of this superfluous, heavy burden once and for all.

In the stand of young oaks Skovoroda turned around and, convinced that he could not be seen from the cemetery, began to play clearly and audibly so that Mykhailo could hear and be sure that his teacher was nearby. After a while, still playing, he began moving toward the cemetery, feeling sorry for the lad. The lad was moving among the crosses and adjusting the sashes.

"Ahoy, Mykhailo!" Hryhoriy called out, afraid for a moment that the lad might have lost his senses.

"I'm here," the boy answered quietly and walked toward him.

"Scared?"

"No..."

Haggard and pale, he was smiling nonetheless, glad that he had not disgraced himself in front of his teacher.

"Well, does the song sound better from afar?"

"Of course!" the lad said cheerfully. "Although it would have sounded even better had I gone into the wood..." He laughed. "My, you're a cunning fox!"

Skovoroda embraced his shoulders and hugged him tight.

"You're a good lad, Mykhailo. A real Cossack! We could just about send you off to the Sich."

"Yesterday three more boys ran away from the seminary dormitory," Mykhailo said.

"To the Zaporozhia?"

"To St. Petersburg, to join the Holstein regiments."

"People have gone mad."

"The call of the emperor!" Mykhailo announced. "I too nearly..."

"God forbid!" Skovoroda exclaimed. "Don't even dare think about it."

"You get a uniform, a military rank, go on expeditions..." the lad said dreamily.

"Transforming yourself from a free person into a marionette, with whom wastrels can play?" Skovoroda asked sternly.

The youth knitted his brows.

"But it's at the behest of the tsar," he said after a while. "His majesty – our emperor!"

"You reason like a pig's head, my boy," Hryhoriy said sharply. "How can he be 'ours'? Did you elect him to the throne? Or perhaps you handed the state and the sceptre over to him?"

"The tsar is sent by the Lord..."

"A fable for fools, invented by the tsars themselves."

They slowly made their way down to the Lopan River. The narrow path twisted among the oaks and lindens. Hryhoriy led the way, healing Mykhailo of his blindness. Thin, tall, sprightly, he moved just as capably along the uneven paths, as he handled his history – from Abraham to Peter the Third, who had been reigning for six months now, after Elizabeth's death, and was forming an army which he dubbed the Holstein regiments.

"Found somewhere to run off to," Skovoroda fretted. "To become the sword and the axe in the hands of the butchers of the people..."

"That sounds frightening," Mykhailo whispered into the back of his neck.

"We need to call a spade a spade when we are talking of what is happening in the world. You're not blind, look around – they're pillaging, choking, selling people!" Meanwhile they emerged from the wood into a clearing and set off side by side. "Once I set about castigating a certain lieutenant for treating his serfs unscrupulously. Well, he (a former knight of freedom, a fighter for truth and equality) read me a whole sermon! That now, ostensibly, the world was different. Now, if you were poor, you were a fool. It did not matter in the least what you were like inside, even if you deserved being hung ten times over – it did not matter. As long as you had a good name and were seen as being honourable. You need to be bold and daring! He who is in essence right, is not really right in our society, but he who can pretend to be right and covers his tracks well – he is right. This is the fashion adopted in today's world and is its saving grace! In short, only those are happy, who are right according to a piece of paper, not according to conscience..."

"But that's a lie!" the youth exclaimed indignantly.

"No, it's true. Verity. Everywhere there is hypocrisy, fraud, denunciation, villainy. At present the world is a banquet of those who rage possessed, a marketplace of the hesitant and a hell of those who are suffering."

They walked on in silence for a long time. The moon had already risen high into the sky and the shadows had become shorter. The silence grew thicker. It seemed there was a magical fairy-tale mirage only a few hundred steps away rather than a city. In the meadow on the far side of the river horses neighed softly and the mire squelched underfoot. Hryhoriy even stopped in his tracks. He grew tense and silent.

> *Oh steed, my fair steed,*
> *With mane of gold...!*

"But what is there to do, then? What can save the nation, the state, the people's faith?" Mykhailo asked agitatedly.

"A republic!" Skovoroda pronounced firmly.

"A republic?" The boy was horrified.

"Yes."

"But are we Hellenes?"

"For all peoples a republic is the original form of state and order. The best form!"

"Why did Athens fall then?"

"The philosophers who nourished social order all died out. And the philosophical monkeys who resembled the sages only through their cloaks and beards, taught the youth not how to worship the serene Minerva, but how to worm their way into the most glorious titles and grow rich, to live their lives in luxury. That is why everything went head over heels in the republic. Donkeys became mules, and mules became geldings, the wolf became the shepherd, the bear the monk... This is a complete disaster! The leadership was transformed into tormentors, the judiciary into bribetakers, the sciences into a terrible instrument of malice. And everything perished! Those who scorn wisdom won't be saved even by a republic."

"Athens fell, so that the new..." Mykhailo began.

But Hryhoriy stopped him from voicing his train of thought.

"Leave Athens in peace! We had Pskov and Novgorod, Hetmanite rule and the Zaporozhian Sich. In what ways weren't they republics? They fell too..."

"But the Hetmanate and Zaporozhia are alive and well."

Skovoroda waved his hand dismissively, said nothing for a while, and then began exaltedly: "The republic in which I too would like to live will be a country of love, friendship and toil! There must be no enmity and hostility. No one would be discriminated against because of old age, gender, or any other differences. Everything would be for everyone, communal! The laws would be humane, wise, as opposed to those which blossom under tyranny. There would be a great brotherhood, a society of concordant people, united through their calling and aspirations – this is the kind of republic which will replace a kingdom of darkness...!"

"When will this happen?"

"Soon. The more you compress a spring, the sooner and more forcefully will it spring back. Nothing is eternal. Slavery too will sink into the Lethe."

"Of its own accord?"

"No, as a result of our anger!"

"Somehow I don't see it happening," Mykhailo sighed. "Unless the people are fuming in silence..."

"To fume in silence is servile."

"But it's frightening to speak out loud, they'll grab you."

"They grabbed Christ too."

"And crucified Him..."

"And He rose from the dead forever in the hearts of the disinherited."

They entered the city past the guard standing at the gate, dozing. Everything was asleep: the churches, buildings, trees and people... Even the moon dozed high in the sky, covered with a small cloud. From somewhere came the sleepy clapper of the nightwatchman and again there was silence.

"Like the silence in one's ear," Mykhailo whispered.

"Just wait till the nightingales assemble..."

"Will that be soon?"

"Aye. They'll be here in a week."

"Well, here we are. Good night to you! I won't be able to sleep all night long..."

"Philosophers don't sleep," Skovoroda said and offered his hand to Mykhailo. "Take care!"

The lad grabbed his hand, squeezed it very tightly and then suddenly bent over and kissed him.

"What's the matter, Mykhailo?!" the teacher was taken aback.

However, the youth had already run off to his home. The door creaked twice and again there was silence.

Moved to tears, Skovoroda returned to his *museum*. He was the richest person in the world! He had a good friend, a student and a disciple. God, what happiness!

*   *   *

With the arrival of summer and the start of the vacations, a courier hurried in from St. Petersburg with an edict. The Holsteiner had displeased the Lord and the Almighty had sent the slaves of the throne and the faith a new majesty, once more a woman, the Empress Catherine, second in number. What, how, and why no one knew. They gathered silently in the synodal church and listened to the tsarist charter. And then those whose rank was fitting swore an oath of allegiance (the second that year) and everyone parted, mute as sheep.

Skovoroda came across Mykhailo in the crowd and walked along beside him.

"Well, your idol is no more," he said in a low voice. "God must have mixed something up..."

Mykhailo placed a finger to his lips and looked about.

Taciturn, scared, he really seemed to have suffered spiritually over what had happened there, in the distant north, in St. Petersburg.

"Nothing is everlasting, not even tsars," Skovoroda thought out loud.

"Quiet, stop it!" the youth whispered, turned to the side and became lost in the crowd of townsfolk.

Skovoroda saw the boy off with his eyes, sighed, and continued on. He was alarmed by Mykhailo's prank, however having grown accustomed to view everything with philosophical restraint, he calmed down and began to deliberate about the future. New rulers always destroyed the things created by their predecessors, so the Holstein regiments would be dispersed. The church lands would not be taken away, at least not yet. In Ukraine, Peter III had not managed either to create or destroy anything – they would destroy Elizabeth's concessions. Count Rozumovsky, the illustrious *hetman*...

"Hryhoriy!" Father Kordet grabbed his arm. He had already received Communion, for his eyes shone with an intoxicated gleam. "What luck, eh? We've got an empress! What would we wretches do without her? Would you have a piece of bread in your cell?" Skovoroda nodded. "Great! And I've got a bottle. What an occasion, my God! How can one not drink for joy!"

> *Licked the backside of the drunken tsar,*
> *Now we can lick the empress'...*

And he began to squat dance. Thank heavens they were already in the monastery and no one could see them.

Skovoroda grabbed him by the shoulders and pushed him into his *museum*.

In the cell Kordet pulled a bottle out of his pocket and a chipped glazed chalice, filled it and drank in silence.

"Vivat!" he yelled afterwards and sang: "A long life, a long life, a lo-o-ong life! We're not Cossacks, Hrytsko, but timorous hungry mice. For a crumb of bread, we bite through each other's throats. And where is concordia, where is accord, national unity?!" He drank a second chalice and filled it again. "We'll drown our sorrow, my friend... Or drink for joy, I should say!"

In Tsarhorod in the market-place
Bayda drinks mead and vodka neat!

The door opened and a perplexed Yasha appeared in the doorway.

"What do you want?" Kordet asked angrily.

"The rector is calling for him," the boy said fearfully and pointed at Hryhoriy.

"Shoo, shoo!" Kordet stamped his feet.

The boy disappeared.

"I'm off then," Hryhoriy said.

"Wait, I completely forgot!" Kordet stopped him. He put down the bottle and muttered: "I told you before, leave this Narcissus in peace..."

"I don't follow. You mean Mykhailo?"

"Who else!"

"Our friendship is in someone's way again?"

"Worse. Your Kovalynsky has begun to convert the devout student flock to heresy and someone denounced him..."

Heavens above! Suddenly forgetting about Kordet and everything in the world apart from Mykhailo and the misfortune which threatened him, Skovoroda went off at a run to the rector. He castigated himself for not having told the lad when and with whom he should discuss all the things he had told him about, and feverishly sought a way, a safe path out of this calamity. But he could find nothing fit, apart from taking all of the guilt on himself.

With this in mind he entered Kostiantyn Brodsky's office.

"Sit down." The rector gestured at an armchair.

He was sullen, grey. Had Hryhoriy not known why he had been summoned, he would have thought that the world's end was imminent and Kostiantyn, who had learnt of this, wanted to say his last farewell.

"Hryhoriy," the rector began slowly. "We all respect your sharp mind, your profound knowledge of history, writing, languages and philosophy. You have a chair, bah, even two, a choir of students, books and a cell. What more do you need? Why are you floundering? What are you seeking?"

"Verity," Skovoroda said calmly.

The old man grimaced, as if he had bitten into a sour apple.

"Verity is like the fire-bird. People seek it, strive to grab it, however no one has ever caught it..."

"To strive is a lot in itself."

"Perhaps too much…"

"Those without desires, aspirations, and hopes are not alive."

"Desires can also be fatal…"

"I know. But as they say in our Chornukhy: if you fear the wolf, you'll never collect any mushrooms."

"Not all mushrooms are edible…"

"Poisonous ones can be seen from far off, everyone can spot them."

"Not every belly can stomach even a good mushroom."

"We have strong stomachs."

"However, as they say, what a mother may do, a baby may not."

"That's the honest truth." Hryhoriy nodded and smiled: "But when the baby is seventeen years old…"

"All the same, seventeen is not forty."

"Verily. What little Ivan does not learn, big Ivan will never know."

"At times those who know less lead a calmer existence."

"Fools lead the calmest of lives."

"And the meek."

"Whoever passes by takes a swipe at them."

"A meek calf suckles two mothers."

"And succumbs to the butt end of an axe."

"Perhaps this is enough?" the rector rose to his feet.

"As you please, father," Skovoroda shrugged his shoulders.

"I have been informed that a student from the Syntaxis class, Mykhailo Kovalynsky, is spreading thoughts contrary to the church's teachings, to say the least. He could not have picked them up in our school…"

"That he could not," Skovoroda agreed. "Barracks are barracks…"

"That's none of your concern!" the rector said sharply.

"Concern is not merely money or slaves…"

"Madman, think what are you saying!"

"To reason is the right of all, even a duty."

"You've already done enough reasoning." He took out his handkerchief and wiped the sweat from his forehead. "God forbid, lest it reaches the authorities… It will result in Siberia for all of us!"

"For speaking the truth?"

"My God, whatever else! Truth is the most frightening thing."

Hryhoriy rose too. Mykhailo! How could he protect the boy, shield him?!

"He repeated my words without thinking," Hryhoriy announced firmly.

"That's not enough," the rector retorted benignly.

"He did not understand them, did not take them to heart and merely repeated them in public to find support for himself, accomplices in his fight with me."

"That's not good enough, Hrytsko."

"What do I do?" Hryhoriy asked in desperation.

"Accept the monk's order."

"Clip my hair?"

"Hide behind the church's back. And in so doing, shield your friend."

Skovoroda nearly let out a scream. A net, another net! Give my assent, knock out the stick, and I'll beat about liked a netted grouse. No, no! And what about my friend? Can I allow him to be ruined? I'll go and tell the colonel that I'm to blame for everything, that I talked the boy into it, coerced him, forced him! Death or imprisonment is preferable...

"Agreed then?"

"No!"

This 'no' was probably so decisive, that it gave no hope for any other answer. Kostiantyn came up to his desk again and sat down heavily.

"Then write a laudatory poem in honour of the Empress' accession to the throne," he said ingratiatingly after a while. "This would be a good shield."

"I am not a poet."

"But you write, I've read your Latin poems myself.

> *'O igitur miseros, o terque quaterque misellos,*
> *Sidere qui prolem sub Pharaonis habent...'"*[58]

There were no bounds to villainy! The poem was from his letter to Mykhailo, recently delivered into the boy's own hands!

"As we can see, you have experience in writing poetry about tsars," the rector said slyly, after a silence. "So, sit down and write an ode."

"No," Hryhoriy retorted and turned to leave.

....

[58]   O wretched are they, three and four times over,
       Who bear offspring under Pharaoh's star...

"Wait!" The rector stopped him angrily, and continued in a more conciliatory tone: "I'll try to stifle the matter. But I entreat you, Hryhoriy, be careful and do not harass Mykhailo! You can go now."

How he reached his *museum* he did not remember. It was already late, dark and overcast. He struck a light, fanned it and lit a candle end. The flame burnt unevenly, dully, so that a step away there was miserly grey twilight, and two steps away – darkness.

He sat staring at the unscrubbed oak boards of the table, in his mind leafing through the moving, sad, and joyous book inscribed with Mykhailo's and his friendship, and he almost wept with sorrow.

The wick burnt down and darkness crowded in from all directions. The flame flickered fearfully, crackled and slowly began to die away...

In the gloom Skovoroda took a new wax candle from his drawer and, lighting it, pressed it into the warm, uncongealed wax. He took out some paper and ink. Dipped in his quill and it set off, sometimes stumbling, then racing across the white field of the paper:

My dearest Mykhailo, greetings!

I see your sincere love toward me, when you consider it better to endure envy and hatred, rather than put an end to our meetings and discussions. Therefore, even though I know that the fiercest animal customarily follows noble actions, as smoke follows fire, I feel sorry for you all the same, because you deserve triple the love in return. However, I will have to desist writing letters to you in future. I have decided to yield to the will of the mob, so that through some indiscretion I don't perchance harm the notion that the words "a true friend is known in the day of adversity" refer to.

You must stop writing your enchanting letters to me too, until this confusion subsides and the flames of hatred are quelled. Therefore, we shall conduct conversations in silence, as absent people do, recalling that Zeus does not always send tempests. Have courage!

Yours, Hryhoriy Savych Skovoroda

He placed the final full stop on the letter, sadly looked about the cell and, extinguishing the candle, went off to the seminary to find Yasha – his Mercury.

THE SEVENTH NET

Two years passed, like snowmelt. But the malice did not die away. Its greatest demon triumphed: Iosaf Mytkevych passed away and Kraisky took over the helm of the eparchy. This stunned everyone who knew Porfyriy. Rumours began to fly that Satan was roaming the world in a long black cowl, that a child with hooves was born somewhere and that in a village church near Belgorod an old icon of the Holy Mother began to weep during the evening service.

The new eparch had much to attend to in Belgorod, however Father Porfyriy maintained a vigilant watch through the eyes of his adherents on the friendship between Skovoroda and Kovalynsky and, gloating, he informed Father Petro or the boy's father in Olshanka about their every meeting. The family suffered, fumed, sought a way out of the calamitous situation.

And it was found at last. In fact, Mykhailo himself came up with the suggestion, and his family merely grasped at it, like a drowning man clutching at straws.

A journey to Kyiv! The city of Volodymyr, with its churches, ruins, and books. Each summer thousands and even tens of thousands of people visited Kyiv. Pilgrims kept coming and coming. Visiting holy places! But the main thing, about which nothing was said of course, was to deprive Mykhailo for at least a month of his friendship with Skovoroda: the fellow's letters, his fanciful judgements about the world and the church.

A light buggy was finally hired in Olshanka to take them to Kyiv. They left on Sunday morning, at the crack of dawn.

And after midday they came across a pilgrim, also making his way to Kyiv. The two struck up a conversation, and the young master took him along with them. So that the old coachman would not be cross, he promised to give him an extra gold coin.

Near Boryspil the buggy broke down and not wanting to wait around, the teacher and pupil went off on foot.

In the morning on the Feast of Maccabaeus, as soon as they emerged from the forest near Darnytsia, they stopped, awestruck by the majesty of the churches, which towered on the hills, flooded with bountiful sunshine, sandwiched between the azure blue of the river and the sky. Hundreds of bells were tolling triumphantly, joyously…

"What beauty!" Mykhailo spread out his hands. He was glowing with rapture. "Verily holy places, the Lord's retreat!"

"God is not to be found in churches, Mykhailo, but in ourselves, in our souls," Hryhoriy checked his enthusiasm.

"But it's so beautiful, so beautiful!"

"You have an eye for beauty. That's good. I always become awestruck when I see this sight…"

"Let's hurry up, or we'll miss the blessing of the poppy seed!"

The youth scooted off and raced down the sandy slope into the valley, along which ran the road to the pontoon bridge over the Dnipro River. Passing carts, Berlin carriages, and drays, he ran down to the river, waving his hands for Hryhoriy to keep up.

Skovoroda was delighted with the boy, rejoicing at his rapture and was endlessly grateful to him for his courage and the ingenuity with which he had invited his teacher along on this pleasant journey. Hryhoriy had not been in Kyiv for ten whole years! How would his former friends and fellow classmates, with whom he had partaken of bread, salt, and water, greet him? Perhaps they wouldn't even admit to knowing him. Some were eminent, well-known people. Samuyil Myslavsky was now the rector of the Academy! He certainly would not have forgotten him. There had always been stiff competition between him and Samus when it came to studies. How the poor fellow had fretted when they praised Hryhoriy instead of him!

"Oh, come see what's happening there!" Mykhailo came running back. "So many carts, people, and soldiers!"

There really was confusion near the bridge. Everyone was hurrying into Kyiv for the church feast, to make a pilgrimage, or on business. Those who hadn't managed to get across in the evening were still waiting in line, while more and more horses and carts kept arriving. Oxen bellowed, horses neighed, people shouted and swore. Here and there people were breaking into song – tired of waiting for the poppy seed feast and the crossing. The travelling public had already downed a glass in honour of the holy martyr.

An old man was playing the bandura. Smoke billowed from dying fires on the Dnipro banks.

Those without a horse or cart were being let across first. Mykhailo had managed to learn this good bit of news and dragged Hryhoriy through this mass of humanity to the bridge.

"Stop! Documents!" They were stopped some five sagenes from the shore by a Russian-speaking official. "The cart yours?"

"No. Ours broke down," Mykhailo explained, handing his documents to the officer.

The fellow quickly glanced through them, then took Hryhoriy's.

"Who are you, a teacher?"

"Yes, your honour."

The fellow eyed him from head to toe with a keen eye, shrugged his shoulders and swept his arm through the air.

"Two coins from each of you. Petrov, collect the money from these woodcocks! Where are you pushing? Stop, stop!" he suddenly hollered in Russian and grabbed a horse by the muzzle. "Any tobacco, wool, wax, sheepskins?"

"No, young sir. What I haven't got, I haven't got," a village beauty answered in fright from the cart.

"Well then!" The officer smoothed down his moustache. "Pay three copecks and pass on. On the way back I'll let you through without paying, if you're a clever lass!"

Creaking, guffaws, songs…

On the far bank Hryhoriy made off to the right along the Dnipro and headed along a path to the city, leaving behind the toll-gate and the road choked with carts, horses, and humanity. They walked along between the riverbank and cliffs overgrown with bushes of sloe, wild fruit trees, and boxthorn.

"Hryhoriy Savych, where's the Lavra Monastery?" the youth asked anxiously. He probably wasn't completely sure that the beauty which had appeared before him back at the forest's edge near Darnytsia was not some delusion, a mirage.

"Beyond the cliff. Another two hundred steps and we'll see it again," Skovoroda placated him.

"The caves as well?"

"They're behind the walls, and underground."

"Do hermits still live in them, surviving only on grasshoppers?"

"They're still there. During the day, for appearance's sake. But at night they go back to their cells and stuff their faces."

"The holy anchorites?" Mykhailo asked in amazement.

"There are no holy ones, only hypocrites."

"And there never were?"

"Maybe once... For instance, the great martyr Varvara, who died somewhere here in Kyiv during pagan times. People become holy only when they suffer, struggle, or blaze paths to the bright sun of verity. But having surmounted lies and darkness, they themselves fear the light, like bats or owls. Such is human nature, such is life."

"What about God? Doesn't the Lord see this, doesn't He punish these renegades, doesn't the earth open up beneath them?"

"My dear friend, there are so many of them, that the whole earth would have already been criss-crossed with cracks!" Skovoroda smiled wryly. "If our God was merciful, kind, just as we call Him in our prayers, then He wouldn't let one lot kill another merely because they pray to the south instead of the east, he wouldn't send floods, wars, and plagues upon the human race. Our God is cruel and vindictive. We created Him ourselves, and He resembles us in everything. God weeps, rages, sleeps, and repents. 'The Lord thought...and created man,' the Bible says. God created the sun, the earth and the creatures living upon it, and 'rested from the work He had done.' Meaning, that He was tired. If it wasn't for this, then we would certainly have ended up with tailless lions, winged horses and tortoises, hares with dog's tails, and all other manner of animals which have remained in God's abyss!"

"There's the Lavra Monastery," Mykhailo said sullenly.

Skovoroda grew silent. He was insane, why did he have to go and spoil the boy's spirits?

"Did you know that it's seven hundred years old?" he asked soon after. "That books have been printed here for a hundred and fifty years, and distributed throughout Rus' and even further afield?"

"Do they still print them here?" Mykhailo's eyes lit up.

"They reprint them," Hryhoriy sighed.

"And can we take a look at all of this?"

"Of course. My relative Yustyn works as a printer there."

"Let's hurry!"

"Don't get too excited," Hryhoriy stopped him. "We'll visit the alma mater first. Besides, there's a church feast today and there'll be great revelling in the Podil area."

Suddenly the bells atop the Lavra began to toll, answered by those from all the other churches – the flowers and poppy seed had been blessed. Now people would be rejoicing, driving their boots into the ground!

Hryhoriy was overcome with memories, old friends appeared before his eyes. He saw them and himself among them, first as boys who had arrived from distant villages and settlements, then as students who spoke Latin, as if they had been born Romans and sucked in this old melodious language with their mother's milk. Pitiable schooldays were replaced by festivals, disputes, choral renditions by the biggest and best choir in the whole empire. The orchestra played Bach, Handel, Scarlatti, as well as works by local composers. Many of the boys wrote chants, psalms, concertos, and music for puppet dramas and interludes.

As he walked at the base of the cliff Hryhoriy imagined the choir singing, the orchestra playing, individual brothers hitting the highest notes in the most difficult parts of the polyphonic songs. And he heard his own voice – youthful, forceful, beautiful.

It seemed to him that as soon as he entered the narrow Podil streets he would immediately shed some fifteen to twenty years and once more become Hrytsko the Student, who swallowed books in a single breath, sang in the choir, and played in the orchestra on anything he could put his hands on. The weariness of the traveller had suddenly left him, his step became light and sprightly.

"My, you're in a real hurry!" Mykhailo groaned behind him. He was rather tired. "You're flying along."

"That I am, Mykhailo," Skovoroda answered merrily. "Into the past, into my youth!" And he launched into an old puppet-show song:

> *There is no better,*
> *There's no place finer,*
> *Than here in our Ukraine!*

In the square near the fairy-tale "Felicial"[59] fountain Skovoroda spied the academy choir from afar. Surrounded by festively dressed people, the choir stood in a sea of flowers, poppyheads, as if in a garden, and prepared to begin the festival with their beautiful singing.

Hryhoriy held back the lad and asked him to be silent. A soft murmur passed over the square like a breeze... Suddenly it was silent. The tall thin regent ascended the dais and raised his hands as if they were wings. A moment more – and the song took wing! Skovoroda had never heard this one. It soared over the dumbfounded crowd, squeezing the soul with grief, filling the chest with joy. What it spoke about, Hryhoriy was unable to discern. He was not even listening attentively but enjoyed it, imbibing it like wine, like water on a hot summer's day, unaware that he was crying. God, the trip from Kharkiv was worth just these few minutes of song.

When the song had finished, Skovoroda stopped a student who was walking past them with a blank expression, and asked: "Tell me, young Cossack, who wrote this marvellous song?"

"Our Berezovsky," the fellow said proudly. "He's standing in the choir there, near the columns on the right."

He was a slender, blond youth with an angelic face, who had become tanned walking through fields side by side with those who grew people's daily bread. Skovoroda drew closer and was able to make out his large, possibly grey or light-blue eyes, which attracted one's gaze like a magnet, subduing and forcing one to forget everything in the world, including oneself.

Meanwhile the choir had begun a reapers' song, which had been performed ten years earlier as well.

"I'm hungry," Mykhailo whispered.

"Just a moment..."

They quietly emerged from the crowd of city folk, Cossacks, and sullen bondsmen, who were visiting their free relatives during the feast and had headed toward the monastery. Looking over the bell tower from all sides, they sat on a bench in the shade and took out onions, bread and lardo from their bags.

....

[59] Now renamed the Samson Fountain.

Hryhoriy was not hungry and, leaving the boy to breakfast alone, he wandered off to the boarding school. Although this squalid domicile had once been damned on many an occasion, he was still drawn to it, for his best years had passed here, his cold and hungry youth, the years of his hopes and aspirations. It was deserted and quiet here – everyone was in the square, in the city, where the festival was getting into full swing. People would be raging here for three days and three nights, according to custom.

Humble greetings to you, my dear alma mater! Somewhere they said (he had heard about it in Kharkiv), in another yard, a high white dormitory had already been built, made of freshly-hewn timber. He felt sadness and joy. Let the boys luxuriate; dirty water would no longer drip onto their wise heads from the ceiling, the drafts would not chill their fervent chests, so defenceless against consumption and various other evils!

He continued slowly on. Pausing beside Sahaidachny's grave, he turned left toward the academy. He heard voices, conversations, footsteps... He was not alone, accompanied by those who were scattered throughout the empire like servants of God and the tsar. There was laughter, jokes, quotes from recently-read books and classes…

"Hryhoriy Savych?" he heard suddenly.

Skovoroda opened his eyes and saw a novice beside him in an old, tattered cassock.

"Yes. How can I help you?"

"The rector is calling for you."

"Father Samiylo?"

"Yes," the fellow said, nodding.

"I'm not alone here," Hryhoriy remembered his friend. "There's a boy from Kharkiv with me, a student from the collegium. He's having breakfast near the bell tower…"

"I'll find him and bring him along."

"Perhaps you could show him our monastery?"

"All right. Please come along!"

The novice brought Hryhoriy to the rector's cell, let him into the antehall, and set off to find the lad from Kharkiv.

Skovoroda stood there a while, growing accustomed to the darkness, and then opened the familiar door.

"Allow me…"

"Come in, come in, Hryhoriy!" Myslavsky stepped forward to greet him. He embraced him, hugged him tight, kissed him. "I'm looking at you and thinking: is it you or not?"

"You've changed too, Samiylo," Hryhoriy said. "Become emaciated, overgrown like an ascetic..."

"Don't even ask," Myslavsky sighed sadly. "Think it's easy to bear this cross of responsibility? And how are you?"

He offered Hryhoriy an old, worn armchair, acquired back in Prokopovych's time, sat down opposite him and prepared to listen.

"I wander and roam," Hryhoriy said. "At present I'm teaching in Kharkiv. Before that I was in Pereyaslav a while. In Kovray I taught a nobleman's son, then visited Moscow with Kalihraf, spent the night in the Trinity Lavra of St. Sergius, where our Liashevetsky is reigning presently."

"You've seen a little of the world," the rector said sorrowfully. Whether he empathised or was envious was hard to tell. "Why do you have such a plebeian appearance?" he asked cautiously. "Do they not pay you well?"

"No. It's more comfortable like this. I feel like a cow in a yoke in camisoles. The pay is fine."

"Well, bless the Lord. But we have a problem here. Last year they revoked the tsarist financial assistance and we live like beggars now, on whatever we can wheedle out of the metropolitan, the Lavra, and benefactors. The empress is squeezing us, turning us into a scarecrow for her pleasure, trying to make us the laughing stock of Europe."

"We heard rumours that the academy was to be turned into a university," Hryhoriy said.

"Had they wanted to, they wouldn't have abandoned the plan handed to the empress by the *hetman*," Myslavsky said. "Only a year has passed since the *hetman* himself is no more. Count Rozumovsky is still there, but the *hetman*..." He spread out his hands in desperation. "Rumiantsev will quickly nobble him! The fellow doesn't like playing games, the Cossacks will weep many a time yet, bathed in whitewash!"

He grew silent, his head drooping onto his chest, as if he had dozed off.

Hryhoriy felt sorry for Myslavsky. Sorry for the hetmanate and the Cossacks, but he was not stunned by the news, for he had long since realised the intentions of the tsars and their sycophants, who made soft beds which were oh so hard to sleep on. No one would ever give the gift of freedom!

"I am labouring over a new statute for the academy." Myslavsky raised his head. "I'm trying to wrangle it so that we can have our cake and eat it… God, how weary I've become during these past three years of being rector! You need a merchant here, not a philosopher – a thaler worth of wheeling and dealing, and a copeck of learning. And everyone with their threats and torment, tugging at me as if I was some string puppet."

Getting up, he began to pace about the cell, miraculously not touching or upsetting any of the books, rolls and sheets which lay everywhere where anything could be placed or stacked. Samiylo was short and somewhat ugly. He was wearing a monk's cassock and was bareheaded, without a cowl. Whitish streaks of hoarfrost covered his temples and beard.

"Missed the alma mater, the city, eh?"

"That I have," Skovoroda admitted frankly. "I even miss the dormitory."

"We're building a new one," Myslavsky announced proudly and knitted his brows. "To do it properly, we should have built it of stone. But what can you do when there's no money!"

"I heard, I heard. Back in Kharkiv."

"Are you in the collegium there?"

"For the moment…"

"What are you teaching – poetics or philosophy?"

"Syntaxis classes. And Greek language."

"Why?" Myslavsky asked gloomily.

"Because I'm not a monk."

"Then join the order."

"No way!" Skovoroda said sharply.

Myslavsky knew Hryhoriy and was not about to ask about the whys and wherefores. He settled into his armchair again and rested his head on his chest.

"I'd invite you here…" he said eventually, "but I fear that we ourselves will soon be dispersed like rats. The empress breathes an ill breath on the academy. And on Ukraine too. In St. Petersburg our former boys, now in various clerical and lay positions, said something to the contrary when she spoke about routing the Hetmanate and getting rid of old customs. Well, her highness became so enraged that she was ready to swallow not only these transgressors, but also the academy which had taught them and the nation that had given birth to them."

"A monarch-philosopher, a monarch-sage, surrounded by the high priests of muses, a true Minerva…"

"What are you mumbling there?" Myslavsky asked.

"Nothing. I recalled Hrytsko Kozytsky and Motonis. I met them in Moscow nine years ago. They dreamed of just such a monarch…"

"O-oh, the Dioscuri will go far now!" Myslavsky said. "They are intelligent, stubborn, and shrewd. I've heard they're no longer in the academy, but functionaries in the royal court. They've caught the empress' eye, for they pleased her in some way in the field of new laws which *she herself* drew up. Victoria! The boys are moving up the ladder."

"Well then, may the Lord help our calf catch the wolf," Skovoroda smiled.

Myslavsky waved his hand through the air. "As the English say, the road to hell is paved with good intentions. Where are you staying?"

"Nowhere as yet."

"Then I invite you to stay with us. As long as I'm here there will always be a cell for you!"

Skovoroda was moved. "God bless you, brother."

There was a knock on the door and, without waiting for permission, someone came inside. Hryhoriy looked and grew speechless: it was the youth from the choir, the composer.

"Forgive me, father…" He stopped, embarrassed. "I thought you were alone…"

"Come in, come in, Maksym," Myslavsky said in a gentle voice and nodded in Hryhoriy's direction: "This is my fellow student, Hryhoriy Savych Skovoroda, a composer as well."

Skovoroda rose and approached the lad.

"I heard your wonderful song today," he said emotionally. "As a composer I'm fit to be your student…"

"Come on, now!" The youth blushed.

"I wept listening to it," Skovoroda admitted sincerely. "You've got talent, exceptional talent!"

"We've been telling him the same thing for God knows how many years," the rector interjected. "And he only laughs…"

"I'm not laughing now." The boy radiated a smile.

"He was presented to Count Rumiantsev… Well, the fellow rubbed his hands with satisfaction. And what a voice, what a voice he has, Hrytsko!

His highness the governor has promised to take our Maksym with him to St. Petersburg."

Myslavsky spoke the last phrase with obvious sadness.

"I'm leaving today," Berezovsky said quietly. "I've just had a messenger from the count."

Twirling his finger through his beard, Myslavsky stared down at his feet.

Skovoroda did not take his gaze off the lad's face, to retain it in his mind, to remember it for life, for he had no hopes of ever meeting him again. St. Petersburg was a large mill, which ground people up like grain.

"Well, then." The rector rose heavily. "Farewell, Maksym. Don't forget us sinful souls. Or your native land." Embracing him and kissing him three times, he added sternly: "Don't hurry and become a court choir soloist, instead learn non-stop from everyone and everywhere! Ask them to send you to Italy."

The youth swallowed the tears which betrayed his feelings: "I'll study. And I won't forget who I am."

Skovoroda kissed Maksym too, took his guelder rose flute from his shirt front, which he had made back in Kovray, and pressed it into the boy's hands.

"Take it, Maksym. This is a magical flute. It dissipates grief and fills the heart with strength. It contains all the songs you have heard from your mother, the wandering minstrels, the commoners, the craftsmen, the students, and even those which you have never heard, but which live in the soul of our people, passed on from generation to generation, immortal like our language and the glory of our ancestors."

"God bless you, father," Maksym said through his tears and kissed the flute, as a Zaporozhian Cossack would have kissed his sabre. "Till death us do part!" He turned around sharply and left the cell.

"Bless his path, oh Lord," Myslavsky whispered.

He came up to the table and began to leaf through some papers. His face became gloomier and gloomier.

"Our most talented people are borne away, as if by floodwaters," he said sorrowfully after a while. "And we are powerless to retain them, to provide them a place under the sun. This is utter nonsense! Instead of thinking lofty thoughts, attending to matters of state and philosophy, I must scrape about in these paragraphs, these miserable points, which stick out like sore thumbs, to make them smooth and rounded, like five-copeck coins!" he hurled the documents onto the table, sat down and closed his eyes.

"Toil away, Samiylo, I'll be off," Skovoroda said softly. "I'm not here alone, but with a lad."

Myslavsky looked up with a start.

"Your son is with you?!"

"No, a pupil, a friend."

"The two of you come then…"

"Thank you, we will."

Hryhoriy left quietly and closed the old oak door behind him. Let him rest, let this martyr, this eternal sufferer sooth his festering heart. He was aching with all the grief, the sorrow and the tears with which fate had so generously endowed the once mighty and joyous tribe of Ruthenians!

∗　∗　∗

The following day Skovoroda took Mykhailo sightseeing in the city. They admired the town hall, its tower reaching far into the heavens like a church bell tower, they walked along the winding narrow streets to Starokyivska Hill. Mykhailo, of course, kept looking back at the enormous statue of Themis, which stood above the entrance to the town hall – she had a sword in one hand and scales in the other. He was no less impressed by the bronze statue of the Saint Michael the Archangel, who plunged a steel spear into the dragon's jaws when the clock struck the hour atop the tower.

"Now that's really something!"

"And in the dark, with each thrust of the spear, sparks fly from the jaws," Hryhoriy said, smiling.

"Shall we take a look?"

"Of course. That's what we came here for."

From the top of the descent, they could see the whole of the Podil district. Bounded by the Dnipro River, the Pochaina River and two ramparts, the churches, houses, and adjacent orchards were herded together like people in a marketplace. Only here and there could one make out the unclear outlines of squares, streets and workshop yards. Around the Prytyka jetty there were countless fishing boats with thin masts, and some larger vessels. Two or three sailboats crawled along sleepily, exhausted by the calm air and the heat. And over on yellowish-green Trukhaniv Island gulls glistened in the sun, as if they were made of silver.

"What beauty, what boundless space!" exclaimed Mykhailo.

"That's Kyiv for you," Hryhoriy sighed. Once more his chest filled with the pain of acerbic melancholy, vaguely resembling the feeling one felt upon returning to one's magical native land after a long absence. He hadn't even realised that this golden-domed, hundred times destroyed mother of all Rus' cities had made such a lasting impression on him. He was curious whether ancient people also appreciated the beauty of nature? Or did they only care about the sun which warmed them, and the warm summer rains which nurtured their grain? But why then did they settle in such pictur-esque places – on river banks, and atop high cliffs.

"Our ancestors must have been poets," Mykhailo said, as if overhearing his thoughts. "Or philosophers…"

"Or simply warriors," Skovoroda replied in turn. "In Serpukhiv I heard the saying: 'Not to grow fat, merely to survive.' A city is not poetic, but mere-ly a tract of land surrounded on all sides by ramparts and palisades, where one can hide from enemies, fend off their attacks, and sit out calamitous times. Fate was generous in granting this glorious old city hard times. Peer into the depths of time to see who attacked it! Our own people, foreigners… And every one burnt and pillaged, trying to erase it from the face of the earth. But it remained standing, our grand old Kyiv. Rising each time from the ashes like a phoenix…"

"You speak as if you were born and grew up in Kyiv," the boy said slyly.

"Because it is the embodiment of history!" Hryhoriy exclaimed and continued walking uphill. He stopped by the gate and spoke slowly, softly, but emotionally about that which had festered in his soul: "It upsets me to watch how flippantly and indifferently people react to their past history."

Mykhailo turned crimson.

"My past is like a mosquito's nose," he immediately countered with a joke. "I'm not even twenty yet…"

"People who respect, know, and love the history of their people live not a lifetime, but for as long as their people, their land, their country exists," Skovoroda continued just as softly, as if deliberating. "Sometimes, it seems to me that I marched on Byzantium with Oleh, baptized the Kyivans with Volodymyr, defended these walls against Batu Khan, routed the Polish nobles alongside Khmelnytsky and liberated my brothers from Tatar slavery with the legendary Sirko... The past is our treasure, it is our roots, the arteries which nourish us with terrestrial juices and without which we cannot blossom, and will wither away. The past rallies us together, gives us energy to overcome hardships, and hope – and this is probably most important. How can one live without hope? Without the certainty that the sun will rise tomorrow, without believing that daylight will dispel darkness, that evil will fall and be replaced by goodness, learning, and happiness, what we have is not life – it is vegetation!"

He became silent once again, thinking. But when they reached the top of the hill and entered the Starokyivska Fortress, where two out of every three passers-by were soldiers, Skovoroda resumed his train of thought: "Knowledge of the past gives us the ability to perceive our nation better and ourselves as a part of it. Most odious are the janissaries,[60] those turncoats who are suspended between shunning their own, and not quite being accepted by the Ottomans. Everything is fine in its own place and within its own dream, and all things natural, pure, and genuine are beautiful." Remaining silent awhile, he smiled. "In St. Petersburg I've seen enough of our powdered monkeys, who have forgotten which mother bore them and nursed them! Although now, even in Kyiv and in our famous Kharkiv, there are enough of these blockheads. This is St. Michael's Golden-Domed Cathedral, a contemporary of the Lavra." He pointed to an extremely tall majestic church and took the boy by the shoulders: "Look how well you and I were able to build at a time when many of today's capitals had not yet existed!"

Near Saint Sophia Cathedral they were overtaken by a group of artisans, some dressed in city garb, others in Cossack dress. Tipsy, merry, aroused, the old men strove to sing something bawdy, exchanging words and jests. A tall broad-shouldered moustached old man stood out from among the revellers. Bare-headed, formidable, he walked decisively, precipitously, as if measuring the street with his feet and making a mental note of what needed to be demolished or built.

....

[60]   Janissaries were members of an elite Turkish army composed of captive Christian boys converted to Islam and brought up in the spirit of religious fanaticism and blind obedience. In Ukrainian the term is used to mean an apostate or traitor.

Although not at once, Skovoroda recognised the old man as Stepan Kovnir, a famous master stonemason and architect.

"Look over there." He nudged Mykhailo, who was admiring the church. "That's Kovnir, who built the bell tower of the Brotherhood Monastery…"

"Where, where?" The boy shuddered.

As if hearing that he was being discussed, Kovnir stopped, threw an intent eye over the two pilgrims, who were dawdling for so long and in such rapture outside Saint Sophia, and took a step toward them.

"Admiring it?" he asked sternly.

"Good day to you, Mister Kovnir." Hryhoriy removed his straw hat. "It is very beautiful!"

Kovnir screwed up his eyes, as if sizing up the solemn old church.

"And how do you know that I'm Kovnir?" he asked shortly thereafter.

"Who doesn't know you in Kyiv!"

"So, you're a Kyivite?"

"No. I studied in the Academy here. And now we've come from Kharkiv to look at this glorious city."

"Boys!" Kovnir called out. "Invite our guests along! Let's not put to shame the guild of stonemasons and bricklayers!"

"We invite you humbly!"

"Join us for some bread and salt!"

"And vodka!"

"Let's visit Motria!"

"Off to Motria's, brothers! We haven't been to Motria's yet!"

The stonemasons took Skovoroda and Mykhailo by the arms and dragged them off to the tavern. There were shouts, guffaws, and clamouring, as if the whole of Kyiv had poured into the now quiet streets of the city of Yaroslav the Wise.

The sprightly publican ran into the street to greet her dear guests. She clucked and twittered: "Lord Almighty, Stepan Demianovych! What wind has brought you here? You haven't dropped by for quite some time. Step inside, please, my dear guests! Varvara, Varka!"

The servant stepped outside carrying a large bottle and a glass on a silver tray, and the keeper herself first treated Kovnir, and then the others. Handing the glass to him she cunningly flashed her blue turquoise eyes:

"Where did you find this child? He's an adorable flower!" She burst out laughing, like a nightingale breaking into song.

Mykhailo turned crimson.

"This is our guest from Kharkiv," Kovnir smoothed his sumptuous grey moustache.

"Don't keep your eye on another's morsel!" added a pockmarked fidgety stonemason and pinched Motria.

"Whoa!" She stamped her foot and turned to Mykhailo again: "Drink up, drink up, young Cossack. Or maybe you want me to bring a glass of milk?"

Mykhailo suddenly emptied the glass and began to cough.

"Woe is me!" Motria feigned alarm. "What's the matter, birdie, went down where the Easter cake goes, instead of where the bread goes?" She moved her hips seductively and, stretching like a cat, strew the azure sparks of her gaze about and floated back inside like a peacock: "Please come inside, my dear guests!"

It was busy and noisy in the tavern. In one corner, their tight uniforms unbuttoned, Russian soldiers were sitting around a bottle. They had obviously been here a while, for they spoke in shouts, and all at once. In the middle of the room, like fatherless children, Cossacks sat drinking gloomily. The Empress had turned them into orphans and soon, as rumour had it, she would be making them into bondsmen or lancers. Almost on the threshold, around a low long table, caroused the city's grey masses. People made merry here as they pleased – thoughtlessly, generously, and recklessly.

The tavern-keeper cleared a table not far from the bar and together with Varka brought out roasts, boiled dishes, vodka, mead, cherry brandy, plum brandy and imported wines on enormous trays.

The eyes of the stonemasons and master-bricklayers nearly popped, amazed at seeing such sumptuous dishes.

"Are you insane, Motria?"

"You'll send us out of here as beggars!"

"Stop whimpering, kiddies," the tavern-keeper placated them. "Mister Kovnir ordered this, and your only concern is to eat and drink…"

"Long live Kovnir!"

"Vivat!"

The overjoyed brethren rushed up to their leader, but the old man stopped them with a peaceful, authoritative gesture.

"Sit down, boys, or I might change my mind. We've had our fill, but our guests might not have had breakfast yet…"

"It's fine, we had breakfast in the monastery," Hryhoriy replied.

"Snatched some molasses with an awl." The master builder smiled, sitting the guests at the table first.

The stonemasons grew silent, laying siege to the table, and the banquet began.

They ate and drank harmoniously. These irrepressible people probably toiled the same way, without undue words, tirelessly, their hands and minds moulding lime and stone into a single beautiful strong whole. They had the large coarse hands of workers and the faces of holy prophets. They of course knew their worth, but never boasted about it; they respected their leader, but did not adulate him, did not crawl before him. And the great master himself did not put on airs in front of mere mortals, but spoke, ate, and drank as an equal among equals, except perhaps as someone older in age.

Kovnir stumbled at the third glass and only brought it to his lips, setting it aside.

"What's wrong, father?" the masons asked worriedly. "Is the vodka bad?"

"No, the spirits are fine," the old man sighed. "It's me that's getting on in years… Seventy is no joke! My health's beginning to play up, lads…"

"Come on now!"

"What's with you?"

"I'm weak and infirm…" he said in Church Slavonic.

"Ho-ho-ho-ho!"

"Remember how you pummelled the church warden, father!"

"But that was a while back…"

"You'd break a bear's neck now, father!"

The old man screwed up his eyes, smoothed his moustache and without hurrying, staidly emptied the glass.

"That's the way, like a true mason!" Riaby called out and, overjoyed, downed another glass.

Suddenly there was silence in the tavern. Even the Russian soldiers grew silent, turning toward the adjacent table. Gloomily, awkwardly, just as they had drunk, the Cossacks rose from their table, settled their bill in gold, and clanking their curved sabres, moved toward the door in a grim procession.

"The Cossacks are carousing at their own funeral," someone said sorrowfully.

"They won't perish," Riaby added. "After all, we're still living..."

"Call this living?" Kovnir turned to him. "We're wasting away, not living! Who am I?"

"You're an architect, father, a great master!" the masons called out in unison. This probably wasn't the first time they had heard the question posed.

"I'm a big bondsman, a monastic slave!" Kovnir struck his palm down on the table. He remained silent a while and then spoke with such grief in his voice, that Hryhoriy's heart turned to stone: "I'm seventy already, I've lived my life, but what have I done, what have I built?"

"Fear God, father," Riaby interjected. "What about the Vasylkiv church!"

Everyone began to talk at once.

"The bookshop in the Lavra!"

"And the kitchen."

"The bell towers!"

"The monks' cells."

"And the Klovsky Palace!"

"The iconostasis in the Church of the Saviour at Berestove...!"

"Rubbish!" The master stopped them menacingly. "All this is a niggardly part of what I might have built with you, lads..."

"There's still time!"

"No. A falcon with tied wings cannot soar, he can only run. Like a rooster, a drake, or a gander. Without freedom, my friends, there is no life, no soaring, no creativity!"

A silence set in. The intoxication disappeared in a flash. With heads bowed, the masons sat completely sober, suffering, like the martyrs who had risen from the dead on the walls of their churches.

Skovoroda studied the artisans' mournful faces and once again his heart filled with a growing desire not to leave, to remain here in Kyiv, where the present was side by side with the past, where there were Kovnirs, who could see and create beauty no worse than the ancients.

"Let's forget our misfortune and sing!" Riaby said unexpectedly.

"Why not."

"A song is like a curative herb..."

"Or alcohol," Riaby added and began in a clear high voice:

Rejoice, my glass,
Make merry, my bottle!

The masons were all smiles and picked up the tune:

Don't weep,
Wheat bun!
There'll be work for you yet…

Some musicians entered with a dulcimer, a violin and a tambourine. The singers fell silent and Riaby made a move to have the musicians join them. But the tavern-keeper intercepted them with a glass of vodka and sat them at the bar, so there would be no brawls among the guests. However, as the saying goes, what must be, will inevitably be. No sooner had the musicians wiped their lips after the vodka than requests came thick and fast from all directions to play some tune – not just anything, but this or that particular dance.

"The *hopak*! The *hopak*!" the masons called out in unison.

"The *kamarinskaya*!" The Russian dragoons did not relent.

"To hell with you!"

"To hell with you!" they yelled back in Russian.

One, then another bottle fell over. Someone tipped over the bench with the masons. There was laughter, uproar, curses…

Skovoroda nodded to Mykhailo and they hastily made their way out of the crowded tavern.

"Where vodka and passions reign supreme, there is nothing for philosophers to do," he said sagaciously, as soon as they emerged onto the populous, festive street.

The sun showed that it was already midday. It burnt so strongly that by the time they reached the fields beyond the ramparts, they were tired and perspiring profusely. In a nearby gully, they found some spring water and, having slaked their thirst, lay down to rest in the dense shade of a willow.

They were woken by the sun and a turtle dove. Moving away from its midday vantage point, the sun had shifted the shadows and the heavenly fire once more began to fry the travellers. Spying people in its wood, the vociferous turtle dove chattered in alarm and darted into the undergrowth.

Having crossed Khreshchaty Ravine, thickly dotted with small distilleries, Skovoroda and Mykhailo caught their breath and made their way up the steep road between the shrubbery and hillocks toward Pechersk. Having passed the tsarist palace and the Pustynno-Mykilsky Monastery, they saw the churches before them and the Lavra bell tower. Although, there was still half a verst of road between them and the Lavra, plus a high rampart, a water-filled moat, and bastions.

The heat subsided a little and the Kharkiv travellers were soon inside the fortress.

Pilgrims were heading toward the Lavra from all directions. Subdued, impressed, in expectation of coming face to face with miracle-working sacraments, places of great spiritual feats achieved by grim ascetics, they flowed in a living river through the prodigious Holy Gates and, spying the Great Lavra Church – the Cathedral of the Assumption – they reverently prostrated themselves and kissed the ground. As was the old custom, the pilgrims had to crawl on their knees all the way to the cathedral.

Hryhoriy had seen this inhuman maltreatment before, this savage custom; all the same, he was bewildered by the crowd of crawling humanity, kissing the ground and making the sign of the cross. Clutching his torment in his heart, he moved along like a giant among pygmies, soaring above the crowded road, his eagle eye barely able to contain the burning storm raging inside his chest. He felt painful vexation for these humiliated, downtrodden, ignorant people; he insufferably wanted to address them with words of truth, to reveal the deception in which they had been swathed by these hypocrites in cassocks, to open their eyes, to teach them self-respect and dignity. But he was unable to, lacking either the power or the courage, or perhaps he himself was constrained by the iron will of habit and doubts...

Coming to his senses, he sought out his friend. Mykhailo was crawling along on his knees, crossing himself, bowing and kissing the sacred road.

Skovoroda turned back, took the lad by the shoulders and stood him on his feet.

"Crawling does not become anyone who strives for verity! Only the ignorant, the spiritually destitute grovel, and the abject who, by bending, reach for power, so that they can bend and break the will of others. You're not one of those."

"But this is the Lavra, it's sacred ground..." Mykhailo whispered.

"Sacred is the ground that bears. Here there is only dust and stone."

"Blessed by the Lord…"

"Just like everything else in this world!"

They stood amid the stream of believers and argued, debating the sacredness of the place.

A few pilgrims joined them – thin, exhausted, covered with the dust of long travels. Listening, they began to get up and nod their heads affirmatively. Hryhoriy's words were passed on from mouth to mouth.

At this point the Lord's servants in black appeared. Pushing aside the others, the chubby shepherds immediately surrounded Skovoroda and spirited him off to one side.

"What are you doing, you devil?" One of the monks grabbed him by the chest when they found themselves in a deserted corner by the bell tower. "Preaching against the church?!"

"Are you an atheist?" another asked through gritted teeth.

"He's probably a Jesuit," a third added.

"Cross yourself!"

"I have no desire to," Skovoroda said calmly. "You're not icons or saints, merely the most ordinary, insolent, satiated of thugs, who have abandoned their consciences and turned the Lord's name into a scarecrow. And you sell God's word piecewise, like traders selling nuts…"

"Shut him up," boomed the voice of an old monk, who looked on in silence as the brethren converted this intruder to the bosom of the church and the faith.

Another moment and the 'baptism' would have begun. But Mykhailo came running up and with him the cathedral's printer, Hryhoriy's distant relative Yustyn.

"Who do I see!" he called out joyously and, spreading out his arms, grabbed Skovoroda in his embrace. "What wind brings you here, Hrytsko? We talked about you only a few days ago. So many of our brethren have gathered here, you know!"

Like defeated dogs, Christ's warriors dropped their heads and slipped off in all directions.

"Have they been preaching here like this a long time?" Hryhoriy asked, watching his long-haired attackers disappearing.

"Ah, take no notice," Yustyn said sagaciously. "Each has his own job…"

"Where the cross has no effect, resort to the fist?"

"No one tolerates heterodoxy nor will they ever..."

"Nonsense! Tolerance is the lever of progress, advancement, and where it is lacking, there is no truth, freedom, or movement, for great and brilliant verity is born of contradiction!"

"Who needs it now?" the printer asked sorrowfully. "There's still semi-verity..."

"It's the same as driving half a cart," Hryhoriy said and manoeuvred Mykhailo toward the printer. "My sincere friend and pupil!"

Yustyn shook the boy's hand.

"Good lad, didn't lose his cool when his teacher fell into a spot of bother... Well then, gentlemen, I graciously invite you into my household!"

"He hasn't seen the Lavra yet." Hryhoriy nodded in Mykhailo's direction. "Perhaps we could first show him the churches, the caves, and your printing works?"

"We'll show him everything," Yustyn smiled languidly. "It won't disappear anywhere! It's remained standing for hundreds of years and, God willing, will remain standing a while longer. However, in my cell, something might disappear, just as smoke disappears and wax melts in the face of fire."

Embracing the waists of his visitors, the printer set off with them across the main street, along which pilgrims kept flowing ceaselessly, leaving the Great Lavra Church on his left, and turned into a street running north toward the Economic Gate.

The cell to which Yustyn shortly brought them was filled with a great clamour and Skovoroda recognised quite a few familiar faces among the brethren. For a moment he imagined that he was a student and had accidentally come across a party organised by the boys somewhere in Podil.

"Attention!" someone drawled in a deep voice and, falling silent, everyone fixed their eyes on the new arrivals.

"Whom has the Lord sent?" the same voice asked in a recitative tone.

"Who-om ha-as the Lo-ord se-ent?" the brethren answered in four-part harmony.

"Don't recognise me?"

"No-oh!"

"Hryhoriy... Skovoroda."

Moving aside tables and chairs, the monks rushed toward their fellow student, whom some hadn't seen for eleven years, others for more. There were embraces, jokes, exclamations!

Hryhoriy was completely moved. In the monk's faces, overgrown with beards, he recognised comrades from the seminary, from classes; one after another their names surfaced. How comical, how different these boys were in cowls and long black robes!

He was seized by the arms and to the accompaniment of the triumphal student hymn, they carried him into the corner under the icons.

> *Gaudeamus igitur*
> *Juvenes duel sumus;*
> *Post jucundam juventutem,*
> *Post molestam senectutem,*
> *Nos habebit humus.*
> *Vivat academia,*
> *Vivat professores...!*[61]

After the fervent joy of the meeting had cooled off, the academy graduates launched into discussions of theology and philosophy. A real dispute began. And not about how the Lord created the stars and the Earth or how Eve committed the original sin, but about life, about the place of a thinking person in the struggle with the devil, who now appeared not in his own image, but in a mask, with a halo of the just and righteous.

"Hryhoriy, stay here!" Yustyn said unexpectedly.

"Forsooth!" the brethren called out in unison.

"And what will I do here?" Hryhoriy asked. "Thrash the pilgrims so that they crawl along on their knees?"

....

[61]   Therefore, let us rejoice
We are young still;
After a joyous youth
And troublesome old age,
We'll return to the earth.
Long live the academy,
Long live the professors...! (Latin)

"What for?" the steward monk piped up. "For that we have novices and the lower ranks."

"Come join us as a printer."

"Or as a choirmaster."

"Sacred work will be found for you," the steward monk embraced his shoulders. "We need intelligent people. Once winter is over, we'll have you tonsured. And then give us a few years and we'll appoint you archimandrite, defender of the retreat and its servants."

"But above all yourselves?"

"And us too," the steward monk agreed and winked at the brethren. "We're not just anything in the Lavra!"

"You're a force?"

"Of course. And what a force!"

"And you stand by truth?"

"Of course, Hrytsko."

"Then why do magnates and nobles drive into the yard in phaetons, instead of crawling along like the poor?" Hryhoriy closed the trap.

Exchanging glances, the monks fell silent.

"They have heavy purses," the steward monk said after a pause. "They can't get them to church otherwise. Might lose them along the way..."

"And what about everyone being equal before the Lord?"

The monks chuckled.

"Hryhoriy, don't hit your head against a brick wall," Brother Yustyn advised quietly.

"You're God's servants!" Hryhoriy called out. "Fighters for human souls, holy servants. What can you teach your neighbour, when you yourselves don't believe your words, your own preaching and sermons?! Oh, holy cassock! How few people have you made venerable and how many have you enchanted, and driven to depravity! The world captures people in various nets: wealth, awards, comfort, pleasure, sanctuaries... The most calamitous of these is the latter. Blessed is he who has not hidden the sanctity of his heart, his destiny and his own happiness inside a cassock. The greatest evils are hypocrisy, deceit and insincerity – these erode the soul, like rust eating away at iron. And you want to ride these three donkey twins into the kingdom of God!"

The monks looked at him in horror, as if he was tearing up the Shroud or some holy book.

"It's already late, brethren," the steward monk said firmly. "Time to pray before bed."

"How true!" Yustyn agreed hastily.

"Farewell."

"God be with you!"

Soon only the three of them remained in the printer's cell. Clearing up as best he could after the brethren's incursion, the host laid out some bedding and embraced Skovoroda by the shoulders.

"I think the same way, brother, but I was afraid to even let out a squeak. This insincerity is like a knife in my heart, and these black robes are like a cage. But I don't know if I have the strength to break free..."

"A person is capable of everything," Hryhoriy said and suddenly sensed that he did not have the strength to stay long in Kyiv. He was drawn into the open steppe, to freedom, among simple and ordinary folk, miserable, poor, but not cunning, like these former friends, who had become satiated shepherds, stepfathers brimming with malice.

A day later, when the time for farewells arrived, the academy brethren again gathered in the printer's cell. They were taciturn and reticent.

"Well then, gentlemen fellow students," Yustyn spoke first. "Hryhoriy is leaving us. We wish you a safe trip, brother, and you too, Mykhailo! Don't remember the bad, if something was not right... P'raps you'll stay, Hrytsko?" he added after a silence.

And the brethren spoke up: "Come on, stay!"

"Enough of wandering about the world!"

"It's time for you to put into shore."

"Everyone knows of your talents, and the Lavra will accept you as a mother takes in her worthy offspring."

"You will be the pillar of the holy church and the showpiece of the monastery!"

Skovoroda smiled.

"Ah, my reverend fathers! I have no desire to multiply your confusion with my presence. There are enough uncouth pillars in God's temple!"

He picked up his straw hat off the bench and, barely able to contain the desire to leave the cell right away, without even saying farewell to the rector, he said: "We are very grateful to you, holy fathers, for your bread and salt and... your lessons. Create whatever you want, but without me."

"Come to your senses!"

"Don't tempt fate!"

"Tame your pride!"

He didn't even look back. Only on top of the cliff, on the far side of the ramparts and the moat, did he take out his handkerchief and wipe away the sweat.

"It's hot..."

"And in the meadow back home beyond the Lopan River, the boys are probably baking potatoes again and singing about *hetman* Sirko." Mykhailo added dreamily.

"And Father Lavrentiy is lying on the hay near the spring, tending to the clouds, in contemplation..."

"Or listening to the bumblebees buzzing in his noggin from the vodka."

Laughing, they continued on their way. And although all around them gilded crosses and domes of wonderful ancient churches burnt in the last rays of sunlight, and the old Dnipro River flowed wide and blue at the foot of the hill, Skovoroda and Mykhailo were no longer in Kyiv. They were on their way; one of them leaving behind a fairytale, the other his youth. Fairytales were beautiful when viewed from afar, and that which faded away was best borne in the heart and should not be relived. Life was like a river, it could not be turned back.

"Kraisky will be furious, when he learns that you came along with me," Mykhailo's voice rang out.

"In vain," Skovoroda whispered and quickened his step.

⎯⎯

THE EIGHTH NET

Misfortune takes many paths. The new archimandrite and rector, Iov Bazylevych, was meek, soft-hearted and sickly. Meanwhile, the bishop lived in Belgorod and did not visit Kharkiv once throughout the entire winter nor did he summon anyone before his stern eyes. And then suddenly – here you had it!

One evening while Hryhoriy and Kordet were sitting in the prefect's cell and reflecting who was right – the Bible or Nicolaus Copernicus – a frightened Yasha Pravytsky burst in and whispered: "The rector is summoning both of you. His grace has just arrived!"

"Coming after me," Kordet sighed. "*Plaudite, cives, plaudite, amici, finita est comoedia!*"[62]

"Intuition?"

"No, logic. Porfyriy Kraisky isn't a person who stops at half measures." He took a bottle from his pocket, uncorked it and emptied it there and then. "Now we can go." He looked about the cell, closed the book and blew out the candle. "*O tempora, o mores!*"[63]

His grace met them warmly. Blessing them, he shook their hands and invited them to sit down.

The meek Iov fell silent in his armchair and only flashed his sparkling eyes.

"Well, how are we keeping?" the bishop asked warmly. This turned out somewhat insincere, for even his smile was crafty, rapacious.

"All right."

"Not bad."

....

[62]   Cheer, citizens, applaud, friends, the comedy is finished! (Latin)
[63]   Oh the times, oh the mores! (Latin)

"The Lord be praised! The Lord be praised... You haven't become bored here?" He screwed up his eyes, like a cat eyeing a mouse. "One and the same thing year after year..."

"No, father," Kordet said calmly. "We are quiet, unenvious, honest people. Trifles are enough for us. We're not hungry for high positions, accumulating land or salting money away in barrels. As the Romans said: *omnia mea mecum porto*."[64]

The bishop smacked his lips: "We could just about take you and place you on icons... Listen, Iov, but this is a wonderful thought. Why not make him a Father Superior!" and he nodded at Kordet. The latter turned white while the rector didn't even twitch. "Father Lavrentiy…" The bishop weighed up the sound of the title. "Father Superior of the Sviatohirsk Monastery... Of course, it'll be a pity for us to part with such a hearty friend," he drawled derisively. "But what can we do, it must be done. God comes first...!"

"I won't leave here," Kordet said through clenched teeth.

The bishop looked up and spoke as if hammering nails into a coffin: "Don't be in a hurry, Lavrentiy. It's never too late to refuse. Think it over, weigh it up. Such a great retreat! It's almost like an eparchy..."

"But I'm a philosopher! Who will I teach there?" Kordet exclaimed.

"The monastic brethren." Kraisky was openly mocking him now. "They've been anxiously awaiting lessons there. Without philosophy they are as if without hands…"

"Are you tormenting me?!" whispered Lavrentiy, getting up.

The meek Iov immediately jumped from his armchair and shielded the bishop.

"Calm down, my son," he raised his bony hand before Kordet. "Everything is God's will."

"No, this is his will!"

"You are mistaken," Iov said quietly. "It was I who begged his grace to send you to Sviatohirsk."

"What for, Iov?" Kordet asked, flabbergasted, reaching for the armchair with his hand.

"So you don't have far to travel. This isn't Siberia..."

---

[64]   I carry all my things with me. (Latin)

176

The bishop was fingering his rosary. The meek Iov stood like a barely living martyr. And Kordet was pale, as if he had been taken down off the cross.

"You are snakes, not people," he said after a while. "May that day be damned when I allowed these hunters to ensnare me in cloaks and cassocks! Hell's torment is a game compared to this earthly suffering! Everywhere there is hypocrisy, perfidy, lies. To magnates a person is not a living soul, a unique creation, but a unit, a log which can be traded, neglected, and utilised according to one's own judgement. Lord, if You can hear me, then spit into their satiated eyes!"

He left quickly.

"In vain have you defended this dolt and troublemaker, Iov," the bishop grumbled. "Because of men like him they still view us with an angry eye in St. Petersburg, and sedition roams the country..."

"Otherwise, we would all have long been serfs," Hryhoriy added.

"What did you say?" the bishop asked.

"We would all have been slaves."

"Hryhoriy, don't try my patience," Kraisky said malevolently. "Think I don't know with whom Mykhailo went to Kyiv? Or not heard what a fuss you created in the Lavra...?"

"You have an informer's flair."

The bishop gritted his teeth.

"Hryhoriy, isn't it time for you to exchange your peasant coat for something more respectable?" the rector interjected. "It somehow doesn't become you... The rich stab us in the eye with you."

"Aren't I free to wear what I wish? After all, I'm not a soldier."

"No, you're free, you're free," Iov made a wry face. "But..."

"You are in the tsar's service and must obey the rules," Kraisky added calmly.

"No, I'm in the service of the people. The community doesn't care what I wear. It's not the peasant coat that teaches, but the head."

"Smart..."

"Which can't be said of you."

The bishop pressed down into his armchair. And suddenly burst into guffaws: "You're simply a buffoon! Everything on your mind is on your tongue. Iov, you must find it fun here! Listen," he addressed Hryhoriy again, "why do you think that I am not wise?"

"A wise shepherd wouldn't have exiled a person such as our Kordet to a monastery, but would have taken him under their wing, warmed him with a kind word and directed his fervent, zealous spirit onto the path of kindness and truth."

"The best path for him is on a transport to hard labour," Kraisky said sharply. "Have you heard his satires and epigrams? He's dissatisfied with everything, hurls mud at everyone!"

"Mud doesn't stick to the clean, only to those who wallow in muck…"

"Out of my sight!" the bishop stamped his feet. "You're birds of a feather! By morning I want you out of Kharkiv!"

"Oh Lord," Iov sighed sorrowfully and drew his head into his shoulders.

Skovoroda stood up, adjusted his belt and although his spirit was seething with fury, he left in silence.

Tyrants loved tears and repentance, while a person's dignity was like a knife in their hearts.

Hryhoriy got up before dawn, washed and, placing his belongings in his bag, quietly left the monastery. He didn't even drop by Lavrentiy's cell: there would be enough time – he would visit him in Sviatohirsk.

He made his way across the misty sleepy city toward Troyitska where Mykhailo was lodging with Father Borys. He did not know himself where he would go or what he would do in this cramped boundless world, where there was no room for haughty injustice and truth to pass each other by. It was a pity to leave Kharkiv, the pupils, and his *museum*, where he enjoyed warmth and comfort. But he also rejoiced that he hadn't yielded to those in power, hadn't submitted to the will of that snitch Kraisky. His only treasure was the freedom of his body and soul, so he had to take care not to be tricked into losing this treasure. Not under any circumstance must one exchange freedom for a slice of bread. How often do we deprecate ourselves before rulers and even those who might provide us food, because we are afraid of being left hungry in body, corrupting our soul out of fear? If it wasn't for this, injustice would never have flourished so luxuriantly in the fields of truth and verity.

Kovalynsky was already awake. Like his teacher, he rose early and immediately began to draw from the spring of knowledge.

He was not surprised by the appearance of his guest. But when he saw the bag, he asked in bewilderment:

"Where are you off to, Savych?"

"Into the world, into the wide world!" Skovoroda said cheerfully, although he felt terribly sad inside. "I was probably destined to spend my life on the road…"

"For long?"

"Who knows."

"And what about us, the collegium?"

"The most reverend Father Porfyriy will bestow his favours upon you!"

"He's here?"

"Arrived yesterday evening."

"When did he manage to drive you out of the collegium?"

"Kordet as well."

"Lord, why do You allow such highhandedness?!" Mykhailo whispered ardently.

"God must have been asleep," Hryhoriy joked. "It was late at night… Well then, farewell, my friend!" he embraced Mykhailo and kissed him.

"Where are you off to now?" the youth asked, bewildered.

"It makes no difference…"

Mykhailo wept soundlessly.

"Damned world, damned people!" he called out in desperation after a while.

"There's no need for that." Hryhoriy stopped him. "Both people and the world are beautiful. Don't judge your nation and humanity by the degenerates. Learn, reason and sow knowledge about you. Tyrants can only rule amid fear and ignorance. But the night cannot last forever. Dawn must come!"

Embracing his friend one more time and kissing him thrice, Hryhoriy left the yard.

"Write!"

"Of course!"

"Don't forget me!"

"Never!"

The mist grew lighter. He could already make out the river and the bare forest beyond. The sandy street was crusted over with a light spring frost, or maybe the earth had warmed up and was exhaling its rigid winter cold. Intoxicated with joy, the sparrows chirped zealously, tempestuously, cheerfully. Rooks called to each other as they built their nests. The air was starting to come alive with greenery and blossom, though spring had not yet arrived.

It floated on the warm wings of a breeze, waking the earth, the birds, and people's hearts.

Perplexed, brimming with thoughts, melodies, and poems, Hryhoriy ascended the right bank of the Lopan. He stopped, surveyed his *museum* and the collegium, then turned left, so that he would be walking into the wind, and made his way south along the road.

* * *

Spring arrived when he was still travelling. He had become tanned, invigorated, weather-beaten. Like the heavenly birds, he neither reaped nor sowed, but he did not go hungry. In each house he was gladly received, the hosts shared everything they had, listened reverently to his preaching and accounts of those cities and lands he had visited or read about. He made a new flute and played to old men in apiaries, to staid elderly people on porches outside churches, and to young people relaxing on the village common. He didn't stay anywhere for long. A day or two passed, and he would be picked up and carried further and further, into unknown villages, apiaries, and settlements.

And so it was until May. Until he reached the settlements near Valky.

The road passed through an old oak forest. Among the fluffy green crowns were the black branches of sessile oaks. Here and there alongside the road wild fruit trees blossomed in clouds. Orioles sang, and Skovoroda yearned to sing as well. Moving along the shadow-mottled road he delighted in the freedom, the movement, the joy of being free, under no obligation to anyone or anything, except for the people who shared their bread with him as if he was family. Admittedly, these kind souls demanded nothing in return for their hospitality, and on the contrary were virtuously grateful for the honour of hosting and feeding him, for the chance of hearing a word or two about what was happening in the world. Blessed people, and sacred was the earth which bore them!

Like a blind man feeling his way along a path, he found the words and melody to songs, which expressed his anxious thoughts, the credo of his life and his philosophy:

Today there is the sceptre and the mace,
Morning risen – only lean glory,
The heart aroused throughout,
Hands and feet tied firmly,
How doth one evade the net?

Like a young mother rejoicing at her firstborn, Hryhoriy rejoiced and trembled at the great marvel of the song's birth. He repeated it again and again, with variations, seeking the best version, and delighted in the words and melody. This was real sacrament! Way back there, near the settlement he had recently passed, there had still been nothing more than thoughts and feelings, but now there was a song, in flesh and blood, a new creature which might perhaps survive not only him, but also everyone now living and yet to be conceived.

Drunk freedom dances early today,
Up in the morning – a barren fate...

Hryhoriy continued the song. And suddenly noticed that an alien melody was intruding upon his. He stopped and ceased singing. In a forest clearing on his right, he could see a house surrounded by birches, and beside it stood sheds, an orchard and an apiary. From somewhere there, from the orchard inundated in a mist of blossom, came the singing. It was a girl. Her voice was restrained, throaty, majestic. She easily managed the low and high notes, despite the fact that she had chosen a difficult Cossack song.

Oh yeah, I would head for Zaporozhia,
But I do not know the way:
Hey, at least I'll stop, I'll stop, and see,
Hey, I'll ask someone the way...

Hryhoriy listened, having completely forgotten about his newly-born psalm. He pictured the girl as being slender, dark-haired, with a plait falling below her waist and eyes filled with a despondent grief... She stood among the cherry trees near the forest, gazed into the deep blue sky framed in white blossom, and poured out her soul. She sang with such inspiration, filling every sound and word with such energy that Hryhoriy's heart went numb. He had never heard such singing, had never met such a girl.

> *Oh yeah, the Cossack went, oh yeah, the young man went*
> *Waving a kerchief about;*
> *Hey, it was for him, for him, that the young girl,*
> *Hey, she shed fine tears...*

Without noticing it, he turned off the road and headed toward the settlement. He regained his senses only after bumping into a low osier fence. And he wandered into the forest again. This was some kind of delusion, sorcery! A respectable man, a teacher goes running off after a girl, like some moustacheless young swain.

His chest burnt, and his heart thumped like mad. He quickened his step. However, he was unable to escape the charms of the song. It pursued him, blinded his eyes, struck his soul with wings and tried to drag him back toward the settlement.

He slowed down only near Valky, sat down on a stump and caught his breath. And burst out laughing: he'd really scampered off – God knows where he was! Around him were ironwoods and lindens. In the distance was the village and the fortress, and on the edge of the forest nearby stood a large apiary, some hundred hives. Above hung an already low pinkish sun. A turtle dove chattered away...

Somewhere near the apiary a nightingale repeated its articulations and warbles in preparation for the evening concert. The air was pure, fresh with the heavy intoxication of flowers and greenery... Paradise, simply paradise! What more did one need? The old beekeeper would probably find something to appease his hunger and somewhere for him to rest his head.

The fear with which he had run away from the settlement was no longer there. There was indifference, exhaustion, and a great lack of desire to leave this blessed place and... this maiden's song. He was afraid to admit it to himself, driving the delusion away; however, it did not leave his heart and echoed from time to time with an alarming, though pleasant, ache. He realised that he was being tempted, that this was a test of his fortitude. Only he didn't know who was testing him. If it was the devil who had contrived such an insidious battle with him, then the fellow ought to watch out! But if it was the Lord...

He wanted to eat and drink. Picking his bag up off the ground, without throwing it over his shoulder, he wandered over to the apiary.

He was met by a tall grey-haired old man. Permeated with the smell of wax, honey and various herbs, the old man looked like a sorcerer, a bee god. Barely smiling, he opened the ramshackle wicket gate and bowed.

"Please step inside. I can offer you bread, honey and spring water!"

"God bless you, father. Bread and water are a Cossack's sustenance! And if you could also find a little hay on which to spend the night, it would be a vagrant's paradise..."

"Of course, we can find some." The beekeeper smiled. "You're welcome to stay the night!"

"Thank you."

They made their way down a path between two rows of hives to a hut lurking beside an old linden.

"Sit down, young fellow," the old man said warmly. "Rest from the road, while I gather what the Lord has sent and we can dine while the lamp's still burning."

He looked at the dying evening sun, freed a bee which had become entangled in his hair and, bending over, entered the hut.

Skovoroda placed his bag under the linden tree, covered it with his straw hat and lay down on the knotgrass.

He took a deep breath; there was a sharp smell of half-dried herbs, roots, flowers, as if someone nearby had mown a magical meadow, where herbs from around the world were flowering... He closed his eyes and immediately heard his mother's tearful voice: "Granny darling, please save the boy!"

"Don't wail, Palazhka. I've cured worse than him. This is only the evil eye, a trifle. I'll whisper a few words and we'll give him a decoction..."

"Poor fellow's fallen asleep," he heard the beekeeper's voice beside him.

"No, father, no," Skovoroda opened his eyes. "I remembered how my mother used to take me as a small boy to an herbalist in the settlements."

He got up and sat cross-legged.

"And did it help?" the beekeeper responded, spreading out a white cloth.

"As you can see."

The old man put down a fresh brown loaf, placed a bowl of honey beside it.

"There's great power in herbs," he said after a while. "Each herb contains a weapon against wounds, ulcers, diseases. If one knew for certain which herb was for what, people would never be ill. Our health is literally under our feet..."

"You're not an herbalist, are you, grandfather?" Hryhoriy asked.

"No." The beekeeper waved his arm dismissively and, crossing himself, picked up the loaf of bread. He cut several slices and began to invite his guest: "Here's the bread, the honey – help yourself. Don't condemn me for being poor. We share what we have."

"It's a king's dinner."

"Eat heartily."

Having checked his hunger, Skovoroda took out his flute.

"Out of guelder rose?" The beekeeper smoothed his moustache. He took it, examined it and, returning it, spoke as if the curative herbs and trees were giving him no peace: "You'd think: what's in a guelder rose? An ordinary bush. No good for a pole, not even a whip handle, except perhaps for the berries as pie filling. But look carefully and ask among the seasoned, knowledgeable people, and you'll have to take your hat off before the dear mother. For colds, coughs or fevers – a tea of guelder rose blossom is excellent. For bellyache you can eat the berries. And for haemorrhaging, wounds – just crush some young bark and apply it."

"And what about whispering some spells?" Hryhoriy asked in a sly voice. He was certain that he had come across an old herbalist.

"That's all nonsense!" The old man waved his hand. "They lead people by the nose. It's not in the whispering, but in the herbs themselves that the power lies."

"Do you heal people?" Hryhoriy did not relent.

"I help them occasionally," the fellow admitted finally. "I give people advice, herbs. People become ill, so one needs to save them somehow."

Skovoroda felt awkward because of the persistence with which he had badgered the beekeeper to find out whether he was an herbalist. In an effort to atone for his trespass, he spoke seriously, demurely, like a colleague: "Of course, one must. One must... I once heard that in India when someone is bitten by a scorpion, they take it and rub it into the fresh wound. And it helps! There are plenty of scorpions there, and so each house has a vessel with them floating in oil."

"Apart from containing poison, their bodies must contain a force to combat it," the old man said after a short while. And asked: "Can you play something for the soul?"

It was already growing dark. In the west a red selvage of glints was still dying away, while in the east the world was swathed in thick gloom. The day was falling asleep, exhausted. Not a rustle. Silence. Stars ran out onto the clear field of the sky...

Hryhoriy brought his guelder rose flute to his lips, took a breath to transform it into the sorrow of a melody and grew silent; the forest maestro himself broke into song overhead. The nightingale gave a tweet or two and then launched into song, warbling away....

"I can't, father," Hryhoriy whispered. "It's impossible to compete with such a singer."

The old man nodded, closed his eyes, listening.

The forest reverberated with song. These songs, these melodies, this evening spring concert did not die away for a moment over the settlements and apiaries, in the riverside undergrowth and impassable brush, in the gullies and the valleys.

"The earth is singing..."

"Forsooth."

As they were bedding down inside the hut hung with all kinds of herbs and blossoms, Hryhoriy again heard the girl's voice over the nightingale's twitter. He strained his ears – it melted away and disappeared. But as soon as he closed his eyes it filled his chest in a wave. His heart hammered away again.

"Father, whose settlement is that in the birch grove?" he asked the beekeeper softly.

"By the roadside?"

"Yes."

"Taken a fancy to the lass?"

"No..."

"Go on! If I could shed forty years... It's Major's settlement."

"So, she's of noble birth?"

"Not at all. Major is his nickname. He's a commoner or a Cossack. They bought the apiary and a slice of forest four years ago and set up house. They've come from far away somewhere."

And as he fell asleep Hryhoriy heard not only the nightingales, but also a grand, sorrowful song about a Cossack who sought a road to the Sich, and about a sweetheart who bathed his tracks in tears.

* * *

She appeared several days later, at noon.

Skovoroda was sitting in the shade and reading a Hebrew Bible given to him by Myslavsky when they parted. There had been a generous shower recently and everything had changed colour, shimmering and glistening. Drinking the dew with the nectar, the meek, wet bees dried their small wings in the sunshine. The trees, the grasses, the flowers – everything strained toward the sun with a rustle.

Swallows soared through the sky earnestly, joyously. Somewhere nearby in the forest, cuckoos counted someone's future years in eager rivalry. Covered in pollen and petals, bedewed, the beekeeper returned from the forest and, sitting deep in thought, sorted through his curative booty.

"A good day to you..." someone's timid voice reached them.

Skovoroda looked up and saw the girl on the path. She was slender, black-haired, with a plait reaching below her waist, and with eyes filled with a kind of desperate grief... It was the Major girl!

"Good health to you too," the beekeeper replied hollowly. "What have you to say, daughter?"

"Something bad is happening to my dad." The girl took a step toward him. "He won't eat or sleep, keeps mentioning our late mother and keeps being horrified by something."

"Has this been going on for long?"

"Since the day before yesterday."

The old man sighed.

"Please help, dear gramps!"

"If only I could, Olenka." The beekeeper spread out his hands. "I heal the body. But his soul is ailing... Hryhoriy, perhaps you can help? This is in your parish."

Skovoroda's eyes were fixed on the forest girl and he could barely make out what was wanted of him.

"How can I help, father?" he replied hoarsely. "I'm no priest..."

"You're a sage, a teacher."

Olena wept silently. Without grimacing or sobbing. Severe, restrained in her grief, she stared into the forest, beyond the apiary, and heavy niggardly tears slowly rolled down her cheeks.

"I'll come, agreed." Hryhoriy put down the Bible. Those tears burnt him, as if they had fallen not on the girl's blouse, but upon his impressionable, tender heart.

Gangly, sweeping like a poplar, the girl stepped lightly, softly forest-like. She was about twenty years old, perhaps more. A kind of dignity, self-respect, or natural wisdom gave her face an extra-terrestrial beauty, more serious than her age warranted, but so attractive that it was impossible to look away.

In an effort to dissipate the girl's charm, Hryhoriy decided to talk with her, to assure himself that she was an ordinary woman and, in the main, to find out something about their life and her father's past, which probably held the key to his illness.

"You live alone with your father?" he asked calmly and deliberately, somewhat indifferently.

"Yes. Why?" The girl grew wary.

"Nothing... Did your mother die long ago?"

"Been five years now."

"Must have been ill a long time, eh?"

"No. She was badly shaken when our house burnt down."

"And father too?"

"Of course. We barely got out..."

"From the fire?"

"From the *palanka*."

"The horde?"

"Not at all! The Tatars were afraid of us," she answered, as if striking with a sabre.

"Who then?"

She said nothing. Squatting, she picked a stalk of bluebells and stole an intent glance at the stranger.

Hryhoriy cowered, realising that the girl was afraid of telling him the whole truth. He reproached himself for his inquisitiveness and sought the quickest way out of this unpleasantness. He had been convinced many a time: if you seek confidence, then don't be secretive yourself. And so therefore once more he resorted to this wondrous expedient.

"I've spent five years teaching students in our famous Kharkiv," he said affably and sincerely, as only simple-minded souls can speak. "They drove me out too."

"And where are you now?" the girl responded immediately.

"Here!" Skovoroda stopped.

She smiled, picked a yellow flower and asked timidly: "Do girls study there?"

He drew his arms apart.

"There are no women in the collegium."

Like girls among Cossacks, impetuous birches flashed white among the oaks. A colourful flood of flowers splashed underfoot. The sun scattered its rays about.

Olena ran out onto the forest clearing.

"There's our house and apiary!" she said joyously. And suddenly faded, knitting her brows.

Without looking back, she went ahead.

Hryhoriy trailed after her as if in a dream. An alarming and joyous premonition of certain upheavals and changes in his capricious fate kept flooding into his chest and intoxicating his heart and brain, relenting, melting, and leaving a mournful emptiness.

Olena waited for him by the gate and led him to the house through a small tidy yard.

Major lay in bed. Thin, swarthy, with a long, hooked nose and arms thrown onto the sheets, he resembled a steppe falcon who had strained his wings in flight and had fallen, utterly exhausted.

"Daddy dear, I've brought you a doctor," Olena said tenderly.

Major didn't bat an eyelid. He was awake, looking somewhere into a corner toward the ceiling, moaning.

"Peace to your house!" Skovoroda announced triumphantly and came up to the ailing man. "Get up, old fellow, and let's have lunch, because I haven't even had breakfast yet!"

The fellow only blinked a lacklustre eye at him and raised an eyebrow. "What's paining you?"

"Nothing... And that's that," he answered.

"Terrified, eh?" Hryhoriy asked. He spoke out loud on purpose, to dispel the oppressive silence of the settlement, into which the host had sunk. "Even the wide world is no longer dear to you, right?"

A slight convulsion passed across the sick man's face.

"You must be a good doctor – it's like you're looking into my soul," he said softly and hoarsely.

"He's all the way from Kharkiv, daddy dear," Olena added.

"I was thinking: you don't look as if you're from Valky..." The patient cheered up. "Curing aristocratic officers there?"

"At times. Most often from vainglory and haughtiness."

"Oh, that's our magnates' greatest ailment now," Major said, sitting up in bed. "They treat Cossacks and commoners like their own cattle... Olena!" he yelled suddenly. "Why are you dallying about there, darling? Hurry up and get us something to eat. Or the dear doctor will wilt completely from hunger."

He threw off the blanket and lowered his bony yellow feet to the floor.

"When you arrived, dear sir, things seemed to clear for me," he began trustfully, and raised a trembling arm: "All I see is smoke, smoke, smoke... Blood dripping from the whip..."

"Do you have a large apiary?" Hryhoriy asked, to distract him from his reminiscences.

Major began to blink rapidly and suddenly smiled: "I hear a bee buzzing... I can smell bee bread and wax... Olena, have you been in the apiary?"

"This morning," she placed some boiled dumplings on the table. "There'll be a rich harvest – the blossom is so lush."

Cheering up, Olena seemed to become even more beautiful: spangles glittered in her eyes, her face reddened while her nimble long arms flew about, weaving here and there.

For a while the men sat in silence and admired this hazel-eyed whirlwind. And then Major again knitted his brows, darkened all over, as if before a storm, and groaned so pitifully, that Hryhoriy's soul filled with pain.

"If only Nastia could see a glimpse of this…"

"There's no need to fret, uncle," Skovoroda took hold of his arm. "One shouldn't have such deep regret for things which have been lost. Better rejoice at what you have left: your life, health, the sun, rest, work, such a lovely daughter…"

"My daughter is genuine gold," Major said. "Hard-working is one thing, but she's a real beauty too…"

"Daddy, go on, tuck in!" The girl blushed and, placing stewed fruit on the table, ran out of the house.

Skovoroda left only toward evening, even though the host was adamant that he should stay. However, Hryhoriy was implacable: woe to the moth which circles around a fire. He promised to come back the next morning, bowed before the girl for her hospitality, and dived into the forest like a fish into water.

∗　∗　∗

From that day on Major rejoiced at Hryhoriy's arrival each day, like a child happy to see its mother. Slowly he recuperated and his faith in life, the world, and humanity returned steadily. The horrors and spectres of the distant past weighed on his mind less and less. Finally, having recovered completely, he revealed to Hryhoriy the grievous experience which had stopped him from living out his last years in Zaporozhia. He recounted with sorrow and pain, but reasonably, without the signs of affliction which had plagued him earlier. When he recalled his wife, he wept furtively, stealthily wiping his miserly Cossack tears, and began to lambast the nobility, which had flourished even in the free Wild Steppe.

They sat in the shade under a young apple tree and chatted quietly, as befitted good people. Taut green buds swooned in the sun above them and a little to one side; against the white background of the dwelling, a magnificent row of peonies burnt with an irrepressible flame. A song of longing came from somewhere in the vegetable patch behind the house. It beckoned, filling the chest with a sharp pain. Hryhoriy could not imagine how he would live without it, and had therefore decided that morning to resume his travels. He had come now to say his final goodbyes, but couldn't bring himself to do so. He sadly eyed this lovely corner and its keeper, caught the sounds of Olena's voice and could not find the strength to break the bonds of goodwill.

"Well then, Ivan Hnatovych," he spoke up at last, "it's time I left!"

"Where to?" Major sensed bad tidings.

"I've been a guest in your Valky much too long..."

"Fear God, Hrytsko!"

"God bless you for your hospitality and your kindness. I'll be off."

"Perhaps we've offended you in some way?"

"No, you were like family to me. I am truly grateful to fate for having brought me to your threshold, but there's no need to abuse its benevolence."

Major began to fuss about in despair, not knowing how to stop his guest, who had appeared in his life like a sun and now wanted to disappear.

"Stay at least a month, at least a few days!"

"I can't."

"Why not?" Major grabbed at his arms.

After a silence and overcoming the desire to submit to fate's kindness, Hryhoriy had to raise his defences a little.

"As one Hungarian Turk once said: I must either drive this camel out or immediately make tracks out of here..."

"What camel? Oh Lord!" the host did not understand the allusion and called out: "Olena, daughter dear, come here quickly!"

The rascal knew whom to call to his aid. Now Hryhoriy might as well heft his feet onto his shoulders and take to his heels posthaste. Instead, he became rooted to the table and saw through the house as she straightened her back in the vegetable patch, blew a lock of hair from her face and made her way to her father.

"Hryhoriy Savych is leaving us!" Major said, as soon as Olena appeared from behind the house.

She stopped, as if tripping over something, smiled sorrowfully and said: "Each has his own path, dad. Only it's a pity my hopes won't be realised..."

"What hopes?" Skovoroda asked sullenly.

"I wanted to ask you to teach me to read and write..."

"You?"

She nodded and blushed.

"Lord Almighty, I completely forgot!" Major clapped his hands. "Teach her, Hryhoriy; don't let her spend her life in ignorance. You told us such lovely things! Although she's a girl, she's intelligent and has a good memory. I showed her the alphabet and by evening she was already reading!"

Well, that was it. Farewell to the villages and people he had wanted to see, the spreading paths of carefree travel, which stretched obediently and gently before his feet, farewell to thoughts which were born only on the road. How could he say 'no' to a person who sought knowledge!

Major was still waving his arms about, passionately arguing, but Hryhoriy did not hear him. He listened in alarm as his recent firm resolve of escaping into the wide world to outsmart human nature was disintegrating to dust inside him. He had been the field of battle, where two opposing forces – the soul and the mind – had met in fierce combat. This battle had been going on inside him for quite a few days now, and still, he could see no end to it.

"To tell you the truth," Major's voice reached him from far off, "I feel much more at ease when you are visiting us or staying somewhere nearby.

"I'll stay," Hryhoriy said wearily. "For a month or two..."

"God bless your kind soul," Major whispered, deeply moved. "I'll be grateful 'til my dying day!"

"I'll go back to weeding then," the girl said hastily and ran off.

"Lessons begin tomorrow morning!" Hryhoriy called after her.

"P'raps I should go to town and buy a Psalter, some paper, and an inkwell full of ink?" Major asked smoothly.

"As you wish," Hryhoriy remarked indifferently and left the yard. "Careful there, mister teacher," he whispered to himself deep in the forest. "This isn't a class of students for you, but a Zaporozhian nymph with the body of Venus and the spirit of a Spartan woman."

* * *

Olena really was unusually clever. By the Feast of Maccabaeus she already knew more than the louts who were accepted into first year at the collegium. And within another week she could freely read Latin.

Impressed by such amazing talent, Hryhoriy gave her a Latin poem (which he had composed recently and had not yet sent to Kovalynsky) and asked her to memorise it by morning. She took it and placed it next to the books in the corner.

"How kind you are, Hryts," she whispered gratefully.

The whole night Hryhoriy dreamt of the poem, the girl, her eyes, her voice. That magical, tender 'Hryts', which she had uttered for the first time, echoed like music through his heart. No, even better! He recalled her words, questions, movements, and smiles and sensed the duel inside him abating, dying away – the soul was victorious. He wasn't worried by this, but on the contrary rejoiced at the mind's defeat. Although now it wasn't the beauty whom he feared, but Olena the close friend, an unusually clever and wise girl, whose intellect was no worse than her figure and face.

He awoke as dawn was breaking. The entrance was hung with an old rug and the hut smelt even more strongly of herbs. The old man slept with a whistle, but when Hryhoriy shifted about, putting his shoes on, he responded meekly:

"Can't sleep, sonny?"

"Like a nightingale in spring."

"Your spring's probably come."

"At forty odd years?"

"Whenever destiny decrees it."

Throwing a coat over his shoulders (the Apple Feast of the Saviour had already passed and the nights were cold), Hryhoriy stepped out of the hut. A mist hung over the apiary and in the valley along the entire length of the forest edge. Thick and white, like milk. The dew had bent the grasses and they responded to each touch with a shower of heavy cold drops. The old shaggy lindens stood in sleepy delirium...

Hryhoriy left the apiary and wandered off to the forest along a path which he had himself beaten during the summer. Holding up the vaults of their crowns, the gangly trees stretched straight up like columns, making it seem as if one was walking about in an endless temple. It was so quiet and sonorous, that every sound – be it the crackle of a twig or the scrape of boots – could probably be heard half a verst away. The mist soon thinned and hung in light skeins, then disappeared completely, and through the trees in the east one could see the birth of a new August day.

Still, it was too early to go to the Majors. And so, before he reached the settlement, Hryhoriy turned to the left. He seemed to be in no hurry, but his heart thudded like a woodpecker striking a hollow trunk. Something incomprehensible, strange, was happening to him: it died away, then hammered quickly, then filled his body with a faint, sharp pain. Each day and each night it drew Hryhoriy into this birch stand, toward the settlement, stopping him from leaving Valky and the apiary, from continuing on his way. He had long since abandoned the Bible, prayed only in the evening, and even then, only when the beekeeper was by his side, and then ever more indifferently, without any pain, recalling those who had done him and other people injustice. There was serenity here, kind people, and an honest piece of bread could be earned not by word-fornication, but through calluses and sweat. Here there was the sincere heart of a woman who could forever become his closest, faithful friend. Here he would be able to read, reason, and expose the hypocritical world in his writings. And there would be happiness – true, earthly, tangible happiness, not something phantasmagorical, like a mist.

Once more he came up to the settlement fence! Oh Hryts, Hryts... No, she said it more tenderly, so... God, was this really not a dream? He touched the wattle fence with his hand, picked up a red apple. No, it wasn't his imagination! He strained his ears: from somewhere beyond the orchard, beyond the apiary (probably in the cowshed), he could hear taut spurts, sounding like a cat purring. Olena was milking the cow. Major must have already left for the fields – he would be ploughing today. Dry oak logs were burning in the oven and something was boiling, bubbling away. Fragrant pears and plums were drying on the hearthstone...

He returned to the forest, got his flute and, leaning back against two birches growing side by side, began to play, losing himself in a dreamy-sad song about the forest, about a girl who was more lovely than anything in the world, and about a vagrant's heart which had known no kindness and dreamed of a happy future.

He came into the yard after the sun had risen over the trees. Olena came running out and greeted him first: "Good day to you, mister teacher."

Hryhoriy looked up at her and she hushed, growing wary. Oh, these girls: they could read everything in one's eyes, as if they were an open book!

"Well, how's the lesson?" he frowned.

"I learnt it yesterday."

"That can't be..."

"By God, it's true. Want me to recite it?"

She brought her brows together so comically and, looking off somewhere into the forest, past the teacher, began to speak in his 'Latin' voice:

Si sit vita beata intus, cur, inquis ad illam
Grex hominum rarus tamque pusillus adit...

"Wonderful!" Hryhoriy stopped her. "Now you're a true Latin."

Sighing joyously, she asked: "What is the poem about?"

"Happiness."

"That's interesting! Can you translate it for me...?"

"'You ask, if life's happiness is in each of us, then why do so few people ever achieve it?'" Skovoroda began elatedly. "Oh, this is because they find it hard to control their soul and because they have not yet learnt to tame their passions. The inexperienced rider gallops along tortuous roads, over hills, and through deep ravines if he has no control over his horse. Those who fail to control an irrational soul with their mind, rush headlong over water and dry land, through sword and fire."

Olena thought for a long time.

"Back home in Kamianske one centenarian Cossack said that his happiness came from the same place as freedom," she said at last. "Must the passion for freedom be tamed too?"

Hryhoriy was flabbergasted at first.

"The old fellow was a wise man, my word," he drawled slowly, giving it careful consideration. "The poem speaks about unrealised aspirations. Striving for them brings people only suffering. Be satisfied with what you have, and you will be happy for life."

"And what about freedom, Hryts? It is always illusory..."

"Oh, you're a philosopher!" Hryhoriy said cheerfully, although inside he immediately felt anxious about his model of happiness.

"What is a philosopher?"

"A person who can think wisely and seek the truth where others cannot. I wouldn't live without freedom," he added resolutely, firmly.

"Me neither!" the girl said fervently.

A wave of happiness rose in Hryhoriy's soul, splashing into his chest and his head. He barely managed to stop himself from embracing this steppe goddess, from pressing her close to his heart. Beauty and intellect...

"Is there anything in the house to breakfast on?" they suddenly heard from outside and the old Major entered the yard. "Or has the girl whiled away the time chatting to the swain…"

"There is, there you are, dad!" Olena dashed into the house.

"Good health to you, Hryhoriy," Major offered his big heavy hand. "Well, how are the lessons going?"

"Good. No, even very good."

"And why not – with such a great teacher!"

"The student carries all the blame."

Major shrugged his shoulders and laughed.

"Ivan Hnatovych," Hryhoriy exclaimed, "you've no idea how clever Olena is! It's simply a marvel! I've been around the world but have yet to meet such a wise and gifted person, let alone a woman!"

"And such a beautiful one?" Major asked. And said sorrowfully: "I thought exactly the same thing when I met my darling Nastia…"

"Beautiful that she is, very beautiful!" Skovoroda admitted frankly.

Major looked back at the door to the house, took the teacher by the arm and led him aside, toward the wattle fence.

"To tell you the truth, I've already heard all this," he whispered conspiratorially.

"Who from?"

"From Olena, of course…"

"She said as much about herself?"

"Why no – about you."

Skovoroda closed his eyes. He was breathless from joy! He did not like being praised, but this time Major's words were like a song to him. He had never guessed that so much happiness could be lurking in a person's praise. Until now he had considered this to be a trick which only had an effect on children and spiritually wretched, envious people. Perhaps he had become childish? Small wonder that it was said that love made fools of wise men, angry men meek and quiet people tempestuous.

"I wanted to tell you, Hrytsko," Major began timidly. "Maybe it's time you ceased your travels and ended this vanity of vanities. Take Olena, this settlement, and live like other people… With me at your side. And my grandchildren."

Although emotionally, he painted the future staidly, thoughtfully, just as he saw it. It was true happiness, earthly and eternal.

Hryhoriy heard him out in silence, then bent over, took his brown right hand, which resembled a loaf of rye bread, and kissed it.

"Olena, dear daughter!" Major called out.

*   *   *

The wedding was held in October. Though neither the Majors nor Skovoroda had any kith or kin here in Valky, kind people were found who helped organise everything properly. There was a betrothal, a wedding bread, and a bridal shower.

Hryhoriy set off after the bride from the beekeeper's yard. Old Mrs. Healer (as she was dubbed), acted as Skovoroda's mother, strewing grain and money upon him, blessing him and seeing him all the way to the gate, where the wedding train was waiting for the groom. Around the cart, generously padded with straw and covered with a colourful carpet, were the best man, the groomsmen and other wedding personages. All were on horseback and armed with sabres; some were in Cossack dress, others in hussar garb. From the middle of summer there were no longer any Cossacks in Slobodian Ukraine, replaced by hussars of her highness the empress.

Hryhoriy was picked up like a colonel and placed on the groom's seat. The carter whipped the horses, the cart lurched forward, and the wedding train set off. The groomsmen, who had already had a drink or two, broke into song.

Skovoroda sat as if chained. Perhaps it was the new, unusual clothes, or the change in status, his role as groom, but something pained his heart and stopped joy from spreading out its wings.

For over a month now Hryhoriy had lived as if in a mist; he was being spun around in the pre-wedding whirlwind, washed and scrubbed, in an effort to turn him from a philosopher and vagrant Cossack into a staid man and a farmer.

"Our groom seems to be grieving!"

"Because he hasn't married for so long!"

"P'raps he's afraid!"

"When this one sinks her fingers into you, lads..."

There was laughter and joking. And more singing. The forest cackled, tearing the melody to pieces, and this spurred the boys on, making them want to sing even more, to utter witticisms and to taunt the no longer young groom, who had certainly trodden on the toes of one of them...

The road was in engulfed in yellow-red flames. The oaks, birches and maples stood in sumptuous garments, strewing gold under the horse's feet with a silent tolling. This road had brought Hryhoriy face to face with his destiny, here he had first heard her beckoning voice and stopped, smitten to his very heart, just as the seagoing Hellenes had been stricken by the singing of the dangerous sirens...

At the gate the guests were met by the bridesmaids. Nimbly dismounting from their graceful Cossack horses and turning up their moustaches, the groomsmen rushed up to the bridegroom, helped him off the cart and led him off to the house.

Never had these twenty to thirty steps from the wattle gate to the threshold seemed so long and so difficult to Skovoroda. He seemed to be ascending a hill where he had never been and where countless novelties and surprises awaited him. How simple life was for these Cossacks, his groomsmen, for the women and girls who had packed the yard! Together, in a community, they were like a river with streams. But he was alone. And also chained in the fetters of intellect, which sought to perceive everything, to seek the Great Truth and to arrive at the essence, the concealed verity of not only the world, the cosmos, but of man himself. Oh, how difficult it was to live for those who knew the price of wisdom and who were aware of their supremacy and superiority in relation to everyone they came into contact with! Such people were martyrs...

Today Olena was like a slender pink hollyhock. She did not fuss about, did not try to weep. Calm, serene, and pensive, she performed her difficult role according to custom staidly and diligently.

The groomsmen dressed her in red boots and sat her on an upturned kneading trough placed in the middle of the room. The bridesmaids asked in a chorus:

"Mister matchmaker, and you too, father and mother, allow your child's plait to be unbraided!"

Olena went pale.

Moved to the hilt, Skovoroda watched the girl who would become his wife today, his companion in grief and joy, his closest and most loyal friend.

He didn't have a drop of doubt: she would warm his heart, which had been cooled by the winds of travel, teach him to live in comfort, bear him children... God, in a year or two he would become a father! And then... Then he would take his sons to Kyiv, to the academy! Samuyil would be surprised...

And at this point a harsh frost entered his soul: "And you, Hryhoriy?! Are you ready to accept the estate of farmer, husband, father?"

"Yes, I am."

"Will you love your wife and children all your life?"

"I will."

"And will you plough, sow and harvest the bread yourself?"

"Certainly..."

"And you won't leave the settlement; you won't ever again want to feel the wind of freedom, to taste water from new springs?"

"I don't know..."

"You'll throw away your books, forget the wise Romans and the great Hellenes, and you won't venture beyond your field in your thoughts?"

"No."

"Your heart will become stale and you will blink with utterly indifferent eyes as your neighbours suffer in the yoke of slavery?"

"That will never happen!"

"You'll do battle with the nobles and defend your people and truth with might and main?"

"Yes. For I am a philosopher and a defender of verity."

"And you will sacrifice to verity your wealth, your peace, and even your own destiny?"

"I will!"

"And their happiness?"

"Whose do you mean?"

"Your wife's, your children's..."

Skovoroda was bathed in a cold sweat. He looked at the bride as if through a mist, looked at the bridesmaids who were dressing her and singing sonorously and sadly:

> *Why weren't the nightingales singing,*
> *When the orchards blossomed,*
> *Why wasn't Olena weeping,*
> *When her plait was unbraided...?*

Once she was dressed, the groomsmen hurriedly removed the trough, and in its place brought out a small bench covered with a sheepskin coat turned inside out. Major took down the icon and, holding it in his hands, sat down on the bench.

"Time to be blessed," someone whispered sharply and nudged Hryhoriy toward the bride, who was already standing before her father.

Major rose, blessed them and, handing the icon to one of the bridesmaids, first kissed his daughter, and then his son-in-law.

"Ivan Hnatovych... Ivan Hnatovych," Hryhoriy began. But he had already been picked up and carried out of the house.

Soon he was back on the cart and watched as *svakhas* and bridesmaids helped Olena onto another cart. Everything proceeded according to tradition, without any hold-ups, like a river flowing along. Now that they were seated and had set off, the *svakhas* began to wail:

> *Oh, early on Sunday morn,*
> *The blue sea shimmered.*
> *There Olena drew water,*
> *After which she began to drown...*

Skovoroda clutched at this tragic word and began to conjugate it: I am drowning, you are drowning, he is drowning, we are drowning... Oh, how many are presently drowned in life's sea! Melted away like the meadow mist... They shouted, dreamed, sought the roots of verity, and swore forever to be knights of holy truth, but then folded their arms and sank to the bottom like rocks. The pygmies...

"And you?"

"I'm not a pygmy!"

"But you're drowning..."

"No, I'm not. I'm only changing my estate. And striving for a little comfort and happiness..."

"That's the justification of all drowning people."

"Nonsense!"

"No, it's true!"

Save me, save me, brother,
Pray do not let me perish,
Pray do not let me perish
There in the deep blue sea...!

Skovoroda lunged to get off the cart, but he was held back by the strong hands of the groomsmen. He slinked like an eagle in a cage, feverishly attempting to find a way out. He realised that he was in fact drowning, sinking to the bottom, where hundreds, thousands, of former brave warriors, fighters, and thinkers were lying. Some had grown weary, drawn by the luring mirage of happiness, while others had simply betrayed the passions of their youth. Drowned people were the most dangerous and most horrifying! They were eternally roasted by the fires of their conscience, and their souls rejoiced at the misfortune of others. Hryhoriy heard their guffaws, felt the touch of their hands, which grabbed at his feet and dragged him toward them into the silent abyss.

The wedding train entered Valky. Crowds lined the wattle fences, the small fry raced after them. There was laughter, stamping, and singing.

Only outside the church did everything die down. Although the service hadn't yet finished, there was a crowd of people on the church atrium. Apart from him and Olena there were two other young couples smitten by happiness, groomsmen, bridesmaids, *svakhas*. A minstrel softly drawled some sad song. Children dashed about among the adults as if in a forest of trees.

Skovoroda jumped down from the cart and, accompanied by his grooms-men, stepped resolutely toward the bride. She greeted him with an alarmed gaze and, warming him with her smile, took hold of his hand.

God, how he didn't want to leave her! He was aware that in doing so he would bring insult and grief to the girl for years to come, maybe even for life, that they would never meet again, never talk...

There was a hubbub, a scraping of feet: the service inside was finishing and the populace of Valky flowed onto the atrium in a cloud. The wedding personages began to fuss about beside their princes and princesses. The priest was about to appear at any moment, to lead them into the church.

"Forgive me, Olena," Hryhoriy said hoarsely.

"For what?"

"Forgive me. I love you very, very much."

Blushing all over, she gratefully squeezed his cold hand.

He answered the grip, lightly freed his hand and, taking advantage of the confusion which arose as the tall grey-haired priest emerged from the church, dived into the crowd.

THE NINTH NET

An honest, good person finds it much harder to cause someone grief, than to suffer themselves. The wronged person has the compassion and support of others. While the wrongdoer has nothing apart from the pangs of conscience and self-admonishment.

Right up until the spring Hryhoriy punished himself with the pain he had inflicted on the good, dear people left behind in distant Valky, who suffered now because of him. He now lived near Kharkiv in the monastery's cottage where seven years earlier his compatriot Nychypir had taken refuge. Rather, he did not live, but slowly smouldered on a fire of self-expiation. By the end of winter, he had dried up and turned yellow, like a debarked oak log. The cowherds, who shared their bread and squalid lodgings with him in the small cramped house, only sighed sadly and sought salvation for him either in milk, or herbs, or simply in friendly conversation.

And something finally helped. Possibly time...

One day in early spring, left alone in the house, Hryhoriy put on his stiff boots, threw on his coat, and hesitantly left the cottage. His lungs filled with tart air steeped in osier and sunshine. To remain on his feet, he was forced to grab hold of the roughly hewn doorpost and wait until the world stopped swimming around him. He stood and breathed, and breathed, imbibing the invisible curative potion; people drank water like this on hot days. The high spring sun of March was generous with its warmth and light. In the sunlit patches the snow was melting and gurgling away in streams. Drips rang out as they struck the ground.

Squinting and reeling like a drunk, Hryhoriy set forth into the half-slumbering world. With a pleasant squelch the brownish slush of the snow gave way under his boots. A gentle, warm breeze swayed the tumescent branches, as if waking the trees and giving momentum and vigour to their life-giving juices. It spurred Hryhoriy on, or flirted with him, tearing off his shaggy old hat, or grovelled at his feet like a faithful dog which had not seen its master for a long while. White clouds sailed across the deep blue sky from the south like geese. Standing in the middle of the orchard and surveying this boundless flock, Hryhoriy became filled with strength, like the resurrected Lazarus. His gaunt, bony body was becoming resilient and strong. It was as if he had been bound up until recently, and now the fetters had been removed and he was given free rein to his thoughts and chest. Breathing deeply and often, he summoned his spirits, drew together his mighty harrowed freedom and directed it toward his own soul, where gloom was still nesting. And everything crumbled and welled up inside him, as if the ice had broken and began to move, incessantly and mightily. An unknown sweet sensation immediately overwhelmed the tiniest fibres of his body and ignited a bonfire. And a moment later that fire, that magical force, was swirling through his veins. Skovoroda scooted off and, without feeling his hands or feet, began to dart about the orchard, feeling liberated. He was driven by fervent rapture, and felt as if he had awakened or been resurrected. Everything heaved before his eyes, gently fusing into a single whole and rang out with joy. The streams, the trees, the cottage, the azure blue of the heavens and the clouds trumpeted glory to the sun, a praise to life, a hosanna to summer, which was already on its way!

When a coach drawn by four horses drew up to the cottage, Skovoroda was standing under an apple tree, weeping quietly.

"Hryhoriy Savych? Skovoroda?" A brilliant young officer ran up to him.

"Yes, that's me."

"His excellency is summoning you!"

"Which excellency?"

"The governor!"

"I don't know such a fellow. We're not acquainted," Hryhoriy said sharply and went back inside the house.

"You are being invited by Yevdokym Oleksiyovych Shcherbynin," the officer announced, catching up to him.

"Ah!" Skovoroda stopped. "I've heard of him... Wait, I'll be a moment."

Brushing his boots with the cowherds' pitch and girding himself with a belt, Hryhoriy left the house and got into the waiting coach. The fellow recoiled and called out to the coachman: "Let's go, let's go!"

Shcherbynin met Hryhoriy on the front steps.

"Hryhoriy Savych, I'm glad to see you in my household! Welcome!" He shook his hand amiably and led him up the stairs past amazed noblemen, lackeys and aides. "I've been told that you're a sage, and besides that a musician. Is that true?"

"I play a little."

"What in particular?"

"The violin, flute, *bandura*, psaltery."

"Oho!" The governor beamed. "You're a veritable treasure! I'm also a lover of music. Every time our regimental orchestra struck up a tune, I would freeze, but my beastly feet strove to march of their own accord about the square."

In the study, which they soon entered, he invited Skovoroda to sit down, sat down beside him and, screwing up his blue eyes framed in white lashes, he suddenly asked: "Why don't you select an estate for yourself?"

"Good sir, our world is like a theatre," Skovoroda said slowly. "To play successfully and with praise one must accept only roles according to one's abilities. A person in the theatre is glorified and exalted not because of the importance of the role, but for his fine acting. I have thought this over many a time and am convinced that in the theatre of the world I can only play the simple and safe role which I am playing at present."

"But perhaps you have an ability to do something quite different, something which would be useful to the state, the world?"

"If there were such, I would have known by now."

"But habit and prejudices…"

"Good sir," Skovoroda would not allow him to finish, "if I suddenly felt that I was able to and wanted to butcher Turks, then without hesitation I would take up a sabre, don a shako, and become a hussar. Toil according to natural inclination is a delight. Why, for example, does a dog guard a flock of sheep day and night, even though it is in danger of being killed by wolves? A horse or a pig wouldn't do this, for they are not created for this, their nature is different."

"And what if a horse is made their protector?"

"The sheep will be unhappy! And the horse too."

"What's it to the horse!"

"To undertake what is not right for you, is a tragedy."

"Even when you are glorified for this and generously paid in gold and medals?"

"No one has become wiser or more talented from receiving medals and gold."

"That's the gospel truth," Shcherbynin sighed. "One can be stupid for all to see – and still be in the royal court, bedecked with awards, while another can be intelligent, clever – and while away his time in the backwaters, at the end of the world."

Hryhoriy barely restrained himself from smiling, or expressing insincere commiseration to the nobleman who had been thrown out of St. Petersburg. Ah, the poor fellow, he so much wanted to get under the tsarina's dress... Or rather her hand! Others were hanging around her there while he, the poor wretch, had to sit here and teach these natives how to submit to their landlords and how to serve her highness the empress. Oh, quite a bit had already been done!

"Are you pleased with your lot?" the governor suddenly asked.

"No. I would rather I not be dragged away by whoever, whenever it pleases them," Skovoroda replied sharply.

"Don't be angry, respected sir, that your learned peace has been upset!" Shcherbynin said, not without a note of wile. "I have not summoned you at my whim, although I've long dreamed of seeing you and to hold discourse with you, but this is a matter of business."

Hryhoriy made himself more comfortable and prepared to listen about this matter of urgency. Interesting, what could he have in common with this out-and-out public servant...

"Her majesty has allowed us the extra classes sought by the collegium," Shcherbynin now spoke officially, in all seriousness. "And recently I wanted to entrust you with the class of etiquette, which has been allowed as well. True, the bishop was against it… All the same, as you can see, I summoned you and have the honour to offer you this noble job."

He smiled affably, pleased with his power and his warmth, and settled into a gilded French armchair.

Hryhoriy was overcome with doubts. He was drawn to books, to pupils and teachers, he wanted to bring people benefit, to impart his knowledge to them, his anxious heart. But he was stopped by those changes which had been taking place these past three to four years. These days the collegium had only perhaps its name in common with that of the past. All the rest the tsarist servants had worked hard to transform into their manner of institution. A lot of Frenchmen, Germans and other foreigners had arrived. The student population had been changed too. For example, he would not have been accepted now, because he wasn't of noble birth, an aristocratic bastard.

"Are you pleased?" Shcherbynin asked.

"I don't know," Skovoroda shrugged his shoulders.

"Oh! Why's that?"

"I don't want to babble like a priest from the pulpit..."

"Then don't babble, dear chap! Teach as you wish. After all, you're not a priest. And consider that we need to educate warriors, obedient servants of the throne. We've no need of philosophers!"

"I'm a philosopher too..."

"You're a pilgrim, a teacher, a lover of the muses and the Bible," Shcherbynin said firmly, as if he had known Hryhoriy all his life, and not just this past half hour. "You're amazed at my familiarity?" He narrowed his eyes slyly. "Such is my position, title and function. I have hundreds of ears..."

"Informers are in fashion now," Hryhoriy said.

"The empire rests firmly on them!" Shcherbynin roared with laughter.

"And on bayonets..."

"Forsooth!" the governor puffed up his chest. "Without us military men the sovereign would be like a conductor without musicians!"

"Profoundly spoken."

"And why not. We're not rustics either! Though we never passed through the academy, we've been in the army from a young age. And that's a school in itself, brother, that none of your collegiums can..." Shcherbynin clicked his fingers and added, becoming gloomy: "If it depended on me, I would teach everyone in military companies. In five to six years, they'd all be like dolls. Like cutlasses – no feelings, no nations, no ancient traditions. One, two – and order everywhere. Forward – forward, back – back! True harmony."

Skovoroda rose to his feet, tired of listening: "All right, I agree."

"That's great!" Shcherbynin picked up a quill. He signed some document and rang a bell. The aide ran in. "Take this order and hand it to the school."

The fellow came up, twirled around and hurried out.

"Congratulations. I wish you success!" Shcherbynin stretched out his hand.

"I agree, your worship, but under one condition," Hryhoriy added.

"Yes?"

"I will teach without any renumeration."

The governor's eyebrows shot up, then fell and covered his eyes with snow.

"I don't understand," he said dryly and coolly. "How will you survive?"

"As I have till now. With the cowherds on the far bank of the Lopan River."

The governor shrugged his shoulders and smiled: "It's easier to empty the sea with a mug than to understand you Little Russians."

"Whichever you find easier," Hryhoriy responded and, saying farewell, left.

*　*　*

Lectures began on the Wednesday of Holy Week. When Hryhoriy ascended the pulpit no one in the class, let alone the collegium, had any inkling of the passions it would cause in Kharkiv and indeed the whole eparchy.

Running his gaze over the students and taking out his manuscript of lessons, Skovoroda cleared his throat and suddenly hurled into the over-crowded auditorium: "The world is asleep! And not just asleep, as it is said of the righteous man: 'If he falls, he won't shatter.' It is sleeping stretched out, in a deep sleep, as if knocked out cold! And the shepherds dare not wake it. No, they even stroke it: 'Sleep, sleep, don't be afraid! This a nice place, there's no need to be scared.'"

The class answered with laughter, zealous clapping.

His soul exploded with joy. Here was the moment for which he had left his isolation and had rushed blindly into the world, into a sea of passions and struggles! But he recalled Kraisky's prickly eyes, Iov's hypocrisy, the governor's military discipline, and he hid in the dark undergrowth of the Bible. The students listened in silence. They exchanged glances, as if surprised by his sudden deviation and seemed disappointed. Yakiv Pravytsky who greeted the start of the lecture most fervently, now sat downcast. Students were talking among themselves on the back benches... Obviously they were sick and tired of this Sunday school biblical morality and the clerical babble, which they had no choice but to swallow. This was great! For a thinking person was a genuine person. The future *homo novus*...

"Do you hear, Christian, with your heathen heart!?" Hryhoriy raised his voice. "Will you be lying on the ground much longer? Will you ever become a human being?"

A quiet murmur passed through the auditorium. Pravytsky lifted his downcast head and his eyes flashed with pride for his teacher and mentor, of whom he was always proud, even when the latter had been driven out.

"Genuine man – some seek him in the absolute rule of Augustus, in the times of Tiberius. Others sniff him out in Jerusalems and Jordans, in fasting or prayers. And still others attempt to find him in lay honours, in sumptuous palaces, in ceremonies, titles, and gold. Not there, not there!"

He spoke emotionally, imbuing each word and phrase with the fire of his soul, his great belief in the fact that true humanity and wisdom lay not where power and pomp reigned, but in the depths of the nation, among its sons who had grown up in hard toil and eternal squalor. As before, he hid in the shadow of the Bible from time to time, but now the students waited in silence for him to step out again and shine with the sun of his thoughts, so sharp, so unlike anything they had ever had hammered into them from this and other pulpits.

After the bell, no one left the classroom. The students clustered around the teacher in a dense bee swarm and showered him with questions.

"Tell us, where does one seek happiness?"

"Happiness is not dependent on the heavens or the earth. Do not seek it across the seas, don't beg for it from another person. You won't find it in palaces, or by crawling all over the Earth, or in holy cities such as Jerusalem. Seek it inside yourself. Understand yourself and live a life which reflects your character..."

"Happy is he who has a chest of gold!"

"With gold you can buy anything but happiness."

"You said our God has many names. Which of them is the most important or the truest?"

"God is intellect, verity."

"Then who created man?"

"Supreme wisdom! Out of ugly and wild monsters it moulded us into people, into animals capable of living in a society, in friendship. We differ from the wild animals because of charity and justice, and from cattle – because of moderation and intellect."

"Then why do priests tell us otherwise?"

"Priests aren't prophets either, they are mere mortals."

"But they're ordained!"

"Ordination and piety are not one and the same thing."

"What about the ceremony, the rite of ordination?"

"Ceremonies are like leaves shielding fruit or husks on grain. When this mask is deprived of its power, only hypocritical semblance and deceit remain."

"That's if the people know that. And what if they don't? Or feign being blind and deaf...?"

"Forsooth, in our times leaves and fruit are so often mixed together, husks with grain, ritual with true essence. Some have even more respect for the mask than piety."

Putting away his notebook, Hryhoriy left the classroom. A crowd of students trailed after him. They crossed the collegium in fervent discussion, past amazed teachers and pupils, and emptied in a river into the monastery yard. Such a thing had never happened before! The new prefect, who had replaced Kordet, decisively plucked two students out of the crowd and began to question them. Sometime later, becoming entangled in the long skirts of his cassock and breathing heavily in agitation, he ran off to the rector.

In a few days almost all the good and decent residents of Kharkiv were talking about the lectures and about the man Skovoroda, who was delivering them. And a week later Bishop Kraisky arrived from Belgorod and ordered that the heretical notebook be brought to him immediately, out of which Hryhoriy lectured on the substance of morality.

Everyone skulked about, awaiting his judgement in silence. He did not dally! In the afternoon of the following day Skovoroda was summoned to the residence of his grace, where the consistory court had already assembled.

"Sit down," Kraisky remarked grimly. He had become more rotund, more authoritative.

He pierced Skovoroda with his eyes, probably hoping to scare him with his unsparing gaze. Meek Iov was fidgeting about, as if he was sitting on something hard and prickly. The priests glanced curiously at the bishop, then at Hryhoriy.

"Is this your text?" Kraisky asked at last, lifting up the open notebook.

"It's mine." Hryhoriy answered.

"Did you write it when you were ill or emaciated after lent and work?"

"No, I wrote it while in good health."

"When did you become a priest?"

"I'm no priest."

"Then why have you gone out of your depth, attempting to understand God and the holy sacraments, which are under seven locks for lay people?"

"I am perceiving nature. It is not anyone's property or secret."

"God is not nature, as you repeat other people's heathen words, but an omnipotent, heavenly tsar. Even children know that!" The bishop raised his voice.

"What is fine for children, is not enough for grown men."

"You doubt the dogmas of the faith?"

"I seek verity."

"Which one?"

"There is only one."

"But how can you strive for something you already have! Jesus revealed verity to us. His apostles chewed over its hard nuts for us. Swallow, and ye shall be satiated..."

"If we are to swallow only chewed mush, then what are teeth for?"

"To hold back a foolish tongue!"

"Jupiter is raging." Skovoroda smiled.

"You're playing the buffoon again. Haven't you forgotten how your last jesting ended?"

"I was driven from the walls of the school, like Lucifer from God's kingdom," Hryhoriy sighed.

"That's just it! I wouldn't want to do the same again," the bishop added emphatically.

"Nor I," Skovoroda spread his arms apart.

His grace intently surveyed his taciturn brethren and suggested: "Burn this notebook, teach normally, and you'll be in God's kingdom."

"You're calling on me to violate the ninth commandment?"

"You've violated it already." The bishop picked up the notebook. "There is so much falsehood here!"

"Woe to the man for whom truth is falsehood," Hryhoriy countered.

The bishop's face became white with rage. Bowing his head, he breathed heavily for a long time.

"You want to teach me the truth?" he said brutally at last. "Who are you? A prophet, an apostle, or a patriarch?!"

"A human being."

"What rank is this?"

"The highest!"

"And so, you have this rank." Kraisky leaned back against his armchair. "How do you say we exalt you now – excellency, illustrious highness, or perhaps majesty?"

"No titles have yet been invented for us humans," Skovoroda said calmly. He knew for certain that this chimerical dispute would not sway Kraisky in the slightest, and he argued only for the sake of Iov and the other members of the court. He didn't expect any of them to come to his aid, however he wanted at least one of them to leave here with a doubt as to the bishop's integrity and the justice of what was happening here today.

"Have you ever seen such an insane fellow!?" Kraisky said contritely, addressing the consistories.

They sat as if they had not heard, their eyes buried in the table. Only meek Iov fidgeted about in his chair and some thin bald priest smiled timidly, catching his grace's formidable gaze.

"Invective is not always the best proof..." Skovoroda began.

"Quiet!" Kraisky yelled. "We're not students and don't need to be lectured by you!"

"I'm silent," Hryhoriy sighed. "The unjust always fear words of truth."

The bishop clenched his fists, which lay like two heavy hammers on the red velvet tablecloth.

"In my opinion, everything is clear," he said, barely able to control himself. "What medicine can't cure, iron will..."

"Inquisitors always liked the end of this recipe best of all," Hryhoriy added. "'What iron can't cure, fire will.'"

"We're not Catholics or inquisitors," Kraisky said forcefully. "We're merciful and long-suffering. But when something begins to rot in a healthy body, it is best to cast it out! Am I not right, holy fathers?"

The latter nodded reluctantly. Only meek Iov drew his head into his shoulders and closed his eyes, as if wanting to become miniscule, to disappear completely.

"Am I right, Iov?" Kraisky fell upon him like a hawk.

"I... I agree... God forbid..."

"Well, that's settled then," the bishop said wearily and threw the notebook at its author. "From now on, you, Hryhoriy Savych Skovoroda, are no longer a teacher here!"

"You did not appoint me, so it's not up to you to drive me out," Skovoroda said hollowly. "The governor..."

"That's not your worry." Kraisky smiled supremely and got up from the table. "I'll settle the matter with him."

Hryhoriy rose too. He took his notebook and slipped it into his pocket. Looking one last time at the completely withered judges, he suddenly understood, sensed with his whole being, that this was it, that he would no longer enter a classroom, would no longer warm his heart in the warmth of the curious, fervent eyes of students nor rejoice watching as children became men, and rustics turned into philosophers. Something snapped in his soul, like the branch of an apple tree heavy with fruit. However, strangely enough, he did not mourn that which had perished, but was enthused by the new green shoot which had sprouted at the break and flourished like grasses after a rainstorm. Strict judges love to watch the torment of the men they have convicted. They would have burst with malice had they peered into Hryhoriy's thoughts only a minute or two after the ritual of his destruction as a teacher.

Oh, *vita nova*, new life... However, he had in fact lived more on the road, than in Kharkiv prior to this. Now everything would fall into place and peace would reign in his soul. Although it was late, at forty-four he had finally understood himself and from now on he would live a life in harmony with his nature, and would not give in to the fanciful dream of serving the people like other educated, meek people. That was not his path. He was a traveller, a champion of verity, an apostle of truth and freedom! He was free to seek, this was his happiness.

* * *

One could teach anywhere – as long as one had something to teach. Hryhoriy had long understood this, so he left Kharkiv and the monastery's cottage without regrets or sorrow. The osier was flowering along the banks of the winding Lopan River, all manner of greenery strained toward the sun, the birds made their nests. Skovoroda didn't feel like leaving all this splendour so suddenly, and without much thought (for he was his own master!), he went upstream along the river. From his travels the previous year he had in mind a wonderful spot – an apiary amid the forest on the Lopan. A bubbling spring on the riverbank, ancient lindens, maples, and ash trees. It was simply a slice of paradise. And Lord Zemborsky, the keeper of the apiary, had invited him to drop by many a time, to live with him. Though he was rich and powerful, he had not become completely aristocratised and did not shun the bitter truth and his enslaved fellow brethren. Well, now he had the opportunity to drop by and live there a while. The pulpit had been taken away from him but pen and paper remained! See how fearfully the bishop had held his ill-fated thesis, as if it were a poisonous snake. The despots feared the truth. They bound it in iron so it wouldn't speak out, or they sprinkled it with gold so it would shine merrily and blind people's eyes. Neither fetters nor gold for him! He would hide in the dark wilderness and, like Plato, would write dialogues, in which he would teach how to understand the world, oneself, and verity.

He quickened his step, yearning to begin on his first original philosophical work, which twenty-five years later he would christen *Narcissus*.

Nothing had changed here in a year, as if time had no power over this small piece of the world. And even the beekeeper – a still young, moustached fellow – though somewhat gloomy – met him with the same avaricious smile and, showing him where the water and food were kept, hurried off somewhere, almost as if he had been expecting Hryhoriy's arrival.

Having snacked, Skovoroda took his books out of his bag, some paper and an inkwell filled with ink, and while the sun was still shining, set to work.

What should he begin with? Who would take part in this debate? Porfyriy, Iov... No, they had no place in a book which endured time and enmity, like this grove and this parcel of land. Kordet, Mykhailo? It was probably not worth bringing their thoughts and judgements before the insatiable eyes of those who smothered the human spirit... Who should he choose? Eureka! Lukash, or Luka. That, apparently, was the name of the taciturn, reclusive beekeeper who reigned here. Well then Luka, we'll talk about our perception of ourselves and prove that the main thing in a person is not the flesh, but their mind!

Let's open the holy Bible…

The mind, thoughts, the heart… What can spread the way thoughts do? Oh heart, you are an abyss, wider than the sea and the sky! Boundless, you embrace everything, and yourself you fit nowhere, into nothing.

What does the holy book tell us then? 'Your eyes will not go blind…'

Lord, how many there still were in this world unseeing in spirit, prostrated, grovelling before good and evil! Sometimes it is a pity to look at these creatures who have missed out on the almighty god of wisdom and have stopped halfway in human progress. Like parrots they repeat stranger's words, unable to live without an idol and with fear in their mind, like the devil fears frankincense.

Man, you are the receptacle of everything that is the best and the worst in the world…

Turning over several stiff, yellowed pages, his eyes rested on an expression similar to his own thoughts, his aim of healing those who had become blinded or had never been able to see: 'Listen to me, you stubborn of heart, you who are far from righteousness!' Hryhoriy took in the meaning of these words, as if testing their weight, their strength; he would whisper them, then utter them at the top of his voice, and slowly the clearing in which he was sitting and where the apiary was located, gradually began to fill with more and more people from the various villages, hamlets and towns he had visited in the past ten years. There were the wicked, the perfidious, the cunning, the haughty, the proud, the kind, the gentle, the meek… But most of them were lost, oppressed by fear, ready to do anything to survive under the enormous stone slab of the state aristocracy, which milled living souls into dust.

Hryhoriy was overcome with a great pity toward these unfortunates. Gradually that compassion was transformed into a fierce hatred directed at the millers and their servants.

Laying aside the Bible, he dipped his pen in the ink and began to write a song, instead of the planned book about understanding one's own self. From whence it had appeared, he could not say, but it had appeared and the unusual melody for this creation rang out. The words too were new and whimsical. This wasn't a psalm or a chant, rather a satire about the oppressors, lined with reflections about his own soul and destiny.

> *Each city has its own customs and rights;*
> *Equally each head has its own insights...*

Only a week later was the beginning of the book put to paper and Luka spoke out as an opponent. (Lukash remained silent.) Skovoroda became so engrossed in this 'dialogue' that he forgot all about food and could not resign himself to the fact that at night he was forced merely to content himself with deliberations about future duels between Luka and his Friend. (The Friend spoke on behalf of the author and argued what Hryhoriy had not finished arguing from the pulpit in Kharkiv.) He could have said of himself, quoting words from *The Song of Songs*: 'I was asleep, but my heart was awake.' His heart was not napping, it grieved for the human soul, trampled by the feet of savage monsters, who didn't give a damn that you were a human being, a rational creature and not some draught horse.

He wrote calmly, with restraint, taking inspiration from the Bible, seeking corroboration for his words in this heavenly book. But from time to time something would suddenly rebel inside him, screaming loudly, and poured out not as philosophical logic, but as satirical, mortal insults clothed in the garb of parables or fables. The world would not allow Hryhoriy to find peace in the wilderness, did not release him from its tight clutches. He fought back, read the Holy Scripture for hours on end, chewing over certain expressions with Luka or Cleopas and several other figures, which he had introduced; however, he could not devote himself entirely to his universal reflections. He struggled vehemently, stubbornly and, it seemed, had finally succeeded sometime in mid-summer.

However, Mykhailo and Yakiv arrived unexpectedly and brought bad news.

∗   ∗   ∗

It was a July morning, permeated with the smell of honey. Lukash had gone off somewhere and Skovoroda sat alone near the hut at a roughly made table. He could not write, an anxiety gripped his heart and mind, which stopped his thoughts from flowing freely. In the cool morning sunshine, which broke through the immobile branches, fast earnest bees whizzed past. A lively magpie whirled about the beekeeper's dwelling like a curious woman, and looked askance at the queer fellow who sat quietly outside for hours on end.

And suddenly, with a squawk, it took wing and disappeared into the undergrowth.

Reluctantly Hryhoriy looked up from his notebook… Heavens above, he had unexpected, but much desired guests! Bareheaded and barefoot, Skovoroda ran to meet the lads who were making their way across the clearing, smiling and squinting in fright at the bees flying around them.

"Mykhailo! Yakiv!"

He embraced them and kissed them as if they were sons whom he hadn't seen for an eternity. The students were moved too.

"You haven't forgotten your teacher. And I thought…"

"Come on, come on, Hryhor Savych!" Kovalynsky answered in a deep voice. He was already twenty. Time was like a river…

"All your friends remember you…"

"And your enemies too," Yakiv added hastily.

Mykhailo grabbed him by the elbow. The boy cringed and turned red.

"Well, how are things here?" Mykhailo asked and threw a deft eye about the apiary, the hut and the table. "Writing something, yes?"

"Yes, I'm writing, my dear Mykhailo. Did you arrive from Kharkiv today?"

"No. Yesterday evening. Spent the night in Huzhvy, with the landlord. Zemborsky brought us here."

"Have you had breakfast?"

"If it hadn't been for breakfast, we would have come earlier," Yakiv piped up and waved his arms about.

"Don't do that!"

"But they're buzzing in my eyes…"

"Let's go into the forest, or they might sting us," Mykhailo said, also looking warily at every bee which flew past.

Making fun of the cowards, Skovoroda led his visitors into the grove.

"Do you live alone here or in the company of the beekeeper?" Mykhailo asked, once they could no longer hear the buzzing of the bees.

"Alone mostly…"

"And you're not oppressed by the solitude?"

"Those who were born to deal with eternity find it more agreeable to live in fields, woods or orchards, than in cities."

"I could never do that," Mykhailo sighed.

"The Magpie asked the Eagle: 'Tell me, don't you get bored forever flying about in the sky?'

'I would never descend to the ground, were it not for bodily needs,' the Eagle replied.

'If I were an Eagle, I would never fly away from the city,' the Magpie announced.

'Me neither, if I was a Magpie,' the Eagle replied."

Mykhailo turned red.

"Hryhor Savych, whose fable is this?" Yakiv asked a little later.

Skovoroda shrugged his shoulders, but did not own up.

"Who knows... What's new with you at the collegium?"

"There are more Vikings now," Mykhailo said.

"How's Iov?"

"Whirling about. He wants to be nice to everyone. He bumped into me in the *museum* recently and asked about you, regretting that you mobilised so many against yourself..."

"Seeing once how various birds attacked the Owl, the Thrush asked the poor wretch: 'Don't you feel bad, that you're being pecked for no reason at all? It's absurd!'

'I don't find it strange,' the Owl replied. 'They peck each other too. And as for feeling bad, I find solace in the fact that I am attacked only by rooks, magpies and crows, while eagles and screech owls leave me alone. And the Athenians respect me too...!'

"And as for me," Hryhoriy added, "it is better to have the love and respect of a single wise person, than of a hundred fools."

"So, this is your fable?" Yakiv asked enthusiastically.

"So, what if it is?"

"It's witty!"

"Yes, it's mine…"

"Hryhor Savych, have you written many fables?"

"I haven't written down one of them yet, but I've already composed fifteen or so."

"Fables?" Mykhailo asked, marvelling. In his mind he failed to associate Skovoroda the philosopher with Skovoroda the fabulist.

"Then tell them all to us!" Yakiv exclaimed jubilantly. He was sixteen, had outgrown childhood, as they say, but had not become a swain. Hryhoriy had first met Mykhailo when he was this old.

Clearing his throat and overcoming his embarrassment, which still overwhelmed him each time he was called upon to read his awkward works, Skovoroda began in a low voice: "The Crow and the Finch. Not far from the lake, in which there were frogs..."

Meanwhile they came out onto the riverbank. Thickly overgrown with reeds and willows, the Kozacha Lopan River, as the residents of Huzhvy had dubbed it, abounded with fish and bird life. Here and there in the small azure stretches pike jumped out of the water and timorous flushes of mallards flew overhead like Tatar arrows.

Clouds sailed above this expanse and the sun shone down.

"Let's sit down boys, there's no truth to be found in walking," Hryhoriy said. He found the best spot – in the shade of an oak tree – and was the first to tumble into the ripe untrampled grass. The students sat down beside him.

"Well, well? So, what happened to the Finch and the Crow?" Yakiv's patience ran out.

Skovoroda embraced the lad and began talking as if he was reading out of a book. Mykhailo listened in silence, while Yakiv voiced his admiration, laughed, got up and sat down again. When Hryhoriy began the last fable about the two dogs, he lowered his voice too.

"A farmer in the village had two dogs. One day a stranger happened to drive past his yard. One of the dogs ran out and barked until the fellow could be seen no more.

'And what did that give you?' the enthusiastic dog was asked by his comrade.

'I thoroughly enjoyed myself...!'

'But not all passers-by need be considered the farmer's enemies,' said the intelligent dog. 'It's not a bad occupation being a dog, but it's bad to bark at everyone regardless.'"

"You've hit the nail right on the head, Hryhor Savych!" Yakiv clapped his hands. "There are so many of these dogs in Kharkiv now! They've been baying at you for the last two months..."

"Be quiet, Yakiv!" Mykhailo called out.

"No, no, go on," Hryhoriy bid him and braced himself, ready to face a fresh calamity.

"What a chatterbox..."

"Why? We intended to tell him anyway..."

"Stop arguing," Skovoroda frowned. "Let's hear it!"

"Alright," Mykhailo said. "But don't get agitated, it's really nothing..."

"You're like a courtesan."

"Iov's clever pupil!" Yakiv added.

Mykhailo measured him with a cold stare, glanced in alarm at his close friend, tanned brown and dripping with sweat, who was hiding from the profanity of the world in this dense wilderness, and said quietly: "Someone is spreading rumours among the Kharkiv populace that you condemn the use of meat, wine, and vodka..."

"The priests call you a heretic and a Manichean follower," Yakiv filled him in.

Mykhailo gave the blabbermouth a furtive punch.

"Apart from that," he continued staidly, "they say that you consider gold, expensive things and sumptuous clothes to be pernicious, and seeing as all this is from God and created by God, they—"

"Say you're a blasphemer!" Yakiv could not stop himself.

Hryhoriy lay down, slipped his hands under his head and, looking at the grey faded sky and the small clouds, which had suddenly turned black, asked gloomily: "And is that all?"

"That's all," Mykhailo said.

"No, no, Hryhor Savych," Yakiv leapt up. "Because you live in the wilderness and shun priests, noblemen, and society in general, they also called you a misanthrope."

What utter calumny! Calling him a misanthrope... Then Socrates, Plato, Erasmus and Seneca were also manhaters too, for they sought solitude so that they could reason. Love and reasoning are not friends of crowds... Had he left the city for his own sake? For whom was he writing his book, the songs, and the fables? From whose eyes was he hoping to remove the wool? A misanthrope, a blasphemer... And a Manichean follower! Forsooth, their lies knew no bounds. These bloodthirsty hyenas in cassocks were ready to sink their teeth into anyone who didn't sing their hosannas to the Lord, which contained no soul, only deceit. Because you don't play the hypocrite, because you say what you think – you are immediately considered a heretic. You are seeking truth and verity, so you must be a blasphemer! You reason for yourself, rather than regurgitate the priests' mantras – that makes you a sectarian, an apostate, and a traitor. Oh Lord! Is man, your earthly likeness, no longer free to reason?! Who has given them the right to chain up this almighty force, to squash the spring of progress which, like destiny, shows the way to the willing, giving them wings, and drags along the retrograde ones by force?!

"Lies!" Hryhoriy announced frostily.

"He quarrelled with the prefect because of you," Yakiv announced and fixed his gaze on Kovalynsky. "If it wasn't for the rector, Mykhailo wouldn't be finishing his studies..."

"And he fought with three students who were spreading the priests' gossip!" Mykhailo refused to be shortchanged.

"And the students believe all this?" Hryhoriy asked.

"Not all of them... Only some."

"Hryhor Savych, if you came along..." Yakiv began timidly.

"Of course, I'll come!" Skovoroda said resolutely.

A mountain seemed to shift from the boys' shoulders. Finding an acorn, Mykhailo hurled it at Yakiv. The fellow threw one back at him. In a moment they had sprung to their feet, come together like two young cocks, and began to wrestle. There was wheezing, guffaws, exclamations.

Smiling, Hryhoriy watched this comical duel and was already devastating his slanderers, leaving no stone unturned, attacking their malicious fabrications and profanities.

*　*　*

Skovoroda arrived in Kharkiv on Monday evening, just as the cream of the community gathered, according to custom, in the governor's home.

The liveried lackey blocked his way at the front door: "You've come to see the cook? Use the back entrance!"

"No. I've come to see Yevdokym Oleksiyovych," Skovoroda said calmly.

"He has guests."

"So?"

"You out of your mind? Wait till I call the orderlies…!"

"Highly respected Cerberus," Hryhoriy stopped him, "please run upstairs and tell your master that Hryhoriy Savych Skovoroda has arrived at his abode!"

The lackey looked the intruder up and down with a steely gaze, grimaced half-smiling, but went all the same, pompously, proudly, like a Roman consul.

In a few minutes the adulator came running out as if he had been scalded. Behind him appeared the governor and his guests.

"Hryhor Savych, a warm welcome! Without you our small orchestra is like a military unit without a right flanker!"

Skovoroda ascended the stairs in silence and greeted them according to the ancient custom: "May God grant you joy!"

The noblemen, priests and officers answered each in his own way. Meek Iov nodded and closed his eyes.

There were only men in the large sumptuously furnished hall. In one corner violins, flutes, *banduras* and psalters lay on stools. Bottles and glasses standing on a small graceful gilded table reflected the colours of the rainbow.

Shcherbynin took Skovoroda aside into a quiet corner and said softly: "You are probably angry at me for not defending you? I resisted, but the bishop got his hackles up like you wouldn't believe…"

"No, I'm not angry," Hryhoriy said. "Every cloud has a silver lining."

Casting an authoritative look at Iov, Shcherbynin continued: "The rector and I…"

Meek Iov came running up like a pup, smiling.

"Skovoroda doesn't believe me that the two of us went at Kraisky with bayonets drawn," the nobleman sought his assistance.

"Believe it, Hrytsko, believe it!" meek Iov bleated. "The governor grieved heart and soul. Me too…"

"Poor fellow!" Hryhoriy stopped him. "You are mortally ill even now, Iov."

"From what? What ailment?" the rector asked in fright. The question was posed so loudly that all present in the hall glued their eyes to him.

"Sycophancy, or servility!"

"You're talking scandal, Hrytsko," Iov whispered and closed his eyes as if clamping his shell shut.

"I haven't come here to create a scandal," Hryhoriy said loudly, so all could hear, "but to refute your calumny and gossip!"

The Kharkiv elite pricked up their ears. The familiar and unfamiliar noblemen and priests crowded around the guest. Curiosity overcame etiquette and aristocratic pride.

"You have called me an apostate and a Manichaean follower because I desist from surfeit. I do not condemn the use of meat and wine, I merely do not condone the immoderate delight in them. For this, gentlemen, harms not only you, the rich, but also those who would be glad for a piece of bread and a mug of *kvas*. You have spread rumours that I consider precious metals and expensive things harmful in themselves. This is absurd! They are harmful when they become a goal in themselves, when they are idolised and amassed in the hands of a precious few. Because of silver and gold, people often lose their mind, and their human face in general. Therein lies the tragedy! And only a new person, who understands himself and the world, will be cleansed and be able to look simply and joyously at all the treasures in this world, as we now look at flowering meadows.

"You call me a manhater or misanthrope, and accuse me of teaching squires to loathe, to disregard certain estates, positions, ranks, and situations... Nonsense! All evil stems from the fact that in the theatre of the world we choose a role not according to our nature, but one that is as big and as important as possible. Tell me, why is there such anxiety and such unrest among the people? Is it not because many are playing roles to which they are unsuited, that is, without being mushrooms, they've crawled into the basket? One such folk shepherd will do more harm than five worthy ones can undo!

"That is why I've always advised the squires I knew to first perceive themselves, to understand their true nature, and then to go and choose a role according to their calling. I had hoped that perhaps in this way the common complaints and grievances might abate, for there are still so many unhappy people. I myself would today abandon my estate and enter another, if I did not know that my fussy and melancholic nature was best suited to the lowliest and solitary role in the theatre. Although I may not serve my dear homeland in this mask, however, I will at least try my darndest not to cause it harm!"

Catching his breath and wiping the sweat from his brow, Skovoroda wanted to leave, but Shcherbynin stopped him.

"Don't hurry off, Hryhoriy," he said politely, even though his blue eyes had turned grey. "You demonstrated so ardently that you respect all estates and all people in this world, and yet you want to run off to join the black masses..."

"This aristocratic invention of yours," Hryhoriy said sharply, "that the common folk are supposedly black – is ludicrous. Just as good-for-nothing as those who assert that soil is supposedly dead. How can a dead mother bear live children? And how could white noblemen have been born from the womb of the black masses?"

Shcherbynin gritted his teeth. The lordlings were already frowning.

"Hryhor Savych," the meek Iov began to fuss, unable to stand not only storms, but their presages as well, "why don't you sing us something instead! A new psalm, for example..."

The company immediately came to life. The noble guests openly rejoiced that instead of unpleasant reproaches and dangerous thorny words they might hear Skovoroda's fine music, which impressed people with its harmony and good composition. They liked and knew his songs.

Skovoroda cast an eye over the familiar faces of the aristocratic colonels, ensigns, judges, and lieutenants who were already halfway along the road to nobility, sanctified by the empress, and agreed. He would sing to them! Let it tickle inside their damned childish noses.

He took a *bandura*, ran his fingers over the strings and, looking into the deep black walnut eyes of Colonel Kulykivsky, who only the previous year had still been master of the entire Kharkiv region, began his 'psalm':

> *Each city has its own customs and rights;*
> *Equally each head has its own insights...*
> *And each heart has its own love, of course,*
> *And each mouth has its own taste for sauce.*
> *But there's only one thing on my mind,*
> *Only one thing will not let me rest.*

He ran a curious, sharp eye over the governor's silent guests.

> *Petro bows double seeking awards,*
> *Merchant Fedka shortchanges his clients.*
> *One builds his house in a brand-new style,*
> *He's deep into debt, believe me, it's true!*

But there's only one thing on my mind,
Only one thing will not let me rest.

The young lords looked at him fearfully, like criminals at a judge. The meek
Iov was grimacing, as if his belly was suddenly aching. Shcherbyrin folded
his arms on his chest and listened with a barely noticeable smile in the
corners of his lips.

This one constantly adds to his lands,
That one imports livestock from abroad,
These breed their dogs for hunting in packs,
And those entertain both day and night –
But there's only one thing on my mind,
Only one thing will not let me rest.

Lawyers treat laws according to whim,
Students' heads ache from heated disputes,
These worry about Cupid's caprice,
They all suffer their own stupid thoughts –
But there's only one thing on my mind,
How to stay sharp till the day I die.

Pausing, he slowed the tempo and, accentuating practically every word,
finished the song in a recitative:

Oh, heartless death, your razor-sharp scythe,
Does not spare even the tsar's long locks!
You don't care, be they peasant or tsar –
You consume them all like flames burn straw.
Only those do not care if you come,
Who have a conscience clear as crystal!

Handing the *bandura* back to Iov and, walking around the stunned noblemen, priests and officers, he left the hall. His soul was weary and yearned
for space, open expanses, confronting thoughts, and freedom!

THE TENTH NET

The world was like a chained Prometheus. Each day bloody wounds were inflicted upon it, and why it hadn't died yet even the gods did not know. As it tore at its chains, a knife was driven into its back, and the Cossacks were buried, and because of the hopelessness and the tears of orphans, mountainous graves were piled over them. The insurgents were asleep, Gonta slept too, torn to pieces by the rabid nobility, the last *hetman* of freedom was clanking his chains somewhere, while the Zaporozhian Cossacks, wiping away their blood, lay down their forelocked heads on the banks of the Danube. *Ave, imperator, morituri te salutant!*[65] *Morituri te salutant...* The condemned salute you... Condemned to eternal slavery, to self-degeneration! The noose of serfdom drew tighter and tighter around the Cossack neck... When Hryhoriy had heard about Omelko Puhach's rebellion in Yayik, he sighed with sorrow and recalled his trip to Moscow with Kalihraf, who was dissuading the Russian muzhiks from free thinking. Strange fellow. There were not a people who did not strive and yearn for liberty! Lord, why have You taken such a dislike to Rus', what have these gentle people done to anger Your omnipotence?

Skovoroda had posed this question for many years now. But God remained mute. Silence was a rock, a cliff which pressed down upon the soul. And Hryhoriy's soul grew more and more distressed. His best friend, Mykhailo, had graduated from the collegium and, like all children of noble birth, had set off to seek glory and honour in St. Petersburg. Peace upon you, words and thoughts sown in the heart of a close friend! Yakiv still remained; having been ordained, he embraced a parish not far from Kharkiv, in Babayi, and invited Skovoroda to join him.

The village stood on a hill, all around it were fields, groves, ponds, and meadows. And in the lowlands a stream ran among the alders and

---

[65]   Hail, Emperor, those who are about to die salute you! (Latin)

willows, gathering water bubbling from springs and wells. Near Kholodna River, in an old forest beyond Kunchyrove, Hryhoriy had taken a liking to a secluded apiary and settled there together with his Bible. After he had turned fifty and left behind the cold corpses of his hopes and aspirations, the holy book had become his closest counsel and interlocutor, the source from which he drew strength and thoughts, the immovable serene temple in which he sought refuge from the bustle and spite of the world, from his expired dreams, and still living despair. For Hryhoriy it was a substitute for everything – children, a wife, wine, wealth, friends... Although, he did have friends in Babayi. They had gathered for several years now and, just like the Ancient Hellenes, conducted discussions on philosophical topics. With time Hryhoriy reploughed these free discussions, sowed them with select seed and committed them to paper for people to judge. Blessed work! Blessed people, who in these fiercely bad times had found the strength to reason and, discarding the stone words of dogma, sought truth for themselves!

In the apiary near Kholodna River, Hryhoriy also began writing his new work, the sixth, about the substance of humankind, the world, and spiritual peace.

How quiet it was in the forest now. A bird tweeted somewhere; the wind rustled the languid leaves, and once more became lost in the tree-tops. Water babbled away in the small well, as if someone unseen had made a flute and was forever testing it out. Blissful stillness... It was hard to imagine that the day before yesterday, at this very same time, passions had seethed here, there was a hubbub as one might perhaps come across in a marketplace. Panas, Yakiv, Yarmolay, and Lohvyn had come – the most ardent brother-sophists from Babayi and the nearby villages. Having had a few drinks, they began to argue and, without relenting, reached the *petra*, the firmament, which for them was Hryhoriy.

"Wherein lies the power of the expression 'perceive yourself'?"

"No! First tell me, what is supreme wisdom and where should it be sought?"

"We advocate spiritual peace and harmony, and all around us there is constant bustle!"

"You're like an Egyptian sphinx..."

"Keep calm, good friends, don't get excited and don't hurry with conclusions," Hryhoriy pacified the brethren. "This talk is equivalent to five winds raising waves on the Black Sea..."

This was where Skovoroda began his new dialogue text, which he called 'The Circle'.

Having related the parable about the imprudent travellers in India, which he had heard in his childhood from a Persian man who had traded in silks, crockery, and carpets, he lay down his pen and reflected. Spiritual peace... The soul was a *mobile perpetuum*, it was perpetually in motion. Its wings were thoughts, advice, opinions, and it either desired something or fled from something. When it desired, it loved, and when it fled – it was afraid. And if it knew not what it desired or what to flee from, then it wondered, suffered, became immersed in doubts, dashing this way and that, whirling about like a magnetic needle, until it too found its hallowed North Pole.

Mankind's path was thorny. Nothing led people astray more than self-assurance, insolence, and arrogance. Take a look at the human crowd and you will see that not only respectable, aged people, but also quite young ones, consider that they are well-armed to withstand all misfortune and are convinced that they have no need of other people's advice or eternal human wisdom, any more than they need spectacles for their eyes. And what if this clever little fellow, like some parrot, learned a few words of another language, and spent time abroad in distinguished company in great cities, picking up a smattering of geometry and astronomy, and managed to experience several dozen romantic and civil adventures? Then don't even come near him! The Platos, Solons, Socrates, Pythagorases, Ciceros of this world are mere butterflies fluttering about in comparison to our learned eagle, who acknowledges only the heights above the clouds and the cosmos. And those will appear, who will fervently greet the new powerful wisdom born in his brain, hitherto hidden from sages behind seven locks. Imagining himself the judge of this world, our great Deus reviews with even greater gusto the treasures of the past and approves or deprecates according to his own judgement, like a jeweller sorting precious stones. To him everything which his pitiable overheated mind cannot fathom is useless.

Slanderers of the wise, defamers of our great ancestors! They hold nothing sacred, save their own maxims.

All around us are those who are trying to show people the path to happiness. Wherever one looks there are only leaders and philosophers, who are convinced that they have long ago shoved both Caesar and Alexander the Great under their belt. They are all-knowing! No sooner have they managed to learn one thing and earned a little fame, than they think they are master of all the sciences from alpha to omega. Funny people! The human lifetime is barely enough to master just one field of science.

The writing progressed easily. Though he was alone, he felt as if he was talking with his friends, replying to their quips and questions, proving the truthfulness of his sharp, uncompromising judgements, which had often frightened his pupils, burdened as they were by rank and wealth. This was a wonderful place for reflection and writing books. In this same apiary only a year earlier he had composed some fifteen fables and parables in just a few weeks. And the dialogues and colloquies... Everything here – the earth, the water and the air – must have been saturated with a fervent creative force...

He didn't even notice Panas, Lohvyn and Yakiv appear. They were somehow not their usual selves – scraggy-looking, meek, like monks after Communion.

"May the Lord grant you joy!" Yakiv was the first to speak up.

Skovoroda lay down his pen and rose to his feet.

"What did you dream of today?" Panas asked. He was smiling as usual, as if in his heart there burnt an everlasting candle of kindness and merriment.

"Nothing. I slept like a saint."

"That cannot be. Before such a meeting one must inevitably have a prophetic dream!"

His heart beat faster. Checking this disobedient little bird, Hryhoriy said mirthfully: "Panas, you're putting on airs! If I am to dream every time you visit me..."

"Hryhor Savych, we're not talking about me!"

"And I thought it was about you," Hryhoriy drawled and surveyed the clearing where the path to Babayi began.

"Appear, Mykhailo!" Yakiv called out meanwhile.

As if in a fairytale, a slender guards officer stepped out from behind an old oak tree.

If Pravytsky hadn't mentioned the name, Skovoroda would never have recognised him as his former student, pupil, and close friend. Grinning,

Mykhailo quickly headed toward him. Meanwhile Skovoroda stood, watched, and imprinted forever in his heart this unique, beautiful, and happy moment. They had been separated five years!

After the joy of the meeting had faded and Kovalynsky had allayed his treacherous tears, Pravytsky embraced both of them and led them to the tablecloth which Panas, Lohvyn, and he had spread out in the shade and crammed with various vessels.

Skovoroda thanked them with his tender gaze and, being the eldest, blessed the festive forest banquet and invited everyone to sit down.

"And where's our Yarmolay, respected guests?" he asked Yakiv, who was filling some small copper goblets.

"He has some urgent business to attend to in Kharkiv."

"Well, how can we start without Bacchus?"

"He'll come running," said Panas. "Yarmolay has a nose for alcohol, like cats have for bacon!"

While they drank a goblet or two, Skovoroda did not take his eyes off the guest. He wanted to talk with him as before, frankly and without rounded, definitive words, but something new, hitherto unknown, had appeared in Mykhailo during these past years, and this stopped him. The guest was definitely acting rather strangely. He would smile tenderly, then wrinkle his forehead and become absorbed in some distant thought of his own, then again run his eyes over the face of his teacher, who had remained unchanged, except perhaps growing thinner and ageing.

"Well, where have you been, what have you seen?" Hryhoriy asked, still unable to overcome the feeling of alienation he felt.

"I served for three years in St. Petersburg at Rozumovsky's side, and then went to France and Switzerland," Mykhailo said slowly. And suddenly he came alive, beaming: "Hryhor Savych, in Lusanne I met a person so like you in body and soul, that I couldn't believe my eyes. He's like your twin brother! We became such close friends, and got on so well, that when we parted we both wept. It seemed to me as if I was taking my leave of you..."

"What is the name of this Lusannian?" Hryhoriy asked.

"Meinhardt Danilo."

"From now on then this person will be my best friend!" Skovoroda said ardently.

"Vivat!" Yakiv supported him, picking up a goblet. "To the health of Skovoroda's good friend!"

Mykhailo drank in silence and unbuttoned his guards peasant coat!

"Mister Mykhailo, why don't you remove it completely," Lohvyn suggested, not having uttered a word before this.

"It probably doesn't get too hot in St. Petersburg," Panas drawled craftily.

Grimacing, Mykhailo took off his uniform and threw it aside.

"It gets so hot there," he said unhappily, "that there's nowhere to hide your soul...!"

"They're raging?"

"As if they were rabid... After Puhach's rout, they set about those who were close by."

"Those who had been enlightening her majesty?"

"Who else! Voltaire, Diderot and Montesquieu gave them no peace, they dreamt of their laurels. The philosophers fought with pen and paper, and were attacked with the butt end of an axe! Whack, whack over the head! This isn't France for you, we aren't used to kid glove treatment... Whack, whack over the head – that's the only morality there is...!"

"The butt end of an axe is the *ultima ratio regum*,"[66] Hryhoriy said and turned to Kovalynsky. "You're intoxicated, Mykhailyk. Perhaps you want to lie down a while?"

"I have never been more sober," the guest said sorrowfully and poured himself some more vodka.

The sad news upset and rankled Skovoroda's soul. He realised that these weren't simply skirmishes and internecine struggles, but something more terrible – people's hopes were being dashed, their belief in the genius of the mind, in common sense, which should have prevailed over vainglory, inertia, and the ambitions of the satiated... Applaud now – the show has finished, the wolves have removed their sheep's masks!

"Have you heard anything about Kozytsky or Motonis?" he asked anxiously.

"Motonis is still in the senate. Secretary of State Kozytsky has already submitted a petition to be relieved of his post. Kozytsky is being hounded more than anyone else, because he headed and defended the recalcitrant ones..."

....

66   The final argument of kings. (Latin)

"Ah, strange fellows, who did they think their sermons were directed at?!" Skovoroda grieved out loud. "Those who are used to meat cannot be won over to grass. No cat has yet let a mouse out of its claws, and no sovereign has relinquished even a crumb of power."

"They believed her words, her promises," Mykhailo muttered.

"If everything which the mighty promised came true, the world would become a paradise," Hryhoriy said. He surveyed his downcast friends and added sagaciously: "However, let's recall Christ's words: 'Woe to you, hypocrites! Woe to you who laugh now!' The sun of truth will rise yet..."

"Until the sun rises, the dew will eat away our eyes," Panas said and exclaimed suddenly: "Oh, Yarmolay!"

A horseman had appeared near the oak behind which Mykhailo had hidden. He stopped his horse, jumped down and, hanging the reins on the saddle-bow, headed toward the group of friends.

"What a keen sense of smell!" Panas yelled merrily. He had tired of the sorrowful wisdom of the conversation. "Smelt it all the way in Kharkiv! Do you want vodka or mead?"

But Yarmolay did not answer.

"Gentlemen, he must have buried his mother-in-law!" Panas guffawed and, jumping to his feet, ran off to meet him.

Yarmolay walked past him, as if he was a stump or tree, stopped heavily a step from the tablecloth, removed his sweaty hat and said quietly and hoarsely: "The Sich is no more, good people..."

"Where's it gone? Have the devils grabbed it?!" Panas asked, still laughing.

"It's been destroyed... The empress sent an army..."

"And what about the Zaporozhian Cossacks?! Were they all killed?"

"No. They dispersed in peace..."

They sat in silence. Yarmolay sat down, not even looking at the generous spread on the tablecloth. Panas grew quiet. Hryhoriy was struck dumb, and only a thought circled like a sad gull in the sky over the Zaporozhian Big Meadow, calling out mournfully and dolefully. He realised that this was the end, that there would be no more Sich, no more Hetmanate, no more Slobodian Regiments. From now on the aggrieved would find no truth in the world, the serf would not hurl words of fierce retribution at his landlord, and youths would no longer muse about the exploits of their grandfathers and great-grandfathers. They had taken away the soul, excised it! The rebels, Pugachov, the St. Petersburg reformers, and the Zaporozhian Cossacks – the snake had finished them all off! Oh Lord, does not Your vigilant, eternal eye see how, by hiding behind Your name, modern day Herods act abominably and drain the blood of the nation, like drawing beer out of a vat? Everything had rotted through, there were corpses everywhere. The Judases no longer kissed treacherously, but simply pointed their finger – and martyrs were being crucified, the Christs of truth and liberty!

When it grew dark the guests went off into the village. Mykhailo went with them, for he had to leave in the morning. Skovoroda was left alone in the apiary. He fell to his knees and prayed the whole night for his native land, for his duped holy nation, trampled underfoot and brought to its Golgotha. And he wept. And prayed again. The night hung over him so very sad, so sorrowfully tearful.

*　*　*

From that day on Hryhoriy knew no peace. Wherever he went, whatever he did, he kept hearing alarmed voices, the cold clank of weapons. And instead of exploring his inner being and writing his book, he listened attentively to the forest, catching the slightest rustle and curling into a ball, deliriously straining to burrow into the earth, to disappear or become a moss-covered rock. Most of all he was afraid of venturing into the apiary and the hut. This was his refuge, his fortress, which could be surrounded at any moment and destroyed, wiped from the face of the earth!

Finally, he could stand it no longer and, gathering his manuscripts, books and flute, left.

He entered Pravytsky's yard before dawn and knocked on his bedroom window. Yakiv appeared soon after and, yawning and scratching his head, asked into the darkness: "Who's there?"

"It's me…"

"Hryhoriy Savych?!"

"Yes."

"Step inside, please." Yakiv moved from the doorway. "I'll make up a bed for you presently…"

"No, my good friend. Thank you. I've come to say goodbye."

"Where are you off to, father?" Pravytsky awoke in a flash.

"I don't know..."

"Lord Almighty! Then stay!"

"There's a dense forest there... It's creepy..."

"Live with me!"

"They'll destroy your house. And you've got children, Yakiv..."

"Who needs it!"

"And the Sich? You, me, our friends – we all reason, and to reason is against the law – it's subversive, sinful. Every moment virtue itself is doing the thinking for us, the prosperously reigning woman-philosopher, the female sapience..."

"Hush, father," Pravytsky whispered. "Someone might hear and denounce you..."

"Forsooth!" Hryhoriy sighed and smiled. "We have learned to make denunciations. A spark has given birth to flames... No sooner have you opened your mouth, and the authorities know everything. One zealous lieutenant at the court denounced his relatives and even himself. Hung himself afterwards... Well then, Father Yakov," he added decisively, "farewell. *Vale!*"

"I'll see you off."

The third roosters were crowing. There was mist in the lowlands. Stars were being extinguished in the sky like candles after divine service. The east began to glow pinkish-white.

"Dawn's breaking," Yakiv said softly.

"The blessed law of nature: darkness is replaced by light, grief by joy," Hryhoriy said.

He was taking broad, unrestrained strides. The morning freshness, the expanse of the fields and meadows gradually filled his long-suffering soul with a new force.

"Are you hoping for a better future?"

"Only matter is eternal. Evil, like everything else, is ephemeral."

"Unfortunately, we are not eternal either. We'll die in pitch darkness..."

"The people are immortal. They will live to see changes."

"I would like to glimpse them too."

"To struggle, Yakiv, that in itself is already a great joy."

"With whom, how?"

"With yourself, first of all. Perceive yourself in the people, and the people in yourself. Don't allow your nature, your soul, to be corrupted. Remain who you are! Everything beautiful is natural."

"But everything flows, everything changes..."

"Flow and change in your own channel. Be like yourself, not someone else."

"That's very hard, father."

"It's not easy for me either... Don't you think that in my old age I wouldn't like to have a roof over my head and a dear soul at my side?"

"Then get one, it's no big deal! I'll find you one..."

"And who will believe my words then?" Hryhoriy asked sharply. "To teach others what you yourself do not believe or live by is equivalent to sowing poppies on stone or catching fish by hand in the sea."

"Oh, those instructors abound!" Yakiv did not relent. "They live like princes and preach that people make do with what the Lord has sent them. They shout about sincerity, but themselves play the hypocrite, beat their chest with their fists and make an oath to loyally serve truth – yet themselves breathe lies, squabble, yearn for wealth and awards..."

"So, you want me to increase the crowd of these Pharisees with my presence, Yakiv?" Hryhoriy asked tersely.

"No. I'm saying that now lies and half-truths reign supreme. Everyone sees this and reconciles themselves to this infamy. Bah, they even believe that it needs to be so, that otherwise the world will collapse."

"Don't lose heart, Yakiv," Hryhoriy said. "It only seems that way. The smooth-tongued assure us most loudly and most often about their 'truth'. Commotion, shouts, and bustle! And not an ounce of sense. You can make your way around the world on untruth, but never return. Recall, for example, the parable about the shepherd who was twice believed that wolves were attacking the flock. The third time, when such a calamity indeed took place, the community didn't even bat an eyelid at the shepherd's shouts... They say lies give birth to their own troubles."

They stopped at the crossroads – it was time to say farewell.

"So where are you off to, father?" Yakiv began wearily. Bedewed, canvas-white all over, he shuffled from foot to foot and looked dolefully at his indefatigable teacher.

Hryhoriy felt sad too. He knew what his presence, his words of support, meant to this kind and inquisitive young priest. Pravytsky was like a flourishing hop bush which grew and strained up, but only along a tall stake. From now on he would wilt, fall to the ground, wither away.

"Ah, I'll just go into the wide world," he said after a pause.

"Come back soon, father. I'm so alone here..."

"We are all solitary, Yakiv. Such are the times."

"So how are we to live?"

"Reason. Seek close friends, unity, or concordia, as Kordet Lavrentiy once said... You're trembling!"

"It's nippy..."

"Run off home or you'll catch cold!"

"In a moment, in a moment, father..."

He drew up sharply, embraced his teacher around the waist and rested his head on his chest.

Skovoroda convulsively swallowed his tears, pressed Yakiv to himself and whispered: "I'm not leaving forever... I'll drop by... Our ilk will spread across the world yet, brother..."

When Pravytsky wandered off home, bent double and arms dangling, Hryhoriy wiped his tears and made off along the road to Rzhavets, toward the large, heavy rising sun. Wasn't it all the same where a vagrant ambled? Everywhere he was a stranger and one of the people, a desired guest and a star flying off into obscurity. He could stop where he fancied, turn off wherever he wanted. Like a bird. Freedom...!

Only in the evening, when he was near Zmiyiv, where the Mzha River flowed into the Siversky Donets, did Hryhoriy realise that he was heading toward the borders of the state, to the Sviatohirsk Hermitage, where Lavren-tiy – that veritable Cossack Mamay in a cassock – had been waiting for him for ten years. Here was someone who would rouse his withered soul, restore his hope and faith!

*　*　*

Hryhoriy had never seen such a marvel. From the greenery of the dense primeval forests along the azure Donets River chimerical white mountains rose into the blue sky. It seemed as if giants had come out onto the riverbank and, turned to stone, stared in amazement at the beauty of the river, the meadows, and the steep groves teeming with nightingales. And one of these giants had a crown upon his head – a church! Small wonder that this magical corner of the world was once named *Sviati Hory*, the Sacred Mountains.

Wherever one looked there was God's wisdom and the unfathomable mark of the creator. Happy were the people who lived and praised the Lord on this land, who delighted in such beauty every day!

Skovoroda found Father Lavrentiy in one of the cells cut out of the chalky, temple-like cliffs. Kordet was lying on a squalid bed covered in rags and dirty threadbare garments. His thin, black legs stuck out of the chaos like two old sledge runners.

"Pray the Lord grant you joy," Hryhoriy said in a suppressed voice.

Although not immediately, the shadow of a thought crossed the monk's face, his eyelids opened and, trembling, revealed two sleepy eyes. Another minute, and the runners of his legs stirred, his thin, frail hand rose and fell.

"Is that you, Hryhoriy, or just a ghost?" his soft joyous voice uttered.

"It's me, it's me!" Hryhoriy stepped closer to the bed.

Kordet sat up, threw aside the black rags and, muttering something, embraced Hryhoriy.

If it wasn't for the voice and Kordet's intelligent brown eyes, he would have thought that he had entered the wrong cell.

Lavrentiy was weeping... No, he wasn't weeping – he was calm, half-alive, as if hewn out of wood, and only tears dripped from the slits of his eyes like birch sap.

"How long has it been since we saw each other," he whispered eventually. "Must be forty years..."

"No, only ten."

"You've confused something, Hrytsko... I was still young then, and now I'm an old man..."

"That's not true!"

Lavrentiy released his visitor from his embrace and sat on the bed.

"It's true," he said quietly, dolefully. "There's not a living speck left in my soul... You haven't brought along a glass of anything, have you?"

"No."

"Pity..."

"Why do you need that? You can barely stand on your feet as it is."

"Ah, it's all the same," Kordet waved his hand. "At least I could befuddle my mind... If only you knew, Hryhoriy, how I've tired of life..."

He bowed his thickly overgrown head and dozed off, breathing frequently and with difficulty.

Hryhoriy sat down on the bench which, like the table, was dirty and empty (books had once reigned supreme in Father Lavrentiy's cell!), and eased the bag off his shoulder. What life can turn a person into! And he had been strong as an oak. What storm had quashed him, what evil thunder had struck him and broken him so badly?

"Where are you these days?" Lavrentiy asked suddenly.

"Nowhere."

"Still wandering about?"

"I'm tired of life. Perhaps I should join the order..."

Kordet opened his eyes and smiled.

"You're always joking, Hrytsko."

"The old woman played around with the wheel..."[67]

"Oh, this is a mighty frightening wheel!" Kordet called out. "It breaks, crushes, and corrupts..."

"Were you Father Superior for long?"

"Seventeen days."

"And then?"

"The bishop sent someone else."

"And this is his work?" Hryhoriy surveyed the squalid cell.

"Yes... He's a master at breaking backs and people's spirits."

"Why did you let yourself fall into his hands? You should have left here! This is no prison."

"It's worse. I escaped more than once – they caught me and stuffed me back inside this burrow of a grave."

"What are you waiting for? You have to do something, find a way out!"

"Enough. The dead must rot..."

"Lavrentiy!" Skovoroda drew up to him. "Don't submit to the demon, fight, be a man! You used to rage like fire, awakening the spiritually extinguished everywhere!"

Lavrentiy lay down, rested his feet on the bedhead and closed his eyes. He responded sometime later: "I've burnt out, brother... There are only ashes left... Even these are being scattered by the wind..."

....

[67] The latter half to the proverb is: ...and became caught in its spokes.

"You can still rise, break free, spread your wings!" Hryhoriy shook him. "Lavrin, do you hear? Let's escape together, today!"

Kordet lay as if he was dead. His long bony legs sailed along, engraved against the background of the wall, making it appear as if the bed was a funeral litter and an invisible person was carrying out Lavrentiy's corpse.

> *They carry the Cossack*
> *And lead his horse along,*
> *The horse bows its dear head...*

He had finished fighting, become exhausted, and died while still being alive. Everything in the world was going head over heels! The strong, fit and mighty were broken like rushes, while those wasted in body and soul flourished, climbing up the ladder. Forests were felled, underbrush grew in their place... Such was the law of nature. It could not stand for the earth, the air, or open spaces to be locked away. If there was nothing good, rubbish would replace it. After all, something had to live and rejoice at the light, the darkness, to sprout new shoots.

"Leave, Hryhoriy," Lavrentiy whispered. "Don't defile yourself with this corpse and don't torment your heart in vain. You probably came running here out of despair. Well, you're a little late, dear brother! Don't seek the living among the dead... Go to the living, save them, Hryhoriy!"

Kordet grew silent. And though Hryhoriy stood over him for a long time yet, he didn't utter a single sound, didn't even stir. He was just barely alive...

Kissing his close friend goodbye, Skovoroda slowly left the cell, put on his straw hat, hoisted his bag onto his shoulder and, bowing his head, wandered off to the river, down the steep wide steps, from which one could clearly see the magical left bank.

However, the magic of the place faded for Hryhoriy. The beauty remained, but it did not warm the soul, instead irritating the weeping wound which Hryhoriy had borne out of the hermitage walls. He became convinced yet again: that, which was visible on the outside, was only an illusion. The essence lay in the kernel, which was hidden under a tough shell. Sometimes the nut appeared clean and full, but break it open and you would be surprised to find the kernel was rotten! Beauty was deceptive, beauty was underhanded. Cruelty, baseness, and treachery lurked within it, like a snake in a flower bed. Never trust the eyes, trust the mind instead, for only the mind is capable of penetrating the mask, of discovering the true value of things... Or perhaps the Lord mixed everything up on purpose, entangling good and evil, beauty and ugliness, the lofty and the base, so that people would forever suffer in their quest for verity? And He sat there, grinning, like a merciless despot who has led his nation into a labyrinth of laws and lawlessness!

*　*　*

To go to the living, to rescue the living – this was all that was left for Hryhoriy to do that frightening summer. Clutching his heart, like a gladiator clutching his wound, and driving away the carrion crows of doubt, he desperately rushed to the aid of the spiritually hungry. He appeased them, fed them, drawing from the bottomless sources of the Bible, elatedly calling forth into the world the harmony of body and soul, aspirations and possibilities... In the evenings, on his own and face to face with his thoughts, he suffered intolerable torment, sought new words, new firmament, a haven to which he could direct all the sufferers, all those wanting to achieve spiritual peace and the ever more ghostly, ever more unattainable firebird of freedom. Everywhere and always, they listened eagerly, nodded their heads, sighed deeply and even wept, but, inevitably, at the end of the conversation everyone begged him to show them the path to freedom. He grew silent, for he did not yet know himself. Meanwhile the people grew sullen, lit their pipes which had become extinguished, forgotten, and left him to his own devices. No, he did not become angry, he was not offended. He understood: spiritual peace when one was enslaved was an absurdity! Slavery was eternal torment. Or bovine calm...

He suffered, sought solutions, but could find none.

The Holy Scriptures were no help either.

And then he met Dolia, on a forest road, not far from Kupiansk. Skovoroda had spied the group of Cossacks from afar. He thought he had imagined it: how could they have appeared here, hundreds of versts from the Sich, on this side of the Line, and the Muscovites, who were garrisoned in regiments along the Orel, Donets and Bereka rivers? He rubbed his eyes – no, they really were Zaporozhian Cossacks! Without horses, black, in ragged clothing, but still armed. They were making their way south. As they drew closer their leader warily brought his hand to his side and cocked his pistol. The whole band followed suit. Skovoroda smiled: the knights had grown fearful.

"Don't worry, boys, I won't beat you up!" he called out with a sneer.

The leader hastily took his hand away from his pistol and did not know where to put it in bewilderment.

Someone made a witty remark. A chuckle spread among the men.

"Watch out we don't give you a whipping," the leader said and then suddenly exclaimed: "Hryhoriy Savych! Lord Almighty, this is what I call a meeting!"

Skovoroda stopped before the swarthy leader of the band and barely recognised him as his old friend and compatriot Nychypir.

"Alive?"

"Jumping for joy!"

"You ran away from your landlord at an opportune time."

"Don't remind me! A pain in his side..."

"Didn't come across him anywhere?"

"Oh, that would have been something to see!" exclaimed one of the Cossacks, who stood pressed tightly around the friends.

"We almost bumped into each other the previous year," Nychypir sighed. "Moscow was but an arm's length away, but luck was not with us..."

"Father, perhaps you should be careful?" the same voice asked.

"He is my compatriot and true friend, he can know everything," Nychypir replied and hugged Hryhoriy. "There were five hundred of us, like gleaming glass," he added sorrowfully. "And now there's only a small handful, as you can see. All perished near Chorny Yar..."

The Zaporozhians bowed their heads.

Hryhoriy removed his straw hat.

"Where you headed?" he asked a while later.

"To the Sich, the Sich, Hryhoriy," Dolia said sagaciously, and the whole band immediately came to life, cheered up. "We're sick and tired of playing hide and seek. We roam the forests like werewolves. You're the first person we've come across in half a month. And even then, we took fright, taking you for a tsarist henchman..."

"Well, how are our brethren there?" asked a stocky old Sich Cossack with one ear sliced clean off. "Still bothering the Turks or have they set about their own lot?"

Skovoroda remained silent. He did not have the courage to tell these poor wretches that their destiny was worse than they imagined.

"Just wait till we reach the Sich," Nychypir said, "I'll show them where the enemy is and against whose vile heads we should be sharpening our sabres!"

"And I'll take a drink from the Dnipro," sighed the Cossack without an ear.

"I'll get myself a horse."

"I've sons waiting for me, they're already fully grown..."

Hryhoriy was in despair. He gritted his teeth tightly and crumpled his hat.

"Hryhor Savych, you're white as a sheet!" Nychypir called out worriedly.

The band grew silent.

"You are now complete orphans," Hryhoriy said, looking into their rueful brown faces.

"As long as the Cossack's mother, the Sich, is alive, a Zaporozhian is no orphan," someone said.

"There is no more Sich and no more Zaporozhia..."

"That's a bad joke, brother!" the earless Cossack flew into a rage.

"I'm not joking."

"You're lying!"

"Wait, Overko," Nychypir stopped him. "Hryhoriy Savych isn't one to lie." He chewed on his sunbleached, yellowed moustache. "When and who?"

"Some twenty days ago. The army which had returned from the Turkish War..."

Hryhoriy recounted what he knew about the peaceful surrender of the Sich, about the brethren's escape somewhere down south, to the Turks.

The band bowed their tempestuous heads lower and lower. After Hryhoriy had fallen silent, they remained speechless too, turned to stone like Lot's wife, who had looked back to see her native city perish.

"This is the Last Judgement." Dolia was the first to speak up.

"May all the tsars and their progeny be damned!"

"And may the earth open up under those who put an end to Cossackdom!"

They cursed, prayed, furtively wiped away tears. And then sat down wearily on the grass by the roadside, no longer hiding, unafraid that their camp might be ambushed. When everything that a person has lived for has been taken away from them, death is no longer frightening.

"We should remember our dear mother," said the old man without the ear and glanced at Dolia. "Let's have the flasks!"

"But we're on expedition!" someone said timidly.

"From now on we're on expedition eternally," Nychypir said. "And forever at home: the Sich is where we are. Join us too, Hryhoriy, and drink with us! Now we are all vagabonds. Like those unfortunate souls for whom there is no place either on earth, or in heaven."

They filled whatever vessel there was – from pots to cupped hands. They drank gloomily, hurriedly, as if wanting to get drunk sooner, to drown their sorrow, to wrench the pain of insult from their hearts. They poured another round and drank again.

But the intoxication did not take: grief cannot be helped through tears or vodka.

"How are we to live now?" Dolia reflected aloud. "Everywhere you show your nose there are enemy bayonets..."

The Cossacks fell silent, pricked up their ears.

"By whatever the Lord sends," Overko said.

"He's already sent enough, thank you for the kindness!" Dolia announced angrily. "If He had His wits about Him, then we'd have our happiness too! But He sits and blinks His eyes like a billy goat!"

Skovoroda looked mournfully at these exiles who had stopped at the crossroads, unable to decide which way to head. Take a left turn, and you lose your head, a right turn – and you lose your soul, and continue on ahead. Who knows what will happen, only there won't be any turning back...

"P'raps we should head for the monastery, brothers, and sit out the bad times there?" Nychypir asked. "I've a friend not far from here..."

"Our bad times are like a dog's wail," Overko said. "We won't have enough backsides to sit it out."

"At least until things die down a little. We'll think of something meanwhile." The leader did not relent. "Father Lavrentiy can help us out!"

"Perhaps."

"Agreed!"

"Agreed!"

The brethren cheered up and began to stir, ready to go even into the devil's maw, anything but under the landlord's yoke.

"Father Lavrentiy is no more," Hryhoriy said. It had fallen to his lot to be the bearer of all bad tidings today.

"Dead?!"

"Withered away on his feet."

Nychypir crossed himself, the band did the same.

A silence fell upon them, thick as the night, heavy as a storm cloud.

"Then we'll go on a spree, boys!" Nychypir called out. "Gladden the saintly souls of Zalizniak, and Gonta, and Pugach!"

"Let's!"

"Revenge!"

"Punishment!"

The leader rose and lifted his baton.

"Hryhoriy, I have a spare sabre..."

"God bless you, father, for the honour and respect." Skovoroda bowed low. "I have another weapon."

"The word – as always?"

"Forsooth."

"Well then, farewell!"

"Fare ye well. May fate[68] protect you!"

"That I certainly will!" Nychypir said gaily and slipped the baton under his belt.

"Overko, take the boys into the forest. Find a stream, rest, and tidy up before our great exploit. I'll see Hryhoriy off."

They said their goodbyes in silence, certain that this was their last meeting.

Dolia left the road, drew his sabre and chopped down a maple sapling.

"I'll make you a staff to remember me by," he said, paring it down. "You can drive the dogs away with it."

A song erupted from the thickets in the direction the band had disappeared. So sad and so relevant to the wretches who sang it, that Hryhoriy could barely breathe as he listened. This was a holy moment – a song was being born or resurrected...

....

[68]   The literal translation of Nychypir Dolia's surname is 'Fate'.

'A good evening to you, green grove!
Take me in at least for the night!'
'I won't let you stay, young Cossack,
For I can sense a price on your head...!

"Hryhor Savych, what's all this happening in the world?" Dolia asked meanwhile.

"They've made a laughing stock of us, father..."

'A good evening to you, dark ravine,
Let Cossack freedom stay at least a night!'
'I won't let you stay, for there'll be woe –
A grey dove is humming mournfully in the meadow...'

"Someone might hear and bring the dragoons here." Skovoroda became alarmed.

"Let them sing, they're lonesome. They've been silent for six months. And as for the dragoons, we'll find them some tasty gifts!"

'Even your enemies are asking about you, Cossack,
Seeking you each day and night in the dark meadow.'
Hey, the dear Cossack calls out to the grove, the grove:
'Come forth, my enemies, it's me inviting you!'

Skovoroda very much wanted to remain here, to clean up by the stream, put on a white shirt and to face death and glory at Dolia's side.

"Here you go, your staff's ready," Nychypir said, handing Hryhoriy his present. "Walk in health. Spread the Cossack truth! Don't wait for the dawn, plough and sow the seed of freedom everywhere. And we'll light the way for you with candles made of the burning palaces of landlords!"

He hugged Hryhoriy, kissed him hastily, as if fearing that it would grow dark soon and he would not have time to light the first candle, and hurried back.

Before he dived into the forest, he raised his hand high and waved.

"Farewell, glorious knights," Skovoroda whispered emotionally. "May the Lord protect you."

*   *   *

God is misfortune and despair. In his travels, Skovoroda came across many people, and everywhere he saw the enslaved Cossack sons, sold into captivity, who used to remember the Lord only at Easter and Christmas, praying like ascetics now. But what about Hryhoriy himself? Hadn't he become glued to the Bible in Babayi for the same reason? During difficult times in history, when people became lonely and felt utterly defenceless, they sought a force which could support them in their spiritual bind and stop them from dying. The stronger ones reasoned, striving to resist the evil. The weaker ones prayed. God was the hope of the weary or the lazy, cowards hid behind Sabaoth, philosophising slyly.

Hryhoriy took out the Bible less and less frequently now. It lay in his bag and, as if reminding him of itself, dug into his side with its stiff covers. Perhaps it felt cramped in the company of Rousseau and Voltaire, which Hryhoriy had acquired from a nobleman who had been glad to get rid of such subversive books.

The Holy Scriptures... The Holy Bible... This horrendous sphinx which forever seeks out people to swallow! It enriched people with dogmas, age-old regurgitated truths, and stopped people from thinking freely for themselves. Those who had entrusted themselves to it, without having understood its fallacy, were the most unfortunate people in the world, for it was better to have a tiny drop of one's own thoughts, than an ocean of other people's.

He could not write. *The Circle*, begun in Babayi, had dried up on those three sheets of paper and at the sentence where he was interrupted by the arrival of his sophist friends. And winter, the arch enemy of muses, was already standing on the doorstep. Then he would not be writing, but rubbing his hands to stay warm.

Finally in the middle of September Skovoroda forced himself to sit down to some creative work on a secluded apiary past Ostrogozhsk, where the lands of Russia began. When freedom and truth have been trampled underfoot, sharp weapons have no right to rust in scabbards.

He diluted the ink which had long since dried up in the inkwell, read through what he had written near the Kholodna River in Babayi and became emotional as he remembered Yakiv, Panas, Lohvyn, and Yarmolay. Wonderful people, such wonderful days spent with them!

"Well then, brethren, let's continue our philosophical dispute."

Happiness is preached, thus, by the historian, the chemist, the physicist, the grammarian, the surveyor, the soldier, and the watchmaker – anyone who puts their mind to it. They no longer wanted to hear the words of the apostles, assuming the role of teacher, and expatiating on all and sundry...

The beekeeper arrived with a cart – time to collect the hives and store them away for the winter.

"Good health to you, old man!" Hryhoriy lay down his pen. "What's there to hear in the world?"

The old man shrugged his shoulders.

"The magnates have let loose completely," he responded after a while. "Ever since the Sich has been destroyed, there is no life because of them. Listen to them, and there never were any Cossacks, and all of us have been cattle since time immemorial. They've forgotten very quickly."

"They'll soon be reminded..."

"There's no one to do it – the boys are now on the Danube."

"What about the *haydamaks*?"

The beekeeper only waved his hand dismissively.

With Hryhoriy's help he placed three hives onto the cart, they surrounded them with hay.

"A few days ago, near Husynka," the beekeeper announced, grabbing hold of the reins, "they routed a detachment led by some fellow named Dolia..."

"And was everyone killed?" Hryhoriy asked mournfully. "No one escaped?"

"I don't know. I'm merely repeating what I heard."

The beekeeper drove off. And Hryhoriy was seized by such grief, such deep sorrow, that he couldn't sit still. He dashed about the elegant forest whispering prayers, or damning the cruel world, until the sun set and darkness fell upon the earth.

After the Feast of Transfiguration, the nights became fresh, the earth cooled down more than it warmed up. Hryhoriy was accustomed to spending the evenings beside the fire, in complete silence, on the verge of gloom and light. Therefore, once it grew dark and cold, Skovoroda struck some fire and lit the logs he had prepared during the day.

He sat on a stump and, watching the flames consume the dry branches, sought at least a drop of sense and logic in the endless punishment which the Lord had inflicted upon His people, upon this beautiful land. All-merciful despot! Like all tyrants, You are in a state of bliss when there's the smell of blood. Blood is the herald of death. Blood is the fire which incinerates courage, ideas, intellect – everything which makes mankind dangerous to gods and despots! This was why so much blood had been spilled in God's name, in honour of the holy faith, which for some reason always seemed to be on the side of the stronger party. Those who were strong had the Lord on their side, and victory too. Ah, hypocrites! It's not enough for you to kill the body, you want to destroy the soul, to break the shoots, so that nothing will grow. The desert is the paradise of tyrants, their hallowed dream, which they strive to achieve as they step over the bodies of their dear ones!

Everything in the world was logical, necessary, wisely veritable. And only God... God, like all things uncertain, lived through constant reminders, daily exclamations, and fear, which His apostles sowed all about them, these Pharisees with aureoles... Crucify, crucify him! And they did. They crucified everywhere! And God remained silent. He will not strike them down with thunder, will not cleave their butchers' heads with a fiery sword. He is holy and strong... Gentle and kind... Fools! Who are you praying to? Will you be saved from crucifixion by the one who sent His only son Jesus off to be tortured?

Everything was a smoke screen, a delusion!

He threw more logs onto the fire and took the Bible and the manuscripts of his writings from his bag.

Everything was smoke, a delusion... He had spent his best years on this caprice! He had read, sought truth, given all he had to surmount its supreme wisdom, to discover the symbols, to uncover the kernel beneath the shell. 'In the beginning God created heaven and earth!' What a jester! Created out of nothing something which had always existed. *Materia aeterna!*[69] Only a childish mind could say that our world had never existed or would be no more. God wept, raged, slept, and repented. While people became pillars of salt, rose into the heavens, rode wagons across the sea floor and through the air, the sun stopped moving like a coach and started backwards; iron

----

[69]   Eternal matter! (Latin)

floated, rivers flowed uphill, fortress walls collapsed from the blaring of trumpets; mountains jumped about like rams, rivers clapped their hands, the dead rose out of their graves, and kasha dropped out of the clouds, with quail to boot!

He opened his *Symphony* written in Zemborsky's forests together with *Narcissus*. Perceive yourself... Get to know your nature... What for? To perceive verity... You strange fellow! Who needs verity? And your soul, your mind! They are all smoke, a delusion... Like David, they bless everywhere with the lips and damn with the heart. Each person worries only about his daily hunk of bread. The soul is worthless. Anyone seeking the truth is a brigand, a rebel, an apostate! Falsehood has spread across the earth... Everything was smoke, a delusion!

He tore up his *Symphony* and laid it on the coals, onto the dying embers. The paper curled up, flapped about like a bird, and suddenly rushed into the sky with high white flames.

Hryhoriy covered his face with his hands and waited – at any moment the sky would be rended by a bolt of lightning and the earth would open up beneath him...

But God remained silent. The starry autumn night was dozing. The world slept soundly, its fettered hands flung out like those of a galley slave. And only the fire, where Skovoroda's thoughts and work were burning, was summoning its last flames in its struggle with the darkness.

THE ELEVENTH NET

Gloomy old age crept up on Hryhoriy across the grey stubble of the years like a fox. The roads became longer, and the days shorter. The earth seemed to have swollen, stretched out. He walked and walked... He couldn't reach his destination, retiring with the sun somewhere halfway, in the fields or in the forest, wondering what had happened to his feet and his heart. Ice was born only to melt... His mortal body was starting to break down. The spirit welled, strove forward, but the body – the body demanded peace. That eternal duel, the cold breath of death!

Hryhoriy had never felt so melancholy as this autumn. He sought solace in the Bible, the wise Hellenes, the sharp minds of the erudite French. However, nothing helped. In the three years since the destruction of the Sich he had aged, succumbed to ailments, and began to await the haven where he would find eternal peace, the way a sailor waited to reach his home port. He said nothing to anyone, but was on the lookout, ready to courageously face the great liberation from injustice, implacable despots, conceited fools, Cerberuses who vigilantly guarded other people's wealth, janissaries who beheaded their fellow countrymen with adulatory zeal...

And suddenly there came a miraculous cure! The illnesses, death, the suffering – everything yielded before a new desire, the ravings of his soul and body. While walking through the village where he had stopped for the winter, he lifted his heavy head and on a cropped tree saw the black hat of the only stork nest in the whole of Burluk. He stopped, astonished. Something shifted in his chest, fluttered with a sharp salty pain, transporting him into childhood, to his native village on the Mnoha River... He needed to go there immediately, to run, take a coach, or fly on wings! There, only there, in his family home with its biblical symbol of holy strength and constancy, would he find the desired peace and tranquillity!

His thoughts swirled about, striking each other with their wings, soaring and falling. His heart thudded earnestly in his chest, no longer running out of steam three to four times a day. And his feet, accustomed to endless travels, filled with energy and bore Hryhoriy back to the dwelling where he had left his bag. He needed to return to his native parts right away! There was happiness there, it was his promised land!

He was given a lift to Kharkiv by the fellow with whom he was staying. And from there he went with the post all the way to Okhtyrka. He waited a day for a lift, but then set out on foot, unable to wait any longer. Faster, faster! The shore was there, the firmament, which he had sought all his life!

It was already late autumn. The trees had thrown off their sumptuous vestments and stood black, grieving like monks at a funeral. In the morning the road was paved with a light frost, but toward noon, warmed by the sun, it became a doomsday of mud. He walked along the verge, moving away from the road, which had been kneaded and rekneaded during the days of bad weather. He walked on, deep in reflection, sifting through everything he had heard, seen and suffered in half a century of searching, hesitating, attempting to perceive the world, nature, and himself as its inseparable part. There were falls, flights, bitter defeats and victories, but the road was straight and truthful. In this bustle, this chaos, where the great and the lowly, lies and truth, good and evil, became intermingled, he did not rush about, did not chose the more comfortable path, but headed toward verity and, like Diogenes, attempted to find Man. But he wasn't sure whether he had found him. Man was like a ghost, a spectre. Occasionally it seemed to him that he had him in his hands, had him all worked out, but a moment later he again grabbed his lamp and kept on seeking…

"What's the matter, are you blind, old man?!" someone asked cheerfully.

"Probably had a drop too much to drink?" another voice said.

Skovoroda regained his senses and only now noticed that he was walking through marshland overgrown with willows and young alder. Some hundred sagenes on his right was a thick stand of birches. And not a soul anywhere. Who had spoken? He must have imagined it…

He reached the shore jumping from mound to mound, bypassing the marshy spots and the water. He sat down and removed his boots. They were thoroughly wet. Soaked! A pretty mess…

"Fine boots there!" someone said beside him. Hryhoriy looked and could not believe his eyes – a mere three steps away Motonis was standing beside a willow! In Cossack dress, with a sabre... Christ!

"Is that you Mykola?" he asked just in case, although he was certain it was a figment of his imagination.

"It's me, it's me, Hryhoriy!" Motonis ran up to him. He embraced him, lifted him to his feet and kissed him. He was so overjoyed that there were tears in his eyes. "When did we last see each other?"

"In Moscow."

"Woe is me! That was more than twenty years ago…"

"How on earth did you appear here, and looking like that?" Hryhoriy asked.

Motonis immediately grew sullen.

"That's a long story, Hrytsko," he said eventually. He gave a low whistle and a strange fellow dressed in a hussar shako, in a tattered peasant coat and bast shoes appeared from behind a willow. "Stand guard, boys, while I go for a walk with my guest," Motonis bid him. He adjusted his sabre, his hat, and gallantly took his friend by the arm: "Please, *mon cher*."

They ventured into the depths of the forest. Hryhoriy threw sideways glances at the aged, though still strong, broad-shouldered and light-footed comrade and former fellow student. He was one of the Dioscuri!

"And where's Kozytsky?" he asked after a while. "You're not taking me to him, are you?"

Motonis stopped and, letting go of Skovoroda's elbow, said hollowly: "Hrytsko killed himself four years ago…"

Skovoroda felt as if he had been struck with the butt end of an axe. Removing his hat, he mourned in his heart the departed fighter for truth, for victory of intellect over intolerance and the vainglory of the mighty.

"How could this have happened?"

"Out of despair…"

"But he had achieved what he wanted. He was at her side and was able to instruct the empress about freedom, truth and kindness."

"That he did. He made translations, wrote lots of articles. For all of twenty years he toiled for freedom, struggling against ignorance, singing a hosanna to wisdom! And he fell, squashed by a government boot."

"But where were you, why didn't you support your bosom buddy?!"

"We were separated. Utterly exhausted, Kozytsky retired and escaped to Moscow. And soon after I was thrown out of the senate, stripped of all ranks and forbidden to serve anywhere."

After a silence, Motonis clutched his sabre and added through clenched teeth: "It was then that Hrytsko committed suicide…"

"So much for your enlightenment," Skovoroda sighed mournfully. "I told you so…"

"Hryhoriy, if only you knew how often we remembered your words that last year!" Motonis said ardently. "Back then we had realised that we had strayed, taken the wrong path and given all our knowledge, our intellect, and our lives to bear a candle before the blind. Once Hrytsko saw that the wisest of the wise was only playing at freedom and played games with those around her only to grab the reins more firmly into her hands, he wept in grief and called himself a Judas, who had sold out his people. And then began the decrees, the trials, the repressions and sudden deaths! Losenko, Barkov, Zolotnytsky, Sichkar, Kozelsky, Poletyka, Tumansky, Berezovsky…"

"Maksym? Him too…?!"

"For six years he studied in Italy, became famous as a composer, became an academic, received the title of *maestro di capella*. But when he returned to St. Petersburg, he was appointed an ordinary chorister. He became depressed, was driven to drink and finally could stand it no longer and slit his throat. They say he had nothing to his name apart from a knife and a flute…"

Hryhoriy wept in silence. Damned Neros and Herods! They camouflage their cruelty with mellifluent words and smiles! Everywhere they preach love of fellow man, meanwhile destroying the best blossom of the nation, its hope and strength. They circle around those who attempt to reason like a white dove and then dive like a ruthless eagle upon the sage who regains his sight and utters words of truth in the temple of falsehood, where the spirit of verity is replaced by an air of flattery and incense smoke. They care nothing about the people, the homeland, or the nation! They should be the salt of the earth, a model of virtue and wisdom, there to lead everyone into a valley of eternal joy…

"I barely escaped," Motonis spoke of himself now, "and made my way here."

"Where to, Mykola?"

"Wait, you'll see presently."

They walked along a fir grove and came out into a forest clearing. Oho, there was a proper camp here! Carts formed into a circle, fires burning inside, horses stood eating out of nosebags, armed woodsmen roamed about…

"Ahoy, Mykola! Who have you brought?" a voice familiar to Hryhoriy called out from the fire.

"A comrade."

"Hurry here!"

"His feet are wet."

"Give him my horse-leather boots."

"Who is that?" Hryhoriy asked.

"*Otaman* Dolia."

"God Almighty, so he's alive?!"

"Why shouldn't he be – he's charmed, neither sword nor bullet can touch him!"

"Just like Harkusha?" Hryhoriy asked. In the past years he had heard many tales about the elusive rebel leader.

"Harkusha is also a sorcerer. When he's in a bind, he can immediately turn into whatever he wishes, without leaving a trace."

"If only someone could charm the lot of us..."

"Unfortunately, it's a fairytale, a figment of people's imagination," Motonis sighed.

"When people believe fairytales they become truth. Take God for instance..."

"Christ, Christ... Hryhoriy, what are you intoning!"

"Whatever is on my mind."

Motonis quickly found the boots on the wagon, fetched some dry foot-cloths and handed them to Hryhoriy. He watched askance as the latter put them on. And then said softly: "You've always been a riddle to me."

"Everything in this world is a riddle. Time will pass, and people will still be struggling to solve them. Only fools think that by having read the Holy Scriptures plus another ten books or so, they have perceived supreme wisdom, reached the bottom of the well of nature's marvels. But the well is inexhaustible!"

"Then why suffer, seek, strive...?"

"Because otherwise there is death. Only the living dead, walking corpses, do not strive to attain verity!"

"Mykola!" Dolia called again. "Hurry here, the dinner's ready!"

"We're coming, *otaman*!" Motonis called out and bowed politely before Skovoroda: "Please, *mon cher*."

When they drew close, Nychypir rose from the log and, spreading out his arms, came toward them.

"Now this is what I call a guest! Hryhoriy, you and I are immortal! Watch out, we'll meet next time in some grove two hundred years hence."

"It's all right for you, father, you're charmed." Skovoroda smiled.

"Fierce hatred has charmed us," Nychypir said passionately. "We have no right to die while our people are in slavery! The earth will not accept us, it will spit us out."

The *haydamaks* grew silent, as if they had entered a temple. They certainly believed their leader's words about their mission in battles for a better destiny, in the immortality of their cause, which they served loyally and in whose name they suffered.

"We are freedom's children and won't allow anyone to keep us tied up like dogs," Nychypir continued to thunder. "We'll destroy all the noblemen, to the last one!"

"The kasha is growing cold, father," someone announced impatiently.

Nychypir became silent, scalding the insolent fellow with an unkind gaze and smiled.

"Overko, my good man, you've grown old, you can't see the world for your kasha."

"Forsooth," Overko said. (This was the same Cossack without the ear!) "The noblemen are coming up like mushrooms after a shower; you can't pick them all... But kasha is a sure thing. Especially with a bit of dried fish!" He winked at Hryhoriy, fetched a spoon and a piece of dried fish from inside his bootleg. "Bless the food, *otaman*!"

Nychypir took the dried roach, smelt it with a whistle and, handing it over to the guest, solemnly sat down at the cauldron, whose fragrance had spread throughout the grove.

They dined in silence, only wheezing and scraping away with their spoons. And after they had finished, Overko ahemmed and drawled dreamily: "A fine kasha... All we need now is a glass of something..."

"That has to be another time," Dolia said decisively and turned toward Skovoroda. "I hope our guest forgives us..."

"It's all the same to me, whether there's a glass to drink or not!" Hryhoriy gladdened them.

"That can't be!" Overko called out. "It's not a pair of boots or pants for you...!"

"And not a pistol!"

"Come on, that's a bit much."

"Forgotten how you drank away your pistol, Overko?"

Joking, they filled their pipes with fragrant tobacco and lit their pipes.

"Well, how's life treating you?" Nychypir embraced his guest.

"I live like the Lord's birds, neither sowing nor reaping..."

"Continually reading, writing, seeking truth in books?"

"Yes, I'm seeking it, father."

"Wasted work, Hrytsko. You won't find it there."

"Where then?"

"On the tip of a sabre!"

"Perhaps... But why then do they fear the word more than a hundred sabres?"

"The world has gone crazy. Some are drunk with power, and others with servile intoxication…"

"And you hope to wake them with your sabre of Damascus steel, father?"

"And what's so bad about this world-waker!" He drew his sabre deftly and raised it into the air. "It's like lightning!"

Having admired it, he put away his sabre, glanced at the sun which was already turning red beyond the black-and-white forest, and hugged Hryhoriy again.

"Countryman, drop your philosophising and come join us!"

"Stay with us, Hrytsko." Motonis cheered up. "We'll attain freedom or die merrily!"

"Stay!"

"We'll butcher all the lords and their lackeys!"

"God bless you, good people, for the honour, the respect." Hryhoriy bowed with restraint. "To hew with the sabre is alien to my nature..."

"You're a coward!"

"Worrying about your own skin!"

"You dog's bone!"

"Traitor!"

Skovoroda heard them out patiently, surveyed the crowd with a gentle intent gaze (almost the entire band had gathered around him) and said quietly, but so that all could hear: "The Knife reproached the Whetstone: 'You don't love us, brother, if you don't want to join our kind and become a knife like us…' 'If I wasn't capable of sharpening,' the Whetstone replied, 'I would have gladly entered your circle. But right now, the reason I love you is because I have no desire to cut anything myself. But if I were to become a knife, Lord Almighty, I alone would never be able to cut as much as all those knives and sabres which I will sharpen in my lifetime. And I hear there's a great shortage of whetstones right now!"

A rather young horseman appeared out of the forest, raced across the clearing and, drawing up before the crowd of *haydamaks*, shouted in alarm: "Father, Harkusha is asking for your help!"

The leader rose to his feet.

"Where is he?"

"On the Hrun-Tashan Road, father, near Liutenski Budyshcha."

"Fetch my horse! Let's hit the road, lads!"

The clearing and the whole grove immediately sprang to life, seething with humanity.

Motonis hurriedly embraced Hryhoriy, kissed him on the cheek and said sorrowfully: "Who knows, if we'll ever meet again in this world. I'm very, very glad that I came across you."

"Me too, Mykola."

"Farewell! *Vita sine libertate, nihil!*"[70]

"Amen!"

A moment later Motonis had mounted his horse. He waved goodbye, let out a whistle, and disappeared into the forest.

The wagons and the horsemen dissolved into the grey twilight one after another. Slowly the hubbub subsided… When the last cart had disappeared into the thickets, Nychypir Dolia stopped his horse beside Hryhoriy, took off his grey hat and said sadly, but brusquely: "Fare ye well, countryman! Who knows when we meet again… Sharpen those pens, dear fellow! Because to tell the truth, our strength has blunted, for what it's worth!" He dug his spurs into the horse's sides. "Farewell!"

"God protect you!" Hryhoriy called after him and sat down heavily.

The fire was barely glowing. The twilight was growing thicker. The heavy autumn darkness was smothering the half-extinguished fires, which became covered in ash, shielding each spark for those great outbursts yet to come,

....

[70]   Life is nothing without freedom! (Latin)

which would raise flames like crimson banners, proclaiming a new Great Day.

Fine cold drops rained down. And then a wind began to blow and brought fluffy wet snow from the darkness.

* * *

Skovoroda arrived in Chornukhy on frozen ground. There was a breath of the near and dear. Like the prodigal son he was ready to fall upon this beautiful earth, to burst into tears of joy and to beg the shadows of his ancestors not to send him away at this difficult time, but to shower him with their love and provide him with at least a small fraction of the earthly paradise he had grown up in and which he had left for the wide world, driven by his thirst for knowledge. Oh, promised land! Forgive those like me our years of travel, vain hopes and wicked captivity, which has kept us at a distance from you! Grant us our last vestige of strength or accept us into your generous bosom. Blessed are the paths leading home, blessed is the infallible firmament, which we strive for during our voyages!

He moved along the road travelled by *chumaks* and celebrated an endless string of meetings. The woods, the orchards, the outcrops, the houses, the trees, the barns – everything here whispered stories of childhood, filling his old, mummified body with youthfulness. What beauty, what bliss! He was brimming with joy, like a spring with water, his chilled soul had been warmed and became immensely kind and all-forgiving.

All the same, something galled him, something stopped him ever more persistently from welcoming this dear, serene haven... He had not been here a quarter of a century. Where trees had grown, there were now black stumps; where there had been beautiful yards of ensigns and Cossacks, there was now wasteland or sad-looking hovels resembling beggars. It seemed as if an epidemic had passed through the village... Although it was a Sunday, Hryhoriy came across no one. Only here and there the sad eyes of children gleamed from windows... Gradually his joy melted, the fog of memories shifted from his eyes and soon, instead of dreaming of the past, Hryhoriy came face to face with reality, seeing things as they were, in all their squalor and ugliness.

From afar he saw his own house. He recognised it by the pear tree and the stork's nest. And almost burst into tears. Lord Almighty, could he really be home, in his native village, on the banks of the Mnoha River?! He closed his eyes and from all directions he was engulfed by everything he had once heard and seen on this earth, on these narrow fortress streets. His grandpa, father, mother, neighbours, his brother and his sister-in-law and their children shouted, wept, laughed, swore, told him of their problems, adventures and dreams…

"A good day to you," someone said beside him.

Skovoroda opened his eyes and answered the old man, who stood with hat slightly raised. No matter how hard he looked, he was unable to recognise him – there had never been an old man like that in the village… He smiled, suddenly recalling that since the day of his departure from here for the academy, forty years had passed. This old man had probably been a youth back then. What time did to people!

He went down the ascent along which the Swedes had once stormed the castle. He paused for a moment by the stream, which ran beside the ramparts down to the Mnoha River and, as if in childhood, tested it to see if the ice was strong. Not bad, one could skate on it… His soul again filled with a sharp stab of joy. Every bush here and every path, even every clod of earth, reminded him of something and spoke to him mutely and passionately.

He could already see the windows and the door of his home, the cart by the barn and the leaning osier fence…

Skovoroda entered the yard and, leaning on his maple staff (his strength had left him), headed toward the house. He took in, caressed everything which had survived from those distant days or was at least similar to the grey witnesses of his childhood. His heart thudded ever more strongly in his chest, it became harder and harder to breathe. Finally, he succumbed completely and sat down on the frozen earthen porch. Now, now, Hryhoriy, keeling over in the wind already? He lacked the strength to cover even a few sagenes… Could his time have come? No, this was not the end, he was not on death's doorstep! He hadn't had a crumb to eat for two days… He would presently soothe his heart and rest.

The heavy oak door creaked open and a boy of six or seven ran out into the yard. Dressed in a sheepskin coat and someone's large boots. He came up to Hryhoriy and timidly handed him a piece of bread. He took it, brought the fragrant crust to his lips and kissed it. He brushed away a tear which clung to his unshaven rough cheek, and asked the small boy: "Who are you?"

"Kyrylets."

"Whose house is this?"

"Ours..."

"Is daddy home?"

"Yes..."

"Come here."

"I don't want to..."

Hryhoriy took out his flute and handed it to the small fellow. He grabbed it, quickly looked it over and stuffed it inside his shirt.

"Can you play?"

"Yep."

"Play something for me."

"Which song?"

"D'you know the one about Hryts?"

"Yep."

"What about the golden-maned horse?"

The boy thought, sedately brought the flute to his lips and began on the wrong note.

"Not like that, Kyrylets!" Hryhoriy stopped him. "Here, let me show you... I'll teach you."

And the flute began to sing as if it was alive. Hryhoriy's very soul floated out through the guelder rose reed in marvellous sounds. And the earth began to come alive, to shed its winter constraints. A thick carpet of knot grass spread through the yard... The garden blossomed with basil, big-mouthed broad beans, sumptuous poppies... The trees became covered in buds, then blossom and leaves, there was an intoxicating smell of pears... Birds burst into song: the cuckoo, the hoopoe, the turtle dove and the nightingale... God, how this inconspicuous little grey bird warbled in the dense ancient pear tree!

And suddenly a scream: "Hryhoriy, dear brother?!"

He shuddered. Near the doorway, his arms raised like wings, stood his completely grey brother. Skovoroda got up and went toward him.

"I heard someone playing!" His brother laughed through his tears. "I said it must be Hryhoriy! But my son didn't believe me, said you probably hadn't been among the living for a long time. But I said, alive or not, it's him all the same, for no one else can play like that..."

"Gramps, grandpa!" the small boy tugged at his coat.

"Want the flute?" Hryhoriy asked, bending over. "Here, play to your heart's desire."

The youngster grabbed it and dashed into the house.

"Eh, what a scoundrel, recognised his grandfather!" Stepan laughed with a toothless mouth. "He's my youngest son's boy, an amusing little fellow... Why are we standing about here, talking, come inside! Oksen, Katria, do you hear, the Lord has sent us joy!" the old man called into the anteroom. "Fetch a bottle and some breakfast! Kyrylets, where are you, go quickly and call Uncle Petro and auntie, and also Auntie Hanna!"

On the threshold the guest was met by a tall portly man in an embroidered shirt and baggy pants and a blonde ox-eyed woman in a shirt and wraparound skirt – a spitting image of Mariana!

"Welcome inside..."

"Peace to your home!" Hryhoriy blessed them, stood his staff next to the oven-forks and embraced his nephew. "You haven't grown up too badly!"

"Always in earth and manure, and the Lord's not stingy with rain," Oksen joked.

"He's taken after you, Hrytsko – has a tongue like a razor," Stepan said.

Hryhoriy looked into Katria's blue eyes and asked in a numb voice: "You wouldn't happen to be from Kovray?"

"No, I'm from Voronky," the woman whispered and blushed.

"We barely managed to convince the landlord," Stepan said sullenly. "Fleeced us of so much money and still bears a grudge."

"Against us all," Oksen buzzed.

"But you're Cossacks!"

"She's a Cossack girl too..."

"And where's your mother?" Hryhoriy asked softly.

"At God's side for the second year, may she rest in peace," Stepan sighed, crossing himself.

There was a stamping of feet in the anteroom, a whirlwind tore the door open, and Kyrylets materialised in the doorway. Behind him stood a mob of relatives.

They became intoxicated quickly, harmoniously, as if in a hurry to get drunk, to drown their souls. After the third glass they even began to sing, and then weep and reproach their venal fate, which had sold itself to the noblemen.

Hryhoriy listened, watched this cascade of pain, and was again filled with the same sadness which he thought he had left at the gate, at the entrance to his native haven. Here, as everywhere else, everything was being smashed, destroyed, and on the ruins of freedom the Judases built their palaces and kennels. What firmament, what *petra* was this, Lord? Where do we now seek peace and truth, in which parts, from which people, which god?!

He was still here but already far away. As if through a wall he would catch a few words, a song, Mariana-Katria's carefree laughter, which broke his heart, already covered in festering wounds.

Like planets about the sun, all the talk, all the thoughts, revolved around enslavement, which advanced on the people in a cloud. Already the people of Voronky, and Kovali, and Kyzlivka, and half of Chornukhy had become serfs...

"This is infamy!" said Hryhoriy and everyone became silent. "All people in the world are made of one and the same dough and so all are equal. Slavery and oppression are alien to human nature, they are an odious invention of the nobility. Who gave one man the right to live his life like a drone and grow rich on the labour of others? Nature or God? Rubbish! The yoke was created by man and man must destroy it. A great brotherhood of equals – here is the kingdom of happiness, love and peace! Labour and friendship are innate notions. Without any landlords, serfs or caesars. Only working people!"

"That's idle talk," Stepan said. "That will never be..."

"Yes, it will!"

"When pigs fly... There are courts, prisons, the army!"

"When patience runs out – the people become like a storm, nothing can stop them."

"Where are those people? There is only fear, oppression, and poverty, everyone has only one thing on their minds – to avoid having to go begging or dying of hunger."

"Our people are asleep," Oksen added.

"Asleep is not yet dead. When the time comes, they'll awaken!"

"Maybe," Stepan agreed peaceably. "Pity, we won't live to see it..."

"Who knows, brother?" Hryhoriy embraced him. "There are brave people who do not sleep and do not let others doze. Who knows, you and I may yet see the day when freedom will be resurrected!"

"Eh, now, Hryhoriy," Stepan drawled. "If only we could live to see the summer and a new harvest…"

"Was there a bad harvest?"

"Apparently not… But there's only a scrap of land left."

"Where's the patrimony?"

"Went to visit the landlord and never returned…"

Petro, the elder of the two nephews, tired of this melancholy discussion, rested his head on his hand and launched into a sad melody:

> *Oh, I didn't sleep one dark night,*
> *And I won't sleep another,*
> *How weary I feel*
> *And my heart's rather sad,*
> *I'm a young Cossack lost for words…*

* * *

On the morning of the third day Hryhoriy prepared to leave.

"Where you off to, uncle?" Katria raised the alarm.

"I've stayed long enough, Katria, it's time to hit the road."

"Dad, he's leaving!"

"What are you doing, brother?" Stepan stopped whittling a spoon. "If something's not right, then say so…"

"Everything is fine, thank you," Hryhoriy stopped him. "Don't be offended, I'll be off. We saw each other, chatted…"

"You're old, exigent, and frail, where will you roam? Stay here and live out the rest of your life in peace."

"Peace was not destined for us, brother. We are grey orphans, strangers in our own home…"

"Hryhoriy, don't say such things!" Stepan stood up. "You're master here! We're not Mussulmen to go breaking old ancestral customs."

"Don't get angry, I'm not on about that."

"Then stay."

"I can't, brother. I know, you'll be ready to share your last piece of bread with me. But will that piece go into my mouth when hungry eyes stare at it," Hryhoriy said in a low voice.

Stepan lowered his heavy grey head, Katria sighed and, furtively wiping her tears, began to gather some trifles for the road for this strange guest.

His brother wanted to see him off. At the gate they stopped and, taking off his hat, Hryhoriy bowed to Katria, the children (Oksen had gone off somewhere), the woodshed, the pear tree, the house, and the stork's nest.

"Wherever I see a stork, I recall our house…" He smiled to fight off the tears.

"They've left it," Stepan waved his hand. "It's been empty for three years."

Hryhoriy's heart contracted unkindly. Everywhere there was death, desolation. One by one everything was passing into oblivion, ground up by the implacable stones of time, captivity and poverty. The age-old firmaments were being destroyed, and in their place yawned gloomy abysses…

"Where you off to now?" Stepan asked, after they had passed the long-neglected fortress ramparts.

Hryhoriy cowered: he was not yet sure himself. And suddenly he said: "To Pereyaslav. I've a good old friend there, Mykyta Haister."

"You've decided that just now?"

"Yes."

Stepan stopped.

"Well then, farewell!"

They kissed three times, firmly shook hands and without looking back, went off in opposite directions.

*　*　*

The last ten to fifteen versts Skovoroda ran, rather than walked. It was as if a whirlwind had placed its wings under him and bore him along to the famous city between the Trubizh and the Alta rivers. During the long dark nights spent in stranger's houses, among strange people, while being alone on the road, he had bitterly nurtured a new goal, a new hope of finding a cosy haven at least until the spring, at least for a few months. The words, uttered unintentionally, overwhelmed his thoughts and his heart. Faster,

faster to Pereyaslav! He had a true friend there, someone he could rely on, it was his promised land!

A wind was blowing from the north, sharp and piercing. And there was the tart smell of snow borne along by large dark clouds. These dragons kept crawling along ever lower, hiding the last scraps of sky. Though it was only noon, the heavy, oppressive greyness – a darkness diluted with drops of light – was already inundating the steppe and extinguishing the already sombre tones. The sparse, withered stubble, haystacks compressed by rain, bleached grass, the green-black patches of winter wheat – everything was gradually falling asleep...

Unexpectedly he found himself on the bare bank of the river and saw the city. As before, the majestic churches towered over it. True, the crosses and domes did not burn with fire, being barely visible in the grey gloom. The Trubizh River was silent under a sheet of ice and only here and there was the deep water still seething, having licked away its icy covering, breaking free of its cold fetters. The fortress walls around the city had collapsed and reminded one of a toothless mouth. There was something creepy about these ruins, this frozen river, the dull gold of the crosses and domes... He recalled his melancholy entry into Chornukhy, the mute desolation of the streets... No, no! Rubbish. The cold wind, the clouds, the weariness of old age – this was the work of the demon, which had covered his thirsty soul with a blanket of sorrow. Lord, do not let me lose faith in Your supreme wisdom and mercy, allow me to draw strength from Your generosity, which You have long since showered upon these steppes and these city ruins!

On his last legs, leaning on his staff, he trudged along the dam road, and then through the streets, where almost everything was as it had been twenty years earlier. This emboldened him, for he did not like the immobile, the long putrefied, even though lately he had begun to fear change, which was for the most part wicked and tragic. Many things had drifted into the past, into obscurity before his very eyes: the Cossack freedoms, the regiments, the Hetmanate, the Sich, the *haydamak* rebellions, and much more. In their place there was slavery. Half of Ukraine was already enserfed, and the same fate awaited the rest of the people.

He passed the collegium, the cathedral, the bell tower and heaved a sigh of relief when he saw that the lieutenant's two poplars were still in place. Bah, they had even grown – twice as high and twice as wide! He stopped, wiped the sweat from his brow and continued slowly, no longer hurrying, no longer fearing that instead of Haister's house he would find a wasteland. At once his heart felt better. The sorrow and fatigue disappeared completely. He even began to hum Mykyta's favourite 'psalm' about the good neighbour and the pike perch that he was lugging to his female friend:

> *The reeds are crackling,*
> *And the water's splashing...*

Was Mykyta still so cheery and lively? He had probably changed, becoming staid and wise, restrained. Come what may, he was probably a grandfather already, with rank and estates... Oh, not a bad yard. It looked prosperous. He didn't seem to have grown any richer, but he hadn't grown poorer either... Would he recognise him? Never. He might even drive him out, thinking he was some beggar. He was a nobleman, after all... There he was himself! Tall, portly, with a luxurious black shock of hair, as if time had no power over him. Standing there and winding up the reins...

"Good day, Mister Haister," Hryhoriy called out, leaning on the low fence.

"Good health to you too," the fellow replied affably, tied the end of the reins up and turned around.

Hryhoriy was stunned: in twenty years Mykyta had not aged one bit, in fact he'd grown younger! Saints above!

"Did you want something, grandpa?" the fellow asked meekly.

Hryhoriy sat down on the sty.

"Mykyta, what's with you?" he said hollowly.

"I'm not Mykyta, grandpa. My name's Bohdan."

Heavens above, so this was little Bohdan, Mykhailo's eldest!

"Is your father home?"

Bohdan frowned, studied the stranger intently and, crossing himself, said: "No, he's not. It's been eight years."

"Passed away?"

"Killed. In Bessarabia."

"And your mother?"

"Passed away too. When she heard that father was killed, something happened to her, and within six months she was no more... Why, did you know them, grandpa?"

"Yes, I knew them, sonny, I knew them well..."

"Then come inside please, warm yourself and have a bite to eat," Bohdan opened the gate. Skovoroda didn't have the strength to take even a step into Mykyta's yard, where there was no Mykyta or his charming Onysia, whom he had 'wrenched' from Lokhvytsia. He hurriedly passed by the gate and wandered back into the city.

"Where are you off to, grandpa?"

"I'll be on my way. I'm running late," Skovoroda mumbled fearfully and quickened his step.

"Who's there, Bohdan darling?" A clear woman's voice reached him from the house.

"Some strange old beggar... I asked him to come inside, but he refused."

Hryhoriy was struck by a headwind, it tore at his coat flaps, strewed snow into his eyes. And the world melted, disappearing in a white whirlwind. He was all alone! Br-r-r... It was frightening, creepy... But then it was better this way. He was free. He could go where he pleased. But which road should he take, which street? Where was Pereyaslav? It had disappeared. He had intercepted it and lost everything now... What an endless snowstorm! An uncontrollable white wind and black snow... Or perhaps it was merely night, broken into countless black splinters... Or day. Yesterday's. No, possibly tomorrow's. It was better to shred the future – the pain was far worse. The past was easier to shred and easier to piece together... Everything was being torn up, thrown into the wintry wind.

> *Quiet, quiet, flows the Danube,*
> *Quieter still the girl brushes her hair...*

Someone was singing. Who would think it, Mykyta Haister! Brought a song back from the Danube. No, it was someone else. Mykyta was still back there... They say the blood came up as red poppies there. The whole steppe was aflame with poppies...

He only regained his senses in the fields beyond the Trubizh River.

It had stopped snowing and the wind had died down somewhat. Shaggy clouds crawled over the lily-white world.

Poppies, poppies...

Damned memory! Where had he seen these flames, these red-black flowers?

At the crossroads he turned right, where his tracks had probably not yet cooled under the covering of snow. He had no intention of returning to Chornukhy, and chose this road just for somewhere to walk. It was all the same to him, he didn't care anymore. His head was like a bell in the wind, booming away. He was burning up inside. He bent over, picked up a handful of snow and placed it in his mouth. Bong, bong… Inside his temples. Why was it so stifling and hot? Summer was here… He pulled at the coat on his chest.

Sweep away the coals, the coals, mother
You'll sure miss, sure miss your daughter…

Someone's wedding! The horses were striking the earth, the musicians putting on a show, the *svakhas* and bridesmaids were singing… Ah, it was his nephew getting married! There he was, Stepan and Katria… Poppies, poppies everywhere! On Katria's sleeves… She smiled – and then he saw that it was Mariana! Lord, where was she going, what was wrong with her?! She sailed along like a ghost, and red-black flowers kept falling from her sleeves onto the ground… Mariana! She had disappeared…

Not bothering to wipe away his cold tears, Skovoroda turned right again. To Kovray, to Kovray! He wanted to see her one last time, and then he could die. That graceful, cheerful, blue-eyed ray of sunshine, his wretched happiness… It was close by, no more than fifty versts away…

Oh, the small girl runs and runs,
With a water nymph on her heels…

Mariana pressed close to him in fright and whispered: "What do you think, have the water nymphs all hidden or are they still roaming about?"

Skovoroda embraced the girl's shoulders… and suddenly let out a scream: she was already an old woman! God, everywhere there was death, ruins, destruction. Take it, take it all, cruel Lord, everything that there is, all that You can see. Ruin it, rub it into dust, only leave Mariana alone! You're silent, screwing up Your eyes with cunning… What have I said that's so funny? I've had enough of Your wisdom, Your deaths, Your terrible laws! I won't venture there, I won't see her. I'll cheat Your satraps, I'll hide her image in the very depths of my heart and won't let You have it!

He hugged his chest with his arms and raced back. Off to Kyiv, to his alma mater! Myslavsky was wise and powerful, he wouldn't let him be preyed upon. He was firmament, he was the *petra*. As Avvakum[71] had intoned: I will step onto the rock and stand guard for all time! The earth is spinning head over heels, rocking away like a rough sea. The snow is black, and white, it is circling, flowing in ribbons... Mariana is beating about in his chest, ready to burst out at any moment...

Exhausted, he sat down under a willow, slowly slid off his bag and pressed his back against the solid trunk. What bliss! It was probably like this in paradise. After growing weary in this world, the soul flew off to Eden and rested under a tree in paradise...

He grabbed a handful of snow and brought it to his lips. It was sweet as spring water... But where was that paradise? In the East? Nonsense! 'The Lord God planted a garden in the east, in Eden.' Where did one have to stand to spy that paradise, in which direction did one need to face?

He closed his eyes and listened to the bells tolling. Bong-bong, clang-clang, bong-bong, clang-clang... How lovely! It was only a pity that one of them was cracked, spoiling the whole melody... clattering and thumping away... Bong-bong, clang-clang... Thump-thump...! Like a cart going over frozen clods. To hell with it all!

"Whoa-ah, stop, my darling Bay!" he heard suddenly.

Skovoroda raised his eyelids and saw a cart, pulled by a single horse. The driver dropped his reins, rubbed his numb hands together and made his way toward him. He was small, blond, dressed in a sheepskin coat and a skirt. *Pardon*, a cassock. He said something as he approached, but Hryhoriy did not hear him. Those damned bells! They couldn't be the Kyiv bells, could they? Or were they tolling in Pereyaslav? Bong-bong, clang-clang...

"I said good day, old man." the monk called out.

Hryhoriy only nodded. His tongue had grown rough and wouldn't move in his mouth.

"Why are you sitting here?"

----

[71]   Avvakum Petrovich (1620–1682) – Russian writer and cleric.

"I'm on my way."

"Where to?"

"Kyiv."

"That's quite some distance, old man," the monk said craftily. "You won't make it by nightfall! On a pilgrimage?"

"No."

"Visiting relatives?"

"I'm off to see Myslavsky... To my alma mater... At the academy there..."

"You're a little late, old man!" The monk spread out his arms. "By ten years! Your Myslavsky has long since been in Muscovy. Tending bears..." He put his hand to Hryhoriy's forehead and said anxiously: "You're burning up, gramps! Hurry, come with me, I'll take you home. Where do you live?"

Bong-bong, clang-clang... Myslavsky was tending bears. Where you going, you brown devil, there's no wolf to keep you in line! Swish, swish with his hunting crop...

"Where do you live, old man?! Who are you, where you from?"

"I'm Daniel Meinhardt, Skovoroda," Hryhoriy mumbled and sang in a soft hoarse voice:

> *There is no better,*
> *There is no finer,*
> *Place than our Ukraine!*

The monk lifted him up and led him off to the cart.

"I'm still alive, where are you dragging me, you Lucifer!" Hryhoriy shouted and resisted.

"Onto the cart, Hryhor Savych. It's soft and warm there... We'll make Drabiv, and stay the night there – and then on to Pryluky and Hustynka... I've a fine horse..."

"The horse, the horse! Can you hear it?"

Hryhoriy broke free and ran off into the fields. Somewhere close by a golden-maned horse was neighing and he could hear its feet squelching through the mire! There it was, flying out like the wind onto the black and white hill and with a shake of its fiery mane, the horse raced off into the steppe, neighing...

"Horsie, horsie! Horsie, horsie!"

There was only the wind, a low rumble and the tolling of the bells. Bong, bong, bong, bong...

He wiped away a tear. Dragging his bag through the snow, he made his way to the cart. Calmly he allowed himself to be laid out in the hay and covered with something warm. And he was consumed by a sudden rush of heat. Bong, bong...

✶

...AND THE FINAL NET

All winter long and throughout spring Hryhoriy struggled with illness and tore at the snares of death. In the scanty cell to which the kind monk had brought him, he had often heard the rustle of wings and the chilling presence of the angel of death, Azrael. However, neither the winter nor the spring became the last in his life. The last ones, those which delineated the extent of his existence, did not come soon, but they came. There were still years of suffering ahead of him, new books written in solitude in apiaries, new translations of works by great wise men and countless discussions with the common folk and the high and mighty. Perceive yourself. Bless the Lord, that he had made the necessary easy, and the unnecessary difficult. There was a great brotherhood, a kingdom of love and friendship. Unequal equality... Meanwhile all around him that love, and brotherhood, and friendship, steadily diminished. One by one Cossack villages said goodbye to their freedom, the most necessary thing was made difficult and unattainable. Hryhoriy saw all this, suffered intolerably and burnt in the flames of his inability to stop this barbarism, to give people back their minds and their charity.

And one day, while walking around the pond in Pan-Ivanivka, to which he had taken such a liking these past few years, he sensed that this was it, that the time to depart had arrived. *Vixi et, quem dederat cursum fortuna peregi!*[72] Actually, he was ready. His manuscript books, which he had had with him, had long since been sent to Mykhailo in St. Petersburg. He had nothing to bequeath. His only wish was to see his closest true friends and pupils one last time, to chat with them before the long road ahead. Mykhailo was meant to buy a settlement sometime now and to return to his hearth and home. And Yakiv was close by, he could be summoned by letter or by word of mouth. He was already a priest. A clever fellow! After reading

---

[72]   I have finished living and have completed the path which fate has provided me! (Latin)

Silenus Alcibiadis, he flew into a rage and blacked out not only the author's name, but also the dedication. This was something new, some misfortune had afflicted Yakiv. He was soft-hearted, he had always been like clay, out of which one could mould whatever one wished.

He sent his letter and waited patiently.

In a few days he awoke with a premonition – it was today! He rose hastily and crawled out of the hut, like Diogenes out of a barrel. He barely managed to straighten himself and after a fit of coughing, went down to the pond.

Despite the number of years he had spent in Pan-Ivanivka, he still could not grow accustomed to this strange corner of the earth. Had he himself wanted to dream up the perfect place, he doubted whether he could have thought up something more picturesque. The deep bed of the river was traversed by a strong wide dam. On the dam stood a mill and some willows. To the right was a pond, looking like a two-pronged powder-horn, in the corner of which was a hillock overgrown with pines. To the left was a ravine filled with tall, slender alders, willows, hops, and various other herbage. Water streamed over the edge of the steep bank. Delicious, cold, and eternal. And beside it stood a park, where the old and the new were united, the natural and the artificial. God, what they didn't have in that park! From the landlord's stone house atop the hill, a shady linden alley went off in the direction of Merla. Near the arbour it split up and spreading out in a five-fingered fan, ran down almost to the pond. This was a smaller pond, the lower one. There was a small well here too. Cattails and guelder rose. To the west was a birch grove, to the east an orchard and poplars. And further on, an oak and a linden, two ancient giants...

He sat down under the oak tree, filled his cupped hand with dew, and refreshed his face. It had puffed up during the night, becoming coarse and alien. His whole body was collapsing, giving up the ghost, not wanting to live any more, refusing to bear a sharp mind and an implacable soul. If it wasn't for his ebullient soul, which knew no weariness and grieved for everything in the world, he would have long ago left this world, which had turned black from woe. He did not fear death and did not cling to every moment, every breath, for he realised that death was just as natural as birth. Everything living had to die one day and it was useless to torment oneself with horrors and strive to entreat the eternal logos to make an exception in his case.

The park, the meadow, the village – everything was waking, greeting the day with a symphony of the most unusual sounds for this place. The rustle of leaves, the cooing of milk spurts striking a bucket, the merry squawk of birds, the creak of the shadoof, the sheep's bleating, the duet of the scythe and the spattle... He closed his eyes – and he was already in Chornukhy, on the enchanting Mnoha River... But something seemed to be missing... Aha, the flute! From his pocket he took the flute Mykhailo had sent him and played slowly, quietly, so as not to upset the sounds of the morning... Beauty, harmony... Just like in paradise...

He didn't know whether it really existed, therefore he wanted to remain here after his death, in this earthly Eden.

Yakiv arrived in the afternoon. Skovoroda met him on the dam, embraced him and did not let go for a long time.

"What's the matter, father?"

"I've missed you..."

"But we saw each other recently!"

"Who knows when we shall meet again, my friend...?"

"Whenever we like," Yakiv said cheerfully. "Either I'll drop by, or you can visit me."

He had become staider, more rotund and there was little of that hearty, straightforward Yasha in him, who had seen Hryhoriy off one early morning on a new journey of escape.

"It's much easier for you, Yakiv," Skovoroda smiled sadly. "When I die, come and visit, don't forget me..."

"Come on now!" Yakiv spread out his arms. "You'll outlive us all, Hryhor Savych. You're only seventy-two. You still look like you could serve in the grenadiers!"

"I'm not joking, my friend," Hryhoriy stopped him. "My time has come..."

Pravytsky gradually sobered and became pensive. He adjusted his cassock, as if preparing to hear confession. Then he asked: "Tired?"

Hryhoriy made no reply. They walked into the park, along the path past the spring.

"Would you like a drink? The water's good here, try it."

"It's no better than ours," Yakiv remarked indifferently. "They bring me Skovorodynivka water every day..."

"What, what?" Skovoroda asked.

The visitor smiled.

"That's the name they've given to a well in Babayi near which Skovoroda lived and wrote his books."

Bewildered, Hryhoriy moved silently along the barely visible path among the herbage, not knowing what to say and how to treat the news. Though he did not suffer from vanity and vainglory, still it was gratifying that people remembered him, that he had not lived his life in vain.

"And at the market in Kharkiv two weeks ago a blind minstrel was singing about Lazarus, and then he went and launched into your 'Each city has its own customs and rights'! He took away half a hatful of coins…"

Lord, was he tempting him on purpose, this devilish Yakiv! However, it was true – Hryhoriy himself had many a time heard his songs being performed by minstrels, priests and simple villagers.

"What's happening in the world?" he asked his visitor.

"And you said you were going to die!" Yakiv called out, gladdened.

"Going to die does not mean I'm dead already."

"Our friend Panas became a grandfather a few days back. Lohvyn drank, drank, and became an inveterate drunkard…" Yakiv turned down two fingers. He became silent, screwed up his forehead and burst out laughing: "Now there was a bit of a commotion at the Soshalskys! The student Kudrytsky came to them to teach the children French. They gave him dinner, put him to bed. And in the morning they looked – and there was his imprint on the sheet, as if done in ink…"

"What news from Poland?"

"They're fighting," Yakiv shrugged his shoulders.

"Have they granted the people freedom?"

"Kosciuszko granted it, but the nobles wouldn't let it out of their hands."

"What about the French?"

"Still fighting."

"Is the republic alive?"

"It lives," Yakiv said in a whisper.

"How are things at home?"

"Quiet."

"Our country is still asleep," Hryhoriy sighed.

"What do you mean?"

"I mean our people, you and me."

"You're always rebelling."

"What kind of rebel am I? I'm only a sower who wants to see the green shoots of fresh growth..."

"You're sowing on rock, Hryhor Savych."

"Our earth is much too trampled and watered with tears, instead of rain."

"That's as good as rock."

"No, stone is dead, while the earth is alive."

Hryhoriy sat down under the linden, tired. Bending down a branch, he smelt a small cluster of blossom. Pravytsky lay in the grass, threw his arms apart and peered into the sky for a long time.

"His grace asked about you. He was passing through," he said eventually.

"A worthy pupil of Kraisky," Skovoroda waved his hand dismissively.

"You're wrong," Yakiv sat up sharply. "He's an educated man, noble, warm."

"One shouldn't judge people by their words, but by their actions."

"What does he do?"

"The same things as Kraisky. They're all birds of a feather."

"It must be true what they say," Yakiv said sadly. "That you're like a ruff."

Skovoroda smiled.

"The ruff is a clever fish, Yakiv. So small and ugly, but try to eat it – you'll choke."

"Is anyone pestering you? You yourself pick on everyone, you're unhappy with everything, always stirring people up..."

"You've been lulled, Yakiv," Hryhoriy stopped him. "They gave you a tasty morsel piece and you fell asleep."

Pravytsky turned red.

"What was I supposed to do?" he pronounced quietly. "The children..."

"I'll step down onto the rock and stand on guard... Remember Avvakum's words?"

"But where's that rock, father?"

"Seek, and ye shall find."

Avoiding looking into his teacher's eyes, Pravytsky walked around the oak tree. He surveyed the crown, the trunk, picked a leaf and smelt it.

"It's ancient... Three hundred years old!" he called out peaceably. "And it will remain standing for as long again..."

"It's no big deal for it to stand. That's what oaks are for."

"His grace wants to visit Pan-Ivanivka and meet you face to face," Yakiv said triumphantly and beamed. He had probably savoured this unique moment the whole way here.

"Really!" Skovoroda pretended to be very glad. "I'm not worthy of such honour. That can never be…"

"By God, it's true!" Pravytsky ran up to him. "He said it himself, in my home. He took copies of your works. Read them, praised them!"

"God Almighty," Skovoroda sighed grievously. "I had hoped to die in peace…"

"The bishop will come in peace. Be humble too, open up your soul to his Reverence, remove the sorrow from your heart and return to the bosom of the church!"

Skovoroda felt sorry for a person who was now speaking a stranger's words so zealously and elatedly, doing the will of someone else and obviously coming here not for a last 'forgive me', but for the kiss of betrayal. No, he was not capable of treachery! He was weak-willed, gentle, ready to do anything for peace, quiet and bliss.

"And what will we have out of this?" Hryhoriy asked, alluding to thirty pieces of silver.

"For me – an archpriest's position in Kharkiv." Yakiv broke his banks. "For you – peace, the laurels of an ascetic, peaceful glorious old age. And after death – the title of a saint!"

Skovoroda could not help laughing.

"Come on, that's nonsense, Yakiv," he said reproachfully. "How can one trade in such things!"

The bishop's emissary dared not raise his eyes. He stood downcast and crumpled up the leaf.

"Teacher, I did not think it would make you indignant," he said after a while. "I figured it would please you."

"Obviously we taught you badly."

"But you seemed…"

"Yakiv, in our bad times, when you're riding a cart, you must look back at the rear wheels. Remember how Father Lavrentiy and I nearly ended up in Siberia!"

"One doesn't forget such things," Yakiv said, frowning. "But Hryhor Savych, each of your works contains the spirit of the Holy Scripture, the history of the holy faith. And only here and there…"

"*Sapienti sat,*[73] as they say!"

"That is true… However, is such cunning deserving of a man?"

"'Be wise as serpents, and harmless as doves.'[74] From the gospel. Christ's own words."

"All the same, I despise cunning!"

"Me too, Yakiv. But we still write, live, and struggle through the prayers of our Jesus. Does the end justify the means?"

"I don't know. Maybe…"

Yakiv's coachman appeared.

"Father, the lords are inviting you and him," he nodded at Skovoroda, "to come and eat."

"And have you eaten yet?"

"They offered me food."

"Well then, let's go." Hryhoriy got up. "Andriy Ivanovych is a hospitable nobleman."

After lunch Yakiv prepared to leave. Skovoroda did not try to stop him, they had seen each other, chatted; he would still see him off. Everything had to continue according to its natural custom, to flow and change. One couldn't step twice into the same river. And if you dammed the water up, stopped it flowing – the water became stagnant, putrid.

Bidding the coachman to catch up to them, they walked ahead slowly. They wanted to be alone, to smooth over their guilt at the vexing altercation, at the unpleasant sediment which remained in the soul of each.

"We probably won't see each other again in this world," Hryhoriy began first. "Don't harbour any ill feelings toward me. I was nasty today…"

"And I was a good-for-nothing, right?"

"Weak-minded."

"Thank you."

"For what?"

"The truth."

----

[73]   Sufficient for the wise. (Latin)

[74]   Matthew 10:16, KJV.

"It is not valued now – everyone is selling, no one wants to buy."

The buggy caught up to them. Skovoroda looked Yakiv over intently, filling his soul forever with his friend's face, his figure. He choked.

"My good friend..."

"Yes, father?"

"I wanted to tell you something..." Hryhoriy rubbed his forehead. "Thrice damned memory..."

"A testament?"

"That's it! Respect each other, don't let the love for freedom and truth be erased from your soul. Don't give in to despair, don't suffer when there are failures, unpleasantness. We are all precursors. Messiahs will come in our tracks in a year or two, maybe even twenty years. And they cannot but come. Nothing is eternal in this world, least of all untruth!"

"Teacher..." Yakiv was deeply moved. "I... I..."

"Get on the cart and go," Skovoroda said firmly. He embraced him, pressed him close and kissed him.

"Perhaps you could come with me? You could live with us..."

"I can't. Thank you. I've promised Mykhailo."

"Lord Almighty, I forgot. I have a letter for you from him!" Yakiv slapped himself on the forehead.

Skovoroda waited on tenterhooks for Pravytsky to find the long-awaited sheet of paper. It seemed to him that the fellow was purposefully looking for it so apathetically, rummaging about in the corners of his cassock, like a chicken on a muck heap... At last! Hryhoriy grabbed the letter, tore off the seal and began reading, welcoming the familiar dear handwriting, the words and phrases. He reached the signature and understood nothing – a thirsty man drank this way, without tasting the water.

"So, what does Mykhailo say?" Yakiv asked jealously.

"I don't know, just a moment..."

He began to read the letter aloud:

"My loving friend, Hryhoriy Savych! I have wanted to write to you since spring. My wish is to see you and live out my life with you. I tried as best I could to buy a village in the Kharkiv lieutenancy, because I'm accustomed to the region and for your sake as well. I had already worked out the terms, but the neighbours prevented me from concluding the sale... My beloved

Meinhardt! Difficult were the consequences of the privileged circle, in which your good friend found himself, after being left on his own. Disheartened, exhausted by the worries of the world, he turned inwards, finally collecting his scattered thoughts into a small basket of wishes. Having assembled them in his usual genial way, he arrived from the capital into the countryside, hoping there to find a haven from life's storms..."

"Where did he move to, which village?" Yakiv interrupted impatiently.

Hryhoriy looked at the bottom of the letter and read:

"The village of Khotetovo, twenty-five versts from Orel..."

Then he continued reading:

"...but even here the world had disfigured everything. In deep solitude he has remained alone, without family, without friends, without acquaintances, in illness, sorrow, disquiet, with no one to keep him company, offer advice or assistance, or compassion..."

He was unable to read further: his heart was seized with pity, the letters became intermingled and floated off. Something rose in his chest, exploded and grew, irrepressible, passionate, overwhelming his feeble old body.

"He is waiting, suffering... Yakiv, do you hear, Yakiv, Mykhailo is in distress! God, I must go... Take a carriage there!"

Embracing Yakiv vehemently and squeezing the letter in his hand, Skovoroda forgot about everything in the world and ran off to get ready for his final journey.

*   *   *

They left early the next morning. The host gave him his best horses and a brand-new travelling coach. He begged and implored him to wait, for rains had set in, but Hryhoriy would not hear of it and strove to leave on foot. Andriy Ivanovych finally relented, and let him go in peace, as they say. He only bid the coachman to watch over the teacher as if he was his own father, to make sure that he wasn't drenched in a downpour or became too hot in the sun. They parted tearfully, for Skovoroda was not leaving to merely visit someone, he was leaving forever.

The Murava Road was well travelled, the horses ran swiftly, the versts were traversed quickly by the new wheels, however Hryhoriy yearned to move faster. Faster, faster, on to the dear, though unknown, village of Khotetovo! There, God willing, was his close friend! How long hadn't they seen each other? Nineteen years now... Mykhailo was pushing fifty... It was hard to believe. All-victorious and implacable time! Was it that long ago that Hryhoriy first met Mykhailo in the collegium yard, and now – God Almighty! – the fellow had survived all the temptations of the world, had found himself, left his misfortune and joys behind and returned to the bosom of village serenity and forthrightness, which he had walked out on, plunging so thoughtlessly into the vanity of vanities...

Faster, faster! There was so little time left to live!

They drove into the village in the evening of the sixth day. The wavering, dim light from several of the closest windows barely broke through the curtain of rain and thick gloom. Hoarse sleepy dogs barked lazily. The coachman didn't push the horses, they found the street themselves and no longer galloped, merely trotting. They stopped at a crossroads. Grumbling and cursing, the coachman got down from his box seat and wandered off into the darkness.

Skovoroda rubbed his numb legs, moved his shoulders about to drive away the weariness which had accompanied him throughout almost the entire journey. He had no time for falling ill, he had to be strong, cheerful, wise. When one went to heal, one had to forget one's own ailments.

"Well, how is it there, old chap?" he asked, hearing that the coachman had returned.

"It's not far."

"Then let's go!"

They stopped to ask directions twice more and finally stopped outside a gate. They shouted and banged – there was no one anywhere. Silence. Swearing, the coachman moved along the fence, found a hole somewhere and crawled into the yard.

"Is there anyone living about?!" he called in a booming deep voice and banged on the door. "Wake up, sir, you've got guests!"

Soon a small light glimmered. Then came the sound of voices, heavy hasty steps, and an enormous black shape crawled into the travelling coach to join Hryhoriy. It grabbed his hand, fixed its lips to him and whispered in a familiar, dear voice:

"God bless you, father! Lord, is this really not a dream? Hryhoriy Savych, my God!"

Hryhoriy stroked his hot head and could not utter a single word, choking with emotion. Everything he had nurtured in his heart for a meeting such as this, for this very moment, had disappeared without a trace. In its place there was a sharp pain in his heart and a ball of tears in his throat.

The coach set off slowly, passed through the gate and stopped in the yard by the porch.

"Sir, where do I put the horses?" the coachman asked.

"Wait a minute, I'll be a moment," Mykhailo whispered tenderly and disappeared into the darkness.

Skovoroda summoned his entire mighty will to recover, to overcome his deathly fatigue and meet his good friend cheerfully. For he had come to cure him!

Mykhailo ran up. He took his old teacher by the arm, helped him down, and without letting go, led him inside.

"Tired? Such a way... The mud, the rain..."

"That's all right, it's nothing," Skovoroda managed to speak after all. "Desire is worse than slavery."

"If only you knew how overjoyed I am, father!"

"I know."

"But how?"

"Because I'm overjoyed myself."

"Your logic is interesting... There are stairs here – careful, don't trip."

"I'm not as old as you think."

"We'll see presently!" and he opened the wide door. The bright light of three large candles splashed into their eyes.

"Well, greetings, greetings," Hryhoriy embraced his good friend and kissed him. "You're all overgrown, like a sectarian. Too lazy to shave?"

"I find it distasteful, father," Mykhailo said, and began to fuss about. "Why have we stopped here? Please, please! Here – there's an armchair, wine... It won't hurt you to have a drink after such a journey."

"Thank you, I'll sit down... Sit down yourself."

"I'll be a minute. I'll just find something to eat."

"We're not hungry. Where's the coachman?"

"Went off to sleep in the hay. I invited him inside, but he refuses, afraid someone might steal the horses…"

"Sit down, sit down, Mykhailyk."

"I'll make your bed first."

"Later."

Mykhailo sat opposite him, poured himself some wine. He had aged, turned grey, looking more like a defrocked priest than a guardsman from St. Petersburg.

"You live alone?" Hryhoriy asked quietly.

"Like an orphan."

"Your wife stayed behind there?"

"Yes, father."

The rain pattered against the black windows. Wind tore into the room through a broken and badly patched large windowpane, rocking the immobile shadows. Mice were scratching and squeaking somewhere, there was a whine in the chimney or the loft.

"Where are your servants?"

"Gone… Or maybe sleeping in the outhouse."

"Did they drive you out of St. Petersburg or did you run away yourself?"

"There was a bit of everything," Mykhailo sighed and said bitterly: "I've ruined my life, teacher… Old age is on the threshold, and there's a desert in my soul. Not a sapling, not a bush, nor a stalk… You die – and it's as if you've never lived… No one to remember you! And what's more terrible – nothing to remember you by. Like the fig tree which bore no fruit."

"Begin from the start."

"It's late."

"Life shouldn't be measured with the yardstick of years, measure it by your deeds."

"I'd be only too glad… But I've no strength, father."

"You've severed your roots. You must return and grow back into the soil."

"I tried, I wanted to buy an estate somewhere near Kharkiv, but you can see where I ended up."

"Sell the place."

"It's dilapidated. No one will give me even half of what I paid for it."

"Then leave."

"How can I? How will I live?"

"You could teach. Go to a school or a collegium."

"I've forgotten everything."

"You'll remember."

"What about the land, the buildings?"

"Give them away."

"To whom?"

"The villagers."

"And what will I do with them? After all, they're mine."

"Set them free."

The candles were melting. The wind rocked their longish flames, and they seemed like fiery poplars on three graves in the steppe.

Mykhailo finished his chalice, uncorked a new bottle of imported wine, poured himself another glass and drank again.

Then he sat there, downcast, staring somewhere into a corner. Finally, he lifted his eyes to the guest and gave a pained smile: "Let's go to sleep, father! It'll be dawn soon. Do you hear the second roosters crowing?"

During the day Hryhoriy felt bad. A dry scratching cough and unbelievable exhaustion chained him to the armchair, though not forcing him to stay in bed. He couldn't even see off the coachman who was returning to Pan-Ivanivka. His body would not obey, begging peace, rest, and quiet.

The rain did not relent. It would come down in a fine drizzle, then rained cats and dogs, then attacked in a taut wave, shaking the building. And it continued, without an end in sight. A day, two days... Seventeen in total.

On the eighteenth Skovoroda could take no more. He lay down the manuscript of his book which he was reading to Mykhailo and declared: "Please send me home."

"Lord preserve you, father." Mykhailo took fright. "Where will you go? This here's your home!" He spread out his arms. "Live here for two hundred years, if you like."

"I'm not thinking about life at present. The time has come to remember that we are all merely visitors on this earth…"

"Why fret over that too, father? The Lord knows well enough who is destined to finish their life where and when."

"I cannot die here," Hryhoriy said firmly.

Mykhailo wanted to say something amusing, but realising in time who was sitting before him, he only sighed. Ever since the conversation which had taken place on the night of Skovoroda's arrival, Lord Kovalynsky began to fear his teacher, his piercing eyes, and his thoughts, which struck like hammers. It was all so easy for him – leave, give away, set free…

Hryhoriy saw that his friend was suffering, expecting a tormenting conversation, and during all these days he didn't aggravate him even once with reproaches.

"Hryhor Savych, you are relentless," Mykhailo said eventually.

"When I die, I'll quieten down."

"Oh no! Your works and your fame will live on. The people know and love you. There are those that hate you, but no one is indifferent."

Skovoroda fitfully drew his head into his shoulders and waved his arms about: "Stop, enough! I didn't achieve even a quarter of what I could have done. I most likely could have been a Socrates or a Cicero. Who am I today? An old beggar who has written some twenty books, in which there's more chaff than grain."

"No, father, no!" Mykhailo called out fervently. "All your books are virtuous and wise, pious and just."

"To hell with it! Our people are sick to death with all this. I've long felt nauseous from piety and justness. I would have given half my life to have been sinful and wanton!"

"What's wrong with you, teacher?"

"It's your 'desert'. I could have nurtured a grove, a wood, but I'm leaving behind only small bushes."

"Such is fate."

"Perhaps… We avoided the nets, and others will need to tear them. I can sense with my soul that they are coming! Can you hear them?"

"No. I've already grown deaf, I'm indifferent to everything."

"Your ears are blocked with gold," he pronounced tersely. And immediately regretted it. Mykhailo turned pale, became covered in sweat. "Sorry. I didn't mean to offend you…"

"You're speaking the truth, father. I am completely disfigured – my heart, and ears, and eyes…"

"Mykhailo, let's leave here together!"

"I can't: there's a vacuum in my chest."

"A human soul is like a living spring: you can drain it to the last drop, and in the morning, it will be full again."

"Mine has become silted."

"We'll clean it out."

"Don't torment me, father!" Mykhailo jumped up from the armchair. "I'll live honestly and quietly, I won't wrong my people, I'll share my last crust with the poor. I'll put you up as an example, and if I can manage, I'll write your biography. But I can't follow in your footsteps and succeed you! Nor could I ever have..."

"That's true." Hryhoriy rose. "It's time I left."

"Stay!"

"No. My soul wills that I leave immediately."

"At least wait until it clears up."

"I cannot wait. I might not make it..."

"Father, what can I send you off in?"

"Do you have a nag?"

"Yes. But there's no carriage!"

"You don't have what is not needed. Can you rustle up a small buggy?"

"Of course."

"Then be kind enough to tell them to harness it."

"All right... But you're not well."

"I'll recuperate when I arrive."

Mykhailo left with a heavy step. Skovoroda dressed, found his half-empty bag and staff, and slowly followed him out. He sat down on the porch, rejoicing: the rain had stopped, blue sky appeared here and there. The Russian village stood black, alien, gloomy, squalid. Not a wattle fence anywhere, not a tree or a flower to be seen... Slaves... Mykhailo's slaves... What a disgrace! He got to his feet and headed for the stable where the horses were being harnessed. Quick, quick, off home, to his native parts!

They said their goodbyes on the outskirts of the village. Mykhailo touched the coachman with his hand and jumped down off the buggy.

"I'll be heading back then," he announced hoarsely.

"All right."

A stony grief seeped into Hryhoriy's heart.

"Farewell," he announced sorrowfully. "We may not see each other again. Never forget what we talked about. Be merciful, wise, always stick to the truth.

Tirelessly seek verity and await our messiah. He will come soon and save the people and bring liberty through his suffering. I have faith that he will be born!"

They kissed and shook hands.

Off he went. The buggy moved quickly. Further and further away. His good friend's figure kept growing smaller, disappearing in the mist of distance, becoming a painful memory.

*　*　*

The day was serene and sunny. The whole of Pan-Ivanivka was drowning in yellow leaves. They had started falling during the night of the first frosts, covering the frozen earth with a colourful blanket. Apart from the oaks and the pines, the trees in the landlord's park stood bare, black, like motionless ghosts, raising their petrified arms to the sky in frightening sorrow. What were they praying for, what were they begging the Lord for? Spring, generous buds, glorious warm downpours? Or perhaps storms and thunder, when every fibre in the body shuddered?!

Who would understand them, who would hear their mute screams...?

Hryhoriy stepped out of the house in which he had lived upon his return, in a cosy room with a window facing the orchard. Helping himself along with the staff, he descended the steps into the sun-drenched park. He stood a while, screwing up his eyes from the flood of colour and sunshine, and wandered off through the autumn gold.

He had no peace today: neighbouring landlords had arrived, they were carousing and drinking, pestering him, asking him to join them, to have a drink. But that was not all. The worst thing was that his body was going numb and he could barely hear his heart in his chest; if it was not for the pain, he would have thought that it was no longer there. Yes, the time had come for him to end his mortal journey. He only felt sorry for his mind – it was as clear as this high sky. The spirit was sprightly, but the body was frail.

The leaves rustled, pushed aside by his weak feet, and everywhere he went Hryhoriy was followed by two furrows. They saddened him, but also led to reflections about the sense of life, a person's path. Those who had left their good mark on this earth should not be afraid of death.

The hut stood solitary, forgotten by everyone, covered in faded leaves. And yet all the same it breathed of withered blossom, honey, pears, apples, and the summer, which had been his last, and about which he hadn't yet reminisced enough... Ah, why grieve in vain? The crossing had to be made somewhere. Life finished and began again... The same eternity from which we come and to which we return. Everything was simple, wise... And terribly eerie.

Someone had left a spade leaning against the hut. Skovoroda picked it up, examined it and taking a handful of leaves, wiped away the rust. The old steel blade glistened in the sun. Well then, Great Spade, you haven't become so worn in vain. You have good experience behind you, if not yours, then that of your ancestors – having dug millions of graves, countless numbers... Well, today there will be another.

He held the spade, surveyed the park with a calm intent gaze and went off to the two mighty giants. The oak had turned bronze, but had not shed its leaves. Beside it cowered the linden, bare as a rock... Way over there was the pond, the poplars, the willows... Beautiful.

A wonderful spot!

He lay his staff on the ground, raked away the grass and the leaves, and began to dig. The blunt spade unwillingly entered the ancient sod, and this made his hands numb, his feet and back ache. He didn't know if he would have enough strength to finish his last endeavour, but he strove hard all the same.

The noblemen were still revelling. Shouting, playing, trying to sing psalms and chants.

Everything in the world was like this: good and evil, darkness and light, sorrow and joy... A great unity! As the common folk said: one half of the world hops, while the other half weeps.

Tired, he would sit down on the edge of the grave and, breathing frequently and with difficulty, he said his farewells to the sky and the sun, the water of the pond and the willows, the fire of the guelder rose, and the tenderness of the graceful poplars... Today, tomorrow, and in a year all this would still be here, unchanged. Only he would be no more...

Been and gone. How strange...

He got up and again heaved the heavy wet earth.

Toward evening he was caught at his work by Andriy Ivanovych.

"Hryhor Savych, what are you up to?" he asked in amazement.

"Digging."

"What?"

"A grave."

"Who for?"

"Myself."

The master took out a handkerchief and wiped the sweat from his brow. Then he muttered: "You're joking... You're pulling my leg."

Hryhoriy crawled out, wiped his boots with some grass and, catching his breath, said: "I'm not joking, sir... When I die, please bury me in this grave."

Andriy Ivanovych immediately sobered up. Mopping his sweat again, he asked worriedly: "Are you feeling poorly? Do you sense that you are going to die soon?"

"Tonight..."

"God Almighty!" Andriy Ivanovych crossed himself. "Then I'll send for a priest..."

"There's no need to hurry," Skovoroda stopped him. "I haven't died yet."

"What about confession and communion, as ritual demands?"

"It's nothing," Hryhoriy said. "Rites were dreamt up by priests and monks."

"You want to die without absolution?" Andriy Ivanovych asked, horrified. "What about God? What about the world, society?"

"Those who have not sinned need not repent."

"Everyone is sinful."

"True. And priests are no exception."

"But they're people..."

"So how can sinners absolve someone's sins?"

"But they're ordained."

"By similar sinners."

"The things you're saying," Andriy Ivanovych whispered, "send shivers down my spine... Why don't we go inside instead and have dinner...?"

"What about your guests?"

"They've all left."

Slowly they made their way up the hill.

The sun was setting, long dark shadows were spreading out. The crimson leaves had faded and lay like miserable rags, which would no longer swoon to the caresses of the wind, no longer drink the potion of sunshine and fly off the branches like wonderful bright-coloured birds...

Andriy Ivanovych was saying something, arguing about something, but Hryhoriy did not hear him. This was his last evening and he was bidding farewell to the evening, the red sun, the shadows, the fallen leaves, to the entire joyous world. He did not begrudge anything – it was all staying behind. He was dying, having suffered his fill.

The middle-aged lady of the house ran out from behind the barn and yelled:

"He's twiddling his thumbs here, and I've already been everywhere looking for him! Come quickly, Andriy, and do something..."

"Why such a fuss?"

"The bishop is coming, you blockhead!" she rested her hands on her sides. "He's staying the night in Zolochiv and will be here tomorrow!"

Andriy Ivanovych was stunned, as if he had swallowed his tongue. He stood there muttering something, glancing in turn at his wife and at Hryhoriy. At last, he regained his senses and barked, as if before a regiment of Cossacks: "Gather all the servants and all the women from the settlement – I want the house to be clean as a church by morning!"

After the landlady had disappeared, he turned to his lodger, totally bewildered, and spread his arms apart: "Forgive me, Hryhoriy Savych, I must run. Such a guest, it's a great honour for me!"

Skovoroda smiled: "Go, go. Farewell! I'll just ask one thing of you: when you bury me, inscribe on a rock or something similar the words: 'The world pursued me, but failed to catch me'. Can you remember that? You can notify his grace of this too."

"All right, all right. I'll do it all!" Andriy Ivanovych called out. "We'll continue this interesting conversation tomorrow!"

Skovoroda barely made it to the porch, and having surmounted all eleven steps, entered the house, where a great confusion was beginning.

His room was peaceful and dark. Putting down the no-longer-needed staff, he struck some fire and lit the candle end. The room suddenly came to life, filled with thick shadows and beyond the window, outside, it became even darker. The world sunk into darkness, disappearing, passing into obscurity, and Hryhoriy had only a small piece of it left, bordered by the cold masonry of the walls, the table, the bed, the chest, and the flame of the candle.

He took off his boots near the door and stood them beside his staff. Raising the lid of the chest, he put on clean clothes. Without feeling the cold or the floor with his feet, he went over to the table, collected his books and manuscripts and carried them to the bed. He carried them carefully, warily, very much afraid lest he drop and scatter them, because he was not sure if he had the strength to pick them up. He placed them at the head of the bed, covered them with his peasant coat and, crossing himself, lay down.

He sighed with relief, wanted to blow out the candle, but changed his mind: let it burn, there was only about a finger's worth of wax left, it would soon be extinguished...

Well, that was that. He had lived his last day. Death was waiting, the logical end to a human life, the sad finale of a tragedy.

Slowly the body grew numb, becoming alien and cold. It had finished suffering, ready to return to the earth and to change into something else, to complete the circle in some other form – as grass, a guelder rose, or maybe an oak tree...

He recalled the guelder rose on the riverbank, from which his grandfather had made him a flute. That first flute, it was the best ever... Oh, how it had played!

Very faintly at first, and then ever more forcefully, that guelder rose music sailed out of his childhood and resounded, spreading through his soul. Slowly he saw Chornukhy sail before his eyes, the Mnoha River, his father and his tearful, but always cheery mother... She was probably upset that she had died without having bid farewell to her pet... Don't cry, mamma! I will soon catch up to you, ma, I'm already on my way...

He was choking on tears...

Soon after, two more women passed over him as clouds – Mariana first, and then Olena... Were they alive, or were they already waiting for him there?

The flute played, grieved, as if the soul of the guelder rose had become a part of this simple music.

Oh horse, my horse,
With mane of gold...

In the end, he had not ridden out into the open fields with a *kobza*, had not sung a song to make the whole world shudder in awe, so that freedom would gleam in the sun, like sharp steel. Obviously that golden-maned wind was destined for someone else...

The guelder rose wept and grieved... Sorrow squeezed his heart: somewhere out there Mykhailo and Yakiv had his creations, his manuscripts, which would not be going forth among the people... A prophet is without honour in his native land... Prophets there were, but they were feared!

His arms and legs were growing cold... Hryhoriy could see the wind, the well, the willows, a sycamore tree… Water gurgled, a turtle dove chattered in the woods... The flute played his song, enunciating the words:

> *Oh, yellow-breasted bird, take care,*
> *Don't build your nest up in the air!*
> *Oh, weave it here among the grasses,*
> *Upon the green-green river banks.*

No, not like that! Oh God... The minstrels had changed it into colloquial Ukrainian... God!

And suddenly a terrible storm-like thought surfaced: it was he, it was he who had written it incorrectly.

He tried to get out of bed – but it was too late... He opened his eyes. The candle was barely flickering.

Gloomy, feeble shadows rocked about, as if lulling him to sleep, appeasing the final pain in his chest.

Suddenly the flickering, dull flame died away and there was no more pain… Darkness...

The flute began to play again… Sorrowful, loud… Then it grew steadily softer and softer…

ABOUT THE TRANSLATOR

Born in Melbourne, Australia in 1954 and educated as an engineer, Yuri Tkacz left the profession to translate a broad range of works from Ukrainian by such authors as Kaczurowskyj, Honchar, Dimarov, Valeriy Shevchuk, Kariuk, Vynnychenko, Yanovsky and Antonenko-Davydovych. He lived and worked in Canada in the 1980s and in Ukraine in the 1990s. His translations of *Hardly Ever Otherwise* by Matios, *Hard Times* by Vyshnia and *The Lawyer from Lychakiv Street* by Kokotiukha have been published by Glagoslav Publications.

THE NIGHT REPORTER:
A 1938 LVIV MURDER MYSTERY

by Yuri Vynnychuk

The events of the novel *The Night Reporter* take place in Lviv in 1938. Journalist Marko Krylovych, nicknamed the "night reporter" for his nightly coverage of the life of the city's underbelly, takes on the investigation of the murder of a candidate for president of the city government. While doing this, he ends up in various love intrigues as well as criminal adventures, sometimes risking his life. Police Commissioner Roman Obukh, who was suspended by administrators from the murder investigation, aids him in an unofficial capacity. Meanwhile, German, and Soviet spies become involved, and Polish counterintelligence also takes an interest in the investigation. The picturesque and vividly described criminal world of Lviv of that time appears before us – dive bars, batyars, and establishments for women of ill repute. The reader will have to unravel riddle after riddle with the characters against the background of the anxious mood of Lviv's residents, who are living in anticipation of war. *The Night Reporter* is a compelling journey into the world of the enthralling multicultural past of the city.

Buy it > www.glagoslav.com

The Lawyer from Lychakiv Street

by Andriy Kokotiukha

At the beginning of the twentieth century, 1908, a young Kyivan, Klym Koshovy miraculously flies the coop and escapes from persecution by tsarist police to Lviv. However, even here he is arrested – near the corpse of a well-known local lawyer, Yevhen Soyka. The deceased had dubious friends and powerful enemies in the city. Suicide or murder?

The search for truth leads Koshovy through the dark labyrinths of Lviv's streets. On his way – facing daring pickpockets, criminal kingpins and Russian terrorist bombers. And Klym is constantly getting in the way of the police commissioner Marek Wichura. The truth will stun Klym, and his new loyal friend Jozef Shatsky. It will forever change the fate of the enigmatic and influential beauty Magda Bohdanovych.

The Complete
KOBZAR
by Taras Shevchenko

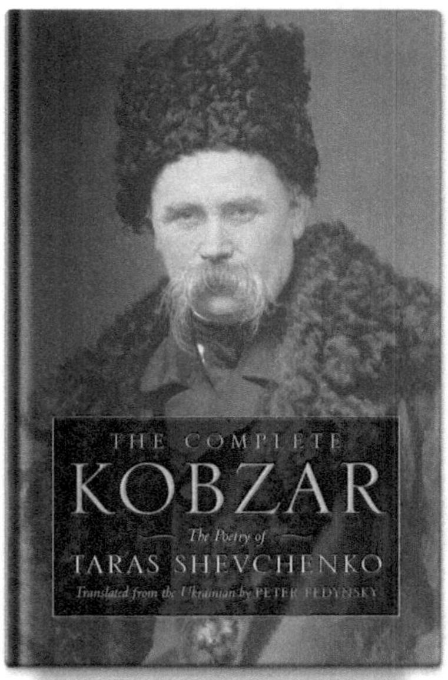

Masterfully fulfilled by Peter Fedynsky, Voice of America journalist
and expert on Ukrainian studies, this first ever English translation
of the complete *Kobzar* brings out Ukraine's rich cultural heritage.

As a foundational text, The *Kobzar* has played an important role in
galvanizing the Ukrainian identity and in the development of
Ukraine's written language and Ukrainian literature. The first
editions had been censored by the Russian czar, but the book still
made an enduring impact on Ukrainian culture. There is no reliable
count of how many editions of the book have been published, but an
official estimate made in 1976 put the figure in Ukraine at 110
during the Soviet period alone. That figure does not include Kobzars
released before and after both in Ukraine and abroad. A multitude of
translations of Shevchenko's verse into Slavic, Germanic and
Romance languages, as well as Chinese, Japanese, Bengali, and many
others attest to his impact on world culture as well.

Buy it > www.glagoslav.com

SEVEN SIGNS OF THE LION

by Michael M. Naydan

The novel *Seven Signs of the Lion* is a magical journey to the city of Lviv in Western Ukraine. Part magical realism, part travelogue, part adventure novel, and part love story, it is a fragmented, hybrid work about a mysterious and mythical place. The hero of the novel Nicholas Bilanchuk is a gatherer of living souls, the unique individuals he meets over the course of his five-month stay in his ancestral homeland. These include the enigmatic Mr. Viktor, who, with one eye that always glimmers, in a dream summons him across the Atlantic Ocean to the city of lions, becoming his spiritual mentor; the genius mathematician Professor Potojbichny (a man of science with a mystical bent and whose name means "man from the other side"); the exquisite beauty Ada, whose name suggests "woman from Hades" in Ukrainian, whose being emanates irresistible sensuality, but who never lets anyone capture her beauty in a picture; the schizophrenic artist Ivan the Ghostseer, who lives in a bohemian hovel of a basement apartment and in an alcohol-induced trance paints the spirits of the city that torment him; and the curly-haired elfin Raya, whose name suggests "paradise" in Ukrainian and who becomes the primary guide and companion for Nicholas on his journey to self-realization...

Buy it > www.glagoslav.com

THE FANTASTIC WORLDS OF YURI VYNNYCHUK

by Yuri Vynnychuk

Yuri Vynnychuk is a master storyteller and satirist, who emerged from the Western Ukrainian underground in Soviet times to become one of Ukraine's most prolific and most prominent writers of today. He is a chameleon who can adapt his narrative voice in a variety of ways and whose style at times is reminiscent of Borges. A master of the short story, he exhibits a great range from exquisite lyrical-philosophical works such as his masterpiece "An Embroidered World," written in the mode of magical realism; to intense psychological studies; to contemplative science fiction and horror tales; and to wicked black humor and satire such as his "Max and Me." Excerpts are also presented in this volume of his longer prose works, including his highly acclaimed novel of wartime Lviv *Tango of Death*, which received the 2012 BBC Ukrainian Book of the Year Award. The translations offered here allow the English-language reader to become acquainted with the many fantastic worlds and lyrical imagination of an extraordinarily versatile writer.

Buy it > www.glagoslav.com

HARDLY EVER OTHERWISE

by Maria Matios

Everything eventually reaches its appointed place in time and space. Maria Matios's dramatic family saga, *Hardly Ever Otherwise*, narrates the story of several western Ukrainian families during the last decades of the Austro-Hungarian Empire, and expands upon the idea that "it isn't time that is important, but the human condition in time."

From the first page, Matios engages her reader with an impeccable style, which she employs to create a rich tapestry of cause and effect, at times depicting a logic that is both bitter and enigmatic. But nothing is ever fully revealed—it is only in the final pages of the novel that the events in the beginning are understood as a necessary part of a larger whole, and the section entitled Seasicknesspresents a compelling argument for why events almost always have to follow a particular course.

Buy it > www.glagoslav.com

HERSTORIES: AN ANTHOLOGY OF NEW UKRAINIAN WOMEN PROSE WRITERS

Women's prose writing has exploded on the literary scene in Ukraine just prior to and following Ukrainian independence in 1991. Over the past two decades scores of fascinating new women authors have emerged. These authors write in a wide variety of styles and genres including short stories, novels, essays, and new journalism. In the collection you will find: realism, magical realism, surrealism, the fantastic, deeply intellectual writing, newly discovered feminist perspectives, philosophical prose, psychological mysteries, confessional prose, and much more.

The volume will include 18 contemporary writers: Lina Kostenko, Emma Andijewska, Nina Bichuya, Sofia Maidanska, Ludmyla Taran, Liuko Dashvar, Maria Matios, Eugenia Kononenko, Oksana Zabuzhko, Iren Rozdobudko, Natalka Sniadanko, Larysa Denysenko, Svitlana Povaljajeva, Svitlana Pyrkalo, Dzvinka Matiash, Irena Karpa, Tanya Malyarchuk, and Sofia Andrukhovych.

Buy it > www.glagoslav.com

THE FRONTIER

28 Contemporary Ukrainian Poets - An Anthology

This anthology reflects a search of the Ukrainian nation for its identity, the roots of which lie deep inside Ukrainian-language poetry. Some of the included poets are well-known locally and internationally; among them are Serhiy Zhadan, Halyna Kruk, Ostap Slyvynsky, Marianna Kijanowska, Oleh Kotsarev, Anna Bagriana and, of course, the living legend of Ukrainian poetry, Vasyl Holoborodko. The next Ukrainian poetic generation also features prominently in the collection. Such poets as Les Beley, Olena Herasymyuk, Myroslav Laiuk, Hanna Malihon, Taras Malkovych, Julia Musakovska, Julia Stahivska and Lyuba Yakimchuk are the ones Ukrainians like to read today, and each of them already has an excellent reputation abroad due to festival appearances and translations to European languages. The work collected here documents poetry in Ukraine responding to challenges of the time by forging a radical new poetic, reconsidering writing techniques and language itself.

Edited and translated from the Ukrainian by Anatoly Kudryavitsky.

A BILINGUAL EDITION

Buy it > www.glagoslav.com

GŁOSY / VOICES

by Jan Polkowski

In December 1970, amid a harsh winter and an even harsher economic situation, the ruling communist regime in Poland chose to drastically raise prices on basic foodstuffs. Just before the Christmas holidays, for example, the price of fish, a staple of the traditional Christmas Eve meal, rose nearly 20%. Frustrated citizens took to the streets to protest, demanding the repeal of the price-hikes. Things took an especially dramatic turn in the northern regions near the Baltic shore — later, the cradle of the Solidarity movement, which would eventually spark the fall of communism in Poland and throughout Central and Eastern Europe — where the government moved against their citizens with the Militia and the Army. Forty-one Poles were murdered by their own government when militiamen and soldiers opened fire with live rounds on the crowds in Gdańsk, Gdynia, Szczecin and Elbląg.

Jan Polkowski's moving poetic cycle *Głosy* [Voices], presented here in its entirety in the English translation of C.S. Kraszewski, is a poetic monument to the dead, their families, and all who were affected by the 'December Events,' as they are sometimes euphemistically referred to.

A BILINGUAL EDITION

Buy it > www.glagoslav.com

Glagoslav Publications Catalogue

- *The Time of Women* by Elena Chizhova
- *Andrei Tarkovsky: A Life on the Cross* by Lyudmila Boyadzhieva
- *Sin* by Zakhar Prilepin
- *Hardly Ever Otherwise* by Maria Matios
- *Khatyn* by Ales Adamovich
- *The Lost Button* by Irene Rozdobudko
- *Christened with Crosses* by Eduard Kochergin
- *The Vital Needs of the Dead* by Igor Sakhnovsky
- *The Sarabande of Sara's Band* by Larysa Denysenko
- *A Poet and Bin Laden* by Hamid Ismailov
- *Zo Gaat Dat in Rusland* (Dutch Edition) by Maria Konjoekova
- *Kobzar* by Taras Shevchenko
- *The Stone Bridge* by Alexander Terekhov
- *Moryak* by Lee Mandel
- *King Stakh's Wild Hunt* by Uladzimir Karatkevich
- *The Hawks of Peace* by Dmitry Rogozin
- *Harlequin's Costume* by Leonid Yuzefovich
- *Depeche Mode* by Serhii Zhadan
- *Groot Slem en Andere Verhalen* (Dutch Edition) by Leonid Andrejev
- *METRO 2033* (Dutch Edition) by Dmitry Glukhovsky
- *METRO 2034* (Dutch Edition) by Dmitry Glukhovsky
- *A Russian Story* by Eugenia Kononenko
- *Herstories, An Anthology of New Ukrainian Women Prose Writers*
- *The Battle of the Sexes Russian Style* by Nadezhda Ptushkina
- *A Book Without Photographs* by Sergey Shargunov
- *Down Among The Fishes* by Natalka Babina
- *disUNITY* by Anatoly Kudryavitsky
- *Sankya* by Zakhar Prilepin
- *Wolf Messing* by Tatiana Lungin
- *Good Stalin* by Victor Erofeyev
- *Solar Plexus* by Rustam Ibragimbekov
- *Don't Call me a Victim!* by Dina Yafasova
- *Poetin* (Dutch Edition) by Chris Hutchins and Alexander Korobko

- *A History of Belarus* by Lubov Bazan
- *Children's Fashion of the Russian Empire* by Alexander Vasiliev
- *Empire of Corruption: The Russian National Pastime* by Vladimir Soloviev
- *Heroes of the 90s: People and Money. The Modern History of Russian Capitalism* by Alexander Solovev, Vladislav Dorofeev and Valeria Bashkirova
- *Fifty Highlights from the Russian Literature* (Dutch Edition) by Maarten Tengbergen
- *Bajesvolk* (Dutch Edition) by Michail Chodorkovsky
- *Dagboek van Keizerin Alexandra* (Dutch Edition)
- *Myths about Russia* by Vladimir Medinskiy
- *Boris Yeltsin: The Decade that Shook the World* by Boris Minaev
- *A Man Of Change: A study of the political life of Boris Yeltsin*
- *Sberbank: The Rebirth of Russia's Financial Giant* by Evgeny Karasyuk
- *To Get Ukraine* by Oleksandr Shyshko
- *Asystole* by Oleg Pavlov
- *Gnedich* by Maria Rybakova
- *Marina Tsvetaeva: The Essential Poetry*
- *Multiple Personalities* by Tatyana Shcherbina
- *The Investigator* by Margarita Khemlin
- *The Exile* by Zinaida Tulub
- *Leo Tolstoy: Flight from Paradise* by Pavel Basinsky
- *Moscow in the 1930* by Natalia Gromova
- *Laurus* (Dutch edition) by Evgenij Vodolazkin
- *Prisoner* by Anna Nemzer
- *The Crime of Chernobyl: The Nuclear Goulag* by Wladimir Tchertkoff
- *Alpine Ballad* by Vasil Bykau
- *The Complete Correspondence of Hryhory Skovoroda*
- *The Tale of Aypi* by Ak Welsapar
- *Selected Poems* by Lydia Grigorieva
- *The Fantastic Worlds of Yuri Vynnychuk*
- *The Garden of Divine Songs and Collected Poetry of Hryhory Skovoroda*
- *Adventures in the Slavic Kitchen: A Book of Essays with Recipes* by Igor Klekh
- *Seven Signs of the Lion* by Michael M. Naydan

- *Forefathers' Eve* by Adam Mickiewicz
- *One-Two* by Igor Eliseev
- *Girls, be Good* by Bojan Babić
- *Time of the Octopus* by Anatoly Kucherena
- *The Grand Harmony* by Bohdan Ihor Antonych
- *The Selected Lyric Poetry Of Maksym Rylsky*
- *The Shining Light* by Galymkair Mutanov
- *The Frontier: 28 Contemporary Ukrainian Poets - An Anthology*
- *Acropolis: The Wawel Plays* by Stanisław Wyspiański
- *Contours of the City* by Attyla Mohylny
- *Conversations Before Silence: The Selected Poetry of Oles Ilchenko*
- *The Secret History of my Sojourn in Russia* by Jaroslav Hašek
- *Mirror Sand: An Anthology of Russian Short Poems*
- *Maybe We're Leaving* by Jan Balaban
- *Death of the Snake Catcher* by Ak Welsapar
- *A Brown Man in Russia* by Vijay Menon
- *Hard Times* by Ostap Vyshnia
- *The Flying Dutchman* by Anatoly Kudryavitsky
- *Nikolai Gumilev's Africa* by Nikolai Gumilev
- *Combustions* by Srđan Srdić
- *The Sonnets* by Adam Mickiewicz
- *Dramatic Works* by Zygmunt Krasiński
- *Four Plays* by Juliusz Słowacki
- *Little Zinnobers* by Elena Chizhova
- *We Are Building Capitalism! Moscow in Transition 1992-1997* by Robert Stephenson
- *The Nuremberg Trials* by Alexander Zvyagintsev
- *The Hemingway Game* by Evgeni Grishkovets
- *A Flame Out at Sea* by Dmitry Novikov
- *Jesus' Cat* by Grig
- *Want a Baby and Other Plays* by Sergei Tretyakov
- *Mikhail Bulgakov: The Life and Times* by Marietta Chudakova
- *Leonardo's Handwriting* by Dina Rubina
- *A Burglar of the Better Sort* by Tytus Czyżewski
- *The Mouseiad and other Mock Epics* by Ignacy Krasicki

- *Ravens before Noah* by Susanna Harutyunyan
- *An English Queen and Stalingrad* by Natalia Kulishenko
- *Point Zero* by Narek Malian
- *Absolute Zero* by Artem Chekh
- *Olanda* by Rafał Wojasiński
- *Robinsons* by Aram Pachyan
- *The Monastery* by Zakhar Prilepin
- *The Selected Poetry of Bohdan Rubchak: Songs of Love, Songs of Death, Songs of the Moon*
- *Mebet* by Alexander Grigorenko
- *The Orchestra* by Vladimir Gonik
- *Everyday Stories* by Mima Mihajlović
- *Slavdom* by Ľudovít Štúr
- *The Code of Civilization* by Vyacheslav Nikonov
- *Where Was the Angel Going?* by Jan Balaban
- *De Zwarte Kip* (Dutch Edition) by Antoni Pogorelski
- *Głosy / Voices* by Jan Polkowski
- *Sergei Tretyakov: A Revolutionary Writer in Stalin's Russia* by Robert Leach
- *Opstand* (Dutch Edition) by Władysław Reymont
- *Dramatic Works* by Cyprian Kamil Norwid
- *The Night Reporter* by Yuri Vynnychuk
- *Children's First Book of Chess* by Natalie Shevando and Matthew McMillion
- *The Revolt of the Animals* by Wladyslaw Reymont
- *Illegal Parnassus* by Bojan Babić
- *Liza's Waterfall: The Hidden Story of a Russian Feminist* by Pavel Basinsky
- *The Vow: A Requiem for the Fifties* by Jiří Kratochvil
- *Duel* by Borys Antonenko-Davydovych
- *Subterranean Fire* by Natalka Bilotserkivets
- *Biography of Sergei Prokofiev* by Igor Vishnevetsky

More coming . . .